TRADING PLACES

EMILY DUVALL

Entangled Publishing, LLC
644 Shrewsbury Commons Ave., STE 181
Shrewsbury, PA 17361
rights@entangledpublishing.com

Amara is an imprint of Entangled Publishing, LLC.

Visit our website at www.entangledpublishing.com.

Edited by Molly Majumder
Cover illustration and design by Elizabeth Turner Stokes
Interior design by Toni Kerr

ISBN 978-1-64937-395-3
Ebook ISBN 978-1-64937-419-6

Manufactured in the United States of America

First Edition September 2023

10 9 8 7 6 5 4 3 2 1

AMARA
an imprint of Entangled Publishing LLC

Hands down, this one goes to Brian

At Entangled, we want our readers to be well-informed. If you would like to know if this book contains any elements that might be of concern for you, please check the back of the book for details.

CHAPTER ONE

Lexi

Here's how things stand.

No one's puked yet. The group of influencers do their thing in pink lace lingerie. Some lap sitting is involved. Tight skin with some boob showing does the trick in the face of distinguished men and open shirt collars.

The auction is for a good cause, I swear. The huge crowd is hot bodies who made the required contributions. We are all committed to raising money for hunger awareness.

I press my lips together in distaste. *Oh my God.* Who dropped the ball and didn't order the Cristal? "Traumatizing," I say at the exact moment the dual confetti cannons spray the room to bursts of cheers and sloppy dancing.

I should let my anger go over the building engineer's firm veto of my request to put in a giant swing in the portrait hall.

Guess we can't get everything we want.

I check the message from my father. *You charged $240,000 in three nights at Necker Island?*

Guilty. But also? Not in the mood for a lecture. Best to skip the part where I rented the whole island. At least he's not bringing up the latest gossip that I wrecked a marriage.

I delete his text. Oopsy.

Who could ever put a price on relaxation? Price tags are mythical creatures like unicorns. I know they're out there. I swipe my diamond-dusted nails over my jaw's ultra-soft skin for proof I have no regrets about using my father's private jet.

A camera lens is suddenly in my face. I push my hand out. "Delete that shot," I say to the hired photographer.

If someone were to take a closer look, they would see a twenty-five-year-old in a Chanel dress hand-stitched for me, Lexi North. The plunging satin neckline in my favorite plum color shows a flawless section of creamy, firm breasts giving off a *look but don't touch* message and a slit showing off thighs made smooth by the white caviar body spa treatment.

Every eyelash is in place. Long, inky, and smooth. Four-inch heels on my feet.

If you took an even closer look, you would see a girl who showed up *not* to raise money to stock community pantries with oatmeal and pasta. I came to see the man I've been pining for since I saw him competing in a polo match in the ninth grade. *Where is he?*

He would be Hudson Hoffman.

The name alone has my heart pounding and my imagination overactive in anticipation of our reunion. I ignore the roar of my empty stomach and square my shoulders, giving a pouty, side-angled look in time for the photographer to click the camera.

"Your lips look luminous. What is that?" Talia asks, sipping her glass of white wine. My best friend could win hair awards with her shiny black hair. She pulls off blunt bangs (harder to achieve than one thinks).

I touch my finger to my lower lip graced by the twenty-four-karat gold-infused lip gloss. "A little something that hasn't hit the market yet." I sweep my hand over my Judith Lieber clutch with room for only three thousand dollars and my phone.

"Hudson just checked in." Everyone needs a Talia in their corner. She always tells me what I want to hear. She stretches her arm with her phone in hand. "I might as well pick the dress I'll wear to your wedding."

"Nonsense." I shake my wrist adorned with a bracelet of chunky diamonds. The heirloom is so popular it has an IG following of 75,000—just shy of my goal of 100,000 by the end of summer. "You'll be my maid of honor. Oh, and, *I hate* to do this, but I'm charging for selfies."

She lowers her arm and stares at me. "You're what?"

"I'm exhausted by people wanting photos with me for free. Supply and demand, sweetie." The solution is perfect for my father's tedious nagging to make something of myself.

He will applaud me for my new photo op initiative enough to get off my back about how shoes don't need to cost two grand. Anything less means I might as well tape rubber and shoestrings together.

My attention moves across the heavy gold framed portraits and marble busts to the crystal arch of the museum entrance. I wrap my fingers around Talia's wrist. Air leaves my chest like someone pulled my mask at an oxygen bar. "There he is."

Talia's drink is halfway to her mouth. "Damn he looks pretty."

Brown hair parted with a touch of gel. The no-tie navy suit with a crisp white shirt shows off his sizable chest. The commanding look scrambling my insides is what I've been waiting for.

Time to put on my best indifferent face. "Hudson," I say, stepping in front of Talia. The two of us are unmoving, looking at each other like no time has passed. "It's so good to see you."

Hudson checks me out with what seems like approval. "You look beautiful, as always."

For three years, I've waited for Hudson to move back to Alexandria, and now he's finally here. Forget my parched mouth. This is exactly as I dreamed.

Next, he will finally tell me how going to California to pursue his law degree was worth the time, but nothing compares to how much he's missed me.

We are going to look perfect this summer. Side by side at the galas and parties. Yacht club jaunts over long weekends. A trip to my summer home in the Hamptons. Mouths are moving in jealous whispers around us.

It was always supposed to be us.

Will there be a ring? Anything is possible.

My heart is swelling. My smile is riding high. This is my future. *He* is my future.

"I can't believe we're living in the same city again." Hudson plucks a glass of wine from a server and gives it a sniff. "How are you?" His detached tone tugs the strangest feeling in my gut.

Come on, Hudson. Skip the pleasantries. Get to the real stuff. *Where are we waking up tomorrow? Are we back on?*

"I've been busy with my fundraising commitments. I'm redefining the swag bag—"

His phone rings and he reaches in his jacket, pulling it out. He presses the phone to his ear. "I'm by the ice sculpture."

Something is off with him, with our energy. The weird vibe calls for reassurance. "It must be overwhelming to be back. I was beginning to think you would live out there permanently."

"Virginia is my home, you know that."

I follow Hudson's gaze over to the life-size ice sculpture, a naked statue of *David* sporting a white fedora.

Usually clothes don't come off until the after party.

"I don't want to waste time." I get to the point. "We agreed when you moved we would keep options open and I have. I think about our times together. We have something between us. We always have. Even when I was dating other people, you were always in the back of my head. I never stopped loving you."

"I met someone," he says crassly, nodding his head at something behind me.

I freeze. Three horrible words. *I. Met. Someone.*

Foolishly, I turn in time to see a dark-haired beauty wearing a beaded dress standing feet away.

No.

I turn back to Hudson.

The spark in his eye lights a match to my jealousy. "That's Isabella."

I'm speechless. Confusion pounds my thoughts. Hudson's grinning?

I've been waiting for this man to return to me like a fool and he's dumping me in front of an audience. He doesn't get to walk away without hearing me out.

"I don't understand." My voice is unreasonably loud, stopping conversations around us.

"What don't you understand?" He grinds out the words with the warmth of concrete. "Isabella and I met at Berkley. She's passionate about so much. Volunteering, the environment, cooking."

"Then I'll bake a chicken." I'm sounding desperate. I don't care. Whoever she is, what she can do, I can do better.

Maybe not a chicken. My personal chef can handle that.

His pitying look says it all. "You? In a kitchen? Sweetheart, we both know you couldn't figure out turning on the burner. Isabella opened my eyes to our lifestyle." He leans in to me. "Did you ever think your spot at Princeton could have gone to someone who would have followed through?"

Tension squeezes my shoulder blades. The stillness in me is as rigid as the hurtful point he's making. His words are like someone blowing out candles on a cake. One insult at a time.

"I don't have to work *and* I left Princeton to realize my life plan." Whatever that was. I'm sure it was good. "You can't fault me for being born into money any more than someone born into poverty."

"The difference is that you live off your father's fortune like you're still sixteen." His hands gesture as if they're blowing up. "Everyone knows Lexi North does not like to get her hands dirty." He straightens his jacket and whispers, "Look at this party."

I break my gaze away to the surrounding gold and pink glam theme. Hudson and I are now the entertainment, undeniable snickering and whispering directed at us.

"You're a joke." He lays down the final slight.

Hudson's cold, demeaning assessment has me holding back tears with the sheer force of willpower.

"I thought who I am would be enough." I cringe at the sound of my own vulnerability. I am still just a girl with a beating heart like the rest of them.

"I'm sure you are. Just not for me." He shrugs and nods to Isabella. "I found someone I believe in." He leaves me to my racing heart and spinning thoughts, adding just before he goes, "But you do look really hot."

I shove my hand to the camera and startle the photographer. "Stop taking photos. *Hudson,*" I call out his name loudly, causing him to turn without an ounce of love in his strained jaw. "If you think I'm so shallow, then you're wrong. Watch this."

I stomp through the parting sea of silent guests and grab a glass of champagne. My destination is the entrance. "Out of my way," I order the doormen.

They push the glass doors open in time for me to stumble out of the museum and onto King's Street, startling a group of women holding ice cream cones. I down my drink and drop the glass.

"Free money!" I shout with tears filling my eyes, careful to step over the shattered glass.

"What are you doing?" Hudson shouts, grabbing my arm.

I shake him off.

I reach into my clutch and pull out my wad of cash and fan it in front of me. People on the street flock to the scene. "See, Hudson? This is me *trying.* How's this for charity?"

People just stare at me. A woman holds up her cell phone and squints at her screen.

I climb onto a bench on unsteady feet. "Who wants cash?"

One fifty at a time, I swipe the bills into the air. There's a pause of hesitation and a guy scoops up the first bill. The crowd jumps in, picking up what they can.

Tomorrow I'll plug the hole in my heart with a refresh from my trust fund.

I throw and throw until the cash runs out, leaving my hands empty. A glimpse over my shoulder shows me Talia, shaking her head at me with parental-like disgust.

I can't go back inside.

Doesn't matter. Talia will be my best friend in the morning because she needs me. They all need my last name to open their doors.

Hudson's hard-lined expression is more than I can face. His attention turns to Isabella clutching his arm. Three years I waited. What a waste.

I turn abruptly and get down, catching myself before my high heel causes me to face-plant. I snap my fingers at the valet. "Get my car."

I don't look back toward the building until my custom-built Audi is in front of me and I take the keys and slam the car door.

I step on the gas, peeling out of there, my only thought to flee from the utter disaster in front of me. Traffic, though, has other plans.

The minivan in front of me is going under the speed limit and the car on the left paces me. I suck in an irritated breath.

Tears are not allowed. I don't cry over men who don't want me. The simmering in my chest creeps up my throat, my hands grip the wheel, and I burst around the minivan with the green light ahead.

A horn honks, startling me from my thoughts and I push the gas pedal at the terrifying moment I see the car in front of me is stopped.

I grip the steering wheel as the car in front of me looms larger—

I scream hard and loud as my car smashes into the back end of the vehicle in front of me with a heavy impact.

Jagged pain hits my neck and I scream again. My knuckles are white, frozen on the wheel, the seatbelt locked against my chest.

Everything turns quiet except for my fast-pounding heartbeats. A wave of delayed shock hits. Someone lays on the horn, startling me into moving my quivering hands.

I don't know what to do first.

Get out of the car. Call for help.

I fumble around in my purse with the contents spilled over the passenger side and push the seat belt button and get out on shaky feet.

There's movement inside the car I hit.

The driver's door opens.

The first thing I notice is his height. My eyes move up his tall, muscled body to a head of ash-blond hair tied back in a scraggly ponytail. He's sporting a faded red Capitals T-shirt and cargo shorts. He turns to me, his gaze riding right down the front of my formfitting gown and back to my face, and he slams his door.

"What were you doing?" he snaps.

"What was *I* doing?" Momentary worry for my life and his vanishes. He doesn't appear to have a scratch on him and, judging by his tone, he makes the same assumption about me.

He comes closer, pausing at the very dented, very damaged back end of his midsize car with rust around the bumper. His hand scrapes his forehead. "This had to happen. Great. Just great."

The words I want to say are stuck in my throat, the panic settling in that it could have been worse. "Thanks for asking if I'm okay," I say to myself, unaware he hears and earning a look with clear meaning. *I am to blame.*

Traffic resumes around us with drivers peering over at us to get a look.

He's on his phone, fingers typing furiously, and he sticks it against his ear. He stalks around the car and gives an idle kick to one of his tires. "I'm reporting an accident."

Accident protocol is new to me. Surely someone shows up and takes care of it all. Unsure about the next steps, I wait until he's off the phone and follow his lead taking photos of the damage.

We wind up standing side by side, our phones out, each of us locked in a passive-aggressive photo challenge. His gaze sneaks to mine, holding for a split second; his green eyes flare and narrow. A cool dose of hatred pierces me. Like I've been skewered by something sharp and hot.

As if my night was going so well already, I have to deal with this guy.

CHAPTER TWO

Lexi

There's a surprising amount of waiting around.

When they finally arrive, the pair of officers get out of their vehicle and walk over to us, assessing the accident. The guy I hit is next to me. My side-eyed glance roams up his shoulder, curious to get another look. He catches me staring, and I turn my focus to my Audi's crumpled hood.

"Good evening, folks." The officer headed in our direction has a clipboard tucked beneath his arm. His partner stays back doing another walk around the cars. "Is anyone hurt?"

The other driver clicks his phone, getting the last picture. "No one's hurt," he says without asking me. My hand rubs the back of my neck from the sting of whiplash. "She ran a red light."

"*He* didn't move on green." The impact happened so fast and this guy is quick to throw me under the bus, inspiring me to ramp things up with a healthy dose of self-protectiveness.

The officer holds up a firm hand. He gives me his attention. "Move your cars out of the lane of traffic, then we'll talk."

Maneuvering in heels around the broken headlights, I get in my car and turn on the engine. Assuming the driver is going to pull ahead, I step on the gas, but he backs up. I lay on the horn as his bumper hits my car and he jerks around in his seat.

I press the horn. "You've got to be kidding me."

We both pull our cars over to the side without further incident and barrel out, trying to reach the officers first. I better get there before this jerk can lie about what happened.

"I'll start with you." At least there's one gentleman. *Ladies first, thank you.* "I'll need your driver's license—"

"Excuse me, officer?" The rough voice behind me has me angling my head to his face as he moves to stand next to me. "Here's my info." He lowers his gaze to mine.

I was wrong about his eye color. They aren't run-of-the-mill green. Struck by the evening light, they showcase green the color of a forest grove, with long inky black eyelashes.

Eyes watching me with a gleam of *I beat you to it.*

His jaw is gloriously firm and the layer of stubble solidifies his need for a shave. My nose turns up at his scraggly ponytail.

I step in front of him, accidentally wobbling on my heel. A firm hand presses on my lower back, steadying me and disappearing.

To my annoyance, the officer takes his license first. "You're Evan Bailey?"

"Yes," Evan responds, turning his back to me like I might steal his identity. He flashes a disgruntled but boyish look over his shoulder. "Could you step aside?"

I move away, staring at his back.

The name Evan suits him. He's blunt in a way I'm not used to from the men in my circles. He's not showing the slightest bit of chivalry.

We might be ten seconds into our dislike for each other, but I pick up on his habit of rubbing his hand under his jaw. Guess I will wait until Evan's done and be ready with a glare each time he nonchalantly looks over his shoulder at me.

The officer ignores my impatient sighs. I need to check

how many people shared my money-throwing video, because it has to be more than the ones sharing my humiliation.

A month later, the officer finally turns to me. "Ma'am? You're next." He collects what he needs.

When it looks like we are near the end of the fender bender fiasco, I order an Uber with a dispassionate sigh. Are there really no luxury options available? "I'll come back for my car another day."

"Ahem." Evan clears his throat and points to the street sign directly in front of my car.

NO PARKING SATURDAY 8:00 P.M. – MONDAY 8:00 A.M.

My shoulders sag. Damn the city's parking rules.

All I want to do is look up photos of Isabella and find reasons why she and Hudson won't last.

The officer tucks the clipboard under his arm. "We're done here. You two have a good evening."

Evan is making progress. He's on his phone. His demeanor is calm. "Alec. It's me, hey… Some woman wasn't paying attention…" His gaze cuts to mine. "Probably on her phone. Bring the truck down."

"I wasn't on my phone," I fire back and google "Tow Truck Companies Alexandria." "And my name is Lexi North, not *some woman*."

The list of tow truck companies is extensive. The choices overwhelm me. I haven't had to have my car towed before, especially on a night when something as minor as making a phone call is needling all my insecurities.

Embarrassment spreads through me, standing in front of Evan, *useless* stamped across my forehead. I need his help with this car situation.

He's on his phone, head angled down, sunlight turning his stubble a soft brown. I wait until his gaze meets mine and he stops speaking.

"Do you have a tow truck company you could recommend?" I ask without pretense.

"I'll call you back," he says, sliding his phone into his back pocket. He moves closer to me, stares at me with less annoyance, acknowledging the shift in my tone. "I do, yes. It's Bailey's Auto Shop."

"Bailey." I type the name in my phone as the officer's words catch up to me. "Didn't the officer call you Mr. Bailey? Is there a connection?"

"It's my brother's shop. I'm Evan." He holds out his hand. I place mine in his, taken aback by his coarse skin and strength. He drops his hand too quickly. "I'll call him."

Money is the best resource I have at my disposal, and my Uber is almost here. "I'll pay you $1,000 to wait with my car and make sure it's towed to your brother's shop."

Evan cracks an even bigger frown. "You're going to pay me a grand when you don't even know me?"

Maybe I should have offered more. "I have somewhere to be and you did offer to call your brother's shop."

"My brother will be happy to assist you when he arrives. *I* have somewhere to be."

Where could he possibly have to go?

My posture inches back tight as a bow. Surely the lure of a woman in a dress and shiny heels will help my case. Evan isn't persuaded. He looks like he might walk away.

"Where are you going? A Caps game?"

He folds his arms, causing the fabric to strain around his lean biceps. Biceps porn is my weakness. There's a lot of muscle beneath his shirt. "Now I'm definitely not going to help you."

My gaze flies to the faded insignia on his shirt. "Why not?"

"A Caps fan would know the season is over. Also, could you be any ruder?"

Oh come on. Throw more money at him. This is turning

into Twenty Questions. "How much do you want?"

He shakes his head slowly. "You had your chance."

Ugh times ten. My opinion of this guy is deteriorating rapidly. "I'll double it."

Evan stops and turns. He holds up two fingers. "Two grand, plus another $1,000 for the inconvenience of staying with your car while you ditch the scene. *And* you admit you're at fault."

I see my error immediately. He knew if I was willing to offer a grand, I would pay more. He's smart and he was stalling. Might as well be the trust fund girl he thinks I am.

"$3,000 is nothing to me." Last month I dropped twice that on the Bottega Veneta floral lace thong currently sticking to my sweaty thighs. Good thing I didn't wear the pair with sequins. "You can have the money, but I won't admit I was at fault."

Evan points above and my gaze follows to the traffic camera attached to a pole. "Guess we'll see about that."

"I guess we will."

Five minutes after I'm out of there, I know I won't see him again. I'll just involve my father and have one of his personal assistants run on down to Bailey's Auto and fetch my car.

I glance at my phone, thrilled to see my Uber is close.

This evening won't be salvaged completely, but I take a selfie with my ruined car in the background and post about the dramatic life-and-death accident.

"North," Evan says, holding out his hand, "I need your key and you need to sign a release allowing me to tow your car to Bailey's."

"Fine. Sure. Great."

A midsize silver SUV pulls up. My ride, my ride, *my ride*.

This is my ticket out of this evening-gone-wrong. I dip my hand into my clutch. *Crap.* The cash. I made it rain money from that park bench but now I have nothing.

I slap my keys in Evan's palm, stepping forward too quickly.

My knee shoots forward and the slit on my tight dress gives an ominous rip all the way up my thigh.

Evan pauses. His gaze rides up my smooth leg.

"Haven't you seen legs before?" I snap and fret over the tear in my dress. Nothing is going right.

My gaze jumps to Evan's and his infuriating wry grin. "Looks better now," Evan remarks and holds his phone out.

I digitally sign my name on his screen, noting the distance to the Uber. "Like I would ever let your hand near my thighs," I mumble. The thought stabs unexpected heat to my core, but I push it away and dismiss the possibility.

Focusing on my next task, beelining it before Evan asks for cash again, I grip my clutch in my palm and take a backward step toward my getaway car. *Dad will send money to the shop. He can send a barcode or something.*

If I seem rushed, he'll know I am about to ditch him without paying. Calmly, I move closer to my Uber. I offer Evan a neutral expression. "Evan, would you open my door?"

He lifts both hands. "Sorry. Since I can't tell the difference between a red and green light, I might not be able to figure out a door handle."

"I'm sure you could. You seem capable."

"I'm capable," he says in a rough voice. "It's just a handle, unless the lady is afraid to get her hands dirty."

The same insinuation Hudson made. I am useless when it comes to doing anything meaningful. Twice tonight I've been told this, and both times the sting is fresh. More so from Evan, since he doesn't know me. Gritting my teeth, almost there.

"I'll take the money now," Evan says, his gaze dropping to my clutch.

I spin around fast on my heel and run to the back passenger door, yanking it open and jamming myself inside. I slam the door and shout at the driver. *"Go."*

The driver eases the car away from the curb and my

shoulders begin to tremble.

"Hey!" Evan yells and I slink down in the subpar car interior. Not even leather seats. "You're not getting your car back without the money!"

I stare at my hands.

Polished and pretty, not a speck of dirt. Tense breaths roll from my mouth.

The torn dress is my battle wound.

Hudson's words from earlier hang around my heart. My accomplishments are...*what*?

Dropped out of college. Lives off Daddy's money. Can't figure out an oven.

I suck in a harsh breath, like someone closed the vents in my lungs, and let the usual hollow feeling take over. Nonsense, I'll throw a party and show him he didn't get to me.

I stare blankly at my bare wrist and my eyes widen.

"No, no, no." Dread anchors down my soul.

The diamond bracelet that belonged to my grandmother was on my wrist. As if this night couldn't get any worse. I just lost a family heirloom. Cheers.

CHAPTER THREE

Evan

I loathe the Lexi Norths of the world.

They think we're all standing around waiting to do them a favor. She upped the price, wouldn't admit she was wrong, and the kicker is, I would have towed her car for free.

I was picking up Cecelia, my twelve-year-old niece. She's my legal responsibility while her mother does time in prison.

"Uncle Ev," CeCe calls from one of the chairs in the customer waiting area of Bailey's Auto Shop. Her head full of dirty blond hair is in a floppy bun taking up half her forehead. "Why couldn't I stay home?"

"Free labor," my brother Alec calls from his office.

Bailey's opens in ten minutes. I unlock the door to the work area, flip on the lights, and perform a cursory check of the vehicle lift. Weak sunlight streams over the concrete floor.

The corner brick building has seen better days. The windows could use a wash and exterior paint is needed around the trim.

I'm feeling it's an Aerosmith kind of morning and switch on the speakers before returning to the customer lounge.

CeCe's on her tablet, sitting in a crappy chair. "Rachel

invited me to a sleepover tonight and King's Dominion tomorrow. She says her mom will pay for me."

I wince. *Park fees.* "You can stay the night, but you can't go to the park."

Her one-shoulder shrug is her latest go-to replacement instead of speaking in full sentences. I was kidding myself if I thought she would paint rocks and watch shows about cats forever.

CeCe anticipates my response. "Knew it."

Christ. I need a new life. I'm only twenty-seven.

It wasn't CeCe's fault my sister Natalie's one-night stand washed his hands of getting someone *like her* pregnant. Those were his exact words. Nice guy, right?

"It's not about the money," I finally say.

"It always is." Emotion swells in her tone. "I wish we had someone else's life."

The immediate reasons why this won't happen come to mind. I am a mechanic with a high school diploma and working on cars in a failing auto shop. Parenthood was thrust upon me when I had barely turned twenty.

CeCe looks at me before looking back at her tablet, a striking image of her mother. Alec was overwhelmed getting Bailey's off the ground when she went to prison, but sometimes I wonder what Natalie was thinking when she named me to care for her.

"You need to see this," CeCe says, her jaw hanging open. "This girl is throwing money to a crowd. There's cash everywhere."

Awesome. I can't wait to check out this lowlife throwing money away. I peer over her shoulder. "Let me see."

Every cell in my body stiffens. Lo and behold, Lexi North. *Hold on.* She's wearing the slinky dress from the night she hit me. The same dress that would look great sliding off the bed and onto my floor.

Noting the date and time confirms this video *is* from that night. Hostility freezes my gut and pushes my pulse over the edge. "She stiffed me," I gripe, my stomach clenching from the inside.

CeCe looks at me while on screen Lexi pushes dollar bills off her hand. "She did?"

I wish I hadn't seen the clip. "Put that away."

CeCe's tender brow wrinkles. "Why would she throw away moncy?"

"She has nothing better to do with her life. I've met her, I know. Her name is Lexi North." The video seals my impression of her. Survey says? No redeeming qualities.

"Evan," Alec calls.

My brother's in his office, the size of a closet. Barely enough for a desk and his ancient laptop the size of a bench.

Alec is a replica of me. Same height and build. Same green eyes. He wears khakis and a Bailey's polo.

Yup. He's my twin brother.

He pulls out a black box from the drawer and places it on the desk. "This was in the Audi I picked up. Do you know who hit your car Saturday night?"

A memory of skin and her dress ripping up her thigh come to mind. An afterthought of glossy russet hair follows. All of it is wiped away like a clean slate.

The word *spoiled* flashes through my mind like a neon sign. "No one I want to know."

"She's an heiress," Alec continues. "Her father is named one of the top hundred richest men in the U.S. He's in real estate. Mostly international. He's a modern Monopoly man."

Lexi seems like she could benefit from landing in jail.

"As I was taking inventory, I found this. It looked like it needed a babysitter." He holds up a bracelet with chunky strands of diamonds. "I'll keep it locked in my desk. Have Tia call her. I want this off our property. *Today.* I don't need to be on the hook for any other financial messes."

No elaboration needed.

Bailey's financial situation has our balance sheets showing more red than black. I take a peek outside his office, but our office manager, Tia, isn't in yet.

The exorbitant rent increase. Loss of customers. This place needs an injection of at least $100,000 to turn it around. No one is going to hand us a jackpot.

Turning the knob to leave his office, I look at my hardworking brother. "A car is one thing almost everyone has. Eventually, they all need repairs. We'll survive."

The bells on the door jingle.

Movement at the entrance stops my words. The door opens.

A sundress on a pair of long legs steals my attention. A swoosh of lustrous brown hair and smooth skin.

Lexi's walking through the front door on her phone. Her dress falls above the knee and breezes up, teasing as to what's underneath.

As she walks past the office to reception, her foot hits the step and she flies with a scream and whole-body face-plants, catching herself on her palms right before her face hits the ground.

The navy sundress billows up like a parachute and falls slowly, giving me an eyeful of the back of her legs and black panties, solving one mystery of the day.

I walk quickly over and crouch in front of Lexi, letting her gaze drift up my work boots, my jeans, my outstretched hand. The rich color of her hair frames her face, giving me an up-close view of her eyes with tiny gold flecks. Pert, pink lips snag my attention with dusty roses blushing on her cheeks.

She makes a face and settles her hand in mine. Soft skin slips against my rough palm.

I hoist her up and she pulls her hand away like fire and smooths her hair and dress, pausing long enough to make fifty wrong assumptions about me all over again.

Alec's standing in the doorway with a wry look in his eye. "Here's your phone."

She takes the phone and releases a huffy breath. "There're two of you?"

"You're in luck," I say.

She gives a fluttery, eye-blinking sigh. Her hand flies up in a dramatic *stop talking* motion. "I'm here to get my car."

"Soon as you pay me." I walk over behind the counter and Tia moves to the side. I type in what she owes and point to the credit card machine. "Whenever you're ready."

"Happily." She swipes her card with vigor. Neither of us take our eyes off the other.

The error button beeps.

She looks down and tries again. Same result. This time she takes out her phone and shows me a barcode screen. "Try scanning this."

"We're not able to do that kind of payment."

"Let me make a phone call." She steps away and I glance over at Alec.

Lexi's voice turns into an angry whisper. Her shoulders hunch and she steps into the tire showroom, talking in a furious hushed voice on her phone.

A slow frown spreads across Alec's face. "She's coming back."

"The money will arrive later today," she says flippantly. "Until then, I left something in my car I need to get."

Lexi's outright judging eyes make me want to stretch this for five more minutes to make her late to whatever brunch she's running to.

I open the door to the garage and gesture for her to walk ahead. "Your car is in the back lot."

She holds her head high and cradles her handbag like a mother protecting her baby. Lexi's presence sets off a series of double takes and throat clearing from the mechanics who have just arrived, which I counter with a head-shaking warning stare.

Lexi quickly gets in her car and rummages around the driver's seat.

Unsatisfied, she moves to the trunk, her gaze intensifying as she makes a show of looking under some bags with too many huffs.

"Evan, I had a bracelet in here. Now it's *not* here." She has half her body in the car and the view of her backside directly in front of me. She eventually backs out and looks at me. "I hate to say this..."

Something tells me she has no trouble with whatever she's about to say.

"Someone from your shop must have stolen it." Her voice is full of fake apologies.

She's not sorry one bit. I bite my tongue. "Why is that the accusation? Do you know how many times we have been accused of an employee stealing anything? Zero." My fingers form the number.

She does the same impatient series of sighs she was doing the first time I met her. Her purse handle falls to the crook of her elbow and she rests her fist against her chest. "I want to speak to the manager."

"Why did you leave something so valuable in your car?" I lean toward her, noticing her, trying *not* to notice the shine of her skin, her fired-up gaze, her thin, perfect lips. A useless short sleeve cardigan I could peel off.

Lexi is a beautiful woman. I won't pretend not to see her. Not a single part of her is as rough as me.

She takes a step closer. "I was in a hurry after the accident. I was in a rush to get home from an auction to raise money for hunger awareness."

She's worse than I thought, using fundraising as an excuse.

"Have you ever been *hungry,* North?"

Her mouth closes. Her eyes wield fresh energy. "The name is Lexi. Did *you* steal my bracelet?"

Wait. She's pinning this on me? "You can't be serious. I went out of my way to have your car towed."

Her face lights like a fuse, the sparks starting in her eyes and working their way to her open mouth. "Is this a scheme to get more money out of me?"

I fold my arms. Defenses up and running on all cylinders. "You mean the money you haven't paid me? You haven't given me a single dollar."

Her expression is unreal. She's not going to pay me. "You know what you are?"

I can't wait to hear this. "I've waited my whole life for Lexi North to tell me who I am. Please. The floor is yours." My hand sweeps wide.

"You're one of those guys who takes advantage of someone like me."

Her rudeness sends me straight off a steep cliff. "You think you know me based on the car accident *you* caused? You're a joke. You come running down here crying about stolen property and blaming people you don't know. You're all the same."

"Oh. What's that supposed to mean?"

I don't have time to get out *that* list. I brush off her question. "Whatever you want it to mean."

Movement stops us cold, both of us startled by the sight of CeCe holding up her tablet. The gift Alec, my mother, and I split three ways to give her at Christmas is causing dread to form in my stomach because I have an idea what she's doing.

Lexi's smile falters. "Hello there," she says sweetly, changing her tune. "What are you doing?"

"Recording you," CeCe says with a cavalier tone. She peeks over the tablet, giving Lexi full view of her innocent brown eyes. "My feed is live. Say hi."

Lexi's abysmal look of stunned humiliation serves her right. "We're having a private conversation. A silly misunderstanding." She looks to me for help and I give her none.

I'm angry about Lexi thinking I stole something and CeCe lying to me. She knows she isn't allowed to be on social media.

"Weren't you throwing cash from a park bench?" CeCe says, knowing exactly who Lexi is. "You should see the angry emojis."

"Turn it off, CeCe. Now."

CeCe ignores me and takes a step back. The determination in her gaze tugs hard on the bad feeling in my stomach. It's the same look her mother gets right before she doesn't back down. "Is your name Lexi North?"

Lexi's mouth is frozen and her face pale as ash. "If you don't turn that off, I'll sue you."

"CeCe," I warn again, reaching for her as she takes another step away.

"You'll sue a minor whose family has no money?" CeCe doesn't bat an eye.

I cringe. My niece is well-versed in terms like "minor" and "litigation" and "rights." *"CeCe."*

"What do you want?" Lexi's voice turns appealing with an unmistakable hitch. "You must want something."

CeCe's eyes glitter with new energy. "My uncle works really hard. Last year he went without Christmas presents so I could have this tablet."

Lexi's smile is full of promises. "If you turn it off, I'll help your family out. How much money do you need?"

My lunge at CeCe's tablet is futile. She evades me and repositions it. "I want to know what it's like to live in your world."

Lexi and I both stare at her, speechless.

"I challenge you, Lexi North," she says, calling her out

in front of her audience, "to trade places with my uncle, Evan Bailey, for two months." Her voice grows more excited. "You live at our house and we live at yours. You have to be a mechanic and he does your job. You live on our money and we live on yours."

"She couldn't survive a day in my life," I chide, and stare at Lexi's dose of hostility.

"Are you kidding? Two months is nothing." Lexi is not backing down and I'm starting to get worried. "You think you have it so rough. *You* have no idea what it's like to be me."

The two of us face each other, look each other in the eye. A stalemate. Fuck me. Who does she think she is? "You're not actually considering this."

"I never back down from a challenge." The steady gleam in her eye tells me she's arrogant enough to do this.

It's the voice in my head I can't stop. An idea sabotages every rational reason to say no. I can't unthink it.

"I'll make you a deal. I'll do this. We can switch places." I jump at the chance, wanting it more than ever. "On one condition. If you quit first, you give me $100,000."

"And if you quit?" she counters coolly, not even a protest at the price.

That's easy. I have never lost a bet. Never went up against a challenge I couldn't figure out, smooth out, or get out of without winning. "Name whatever you want."

"Do you have the bracelet?" she asks.

"I do." Alec is making his way over. Time to nail this down. "It's in our safe."

"If you drop out first, you give it back."

I can't believe she's not asking for more. She could ask for the shop or a lifetime of free tire rotations. "If I win, though, I keep it and pawn it."

She shrugs. "You won't last. I'm guessing it'll be back on my wrist in a few days." Lexi holds out her hand. "Do we have a deal?"

Our fingers close around one another. This is happening. "Deal."

She's doing this for an ugly bracelet I was going to give back to her anyway.

What an easy win this will be.

Not only will I save Bailey's, I will have the chance to prove Lexi North wrong. I am not sure which part of this will be more satisfying.

CHAPTER FOUR

Lexi

I went too far.

CeCe is half my age and I'm the one sinking in self-imposed quicksand. I should have backed down.

Also, I'm trending. On multiple platforms. Multiple IG accounts are rapidly gaining likes. TikTok user @EvanWhatDidYouDo boasts more followers than my grandmother's bracelet I gambled away as a bargaining chip.

I can't stomach watching "The Bet" video. The list of regrets climbs to new heights along with a hundred tightly wound knots in the pit of my belly.

Fast-flying judgment directed at me is spreading like wind on a forest fire.

Celebrities and everyone else alike are tossing their two cents into the fountain of public opinion.

The old adage *walk a mile in someone else's shoes* is trending #IStandWithEvan #TradingPlaces #HeiressFail.

It's hard to explain what I was thinking, and based on social media commentary, no one thinks I was. I got caught up in the moment, threw my grandmother's irreplaceable bracelet into the mix like collateral damage, and wound up fueling continued bad public opinion about me.

My plans to derail this bet must move quickly.

Which is how I landed at North Property headquarters in my father's office.

"Lexington." My father's gruff voice fills his cushy office.

Big, ornate antique windows and wainscotting give his office the feel of a different era. I look toward the door, wondering when the team of publicists will arrive.

"This bet you made with this young man." His voice is concerning.

Mentally, I'm sliding farther into my chair. "I can explain."

My father sits at the head of boardroom tables. His presence in my life has been hands-off; we show face at holidays and photo-ops. "Not this time."

Things my father and I have in common. Wait. There's just one. My trust fund.

This is the way we function. Hugging is something other families do. Our texts are few. I have long accepted that my family defies the term close-knit. We're loose-knit.

Sometimes I wonder where my family went wrong. I'm the one with hope hiding in her heart that one day he will look at me from behind his desk and ask me something as basic as *how are you doing?* But I have a much more pressing issue. "My credit cards aren't working."

His hand splays on his desk and he taps his fourth finger methodically, his gaze finally settling on me. My internal temperature drops a notch at the displeasure etched in his squinty gaze. "I'm the one who cut them off."

I talk fast, racing against a ticking clock. "I have a plan. I'm not going through with the bet. I'll pay Evan the $100,000 plus an inconvenience bonus." I hold my breath.

"No."

"*No?*" That's a word I don't hear often.

"This senseless, childish bet you made was your last chance."

Crap. There's nowhere to go from here. My father's long sigh is not a good sign. "This man, Evan Bailey," he says with unnerving calm, "I had my lawyers look into him."

"Why would you—"

His hand flies up like an auction sign. Edward North is not a happy man. "Did you promise to pay him for towing your car and then fail to give him cash?"

Fear slides through me, rooting itself. "I was going to pay him, but my cards weren't working."

"You also selfishly gambled with your grandmother's bracelet, entrusted in your care. She gave that to you right before she died."

Guilty on all counts. This is so much easier when we're not in person. Unease prickles through me, causing the hairs on my arms to stand up. "I did."

His disgruntled sigh is a siren in the distance, warning of the louder noise to come. "Four years ago you quit college."

Oh no, we're going down Lexi's list of failures. "Not this again."

"Yes, *this again,*" he continues, snapping forward. "I've looked the other way for too long. Do you know what I see?"

My shoulders would hunch if that were allowed. Straight-faced and taking it like I always do, I listen.

"The world sees my only child, my heir, as a spoiled brat. A woman who throws out money from a park bench."

I wince. "You saw that."

"Every goddamn employee in this company saw it." His disapproving lip twist is holding, and his eyes reduce to slits. "You don't take anything seriously. Not even your charity work." He pauses, swiveling his laptop in my direction. "Members of the Alexandria Foundation complain about your lack of caring when it comes to planning fundraising events. Has it ever occurred to you that there's a reason you don't work here?"

Sharpen the blade, Dad. Go on. Right between the ribs.

I am always fine about our lack of closeness until he pokes at this particular bruise. The one time I worked here, he had someone in Human Resources fire me. He couldn't even tell me face-to-face. "You're bringing up ancient history."

The chair creaks as he throws his weight forward. "Do you have any idea what you spend in a day? A trip to Paris on a whim. Waking up my aviation team for an unplanned trip to Beverly Hills at three in the morning." He taps his finger on the spreadsheet open on the screen. "I see every penny you spend."

My shoulders sag. Nothing like a bar graph to break down my spending habits.

"North Properties was built on the back of hard work." His voice raises precariously, heading somewhere desolate. "I've had enough. Enough of your irresponsible spending. Your lack of judgment." His tone grows irate with each new declaration. "How you are portrayed."

I will not waste tears on him. The mantra starts slow. The tears build anyway. He doesn't even know me.

Now I see where he's going and I'm nails-digging-into-the-armrest scared. "If I could just have access to my trust—"

"You're not buying your way out of the bet. You're going to fix this."

I don't want to know how.

"You leave me no choice but to take extreme measures."

Panic explodes in my chest. "What measures?"

"I'm cutting you off financially for the entire length of the bet."

Noooooo. This can't be. I live and breathe off my monthly trust. "I can't live in Evan's house."

His fist comes down on the table, causing the pens to jump. "It's not a choice. To make sure you're accountable, I'm going to add my own third-party term. If you don't go through with this for the full two months—if you quit, I will cut you off forever.

Your inheritance will be withdrawn indefinitely."

My shocked jaw hangs open. Anxiety the size of the universe casts a shadow over me. Anger at myself courses through my veins. I should have backed down. "You can't do that."

He is not interested in my rebuttal. "I set the terms of your inheritance. Legally, I assure you, I can. Your bank accounts are already frozen."

Desperate times, folks. Desperate. Times. "Evan could be dangerous."

He waves an indifferent hand. "He doesn't have so much as a parking ticket and he's raising his niece. His actions are commendable. Single parenting is harder than you could ever imagine."

If he is referring to having full custody of me after the divorce, he doesn't get to make the argument he sacrificed anything beyond tee times to raise me.

With my chin up, I challenge him coolly. "What would you know about that?"

He sits up straighter. "You're going to live Evan's life. You're going to put in the work. Either right the wrong you've done, on my terms, or be cut off."

The fuse ignites on a very short wick. "Evan will take advantage of this."

"Not as much as you have." My time is up, my father's attention focused on his screen, dismissing me with a final, "You're to go to see Evan right away. He's expecting you."

If only I had kept under my father's radar, I wouldn't be in this position.

My father gets up and grabs his suit jacket. "See yourself out."

A knot spreads and claws at my stomach.

I wish I had a different family. The kind where a mother stays with her child until she learns how to ride her bike instead of falling repeatedly because she has to learn on her own. I idly rub my right elbow where I broke my arm. I wish I had a father who baked cookies with me instead of telling me to stay out of our chef's way.

My theme as of late rises in front of me. Hudson doesn't think I'm capable of lifting a finger. Evan looks at me like I'm wasting space. My father sees me as spoiled.

Am I *that* bad?

Do they not see there's more to me?

I could use a friend. I can't make myself get up and leave his office. Reaching out to Talia, I know she'll be waiting to help me with a bottle of bubbly and an appointment at the spa.

Funny, but she hasn't returned my texts after the auction.

CHAPTER FIVE

Lexi

Not loving the faded brick building with bars on the windows and peeled-off letters on the front door.

BA LEY'S A TO SH P.

The rusty signs. BRAKE ALIGNMENT. TIRES. LUBE SERVICE.

A guy walks in front of me and opens it. "Miss? Are you going inside?"

Decision time. Yes. No. No. "Don't really have a choice, do I?"

He gives me a funny look and opens the door.

The waiting room at Bailey's gets a Lexi North quick D minus grade.

Leather chairs with splits. A coffee machine plucked from a time capsule. Let's not fail to mention the framed employee group shot.

I wouldn't say the woman seated behind the counter greets me with a smile. "Ms. North. I'm Tia Carter, officially known as the office manager. Unofficially, I run this place." She watches with bated breath.

A dramatic lip pop follows. At least there's another woman present.

My father might have looked into Evan's background, but what about his coworkers? Surrounded by men all day in an atmosphere that has only magazines about race car drivers isn't exactly twenty-first century.

I go up to the counter on which rests a canister of free pens stamped with BAILEY'S. "Where's Evan?"

She points a finger in the direction of the garage. "Through the door. You'll have to shout. The boys like their music loud."

How very organized. Yelling names.

I open the door, assaulted by screeching heavy metal like someone's in chains, and a windowless room. My gaze moves over the cars with popped hoods and staff—all men, hunched over engines or beneath cars with feet sticking out.

"Hello?" I shout against the raging voices.

A guy close to my height, with nickel-sized flesh tunnels in his ears, makes his way over. "Help you with something?"

"Evan Bailey!" I yell at the exact time the music cuts off. Faces turn abruptly toward me. A tool drops. Quieter, I ask again, "I need to speak with him."

A saw cuts across something at the back of the garage.

The guy turns. "Ev."

Evan appears from around a corner with a welder's face shield pushed up. He takes it off, along with gloves, and makes his way over.

This is the first time I really look at Evan unhurriedly.

My eyes drink in his unmistakable masculinity. A jaw covered by a layer of stubble. His ever-present undercurrent of confidence goes with the touch of grease on his cheek. The flicker of his green-eyed gaze meets mine like he is ready for whatever fight I brought.

Which I did. I'm just doing it in three-inch heels and my favorite Dior sundress, which should score points with Evan. Men can't resist bare shoulders. They are easily distracted by skin.

Drop this man into a three-piece suit and someone *please* cut off his ponytail and heads would turn. What's under his mechanic work shirt is promising all muscle and tense abs, but I turn my nose up at the thought.

Unless I get him on board with getting out of this thing, *he* will be the reason I lose my inheritance. Despite my father's pep talk, I'm not accepting this as the fate of my summer just yet.

"I'm surprised you showed," he says harshly and drops his work gloves on a table.

"Why wouldn't I?" The music switches to a lower volume. "Could we—could we talk? Preferably not at the heavy metal concert?" I point to one of the speakers.

He doesn't say anything and heads outside. I follow him, sensing hard stares on my backside. Evan offers no middle ground in his expression.

"My father told me you've been made aware we're supposed to do this bet. I was thinking we could end this thing. We could team up." This next part gets tricky. "We could pretend we're switching lives and I'll pay you double at the end. We could meet occasionally and throw in video proof. Me: hanging around here. You: lounging in my backyard pool."

Evan's *hell no* expression is not encouraging. He shakes his head. "No way, North."

"Evan. Please. I—uh—" Why does he need convincing? I thought he would welcome this second chance with open arms. Arms currently stealing my attention with thoughts of being held in them.

He rubs his hand over his jaw. His gaze is suddenly skeptical, his voice flat. "I'm not thrilled with this, either, but I have my reasons. Among those is for my niece CeCe, the bet-master. As much as I disagree with her actions, we both agreed in front of her. We promised, and I keep my promises."

Parents break promises all the time.

My father did say he is raising his niece. Whatever the story is there, it's irrelevant. "She's a young girl, surely she understands people sometimes change their minds. Where are her parents?"

A flicker of mistrust flashes in his eyes, like I get whenever someone asks me about my mother. "Not around."

Looks like I can't appeal to them. "How about I set her up with a college fund?" Nothing like a top-rated education awaiting her future.

His gaze lands on my shoulders. My tactic is working until his eyes crinkle. "That's low, trying to appeal to CeCe's educational future. Nice try."

Ugh! "I thought you'd be more flexible."

"I'm flexible." The gruffness of his tone makes me sensitive to his six-foot-two frame. "But not when it comes to what's best for my family. A few weeks at your house will be a vacation. I'm not backing out. Unless you're late to a spa appointment, I suggest we figure out the ground rules." His determined gaze meets mine. "We're doing this, North."

My nose lifts. "You think you know everything about me."

"Don't I?" He shrugs and folds his arms over his chest.

He can think what he wants. The pile of used tires next to him has my skin crawling. I want to get out of here. The sooner the better. "Is there somewhere more private we can talk than this used car lot?"

Evan's shot of laughter isn't comforting. He goes back toward the garage, his steps brimming with swagger. The way he walks is like Hudson, except more controlled.

I hate that I'm thinking of Hudson. He's probably picking out engagement rings with Isabella and I'm in a glorified junkyard.

Evan doesn't hold the door for me and it shuts in my face. "Lacks gentleman qualities," I mumble.

I pause in the waiting area. One of the customers peers

over her magazine.

"Give me a sec," Evan says, wearing a scowl like a fashion statement. He leans toward the computer, reading something on the screen. "Grab coffee if you want."

I grimace. Is he referring to the pot o' river water? "Is that powdered creamer?"

Evan and Tia jerk their heads to me.

"Tell you what, North," he says too eagerly. "Why don't you wait here while I find the nearest local farm and bring back fresh creamer."

"No thanks on the coffee." He goes into an office and I follow. Evan grabs a bottle of water from a fridge. "I'll take one."

Evan's mouth upturns at the corners. He puts his water bottle to his mouth and takes a long sip and walks his fingers in front of him. "The fridge is right there."

So this is how it's going to be. "I'm your guest."

"True," he says, elongating the word, and screws the cap back on the bottle. His deep green eyes make a noticeable effort looking at my hands. "I'm no doctor, either, but it looks like you have two working hands."

"Just—" I groan internally and take a seat at the circular table smudged with greasy finger stains and crumbs. "Forget the water."

He walks around the table. "Would you mind taking notes? Unless your fingers are damaged beyond repair?"

His fingers are tarnished in a light black color. I take out my phone, typing this up in an email. "We'll start with the essentials. Addresses, house staff names, schedules." A glance at his hard expression and I add, "Expectations."

Evan braces his hand next to my phone, looking over my shoulder, practically leaning on me. He sees the signature line. *Paige Lexington Serena Louise North.*

His brow furrows. "How many names do you have?"

I angle my head to his, our jaws nearly touching. His gaze drops to my face. Everything about him is so...stubborn. My throat clears. "Some breathing room, please."

Evan pushes off the table and pulls out the chair, taking a seat next to me, dragging it to the other side of the table with a screech causing ripples of agony up my spine.

"Do you mind?" I blurt.

"This good enough?"

"Yes." Back to the information gathering. "What's your address?"

"Why don't you go by your first name?" he asks, scratching his jaw. Evan's stubble unintentionally holds my interest.

My fingers pause on the keys. "It's a family tradition."

I inhale long and slow through my nose. "Moving on. What about you? Is there an apartment number I'll need to know?"

"Sorry to disappoint your vision of me living in a trailer. I own a house, North."

I type in the address he tells me. The location is not familiar to me, but then again, I don't spend much time out of my five-star bubble.

"What about you? Where do you live?" he asks.

"I live on Princess Street," I say proudly, typing out the info. "Why is your jaw hanging open?"

"You actually live on Princess Street? You don't see the irony?"

"No," I say, downplaying his statement, knowing he's spot-on. "According to CeCe's rules, we have to live on what the other makes." Fingers poised and ready, we make eye contact. "How much do you make?"

"$29,000," he says without blinking.

"For the whole year?"

He nods, maintaining an undeniable look of pride. "I'm an hourly employee without benefits. And you?"

"$50,000 *a month.*" At least, that's what I was told. We stare point blank at each other silently calculating, understanding, and causing reality to cement my feet.

"What do you do for a living?" he asks, leaning back casually, highlighting the broadness of his chest.

There has never been a time I want to whip out a fancy title and all-important role more than now, because I sense what I'm about to say will only fuel the stereotype that is my life.

"I live off my trust fund," I say quietly and feign interest in my phone. Having all this money clearly works against me with him. He doesn't need to know my entire financial future is at stake. "I don't work."

"What do you do all day?"

Darn. He asks only questions I want to avoid.

I clear my throat. "Tennis lessons, brunching, then there's the gallery openings and polo matches." Evan's eyes get smaller. "I keep busy."

Evan doesn't react. "So. You don't work," he concludes annoyingly.

"You'll see."

"What if daddy's money runs out one day?"

He doesn't know the depth of fear in my pulse at that possibility. I need only to outlast Evan. "My bills are online. Those are subtracted automatically. I'll leave you cash leftover after bills. Will you do the same?"

He hesitates. "Don't you want to do something with your life aside from spend your father's money?"

Dropping my phone accidentally, my gaze goes to his lap. He notices and I swoop down to grab my phone. "I volunteer for charities."

God help me, the committee, and the greater city of Alexandria. Evan Bailey is going to be unleashed on society. His rigidity is like someone about to snap, but he's bound to this for the money and, like it or not, I am too.

Then, a miracle descends upon me. A bright spot takes

shape, one I overlooked. "Isn't working here going to be a problem for me? I know nothing about cars." The only applications I ever fill out are my medical history at the spa and my preferred level of pressure during a back massage.

"Alec will take care of logistics. We train mechanics from scratch all the time. By the end of two months, you'll be changing oil."

I have no intention of doing anything of the sort. I'll keep a low profile and help Tia with office tasks. "Lovely."

"Also. CeCe will stay with me. I'm her legal guardian."

For the second time, I am curious about the *why* and *how* of that statement, but Evan's as likely to answer as changing his mind. Pushing the chair back, I get to my feet.

The hem of my skirt falls to my knees and he notices. "When are we starting this thing?"

"Tomorrow."

We're already toes-deep into this and I want to run to the nearest airport. "Be at my house at nine o'clock. I need to be there when you move in."

He remains seated, tipping the chair back. "Why? To make sure I don't run off with the copper pots?"

"To make sure you know where everything is." My hand falls to the doorknob.

Evan and I lock eyes. It's not like we will even see each other.

He stands up and walks over. His hand clamps above mine and opens the door wider. "Once we trade house keys, there's no going back." Every part of me wants to run, but I can't. Not when I look into Evan's eyes and the nerves in my stomach peak. Of all the people to make this deal with, I made the mistake of stumbling upon Evan, a determined man who wants his money.

CHAPTER SIX

Evan

I'm cranky. It's been months since I've been laid, and the woman I exchanged numbers with at the bar last weekend (she had a fantasy about being with a mechanic) told me to call her when the bet was over. Thanks, Lexi.

Her home is a welcoming committee of white brick and black window shutters. Ivy partially suffocates the face of her house and the shrubbery has been sculpted with a surgeon's precision.

It's all very closed-off, with invisible borders.

One bag is in my hand as I approach her house and knock on the door.

And wait.

Another knock. More waiting.

I look over my shoulder at the cobblestone sidewalks lining streets with leafy trees shading luxury vehicles. Mine looks out of place among the Tesla Roadsters and G-Class Mercedes.

Her life is one big ride on a gilded slide straight into a pool of cash. Every adult in my life has a J-O-B, and this girl is trading in her house keys for a piece of jewelry.

She is either bored or lazy with a side of self-absorbed.

Saving Alec's shop is the priority, to not slip into the *Bankrupt Zone*.

I lean toward the door, listening. We have footsteps—finally.

Lexi answers like she's going to tea in a sundress and I'm the unwanted guy about to solicit pest control. "Evan," she says coldly. "I heard the first ten knocks."

"You weren't answering," I fire back, noticing her ruffled sleeves block my view of her creamy shoulders. "What happened? Were you stuck in your tall tower?"

"It was a lovelier view from up there." Her gaze darts to my hand. "Is that your only bag?"

For now, yes. CeCe's are in the trunk. "Yes. Why?" Protective of my ratty but beloved bag with concert tees and cargo shorts, I lean against her doorframe. My gaze follows to the pyramid of luggage at the base of the stairs stamped with an interlocking *L* and *V*. "You realize you aren't going to a coronation."

Her mouth settles into her usual frown. Maybe she was born frowning and no one ever taught her how to smile. She crooks her finger for me to follow. "I packed enough so I wouldn't have to come back here."

"That makes two of us."

She walks ahead, leaving me to follow, her hair springy against her back. Wonder what it would be like gathered in my palm.

The foyer is triple the space of my bedroom. The furniture—from what I see—is bright, clean white with metallic accents.

She fits the scene. Polished and put together as the details of her sparkling chandeliers.

She can keep her opinions locked in that mouth of hers, but it's clear what she thinks of me in every glance. She stops at the large island in the center of the kitchen. Fresh flowers grace the space next to her like she's going to be photographed.

"Flowers are a complete waste of money," I comment.

"To you, maybe," she says, opening a drawer and retrieving a pen. "It's not a crime to buy things that make you happy."

"I'm willing to bet nothing makes you happy." I fiddle with one of the petals. Bet she spends more on flowers than I spend on groceries. "You don't hear the stems crying?"

"I do." Lexi's unmistakable dark, long lashes are like the supporting actress of her attention-stealing eyes. "They're begging not to be left with you." She waits for me like she doesn't trust me not to speak. "Can we get on with this?"

"Please."

She glares at me. "I have one rule I need you to follow. No overnight guests. Except for CeCe, obviously."

Her practiced tone makes me think this scenario kept her awake most of the night.

"You're being specific about female guests, right?" I haven't brought a woman back to my house. The ironclad rule is one I do not break. No overnight adult guests. Male or female. No random women. No drunk friends crashing on my couch.

"Anyone," she clarifies and plucks the lone wilted flower from the vase, tossing it in the trash.

The guys at the shop come to mind. My best friends.

Josh smoking his cigarette, taking up space on Lexi's white couch or Brandon sipping his beloved Big Gulp. Alec would re-fluff the pillows.

"Same goes for you. No parties in my house or dudes stopping by."

She gives a snooty snort. "That won't happen."

I tip up a corner of my mouth. "Do you have a boyfriend?"

Her mouth parts, but her eyes betray her. I hit a nerve. "How long have you been waiting to ask me?"

Of course, she follows up with a dose of conceit. "About three seconds. Sorry, North, you're not my type." This is not entirely true. Physically, yes. Personality-wise, let me file Lexi and all four of her first names under HELL NO.

She isn't disappointed by my declaration, and Lexi does what Lexi does best. Her face remains humorless. "I don't have a boyfriend. He's...it's complicated."

Let me just pound that nail into the coffin. She told me everything I needed to know. She wants him and he doesn't want her. "Complicated, how?" I rest my elbows on the counter, leaning toward her with a dead-serious look. "Is he the chauffeur?"

If there was a layer below ice level, Lexi's frigid expression turns that cold. "My ex-boyfriend is taking time to figure out stuff," she says plainly.

"He's dating someone," I say the words slowly, enjoying the irritated look rising in her expression. "Who's not you. And you're wondering if he's happier with her."

She closes her eyes tightly and inhales a long breath. "How about I give you the tour? I have other important information to go over."

"What could be more important than understanding your dating life, since I'm down on my knees begging for a chance with you?"

She nods and my eyes go straight for the subtle bounce of her glossy hair. "Might want to wear kneepads for all that waiting."

"Any time."

"*Moving on.* I've made an appointment with a stylist. Don't think you're going to get by with that duo." She gestures to my shirt and lower, to my favorite faded cargo shorts with un-ironed pocket flaps. "What is Black Sabbath, anyway?"

"You don't know who Black Sabbath is? You're truly a disappointment." She steps next to me, her arms touch mine. "I am who I am." I wiggle the front of my shirt. "I've been dressing myself since I was three."

Lexi's eyes rake over me, her breath fills with disdain every microinch her gaze moves. "Yes. And tragedies sometimes go unnoticed for years."

I am starting to see why her "boyfriend" is dating someone else. "Are you always so charming, North?"

She ignores my question. "Here's the pin for the safe in my office. Inside you'll find eight weeks' worth of money. Spend it any way you want."

"I could have your house repainted in something other than white."

Her glare is response enough for me. "Is there anything you want to give me a heads-up about? Crime in your neighborhood?"

A grin breaks out on my face. "Was that a joke, North? Don't worry, I left the caution tape up on my front door. You can have the pleasure of ripping that off. What's this?" I scowl at the printout.

"A cheat sheet. How to dress well as a man," she comments without meeting my gaze.

"Hang on." My hand catches her arm, drawing her back to me. The feel of her skin beneath my fingertips jolts an unexpected reaction. A swish of need, of bottled energy. "The ends of my shoes must be round, not pointed. When wearing a jacket, fasten the middle button." I look at her. She twists her earring and pretends to be interested in her shoes. "You suggest I buy a watch from Cartier or Tiffany's. Wear the watch but make sure it's not visible. No denim or cargo Monday-Friday. Play around with color?"

I glance at her with a hard glare.

She gives me a doe-eyed gaze and clears her throat. "Fashion is for the whole body. You want to survive in my world? Learn to fit in."

My hand flattens over hers, dominating every inch of her fingers, and acutely aware of the heat where our flesh touches.

"Underwear should be kept simple." I put the paper on the

table and tap my finger on her suggestion, holding her gaze. I keep my face close to hers, her mouth in direct line with mine. "Who said I wear underwear?"

Her cheeks bloom a gorgeous color that I imagine stretches down the length of her. "I would highly recommend—"

I take her list and wad it in my hand and toss it over my shoulder. "Show me the house."

I'll make a guy confession. Her house is nine thousand square feet, but I'm curious about only one room. Her bedroom. It's the last stop on the house tour.

"This is where the great Lexi North sleeps," I comment at the large bed with a fabric covered headboard with crystal buttons.

She'll find out that my bed makes noise. The headboard, although I've never tested it, will bang against the wall when I finally do let a woman sleep over.

I can't wait to clear her bed of the throw pillows. In fact, the room is all the same gray with the exception of a built-in nook between shelves I make a mental note to recreate in CeCe's room.

"What's with the color scheme? Some kind of artistic cry from the inside?"

"I love the color," she answers with a frown. "Gray is versatile in any light."

Yeah, I don't care about any of that. Running and jumping onto her bed, I full-frontal, spread-eagle it and sink my head into the mattress. The pillows topple over me. "I got the better end of the deal."

"Please get off my bed."

It was worth the horrified look on her face. I prop up on my elbows, chest stretched broad. It happens before I can stop it, the urge to pull her on top of me. "Is it the wrinkled sheets?"

"Wrinkled sheets are not a problem. It's the six-foot-however tall body of yours messing them up. Do you have any idea how big you are?"

"Uh-huh," I say, straight-faced and aware of pink blooming on her cheeks. "No one's ever complained about that before."

She grabs a pillow and flashes her angry eyes at me before throwing it at my face. "You're *not* sleeping in my bed." She storms out of the room. "You're staying in the guest room."

"Which one?" I call after her. "You have eight of them."

Lexi's house has almost too many amenities. She has a pool, and, get this, a staff. A housekeeper, gardeners, a personal trainer, and a shopper.

I am still trying to nail down *what* she does all day if everyone is doing her life for her. She spends too much time over-informing me like I get when customers think they know more about their cars than I do.

"Are you listening?" she blurts.

"No."

She huffs. "Don't wear shoes upstairs. Don't use regular towels for the pool. Don't drink any of the wine in the cellar."

Oh. My. Gosh. She needs to go. I start to usher her toward her mountain of luggage. "You're a working girl now. You might want to get yourself over to Bailey's. Time is money, North."

The two of us face off in the foyer much like when we were cornered into making the bet. She's all fierce vibes and hating life. "Before I go, there is one important thing."

"Does it involve brushing up on my racquetball skills?"

"We haven't gotten to the part where you take over my spot at the Alexandria Foundation. My friends on the board are aware of...*you*."

Her long stare is like she's waiting for the cavalry. "Do you own a tuxedo?"

"Now you're stalling."

She grabs my keys off the counter with so much hostility, I feel bad for the keys. "Are you going to help me with my bags?"

"Not a chance. I'm going outside to relax by your—I mean *my* pool."

My footsteps get me outside and away from her.

I am stretched out on the lounge chair with my eyes closed and my breath calm while I listen to her make several trips to my car to load up her luggage.

Doors slam. My car engine starts. She doesn't bother saying goodbye.

A bead of sweat rolls down the back of my neck. The humid June air sticks to my skin. Maybe I should move to the cabana. *Nah*.

There's a ton of shade and a brilliantly clear pool that is calling my name.

I strip off my clothes and dive butt naked into the cool water.

Oh hell yes. I float on my back.

I haven't skinny-dipped since I was a teen. I close my eyes and think back to those days. Long summer nights with endless possibilities, ignorant of heartache, and wanting nothing more than to love beyond measure—and be loved in return, without conditions.

Now my life comes attached to a young girl I'm trying to give the world to, and most days, I feel like I'm falling short.

Maybe this summer will be good for CeCe.

We'll stay up late watching movies in Lexi's theater room. Do weekend beach trips. According to Lexi's list, she has a house in St. Martin, but neither of us have passports. CeCe wanted to go to New York City forever to see a play. I'll start with that, booking something for— A loud scream causes my eyes to fly open and I stand up, the water covering me from the waist down.

"WHAT are you doing?" Lexi stands next to the lounge chair holding her hand up, blocking her view.

My hands dive underwater to cover my junk. "Why are you

still here?" I shout and swim to the edge of the pool and rest my arms on the concrete so all she can see are my shoulders and arms. "You can lower your hand."

"I forgot something. I had to come back." She slowly brings her hand to her side as if I've traumatized her. "You're naked in my pool."

I wipe water off my face. "Very observant. They teach you that at Harvard?"

"I didn't go to Harvard," she quips. "Could you put some clothes on?"

"Depends. Are you staying or going?"

"I'm *not* staying."

"Then I'm staying as I am. You can't see anything from there."

She sneaks a look down my arm and I catch her gaze, relishing in the mortification. She was *looking*. We both know it. An alluring color of pink blushes right up her cheeks.

"Put a bathing suit on next time. That's a rule."

My gaze climbs up her smooth legs. I'm going to wonder what she would look like naked in this pool.

She looks ready to reach down and strangle me. "In three seconds I'm getting back to swimming. One...two..."

She grumbles and grabs my clothes, tossing them in the pool. "There. Now you can reach your clothes."

She's a piece of work. Grabbing my soaked clothes, a laugh slips, which makes her glare at me more. Good. Hate me.

Once she leaves, I towel off and wrap it around my waist.

My afternoon is spent napping on a chair, eating the food in her fridge, doing nothing. It's not in my nature to do nothing. My favorite place to be is at the shop with Alec and the guys.

Bringing up my phone screen, I research Lexi.

The pot of gold I hit is article after article, mostly from gossip sites. There's no shortage of Lexi posing in front of cameras. The most recent is from an awards ceremony.

Lexi's wearing a dress held together by air and a hairstyle from space, contradicting the natural beauty she had when she opened her door today. Other articles give me pause.

Lexi North ruins another marriage... Lexi North to blame for divorce of high-profile attorney...

I scroll farther down. The next headlines are about her and Hudson Hoffman.

I sit up like I've been hit with a hammer.

Hudson Hoffman.

The Hoffman name sums up everything I need to know about Lexi.

It shines a spotlight on a connection my family and I have worked hard to keep hidden from CeCe. If Lexi is tangled up with a Hoffman, then I stepped on a landmine.

CHAPTER SEVEN

Lexi

I'm not going to Bailey's. I called in sick, relying on a fake cough.

I'm parked in Evan's driveway not ready to walk through his front door. My hands are oh-so-heavy on the steering wheel.

The sound of a lone beat in my heart is like a death drum. I ignore the ring of funk with wadded-up straw wrappers in Evan's cup holders.

His rough-around-the-edges personality doesn't fit with raising a teenage girl.

Where is her mother? Not that my mother is anything to brag about.

She checks nearly every box in the *I Got Parenting Wrong* category, and yet, she holds the illustrious title of giving birth to me, and for that, there's an empty slot in my heart waiting for her. My dad and I are about as close as the north and south poles, making the two sides of my parental equation less than noteworthy.

Going to her for financial help is not an option. I would rather starve than crawl up to her Manhattan apartment and ask for money.

CeCe's better off without a mother.

But raised by Evan? That has to be rough, sweetheart.

A message on my phone breaks up my thoughts.

Evan: *Help. I'm lost in your butler's pantry.*

Is he for real? I don't answer.

Evan: *Since you banned me from drinking your wine, the same is true for you. Don't touch my Miller Lite.*

I snort loud and unladylike.

Me: *I won't touch anything of yours.*

Evan: *You sure about that, North?*

Yes, Evan. I am sure.

Even if he's a whole lot of man. The guy has no shame. Twenty bucks says he is doing the backstroke naked in my pool.

I might have gotten a glimpse.

Evan lives in the same city but the neighborhood is a different planet. A groan rumbles through my throat. Aboveground wiring and multiple satellite dishes on the roofs do nothing for curb appeal.

Grubby outdoor furniture sits on porches. Rusty play equipment is in one yard. A dated RV with flat tires is parked on the lawn of another.

I can overlook the mural of license plates hanging from the neighbor's fence.

What causes my lips to push firmly together is the house with a truck parked on cinder blocks.

Big breath. Breathe in and out.

Evan's house is an ugly, dilapidated Cape Cod meets creative add-on. Spruced up with dirty siding. Instead of grabbing my bags, I grab my phone. I need something to look forward to and it isn't going to be the collection of plastic flamingos in the neighboring yard.

Talia hasn't texted since the auction. I start with her. *In need of a friend willing to buy me lunch and a glass of prosecco.*

Talia: *I'm working.*

I snub the pervasive feeling that she's ignoring me.

Three more texts are sent to friends to get lunch on the schedule. All the responses are some form of *Not today love XOXO*.

"This is temporary," I say, opening the car door and walking up steps with Christmas lights wrapped around the porch.

I jam the key in the lock and twist, pushing open the squeaky door.

Something large and gray with four legs darts across the floor.

I erupt in a high-pitched scream and spin around, running back through the door, and slam face-first into a solid mass of muscle with arms. "I thought you were swimming."

Evan's uneasy stare meets mine. His fingers curl around my biceps. "I had to get CeCe from her friend's house." His gaze holds mine for a split second. "I forgot to tell you CeCe has a cat."

"That's a big detail not to mention."

He shrugs. "Now you know."

My tirade fades at CeCe standing in the doorway.

"Hi Lexi," she says, checking me out like I'm an alien without a ship. She looks like Evan, with the same dark blond hair. Her too-long bangs and untidy split ends could use a trip to the salon.

CeCe's tight-lipped mouth also has an uncanny similarity to Evan's.

She walks past me, shyly looking at me with her brown eyes. The moving four-footed furball appears from behind the couch and trots after her. They disappear into another room.

My attention refocuses on Evan.

Are his eyes always so green? I've had friends undergo iris implant surgery to achieve that color. All I see is how the pool water trailed down his neck this morning and the clear color of his eyes as I tried not to look at the rest of him. "What are you doing here?"

"CeCe forgot her swimsuit."

They came back for a swimsuit. I can't help myself. "She can buy a new one."

"Thanks for the tip." Evan's gaze lingers like his words are more for me than her. "We didn't mean to scare you. The cat's name is Bowser. Feed her or she'll pee on the bed."

My jaw opens in horror. I want to cry. And run away.

"I'm kidding." Evan shoots me a derisive look. "Is everything so life-and-death with you?"

No, just with him. "Keep telling yourself you're hilarious and one day you might be. What sort of a name is Bowser anyway?"

His eyebrow quirks. "Are you for real? You don't know who Bowser is? Then again, you didn't know Black Sabbath. Is it all pop culture you have something against or references starting with the letter *B*?"

"None of the above," I answer, covering my tracks. "I know who Bowser is." He's having none of my snideness.

Evan waits patiently. His challenging gaze is unremitting. "Who is he then?"

"A superhero. *Obviously*. With a sword and shield." *There*. My answer is generic enough. Should be a win for me. "I didn't watch American cartoons growing up. Only French ones."

Evan makes a constipated face. "That sounds miserable."

Miserable is spending more time with a nanny than my family. Evan doesn't want to hear woe-is-me. He will roll his eyes and go hard on me for such shallowness. "My parents wanted me to be cultured."

Evan's shot of laughter causes me to look twice at him. "*Oh*. You're going to get cultured."

I start to walk away and his hand touches my waist, light enough to not be a big deal, but my body notices. He holds his phone in front of him like I should read the screen. The message is from Alec.

Alec: *Lexi bailed on work.*

Alec: *Remind her she doesn't get paid if she doesn't show.*

Sliding my gaze up to Evan's, he's waiting with raised eyebrows. "Thought you might want to see that."

A pathetic cough escapes my throat. "I wasn't feeling well."

He puts the back of his hand to my forehead and presses softly. His eyes stay with mine, his mouth upturned. "You look fine to me."

"What are you doing?" I act offended, but don't push his hand away, either.

"Taking your temperature." He lowers his hand to his side. "You don't have a fever. In case you were torn about going to the emergency room."

"How very scientific of you." I add another cough. "No more stopping by without warning. Technically, you're on my property now. Second." My head shakes. "Why are you looking at me like that?"

Evan turns fully to me, his chest an inch from bumping into my nose. He touches the underside of my chin, angling my face toward his. "You can call it quits at any time. Say the word and you go back home."

Steady, incessant heat trickles down to my breasts. All because his slightly rough hand is on my skin. *If only I could quit.* "I'm in this for the long haul."

His fingers shift, cupping my chin gently, raising my awareness with heat rising in his gaze and a smirk on his mouth I want to erase. "We'll see about that. Speaking of friends. Stay away from a guy named Sticky."

"Who's Sticky?" Subtle panic takes root as Evan goes down the hall and I follow as he knocks a closed door with the back of his hand. "WHO'S STICKY?"

"Are you making the swimsuit from scratch?" Evan says and waits until she opens the door.

We file into her room. Four walls doused in an unappealing purple paint and faded butterfly decals.

Evan looks at me taking in her twin bed crammed next to a scuffed dresser and a light switch with peeled-off sticker marks. Our eyes lock in understanding, and it's clear humility overcomes him. He can put on the best, most confident front, but we both know this room is dingy and sad. They don't have much of anything.

My fingers move over the books on her nightstand, a stack of paperbacks about horses.

CeCe sees me staring. I can't believe she was bold enough to challenge Evan and me into this position. I mean, good for her. Bad for me.

"Are you into horses?" I ask, keenly aware of Evan watching me.

"I love horses," she says.

I am going to connect the dots here that she does not ride. "You have access to my family's stables in Potomac. My father has fourteen horses and access to riding lessons, a trainer, and equipment."

"Oh my God. Yes, yes, *yes.*" CeCe's frown climbs into a jaw-dropping smile with a renewed fresh-faced contagious energy.

"No horseback riding," Evan remarks, shutting out CeCe's excitement. "She could fall off. I like her spine functioning normally."

CeCe goes painfully silent. She grabs a few books worn at the corners. "I knew you'd say no." She persists like a wildflower, strong and determined to make her place among thorny roses.

Her comment gives me pause. I don't see the harm. "You could always check out the stables."

"We'll talk about it later." Evan's reprimanding voice has CeCe off in a huff, leaving him rubbing his shoulder impatiently. "Don't make offers without my permission. I don't want her riding horses. Period."

"I was offering. Not loading her up on meth." I didn't think what I suggested was wrong, but now I'm in the middle of a tug-of-war. "Taking her to the stable isn't a big deal."

"To you, maybe." Evan doesn't move from the doorway. We stare at each other with leveling gazes. "Make sure your cough is better by tomorrow, North."

"The name is Lexi," I shout, exasperated at the sound of the closing front door.

My solo source of support is Bowser sitting on her heinie in the doorway. She stretches at my favorite Gucci platform sandal and digs her claw in, getting stuck. "No!" I scoop her up and the fabric tears. "I'm sorry about your name, don't take it out on my shoes."

Bowser and I journey through the two-bedroom house. My toes curl in disgust from the feel of the carpet. Safe to say I won't be taking any relaxing baths here.

The vacation homes I stay at are made to feel like a hotel. This feels like someone's *home*. I don't see how I'm going to be at ease. Thanks, fate.

"Should we see where Evan sleeps?" I say to Bowser.

Let's not go out on a limb and say I'm curious about Evan's bedroom.

His queen-size bed takes up most of the space and the headboard looks ready to fall between the mattress and the wall. Probably from Evan having constant sex.

Warmth burns my cheeks at that unexpected thought. Evan, taking up the bed. His hands, his mouth, dominating. The mattress shifting beneath me. I saw the way he looked at my decorative pillows, like they were wasted space meant for occupying in other ways.

"What do we have here?" On his nightstand is a book. *Dudes Who Braid Hair.*

A quick perusal through the braid book is followed by a one-foot journey to his closet.

"How depressing."

This calls for a humble brag. I understand men's fashion. I love the way a man looks in the right clothes. Evan's hangers are full of hoodie sweatshirts and a lone plaid button-down. Bowser swipes at the sleeve.

I push it all to the side, since I need to fit my wardrobe in these Porta Potty sized accommodations.

Interestingly enough—he is surprisingly neat. Clothes folded perfectly in his drawers. Socks folded over. He wears boxers.

"I pegged him for a boxer brief man."

Bowser yawns and paws at the carpet, stretching her back. Disrupting her relaxation, I go to the kitchen and do my homework. Evan's kitchen cabinets are loaded with Top Ramen and canned soup.

Evan's "list" is a model in concise handwriting as neat as the folded clothes in his drawers.

Bailey House Rules
Mow the lawn
Keep the house clean
Feed Bowser
Change litter box
Don't get attached to my house
Don't use my body wash

Finding a spot on the end of his couch, I rest my hands on my knees. A stab of emptiness steals my breath at the hopes I had for this year. Summer was my favorite season until this one. Long nights. Late mornings. Hudson has been a staple from June to August since we were teenagers.

He was moving on this whole time. The hurt doubles in my heart. Is he really not mine anymore?

I have bigger problems set to the tune of my needy stomach. What am I supposed to do for food? Bowser saunters into the room, meowing. "Don't look at me, I can't feed myself. What do you eat, anyway?"

I text Evan. *How many times a day does Bowser eat?*

Evan: *Twice a day. Refill the dry food each morning. Give her one half canned food in the evenlng*

Evan: *The poop scooper for the litter box is in the garage*

Evan: *Put her crap in a grocery bag*

Me: *Here I was hoping for a welcome basket*

Evan: *You didn't see the unopened pack of chewing gum?*

I frown at Bowser. My screen flashes with a video call from Hudson. I perk up. What's this? Trouble in Isabella paradise?

"Do you have a sec?" he says, embodying the word handsome from the *h* to the *e*. Coiffed hair complements the crookedness of his mouth and the object of girls' obsession at our boarding school.

After he royally dumped me, I do what I do best. Feign indifference. "If you can make it quick. What's up?"

"I need to apologize for the way I told you about Isabella. I don't want you to feel like you mean nothing to me."

His words are gray as my bedroom, with room for interpretation. "There's not much to apologize for," I say coolly, shelving the hurt. "I appreciate the acknowledgment."

"So listen. Tell me you're not following through with this bet."

This is the real reason he called. "I am. For only a few weeks."

Doubt fills his expression. "Does your father know?"

His punch to the gut gets under my skin. Hudson doesn't have many faults other than being ridiculously handsome, but one of them is tossing my father's name at me like I'm five. "My father is supportive." Mentally, I use air quotes around *supportive.*

"Really? Is your father aware Evan's sister, Natalie Bailey, is in prison for the armed robbery of a gas station attendant?"

Excuse me. *What?* I scare Bowser right off the back of the couch. Now we're adding major crimes to the Bailey family. My pulse quickens at the spiraling revelation. A minor fib is in order. "I'm aware."

"You're okay with it?" He eyes me suspiciously. "Do you need legal help?"

Oh how I would like to lean on the dynamic of Hudson's legal skills. "My father's lawyers are involved." Enough said. Enough of Hudson digging around.

"I'm sorry, Lexi, and I'm here for you. Even if we're not together."

There it is. Lifting me up to put me down. *Thank you for reminding me.*

The screen turns blank and he's gone.

My gaze lowers to the scratched coffee table. What am I supposed to make of his call? "Why does Evan have three remotes?"

I take a photo and send him a message. *How do I know which one to use?*

Evan's reply is my screenshot with the remotes circled and an explanation for each.

Evan: *I can't find your remote*

Evan: *Or my masculinity*

Me: *Television is voice activated. What's your wifi PW?*

Evan: *I have wifi?*

"Forget this," I say, too out of sorts to deal with his multiple remotes.

With nothing better to do than try not to touch anything, I try to read up on Natalie Bailey. There is not much information about the case. She put a gun to a gas station attendant's head. She took a plea and avoided trial. Only a brief mention of her having a daughter. All of this information is overflowing my brain.

"Okay," I say to Bowser, "we know CeCe's mom is in prison. Where's her dad?"

CHAPTER EIGHT

Evan

My first morning waking up in Lexi's house presents a problem. No, no, it wasn't the ultra-soft sheets or her bed or the automatic window shades. The walk-in shower in Lexi's bathroom with a stainless steel grid descending from the ceiling isn't an issue.

I cannot. For the life of me. Figure out why two floating marble benches stick out from the opposite wall.

Wearing nothing but boxers and a bad attitude, I attach a photo of this odd, stacked bench with about four feet of space between and send Lexi a message.

Me: *What am I looking at?*

Lexi: *A horizontal shower.*

I have to read that twice. **Me:** *What the fuck is that?*

Lexi: *How very articulate you are.*

I scratch my junk while tiny green dots move on the screen.

Lexi: *Lie on your stomach and personalized water pressure streams down to relieve your stress points.*

I cover my crown jewels with my hand. "Don't worry, I won't make you," I say.

Exhaling a thin breath, I type fast. *Thanks for the English lesson. Let me try again. No man wants to lie face down with his balls on a cold slab of marble. I have ten other suggestions for how I want my "stress points" worked and—* A pleasant warmth rises against the soles of my feet, like the tiles are heating. *Showers are meant to be VERTICAL. Articulate enough for you?*

Lexi escalates with a second-stage phone contact. She calls.

I answer with a terse, "What?"

"Do you know how much sleep I got last night?" Her fired-up voice has me moving the phone away from my ears.

"Only twelve hours?"

"Hardly any. Your neighbor had half the street at her house. I opened a window and yelled at her."

"You did what?"

I bet she's holding her chin high. "I couldn't sleep. What was I supposed to do*?*"

"Invest in ear plugs." *Christ.* How did she rile me so fast? I move my hand up my jaw, scratching my skin against the stubble.

"I will. Soon as you stop bitching about your shower insecurities."

I snort loudly. "I don't expect you to find anything redeemable about my life." None of this is surprising. I saw the way Lexi looked at my house. I anticipated it, even.

"I'm so sorry your cracked kitchen tiles aren't on my list of things to love. There *is* one thing I adore." Warning bells go off in my head to not trust her next words.

"The sound of the door when you leave my house?"

"Your cat. She sleeps next to me."

Bowser. The traitor. Lying next to Lexi in *my* bed. Phone pressed to my ear, I step inside the walk-in shower and stop short of crouching down to assess a panel of buttons flush to the wall. "She's not allowed in my bed."

Lexi continues talking while I fight back the sudden

overwhelming reaction to the thought of having her against me.

Her long hair sprawled over my pillow. Her naked body beneath me. Bowser relegated to some faraway island. Lexi holding on to me. Saying my name. Shit. My cock is responding.

"Evan," she says rudely. "Were you listening?"

"No." I stare at the bulge in my boxers. Women don't have to worry about this. "I'm thinking which hotel room to rent so I can take a normal shower."

"Fine."

"*Fine.*"

I toss my phone on the counter and face the music. I mentally give a middle finger to the gravity-defying bench and do a Rocky-style jog-in-place in front of the marble shower area with six dials and eight jet stream holes. I crack my neck. "You rebuild transmissions, you can do this. *It's a shower.*"

Pulling the rubber band from my hair, I shake my hair out.

I go to town, turning on every spout and pressing every button. Hard blasts of water shoot from the jets assaulting my chest and thighs, hitting me in the cheeks and groin. Blindly, I scramble to get out of the line of fire and push another button and the nozzle-style spray stops abruptly.

A curtain of the softest raindrops falls from the stainless steel overhead fixture. The column of water changes color to the most delicate shades of alternating blue synchronizing with a mashup of pop and rap thumping from the sound system. A calming, warm mist begins with the sound of birds chirping and perfumed water.

This is...nice. *Really nice.* My mouth snaps to a frown. I won't tell Lexi.

I walk out of the shower a different man. One who's been beaten down, smells like citrus, and possibly went clubbing—I can't be sure.

CeCe's yelp has me throwing on a shirt and athletic shorts and rushing down the hall. "What's wrong?" I ask, entering the open door of the guest room and moving past the white walls with gold-and-white canvases of women in dresses.

"Check this out," she says, sitting on a furry bench in her all-white marble bathroom.

My breathing slows. She's okay. She still has two eyeballs, so that's good. I turn my interest to the oval countertop mirror in front of her.

She moves her face up close to the lighted mirror.

"Good morning," says a female, British speaking AI, "your skin is hydrated, supple, and smooth. Your blemishes will go away in five to seven days with proper care. I suggest a face soap with salicylic acid. Your skin care score is: excellent."

"Scoot over," I say, taking a seat on the bench, and put my face up to the mirror, confident in my skin care regimen of *I don't give a shit.*

"Did you have a bad night?" the AI says. "Your skin is dry, rough, and in need of moisturizer. I suggest a vitamin-infused cucumber mask, increased REM sleep, and more water in your diet. Your skin care score is: needs improvement."

I look at CeCe. "She's not human."

"Did you *see* my closet?" We both turn around on the bench. "Open wardrobe."

A soft humming noise ensues as I watch in horror. Garment racks move on a belt and for the grand finale, an entire wall of individual, lighted cubbies moves forward, each one empty like they're waiting to store my organs.

"I need coffee," I say, ditching CeCe. Halfway down Lexi's spiral staircase, the doorbell rings. "What now?"

I answer the door to a shot of bright sunlight and a petite woman with freckles. "Hi. You must be Evan," she says. Her red-haired ponytail bobs and her green eyes sparkle. "I'm Chef Sofia, your private chef."

"I can pour milk and cereal in a bowl, thanks." I close the door. No chefs. No horizontal showers.

CeCe stomps past me and opens the door. "He's kidding. Come in."

I stare her down. "I wasn't."

"Do we tell you what we want to eat?" CeCe asks as we move into the kitchen. "How does this work?"

"I set the menu a week before and you use an app to make changes or request a meal." Sofia opens a closet like she knows where every fork and pan is. She grabs chef's whites.

I take a seat at the counter. "Right, but every day? Every meal?"

"As much as you want." Chef opens the fridge and gets to work. "I thought we'd do an omelet bar with first of the season spinach, feta from a local farm, with a side of brioche French toast and handpicked strawberries and homemade whipped cream."

All of it is topped with edible flowers and fresh-squeezed orange juice. The fruit buffet alone must cost a fortune. I take a photo and send it to Lexi. *How's your breakfast?*

She sends me a photo of a dry packet of oatmeal. *I'm overwhelmed by the microwaveable options.*

Me: *Then you'll be happy about the Flapsticks in the freezer.*

CeCe inhales every bite.

"Slow down," I say, trying my best to do the same. This beats Waffle House.

I scrape my plate clean. I get up to take my plate to the dishwasher.

"I handle the dishes," Chef Sofia intervenes with a direct voice and takes my plate.

"CeCe and I put our own dishes in the dishwasher."

"No," Sofia insists. "This is my job, understood?"

"Uncle Evan's life skills," CeCe mimics my voice. "He understands."

"You do a bad impression of me."

After Chef Sofia cleans every last inch of the stovetop and leaves us comatose, Lexi's house is a revolving door of housekeeping staff. I stand around like deadwood not knowing what to do.

The kitchen is the least likely place the cleaning crew will ask me to lift my feet to dust. I play around with the buttons on the fridge. It also starts talking, "Time to reorder yogurt, French morel mushrooms, and tampons."

CeCe and I don't look at each other. I press the refrigerator's *no talking* mode.

"What are we doing today?" CeCe says. "Can I have friends over?"

"Lexi doesn't want houseguests and I haven't looked at our schedule." I am strategically putting that off.

"I love Lexi's house. Did you see the workout room? It looks like the dance studio I used to go to."

This entire morning grates on my patience. "Uncle Alec and I used to lift weights in Grandma's driveway. No one needs a workout room."

"You're not even going to try to like it, are you? You never try anything new. You tell me I have to, but you don't."

"CeCe. That's not true. I just ate a meal for three." I fling my arm out. I hate it when she corners me with my own arguments. "I don't want you to get used to all this."

She shrugs. "Yeah, that would be awful."

"You still do chores while we're here. Got it?" She needs to do things for herself. Soon as I say it, another thought comes to mind. *So does Lexi.* I paddle that thought down the river of *not my problem*.

"Why does she have so many pillows?"

A soft laugh leaves my mouth. Probably to support her massive ego. "Maybe she likes pillows."

"Why does everyone hate Lexi?"

In need of more caffeine, I play around with a dial on the

coffee machine. "Who is everyone?"

"Everyone online."

"What are they saying?" I use social media only for Bailey's-related posts.

"She's what's wrong with the rich."

"You mean people you've never met are saying things about a person they've never met? Make up your own mind about people after you meet them. Do *you* hate Lexi?"

CeCe starts picking at her nails. "No."

My mood turns salty. I am genuinely stumped by the coffeemaker. "When you made the bet, you said some things." I wade carefully around this subject. She's not wrong to wish she had *more*. "You know we have a good life, right? We have what matters. You have Grandma and Uncle Alec. We have each other."

Uncertainty flares in her eyes.

If raising a girl could come with a playbook like my beloved Capitals, I would pay. I am in the defensive zone.

"Speaking of social media, hand it over. You lost your tablet for one month."

She's in the offensive zone. "Yeah. *I know.* You told me I can't have a social media account until I'm ninety."

"Yet you went behind my back and, when I asked you to stop recording, you didn't." If it were up to me, I would delete the post and her account. If not for Alec's warning: *Do not delete the account. It will hold Lexi legally accountable.*

CeCe may not win *Niece of the Year,* but she stood up for us. Punishing her for sticking up for herself is one of those parenting loopholes I walk around on sensitive feet. Looks like we will settle for surviving in the neutral zone.

She hops off the barstool and pushes it in. "Could I skip visiting my mom while we're living here?"

It feels strange talking about this in a house with two industrial dishwashers.

I resist the urge to touch the top of her head like she is five with pigtails, though my heart will always want to. This is CeCe drawing lines. She needs to know she can say no and be heard. Parenting her isn't all about my comfort level with letting go. It's about her letting go, too. The choice will hurt Natalie, but CeCe is trusting me to listen.

"I'll talk to her."

"What about my dad?" she asks, stirring up a hurricane of emotions.

Stillness overcomes me. She has no idea who he is and how she ended up living with me. It's a topic my family and I never broach. "What about him?"

"Does he know Mom's in prison?"

He knows. He knows and I can't tell you. She wants to ask more, but I reroute the subject. "How would you feel about going to New York while we're living it up?"

CHAPTER NINE

Lexi

"I can do this," I say to Bowser, placing my many product bottles on a plastic shower shelf. "I won't pay attention to the rust ring around the drain or the black substance at the tiled corners." I pick up Evan's nightmare all-in-one shampoo/conditioner/body wash. "Do you see this? He uses the same soap for his feet and his head."

There is also nowhere to place my La Prairie and Dior skin care or hand carved cypress body brush next to Evan's dried toothpaste holder on the pedestal sink.

I take a head-to-toe deep breath and clasp my hands, stretching my arms in front of me. "It's just a shower."

Here goes nothing. A blast of hard water hits my face and I duck around the water, grabbing onto the shower curtain. The rod unmounts from the wall, slamming down and hitting me on the head. "Ow," I say, pushing off the metal pole and slick curtain while reaching blindly for the faucet handle.

The weight of all my bottles brings down the shelf, rolling into the tub and tripping me up. I yelp and immediately sputter as I swallow a mouthful of water. *All my inheritance. All my inheritance! I have to get through this or I'll have to live like this forever!*

. . .

Evan's thin yarn ball of a towel is tucked at my breasts. Water drips down my back and I sit on the edge of his bed. My breath rises with tension, fresh off little sleep in a room with a creaky fan and no air flow.

Me: *Didn't know I needed protective gear for the shower*
Evan: *Didn't know your shower was going to deflower me*
Me: *I'll pay you to use my shower*
Evan: *Not in your budget, North*
Evan: *Check the backyard for the old baby pool*
Me: *Your shower curtain fell down*
Evan: *So...put it back up*

"He's useless," I complain to Bowser and head for the kitchen. I need breakfast.

I take a photo of my options and send him my grievances. *Bagged cereal and a collection of hot sauces.*

Evan sends me a photo of fresh raspberries, poached eggs with hollandaise, and a latte with foam shaped into two hearts. *No hot sauce needed on my end, thanks.*

"That was completely unnecessary."

What is essential is using Evan's cash for the venti mocha with whipped cream and extra caramel drizzle on my way to Bailey's.

Tia looks up from her computer, her ear pressed to the phone. Her heart-shaped face shows off a small chin. She pauses long enough to accept my presence and the coffee drink in hand. "You're late."

This is record punctuality for me. "Do we count thirty minutes as late?"

She stops typing and stares at me. "At Bailey's, we do." She swivels around in her chair, grabbing a folder, talking to herself. Her brown eyes stay on me for a heartbeat too long. Tia's eyebrows go up higher. Her strong, defined brows have the appearance of someone who knows what to do with brow gel and a pomade pencil.

"Where's the restroom?" I need to check my mascara.

Tia points to my right and I retreat to remind myself I can do this.

When I come out, Alec sticks his head out of his office. "Lexi, a word."

This is my fate. Evan *had* to have a twin. I can't escape the Bailey dudes, though Alec's style is more acceptable with his slacks and a button-down shirt. He is a preview of what his darling brother would look like without the stubble and constant scrutinizing gaze.

"Do you do anything online?" I ask innocently. "Or is this the place where trees go to die?"

Seated behind a stack of documents as tall as the Empire State Building, Alec reaches behind his desk to a pile of shirts and tosses one at me. "We wear these on Fridays. Josh will get you a jumpsuit."

A disdainful sigh is all I manage.

He glances at his computer screen distractedly. "I get you don't want to be here. I'm not a fan of the arrangement."

"Then why did you agree to it?"

Alec's focus turns to me. "I support my brother."

Fair enough.

"All of our mechanics-in-training are held to Bailey's standards. If you're late three times in a row, you don't work for a day."

"That's the punishment?"

"*Be courteous.* This is my business, not a vacation. If you're not physically here, you don't get paid. You get money only for the time you check in and check out. When you're late, that cuts into your paycheck." Alec dismisses me by turning his attention to his laptop. "Find Josh in the garage, he has work for you."

What? I get my pay docked for being late? Is that a thing?
I'm reeling over that concept as I head out to find Josh.

The garage is divided into two sides; the one farther away
has a car lifted off the floor. The lane closest to me has a line of
cars. Half a dozen guys are spread out, some with their noses
in an open hood and another connecting a pump to a tire.

No one looks in my direction. "Excuse me? Hello?" I hold
up my hand hoping for a day of sitting in front of a fan and
examining my cuticles.

A stocky guy with dimples strolls in from one of the garage
doors. "I'm Josh," he says and points to the employees. "That's
Brandon, Garcia, and…"

I take in the grubby walls and dirty equipment. My
sensitive nostrils breathe in the faint smell of cigarettes. It's
like someone peeked inside my brain and drew up a blueprint
for my own personal purgatory.

"Each morning, soon as you arrive, sign in on this computer."
The desktop is cluttered with AC/DC stickers on what I think
might be a bunny with boobs or a frowny face.

"Do you want me to sign in now?"

"Unless you've got somewhere else to be?" Josh waits while
I push the keys and follow the password prompt.

"There. Done." I sand my hands together.

"Your shift starts at six o-clock each morning. You were
late today, so that counts as a tardy."

"Don't I get a pass? It's my first day." I'm still processing
starts each day at six o-clock.

"No free passes." He points to a chalkboard hanging
beneath the wall clock. "Check the job board when you arrive
and you get a thirty-minute lunch break."

In my haste this morning, lunch wasn't even a thought in
my mind. I'm sure there are restaurants nearby.

"You're on car detailing today. Each car that comes
through, vacuum the front seats, wipe down the dash, and

put a seat liner in before you drive the car around the corner to the pickup lot. Brandon, show Lexi the supply room."

Brandon takes a loud slurp on his Big Gulp like he just found the last drop of liquid. Brandon's a lanky guy. No hips. One long torso. Nice eyes that don't go with the arm sleeve tattoos. His thin beard looks more penciled-in than full-out man scruff like Evan.

Garcia whistles and rolls up each garage door in time for a customer to drive up. Everyone jumps into action. Machines hum.

I follow Brandon to the stockroom, an obnoxious setting of unfiltered light. "No one's concerned about their corneas?" I mention and steer clear of the rows of organized bins and products.

Brandon's busy grabbing parts. "Dash cleaners are right here. Grab the ones with the red lettering. When you clean the dash, spray the towel first. Remove the foot liners. Shake them out and vacuum the entire front seats."

"What's the scoop around here? Are you all friends? I'm sure whatever Evan told you about me isn't true."

His steady gaze says otherwise. "We look out for one another. I've known him since high school."

I'll cross him off the helpful list.

"Don't forget to put on the jumpsuit." He points to a rack of hanging gray one-piece fashion disasters.

Might as well wear a bag. I put on the uniform and zip it up, swimming in the oversized, non-tailored outfit.

Brandon leaves me in the stockroom. Talia has not returned my texts, and this is the longest we have gone without speaking. I'm left with no choice but to call her.

Her voicemail is all I get. "Hey, it's me. Any chance you want to meet this weekend? I could use a de-stressing hydration facial. The one with the jellyfish eggs and a manicure. Call me."

I could use a real meal, too. Breakfast consisted of the

rapidly ripening fruit in Evan's house.

Stalling on purpose, I text Evan. *I'm appalled by the bathroom conditions at Bailey's.*

Evan: *Specifically, which conditions?*

The seating options in the stockroom are none, forcing me to shimmy my butt onto an unmarked barrel. I inhale a mild scent of oil. **Me:** *No seat liners. I have to share a seat with hairy men.*

Evan: *How do you know they're hairy?*

Me: *Are you aware the dispensers in the bathroom give powder soap?*

Evan: *Sorry, I'm enjoying utilizing the virtual trainer in your workout room. What's the problem exactly?*

Me: *How do you work in these conditions?*

Evan: *How do you manage with only one massaging bidet?*

"Let's go," Josh says, knocking at the door, "the cars won't clean themselves."

Evan is easing into *my* morning with fresh-squeezed orange juice and having his bed made by the housekeeping staff. Then he's off to sampling chocolates at a friend-of-a-friend's business opening.

I push the most unattractive safety goggles up my nose and grab a bunch of products. Good luck with that, Evan.

My first car is at the front of a line with the passenger door open. I grab a pair of gloves lying around because there's no way I'm bare-handing floor liners. I try not to squirm at the linty insides.

Josh has his head stuck in a hood. Brandon is doing something involving a thingy that shoots sparks, and the rest of the guys are like bees in and out of hives.

I pull the first floor mat out of the driver's side. Grass and hay stick to the mat and I give a dainty, one-handed shake. The safety goggles slide down my nose because it's a million degrees. My mascara sweats into my eyes and stings but taking the cumbersome gloves off is a process like the time I had to wear a spandex top with nylon overlay for a stint on the runway at a haute fashion show in NYC.

I wipe my mascara on my arms.

A throat clears and I catch Josh looking over from the open car hood. "That's not done."

Whatever is stuck to this mat isn't budging. "Back you go," I say, placing it in the car and skipping the passenger floor mat. I use the black spray bottle and wipe down the dash.

My neck pulls back at the odor. Like someone mixed rotten eggs with sour milk. "That's disgusting." I use my shirt to cover my nostrils.

Why I need to use a seat protector in this car with two broken visors is a question mark. I shut the door and start the engine.

All I need to do now is drive the car around the corner to the lot where cars wait with numbered signs hanging from the rearview mirrors.

One car down, the rest of the day to go.

I lose count of how many cars I get to the lot in record time. In between cars, I retreat to the stock room and sit on the barrel.

This calls for a triumphant text to Evan. *You call this work? My morning has been pleasant, driving cars around to the lot.*

Evan: *All the cars made it in one piece?*

I frown at the phone. *Does that not happen when you're here?*

Evan: *Are you offering some kind of instruction, North?*

Me: *I'm informing you that I can tough this out.*

Evan: *So, no instruction then.*

Me: *The dash cleaner stinks.*

Me: *The towels are rough, consider replacing.*

Evan: *I'll take that into consideration. When I'm thinking of things that require a gentler touch.*

Heat slashes me from front to back and back again.

Evan: *Hang on. The dash cleaner is odorless.*

The stockroom door opens and I keep my phone from falling. "What are you doing?" Josh says, catching me slacking.

Alec appears in the doorway. "You. Come with me."

Alec takes me to the last car I detailed. He opens the door and squeezes his massive body in headfirst. "Mother f—" is so quiet I almost don't hear his voice.

He backs out and faces me.

"What's wrong?" I ask, gearing up from the inside out.

"What are you using to clean the dash?"

Josh is holding the evidence in question. "Whatever's in that bottle."

He cranes his neck to the sky and squeezes his eyes shut. "This is ammonia," Alec says harshly.

"There's not a label on the bottle."

"You were supposed to use the one with red lettering. Didn't Brandon tell you?"

My pause is confirmation that he did.

"You're not using seat liners, either," Alec says, all but breathing fire.

"They're impossible to get out of the box while I'm wearing gloves."

"So take the gloves off." He makes a motion for me to spin around. "Turn."

"I knew it. You guys want to check out my butt. I'm going to complain. To someone."

He takes a step toward me making my shoulders stand taller. "We have customers in the waiting room who brought their cars in this morning. They *came back* to show me their dashboards have cracks *and* they have oil stains on their seats. Oil that came from you. You were the last person in those cars."

Oh shit. Think. What did I sit on? The barrel in the stock room.

I incline my waist inward and try to look at my backside. I move my hand over one of my cheeks and find my hand printed with black gunk. My gaze inches up to Alec's.

I mentally slide off my high horse.

"Now we have to foot the bill for cleaning and repairs." Alec talks over me in a way that shuts down my soul.

"I thought I was doing a good job."

"Don't you dare go near a car without my permission."

CHAPTER TEN

Evan

"There's a dress code?" I say to the woman with a drab expression bearing a striking resemblance to the framed portrait of a basset hound hanging on the wall behind her.

Lexi's schedule led me and CeCe to the Marmont Country Club for her weekly golf tee time.

The club manager's not-so-discreet gaze moves down my Metallica shirt and over my athletic shorts. "Mr. Bailey," she says, moving her finger over her thick gold necklace. "Right through those doors you'll find the club pro shop. You'll find a wonderful selection of proper attire." She doesn't smile when she adds, "Along with club rentals."

My thoughts race with impulsive action. No one kicks me out of a place because of my clothes.

CeCe's imploring look hits home, her cheeks beet red. "Can't we just buy the clothes?" she says. "Lexi left you money."

I rub the underside of my chin forcefully. Her logic is accurate. "The website didn't say we had to dress a certain way."

The manager's thin lips press together forcefully and the twinkle in her eyes tells me she is enjoying this. "Dress requirements are implied."

Yeah, to everyone outside this replica of Buckingham Palace. My stomach bottoms out when CeCe won't make eye contact with me. "Fine. We'll go to the pro shop. Which way?"

The manager points behind me and I put my hand on CeCe's shoulder, turning her around. We move past the gold vases with bouquets of white roses. A place with red-carpet floors and a Titanic-esque staircase.

CeCe and I don't have much time before meeting two of her friends for our tee time. One is named Talia Sato and the other, Elena Wilshire. No idea who they are to Lexi.

The pro shop is a cologne-scented trap of pink polos and pleated pants. If I'm going to lose this battle, I lose on my terms. "CeCe, this rack over here."

She meets me at the circular rack in the far corner with a yellow SALE sign.

"We're going to spend only what we would at home." The hell if I need to dip into Lexi's mound of cash stuffed in her safe like a drug deal score. I sift through the selection, finding plaid pants a size too small but discounted. "These will do."

CeCe and I disappear into our respective lounges. The men's changing room has hardwood lockers and a sauna—I'll steer clear of that. Fresh robes are hanging from each locker.

I take a photo of the robes and send the image to Brandon, Josh, and Alec. *How come we don't hang out in robes?*
Brandon: *The fuck?*
Josh: *What Brandon just said.*
Alec: *They look soft.*

I move the robe out of my way. I won't be strolling around the locker with a cigar in my mouth and hands in my pockets. A male voice from another section of the locker room speaks. "I got screwed on the Kepler stock. No, it wasn't five mil, it was fifteen."

I turn my back, as he sounds like he's heading in this

direction. Just because I'm here, putting each leg into my plaid pants, doesn't mean I have to see the look he'll give me when he realizes one dollar to me isn't one million dollars.

Maybe I shouldn't have bought a smaller size.

My thighs pack into these pants like sausages. I squeeze my buttocks and get the zipper up, attempting to squat to loosen the material. They fit—barely, and I top the look off with a neon green polo with a tiger-claw slash.

The clothing hurdle is no match for me.

I hang my athletic shorts in the locker and simultaneously look for a lock, finding none. I frown and text her highness. *Do they not believe in locks at Marmont?*

Lexi: *There's never been a problem with theft.*

Lexi: *Afraid someone will steal your cargo shorts?*

Those are replaceable. It's the other item I'm not willing to let someone run off with.

Me: *What do you have against cargo shorts?*

Lexi: *They drag down the male form.*

Me: *Doesn't that happen naturally?*

Lexi: *What's the problem, Evan?*

Me: *Without a lock, someone might steal my limited-edition Master of Puppets shirt.*

Lexi: *You're into puppets?*

"You didn't hear that," I say to the iconic album cover on my tee and take a photo of my current outfit and send. *If someone takes it I'll be forced to wear this ensemble home.*

A GIF pops up on my screen of Bigfoot, smiling and dressed in a striped jacket with a crooked bowtie.

She might have nailed my look. *That's a good-looking beast.*

Lexi: *Could you do me a favor?*

I walk over to the bathroom counter illuminated with soft lighting and individually wrapped shaving kits and baskets of bottled water. **Me:** *Only if you tell me if the water bottles* *are free.*

Lexi: *They're free.*

Lexi: *You'll be golfing with my friend Talia. Find out if I've done something to upset her.*

Lexi: *She hasn't responded to my texts lately.*

I don't get involved in girl drama, especially with women I haven't met.

Me: *You have friends?*

Regret stabs my conscience. I wince and unsend with panicked fingers. That went too far.

Me: *I didn't mean that*

I can't do anything about my comment, but I can make a choice about these lockers. The clothes stay. The wallet comes with. I stuff the faded leather wallet in my back pocket, making me look like I have a growth on my right cheek.

A golf course is not my natural habitat. The *whoosh* of a club swinging has my eyes peeled for golf balls in the air. Signs to the golf carts lead me down walkways of tall hedges and rosebushes.

My plan is to wing it. Golf isn't hard.

I spot CeCe, struck by how she seems another inch taller. She's already been baptized in the lessons of the real world. Life is not fair. Bad things happen. Parents go to jail. Another layer of unfairness is added because she was born on an unequal playing field. I try to be one step ahead of her and level out the obstacles.

Yet she fits right in to this scene, wearing a black pleated golf skirt and purple polo. Her hair went from messy to a braid and she's happily chatting with two women. "Lexi's house is so cool," she says, "my shower has a waterfall mode…"

All three ladies turn to me.

"You must be Evan," the shorter of the two women says. She's a tiny thing with sooty black hair swishing over her shoulders and intriguing dark eyes. "I'm Talia Sato." She greets me with a raised hand and wiggly fingers.

Talia is the friend Lexi wanted me to play go-between and sort out problems that aren't mine. Meeting Talia makes me more curious than well-intended.

"Finally, I get to meet the infamous Evan Bailey." My attention is thwarted by a blonde with eyes the color of a cloudless afternoon sky. She extends her hand, which I take. "Elena Wilshire. Cochair of the Alexandria Foundation. We'll be working together."

I rub my temple methodically. "That gala thing Lexi told me about."

Elena's even mouth parts into a wide grin. "I thought we could ride over to the ninth hole together and give ourselves a chance to get to know each other. I'm sure you have questions about the gala."

No, not really. A dumb event where people pay money per plate.

"We've never played golf before," CeCe says innocently, and I squirm.

"Your newbie status is not a problem," Talia says. "We'll help you."

"You're with CeCe and I'll assist Evan." Elena picks up my rental clubs and secures them in the back of the golf cart.

I look over my shoulder at CeCe, but she's shoulder-to-shoulder with Talia and not at all in need of my help.

"I simply couldn't believe it when I heard about the bet," Elena says, driving the golf cart over the straight path, past the signs to the clubhouse and water station. "Between you and me, Lexi's been an absolute disaster planning the gala. I gave her the swag bag job to give her something to do. I hope you at least respond to emails."

"I'm not much of an emailer." It seems Elena can be counted on to not hold back, which makes me wary, but I'm getting the inside scoop on the woman currently sleeping in my bed.

"Yes, well, Lexi's life doesn't represent all socialites. I work for a large corporation writing grants for city funding. Talia's a lawyer at her family's firm. Personally, I'm distancing myself from Lexi. I couldn't believe she tossed money out like that. That's no one I want to be associated with."

I curse. My phone vibrates and I wrestle it from my pocket, nervous at the sight of Lexi's name, eager to see if my apology for the friendless comment was accepted.

Lexi: *Have you ever golfed?*

She didn't acknowledge it. **Me:** *Do you count mini golf?*

"Golf is all about getting the ball in the hole with the fewest strokes." The path turns bumpy and I reach for the roof handle until Elena comes to a stop in front of a tree. "Grab your driver." She pulls out a club with a big, fat rounded end. "This one."

The four of us meet at the tee-off area. Talia jumps into action. She's at my side. "Evan. Let's see your stance."

I straighten my legs like they do on television and loosen my arms. I whack an invisible ball.

"Let me show you." Talia's eyes are not to be ignored, and a swath of tiny freckles over her nose highlights her beauty. Her glassy, tight skin shines. She shows me how to stand and points out a white flag on a pole in the distance.

"I'm supposed to hit it all the way there?"

CeCe manages to win their praises but every shot I take is off to the side or in the rough or rolling down a sand trap. The sun beats down, I'm sweaty and my lower back aches right as we arrive at the fifteenth hole.

In no way is this fun. Golf carts zip past. People hang out on the edges of the course with nothing better to do than watch.

Talia is poised next to me, one foot crossed over the other. Hand placed on the golf club. "How's Lexi?" she asks coyly.

"I wouldn't know. How long have you been friends?"

"Since we were kids." Talia does a tight fist close at CeCe's graceful swing. "She's a natural."

"Have you talked to her since the bet?" I ask, grabbing a bottle of water from the golf bag.

Talia examines a plain silver ring on her finger. "She'll only ask to borrow money. It's nice not to feel used."

A funny feeling hits me. Sadness for Lexi overcomes me. I see a deeper image of Lexi with blinders on about how people view her. How she treats them might say something about how she treats herself.

"Evan, you're up," Elena calls, stepping away from the tee.

"I'm starving," CeCe says, walking around her clubs.

"We'll have lunch at the clubhouse after," Elena says. Two golf carts encroach on our territory, waiting for us to finish. "Go on, Evan."

I bend over to put the golf ball on the tee, making the mistake of not loosening my knees and a loud rip right down my ass splits my pants in half.

A string of mumbled expletives drops from my mouth and slowly, I stand, eventually turning around to take the heat. Talia's hand covers her mouth hanging open, and Elena throws her head back in laughter, scaring wildlife out of the brush.

CeCe's mortification tugs at my soul.

"Let me get you back to the clubhouse," Elena says.

Not ten minutes later I drive us to the clubhouse and return the cart. The attendant waits expectantly until Elena pulls out a fifty, handing the crisp green bill to him. "Thank you," she says, and to me, "Don't sweat it, I got you covered."

"He got fifty bucks for taking our cart?"

"I would have given him more, but that's all I had on me."

Soon as CeCe and I are in the car, a message appears from Lexi. *I can't find you on IG or TikTok or anywhere.*

I have only an IG account, which has a handful of followers, all employees of Bailey's. **Me:** *It's @EvaanBailey*

Lexi: *You misspelled your own name?*

Me: *EvanBailey was taken*

Lexi: *Check out @EvansPonytail*

CeCe cranes her neck to get a look at my phone. "Do it. Look up the account."

I login and take a look, clicking on the account she mentioned. "Oh come on. Who was taking a video?" I curse silently at the nearly 50,000 likes of me bending over and the rip seen round the world. All set to Flo Rida's "Low."

"That's a lot of likes," CeCe says, grabbing my phone and adding a heart. "I just gave you one more."

CeCe clicks on the hashtags. Thousands of likes and reposts and cross-posts exist, all of me and Lexi. We're *everywhere*. Since when did this blow up? Lexi and I are in every corner of IG, we're tagged by local news stations and celebrities. "What the hell?" I say, feeling like an idiot.

I don't want this kind of attention. That wasn't the point of this. **Me:** *I'm deleting my account.*

Lexi: *You can't. You have to have one to truly live my life*

I don't know why this leaves a gut-wrenching feeling in my stomach.

Lexi: *Set your account to public*

Me: *That means you set your accounts to private*

I show CeCe the texts. "You kind of did this to yourself," she says, folding her arms. "You bought the pants."

I set my account to public.

CHAPTER ELEVEN

Lexi

What *is* that obnoxious sound? Bottles smashing and a heavy engine?

I push Evan's comforter away from my sticky legs. It's different when I'm the one stumbling home with my heels hanging from my fingertips and crashing into bed at dawn, oblivious to street noises.

Getting woken up when I could sleep five more hours? Brutal.

Bowser's loud as a lawn mower on my head. "Can you purr any quieter?" Groggy, with sweat sticking to my temple, I push my lavender weighted sleep mask up and simultaneously move her.

That sound *again*. Glass breaking and squeaky brakes. It's coming closer.

I get out of bed and pry open the window in time to see the trash truck stop at my neighbor's house. A guy in a reflective suit hops off and dumps the trash into the back of the truck.

They roll right on by my house because...

The blinds snap closed. "Today was trash day. Don't they come at like noon?" I whine to Bowser. She hops off the bed, having none of my complaining shenanigans.

I grab my phone and text Evan. *You didn't tell me today was trash day.*

Evan: *Check the fridge.*

I wrap my mulberry silk robe around me and slide my feet into my house sandals, moving quickly, armed with the goal of proving him wrong.

My hurried gaze moves over the shopping list and Caps season schedule. There. In bold letters. It's today.

Evan: *I hear the sound of the trash truck rolling past.*

Me: *Can I call them up and have them come back?*

Evan: *Sure. Tell them your name is Lexi North.*

Evan: *Don't forget to snap your fingers.*

An irate scoff rolls off my throat and I lift Bowser from the counter. "How on Earth do you live with him?"

Me: *Why aren't you asleep?*

Evan: *You keep texting*

Three eye-rolling headshakes later, I open the fridge. "How many mustard types does one person need?" I grab the eggs and sink in a puddle of homesickness for Chef Sofia.

Evan does have almost a full carton of eggs. Which would be awesome if I knew how to make them. I take thirty seconds to find a video and prop my phone against Evan's toaster, which has bits of bagel seeds on top.

"Start with a nonstick pan," I repeat the instructor's commands on the video.

I open Evan's organized cupboards and shut them until I find a dark, coated pan. Nonstick, maybe?

I shrug and crack the eggs into the pan, mimicking what the instructor does. The gas burner heats the pan. *Good so far.* Broken shells fall into the utensil, and I pick them out, squirming from the slimy consistency.

Attempt number two is slightly better.

"Evan thinks I can't fend for myself. Do you know what

he's doing? Probably spreading out all over *my* bed."

Evan's rigid muscles taking up considerable mattress real estate. His large, broken-nail, calloused hands resting against his uncalloused parts. His abs tensing. His gaze, hard and smoldering. Sheet tented between his thighs.

Sizzle and smoke throw me out of my thoughts. "My eggs!" They're burning. I grab a metal spoon, knocking over my phone as the instructor carries on about not burning your eggs.

I drag-scoop the eggs, leaving scratch marks in the pan. In my clumsy haste to get breakfast onto the plate, one of the eggs slides out of the angled pan and slips down the narrow gap between stove and counter.

Since no one is showing up to deal with this, I grip the ends of the stove and pull, but it goes only so far and I have to get myself mentally prepped to use the shower.

My morning officially is on a dive-bombing path with trash piled up in the garage waiting for next week's collection. I bite into the lone, semi-burnt egg, crunching a shell bit between bites.

As if I didn't need more reasons to frown, I drive in bumper-to-bumper traffic. Muggy morning air drapes like a tarp over the city. I sweat—everywhere—by the time I step inside Bailey's garage.

Josh, Brandon, and Garcia are huddled together with serious head-nodding like it's the meeting of the minds. Garcia runs his hand over his buzz haircut and the diamond earring on his ear.

They stop talking as soon as I set my bag down.

"Don't stop on my account," I say with a hangry, tart edge.

"You're late," Josh says, tapping the watch on his wrist. He points to the job board with a second tally next to my name. Strike two.

Brandon reaches for his extra-large iced coffee covered in condensation. "We were just talking about you."

I lift my brows, relying on strong nonverbal cues to get my point across.

"We have a bet going," he says.

"About me?"

"See those tires?" Josh says, pointing to Tire Land clustered at the farthest corner on the lot.

"They're hard to miss," I say, yawning.

"On the other side of that fence, there's a dumpster. The tires go in there. A truck is coming to pick them up later today." Josh's tone suggests doubts in my ability.

"Isn't this more of a job for Brandon? Or one of the other guys?"

The other employees start moving like they're not an option.

Josh stretches his arms out, cracking his knuckles. "This is where you come in. We each placed a bet for how long we think it will take you to clear all the tires."

I can't help my snobby snort. "I'm dying to hear what the winner gets."

"Whoever guesses the closest time to you completing the task gets lunch paid for."

Lunch. Now I'm interested. Given this morning's egg antics, I didn't have time to grab the oatmeal packet in Evan's pantry, but I did have time to spend more of his money on my iced latte. "Go on. Play your games. If I do this in two hours or less, I get lunch and I control the music in this place for a week."

"Deal," Brandon says, sunlight hitting his nearly there beard, turning his hair lighter.

Josh clasps his hands. "Timer starts as soon as Lexi picks up her first tire."

From my bag in the breakroom, I grab my phone and earbuds. I plug them into my ears and put on classical music.

The dumpster is over five feet high, presenting more than

one problem. I manhandle the tire and get it to the dumpster by using a stepladder. Sweat pools at my pits and neck, but I feel…good, free, a private moment for me.

I get into a groove, one tire at a time, rolling them because my biceps ache and my lower back pinches. The music crescendos with each movement.

I hurdle the tire over the space above the dumpster, getting fancy, doing circles and running up the steps tossing in the tires.

I take a photo of the tire piles I have yet to move to the dumpster and send Evan a photo. *Today is tire death trap day.*

He sends me a photo from a cabana at Marmont, a charcuterie board in front of him. *Not for me.*

Me: *Can you do something about the rising water levels of your shower?*

Evan: *Can I? No. I play tennis this afternoon. After that, working on my tan.*

Evan: *You could unclog the drain yourself.*

That sounds as fun as a hangover.

Evan: *How is the whole cooking thing going?*

Sorry dude, about the eggs decomposing between your stove and counter. **Me:** *No problems.*

Evan: *I'll believe it when I see hard evidence.*

Me: *It's like you don't trust me.*

Evan: *I don't.*

I stiffen at the partial smile tipping the corner of my mouth. No, I do not have magical abilities to interpret the tone of texts, but I visualize Evan's look when he typed his response. The stomach-flipping induced collaboration of amused, cranky, and yet *soft.* A look that is so classically him.

Evan: *BTW why are people sending me DMs about being*

the face of a men's shaving cream and lumberjack shirts?

What? He's already reached influencer status? I'm running out of time with this tire task but I stop and bring up his page. *You have 250,000 followers? How many did you have yesterday?*

Evan: *IDK ten?*

Me: *Took me years to get that many*

Evan: *We can't all be All-Stars*

He sends me a screenshot of me arriving at Bailey's with my latte. *Might want to take the free financial advice people are giving you: "From @SocaliateOnABudget Lexi could save money by making coffee at home."* No. Not the coffee. I'm holding on to the last thread of normalcy.

Me: *BTW. How can I pull the stove out from the wall? I dropped something I need to clean.*

My phone rings. Evan's four-alarm voice has me yanking the earbuds out of my ears. "Do not move the oven from the wall. It's gas."

"I didn't even move it half an inch," I say, starting to pace. Josh makes a *you're on the clock* signal.

"Move it back."

"*I will.*"

I wish I hadn't answered.

I turn up Beethoven's *Symphony No. 5 in C Minor* and grab the next tire, running like the wind up the stepladder. My gloved hand tosses it discus style and overcompensating with upper body momentum. The tire flies forward, and my thighs hit the edge of the dumpster. I'm propelled forward in a slow fall toward the tires, twisting awkwardly to settle into the middle of one.

An awkward twist of my wrist allows me to reach my side pocket and pull out my phone. Evan's sent me a photo of a beer in hand and a near-empty pool. *Getting crowded. Who can I complain to?*

My butt sinks farther. If I don't get out of here, I'll be

recycled into a piece of art or become the next big thing in table trends. Nothing left to do but call Bailey's.

"Bailey's Auto Shop, this is Tia," she says, sounding like she has a hundred other things to do and answering the phone isn't one of them.

"Tia, it's Lexi," I say, attempting to pull myself up. "I fell into the tire dumpster."

"You fell in?" she says, and I try not to take her gasp of laughter personally. "Don't move. Someone will come help you."

It's a mechanic stampede coming toward me, with Josh in the lead.

"No one's ever fallen in before," Brandon says, climbing up the stepladder. He leans his too-skinny body forward and holds out his hand. "Let's get you out."

I climb over the side like I'm dismounting a horse.

"How did you manage to do that?" Josh says, looking at the stepladder. "Are you okay?"

"I should take the day off to deal with the stress."

"Let's not get dramatic," Josh says. "You won, by the way. Lunch and you get to play DJ."

Grime-covered and genuinely afraid I will smell like rubber indefinitely, I pull up to Evan's house hours later and go straight for the shower. The hot water helps, until I pick up my shampoo. Empty. Same situation for the conditioner. I squeeze the last drop of body wash before giving in out of sheer frustration and grab Evan's efficient all-in-one soap.

I use Evan's body wash. I really use it. Squeeze the bottle until it crimps in the middle and douse it over my hair and shoulders. His soap is a burst of forest and crisp air. And I can't get enough.

An attachment is waiting for me. Evan sent a gif of a race car pit crew rolling tires to the car. *I'm stopping by.*

There's a knock on the door. "He's already here?" I rush to answer with my hair dripping around my robe.

I tighten the robe belt and let him in. "Hi," I say briskly. "I'm checking on my oven," he says grumpily and looks at my robe like it's offending him. I'm too fatigued to ask.

"How do you know if the oven's leaking gas?" I ask, thinking I should have asked earlier.

"You don't. That's the problem." He wastes no time, busying himself craning his neck behind the oven. "The adaptor looks fine." He shoves the entire unit toward the wall, making it look like nothing, and looks over the box at the state of the kitchen: mac-and-cheese boxes, dirty dishes in the sink, and Bowser's empty bowl.

"I was just about to feed her." I feel the need to explain. For once, I don't want his judgmental stare. "Since you're here, could you unclog the shower drain?"

"Nope."

He disappears down the hall, and my shoulders slump.

"Get in here, North," Evan calls, and I find him in his bathroom on his knees looking over the tub. He's got a coiled metal tube with a red handle. "This is called a snake. Look up a video online and learn."

I sit next to him, settling my butt on my heels. "What if I break the drain?"

"Then you'll pay for repairs." His gaze meets mine and his eyes reduce to slits. "You smell like my body wash."

"No idea what you're talking about." I give a faux sniff of my shoulder and shrug. "Are you staying?"

"Elena invited me out for drinks to get me caught up with my swag bag responsibilities."

I bristle. Elena and Evan having cocktails? "Your evening sounds posh."

He gets up. "Yours will be hairy. You have fun here."

Bowser scurries into the bathroom at the same time Evan leaves. She rubs her back into my side. "I'm sure Elena will get him all caught up."

CHAPTER TWELVE

Lexi

"I'm going to make it," I say out loud. My handbag hits my back and my feet pound the pavement. Bailey's is two blocks away. I don't even care when the group of teens near a coffee shop hold out their phones to record me.

This morning's circumstances are not my fault, I promise.

I hit the snooze only twice, followed by a mad dash to find the last roll of toilet paper, afterward, dropped my bagel (cream cheese side down). Traffic conspired against me and this is the *one* morning I haven't been able to find closer parking.

If I'm late, I get my third strike.

The corner building comes into sight. Almost there. One of the mechanics drops his cigarette butt and stamps it out. "Josh, check this out," he shouts. "Incoming!"

Not one, but several, of the staff crane their necks outside the garage. A shot of adrenaline boosts me across the floor of the work area.

I put my hands on my knees, releasing jagged breaths, and my handbag slides down my wrist with a *thud*.

Josh points to the wall clock. "Five minutes late," he says.

"What? *No.* Your clock is fast." My tone is all cynicism. "You saw. I was booking it."

"Brandon, what does your phone say?" Josh asks without looking at him.

"Same as the wall clock," Brandon says nonchalantly.

"You're late," Alec's voice booms over the speaker.

Josh points up to the speaker. "You heard the man. Rules are rules. Don't come in tomorrow." Josh clicks the mouse on the garage's computer. He brings up the car history for the red Sonata in the garage's first position. "I thought you'd be celebrating."

Celebrating? *No.* "I tried," I say. "This isn't fair."

Josh keeps his back to me, his bull neck broken by a thin silver chain. "What's not fair is the rest of us who make it on time."

Evan doesn't help. He chooses this moment to message me. *I was disappointed to find out my tennis instructor was only a two-time Olympian.*

The job board reflects the state of my life. My name is next to replacing cabin air filters and general cleaning, which is a catch-all for sanitizing the waiting room, wiping down floors, and unclogging toilets.

The first customer parks at the garage entrance and Brandon's opening the driver's door.

This is where I come in. Brandon hands me the dirty filter and I show the customer the dire state of the air in their car. Their eyes say no before I finish explaining. "The last time you had this replaced was two years ago."

The customer, a middle-aged woman with a chip on her shoulder, shakes her head full of curly hair. "I don't want it replaced."

This is going down the path of earning my seventh rejection. "May I ask why?"

She looks caught off guard. "No. I don't want it replaced."

I hold the filter in front of her and swipe my hand through dirty fuzz. "You're okay with breathing this? They're seventeen dollars to replace. I'll even knock it down to ten."

I have no idea if I can do that.

She sighs. "Fine. I'll do it for that price."

I look over my shoulder and give Brandon a thumb's up. "Tell Tia at the front desk this is the Lexi discount."

"You can't negotiate the price," Josh comes down hard on me, as soon as Tia had three customers in a row with the Lexi discount.

"Why not? You never offer incentives for customers."

"It's a car business, not a boutique." He hands me a tray of screws. "You're off cabin filters. These need to be sorted."

"Isn't bringing in some cash better than nothing?"

"Not when we lose money."

"I've seen the markups, you're not losing." My fingers grip the tray and he releases too soon, I pull too hard, and hundreds of small screws fly into the air, raining down sharp metal objects.

When the damage is done and every eye in the shop is on me, Alec's voice comes over the intercom. "Lexi. In my office. *Now.*"

"Where do I rent a cabana?" I ask the lone staff member wearing a black two-piece and holding a piece of greasy pizza. "I also need a drink menu."

I have earned both.

"We don't have cabanas," she says and points to a sign on the wall. No ALCOHOLIC BEVERAGES. A string dangles around her neck with a whistle on the end. *Lifeguard/front desk receptionist?* "What's your name?"

"Lexi North. I'm on Evan Bailey's guest list."

Gateway Community Pool seemed like a good idea to ease Alec's principal's-office-style lecture about how I can't change prices.

She plops her slice of pizza on a paper plate with an uncontained smile. "Oh. *Oh*. I know you." She proceeds to whip out her phone and bring up TikTok. "Have you seen this?"

The video clip is forty-five seconds of me running to Bailey's set to *Chariots of Fire*. *#SocialiteHustle #FootStrike #RunnersGlow*.

Gateway is no Marmont. For one, there are no staff members carrying smoothies or duck fat fries. All the lounge chairs are taken, and other people brought their own.

I move around a toddler sitting on the cement crying her eyes out. If I had taken the time to look this place up, I would have stayed at home.

Kids run across a patch of lawn, their slick, grass-covered feet go from ground to pool. My hand clenches around my bag strap and I turn.

"Lexi," someone calls my name.

CeCe is heading toward me. Her simple one piece has a slash of blue up the side.

"I like your swimsuit," I say genuinely.

"I'm not allowed to wear a bikini," she says with disappointment. "My uncle's rules."

Evan is a stickler for rules, something I am learning about him. Looking at CeCe, my interest in her guardian is plucked like a violin string.

"Bikinis can be a source of unfortunate tan lines." My words fade as my gaze shifts over her head to the tall figure behind the pot-bellied dad carrying two kids and chasing after a third hitting everyone in his path with a pool noodle.

Evan in swim shorts.

I lower my gold-plated Cartier sunglasses half an inch, as if the polarized lenses are playing tricks on me. His beautiful, just-enough toned torso with a golden trail of hair down to his waistband steals my focus. A stern focus disrupted by the satisfaction in his gaze of catching me staring.

A stray water drop threads down his chest, disappearing into the grooves of his abs. His hands sink into his hips. "You can stop looking."

I stab a finger at his chest. Skin-to-skin contact is a mistake. "What are you doing here?"

"CeCe wanted to see her friends." Evan lifts his hands in surrender. "I can't leave her unattended. Pool rules."

A long glance at the crowded water and I miss my pool like a parent seeing their child off to college. Evan's presence isn't helping. I am sure he has heard about my string of mess-ups at the shop. "I'm leaving, so it doesn't matter."

A muscle in Evan's jaw ticks. "That's ridiculous, North. Have some fun." He smacks my upper arm hard enough to cause my hand to clench my bag strap.

"This isn't my idea of a good time."

"What is your idea of fun? Wine tasting and ballroom dancing?"

CeCe lifts a brow. "Yeah. What do you like to do for fun?"

The question should be easy, but I can't seem to find the right answer.

"I do stuff. Attending the U.S. Open, competing in equestrian events, spending the weekend in St. Tropez—"

"I mean everyday fun," Evan clarifies with a voice warm as a bed of coals. "Something that makes you happy. Not posting videos of shoes."

"While we're on the topic, *you* haven't posted anything since you split your pants."

He scoffs. "I'm gaining new followers without doing a thing."

"We could do one now. Before I go."

"This is going to be so embarrassing," CeCe says. "I'm

going to hang out with my friends."

Evan scoops his arm around my lower back, guiding me forward, the tips of his fingers press into my waist. "Stay."

My skin starts to feel fizzy, and I think that's a burst of flutters in my belly.

I plop down my bag while Evan sprays his shoulders with sunblock, using enough to patch the hole in the ozone.

My throat goes tight at the thought of Evan's hand rubbing sunblock over my back, his fingers gliding between my bathing suit straps. His rule-following attitude would leave no square of skin untouched.

"What am I supposed to say in a video to people I've never met?" he asks suspiciously, like he loves to hate this idea.

"Introduce yourself. Tell them your name, why you're making a video. Give a glimpse of how this experience is life-changing." I get my phone out. "We can edit it if you don't like a portion."

"Nothing about the bet will change who I am." Evan deliberately stares at me. "This is dumb. Put your phone away."

Witnessing Evan's flustered reaction is new for me. "Maybe try it at home later. When you're comfortable and there's not a kid dry humping the towel pretending to be a dolphin in the background."

This scene ties into my next problem. Something that has been on the edge of my thoughts since arriving.

My bathing suits are of the tiny-string triangle-coverage variety, meant to be worn on white sand beaches with champagne delivered in a bucket of ice.

I have a decent sized chest that fills out a bathing suit. None of that translates well for me at Gateway Community Pool.

"Evan," I whisper to him, pulling his gaze away from two women making sexy eyes at him. "I have a problem. My swimsuit isn't…quite…appropriate."

Belatedly, his gaze drags down my front as if now he wants to see more than he did five minutes ago. His hand touches my waist, scoring my skin with heat. "I'm sure it's fine. A swimsuit is a swimsuit."

A quick removal of the cover-up and his eyes turn hard. His deep, green-eyed reaction sets off a trip wire of blush up my front, over my cheeks. He points to my cleavage. "That's not a swimsuit, North."

"It was designed by—"

"No one cares about that when you're wearing a coaster." It seems to pain him to look at me when all I want to do is appear more comfortable than I feel. I hastily grab the cover-up, but Evan's fingers close around my wrist. "Leave it off," he orders with a husky drop of his voice.

The rubber band holding Evan's ponytail breaks and I quietly gasp. His dirty blond hair falls past his shoulders.

Holy hell. He's breathtakingly hot.

"I have a spare rubber band." I dig around my pool bag until I find one. Standing in front of Evan, our toes touch. My bikini top almost touches his chest and I lift onto my tiptoes, reaching behind his neck with both hands. "Let me."

Evan is stock-still, holding his breath, and my hands work around his neck, coiling his hair into a man bun. Our eyes lock and stay on each other.

"I'm going to puke," a kid wails, running past us at the repeated blow of the lifeguard whistle.

That's my cue to get in the water.

The steps are crowded with a mermaid club of girls acting like gatekeepers. Moms are on the sidelines, standing in the water, chatting. Their conversations halt at the sight of me.

No one would think twice if I were on a yacht.

Standing in the shallow end, I keep moving to avoid the tide of teenage boys playing water football. A wave of water splashes in my face from the pimply faced boys gliding by.

Whack.

A yelp leaves my mouth at the squishy football hitting my head. Evan takes a seat on the edge, his long, muscular calves hitting the water. His vibrant eyes mix with the golden sun.

A nervous jolt runs through me that I'm looking at him differently. He has my attention and I don't know if I want that to stop.

"This is where Alec and I spent our summer afternoons," he says fondly as I swim over. "I have great memories of this pool. I had my first kiss here. Watch out," he says so calmly I almost don't turn in time to see the junior football league swimming right toward me.

A cry for help is met with Evan's hand. Our fingers clasp and he hoists me out, plopping me against him, and our hands slide off each other's. My slick thigh pushes against his solid, dry leg. Beads of water slide down my cleavage. "Where did this alleged first kiss take place?"

He points across the grass to a row of trees. "Right over there."

I imagine Evan having his first kiss. "How romantic."

"What about you, North? Where'd you have your first kiss? Or are you still waiting to experience that rite of passage?"

It's oddly refreshing to have someone ask about that instead of which marriage I supposedly ruined. "No one's asked me that in a long time." Inadvertently shifting my bottom, I press closer against Evan and promptly scoot away. "In Hudson Hoffman's bedroom." It's either the intense sun or the kids, but those memories feel like forever ago.

"Hudson Hoffman," Evan says with distaste. "He has an older brother, Craig."

I give him a side-eyed glance. "Yes, Craig Hoffman. How did you know?"

"I looked you up, North."

"Then you know everything about me."

"I'm a big boy, I form my own opinions. What's the story with you and Hudson?"

"We were together until he went to California, and now he's back with a serious girlfriend." Evan's gaze drops to my mouth and lower, sweeping over my cleavage and back to my eyes. My breath holds at the look of softness in his gaze, and my heart beats wildly. "What are you going to do when CeCe has her first kiss?"

"She doesn't even know boys exist."

I watch her with her friends avoiding a group of lanky boys. "Keeping your head in the sand will do wonders for your skin." He gives me a hostile stare, but I take my point.

"Can you explain to me why swag bags are necessary for the Alcott gala? Give me one good reason why that money shouldn't be given to the cause you're supporting."

"Swag items are donated, for one. Second, the better the merchandise, the more people post about the event and will want to attend next year. The better attended the event, the more money we raise."

CeCe flags Evan over and he gets to his feet.

Evan immediately grabs his ringing phone as I struggle to put on my cover-up. The mesh fabric bunches at my waist. Evan's hand is faster.

"That would be good," he says to the person on the phone while his fingers tug at my cover-up and he yanks it slowly over my rear, straightening the fabric, the tops of his fingers grazing my thigh.

Okay, he needs to stop affecting me like this.

He stays close, sounding like his call is ending, and my fingers brush his back. Evan stiffens, and I pull my hand away. "I'll see you in a few." He sets the phone on a table and faces me. "My mother will be here in ten minutes to get CeCe." He grabs a bag of cheeseballs. "In case you get hungry."

"Cheeseballs and chlorine. I'll pass." I look at him, knowing, feeling, thinking about subjects I don't want to think about. His gaze when sitting at the pool was unmistakable, and so was my reaction. Feeling sure about what I'm about to ask, I put myself out there. "If you want to stay, I might stick around."

"No can do, North, I have somewhere to be," he says without elaborating.

Evan puts his shirt on and grabs his sunglasses. "Too bad you wasted all that time checking me out."

"Yes, because that went only one way." I hoist my bag over my shoulder, giving him a proper glare.

My high-and-mighty attitude crumples when I think about tomorrow. No Bailey's. And no money.

CHAPTER THIRTEEN

Evan

It's not always easy to be a dude. Lexi stretched against me and putting my hair in a bun was torture. Her breasts, cushy against her top, make me want to glide my fingers beneath the fabric and feel her nipples turn hard against my palms.

Here I'm the one holding onto those few minutes at the pool.

She had seemed different. Introspective, even. Instead of bringing her Lexi A-game snobbery, she hung out next to me with our legs in the water talking about first kisses.

Where is Hudson now, when she has nothing?

The questions I asked about Craig didn't ease my nerves about our too-close connection. As long as I keep the Hoffmans at arm's length, I should be fine.

My schedule today includes an appointment at a place called Christine's. I approach the building and take out my phone.

Alec: *Lexi got a third strike*
Me: *When*
Alec: *Yesterday*

She didn't say anything to me at the pool.

"This is going to be worse than her shower," I mumble, opening the door.

The day spa is in a historic building with big green shutters and antique windows. I prepare myself for the torture about to unfold anticipating big hands kneading my muscles with oil. A woman with oversized sunglasses emerges from the spa, fulfilling every cliché I have about these places, and apprehension whitewashes me from head to toe.

The receptionist greets me with a tranquil, "You must be Mr. Bailey."

"The one and only." I scratch the back of my neck, smoothing a sweat bead.

An entire shelf is filled with lotions and candles. Orchids are tucked into wall niches.

Her perky demeanor is the opposite of my mood. "I have you booked for the Sugar Plum Fairy package." She nods at the sleek case of nail polish embedded in the wall like an artifact. "Go ahead and pick your color."

Hell no and a horrified scowl break out on my lips, uncaring about the second receptionist looking on. "That's not happening."

"A clear coat will be fine for Mr. Bailey." Lexi's voice causes me to turn around, giving me an eyeful with her brilliant brown eyes.

We wordlessly acknowledge each other with a slight tweak.

I have thought about her naked. More than once.

"You're supposed to be working," I keep my tone neutral, seeing if she bites.

"I took the day off," she says, making brief eye contact, triggering all sorts of bullshit detectors. "I thought you could use moral support."

"Is everything going okay at the shop?"

She pokes my chest with her finger, pushing her nail into me. "Never better." A stiff nod and she releases her finger.

"Put us next to each other."

The receptionist doesn't hide her smirk. "Certainly, Ms. North. Would you care for prosecco or coffee?"

Acute awareness overcomes me. Quiet concern garnishes my words as I tap Lexi's shoulder. "How much does it cost?"

This time Lexi sees past my scowl, and her expression tempers. "They're free," she says discreetly, giving my arm a squeeze. "I'll have the honey lavender cinnamon cold latte. And we need to talk."

"About your drink choices? Definitely."

She gives a halfhearted eye roll and leads me to follow the receptionist.

This place has too many closed doors and secretive music.

The room we're shown to is spacious, with windows overlooking the city. Oversized leather chairs are set up like the massage chairs in the mall. Staff wearing all black work from stools at the base of small foot tubs.

"Take off your shoes," Lexi says, slipping out of sandals and immersing her feet in the water. She turns on her massage chair and closes her eyes, taking a deep breath. Her chest bounces and pushes forward from the motion, her eyes are closed. This is encroaching on indecent. "If you're still standing, sit down. The chair doesn't bite."

"I was thinking—" I can't believe I'm about to say this. "You make posting videos look easy. Could you help me again? I could say my feet are about to be violated."

"Don't say that." She sits up and holds out her hand. "Just tell them you're nervous. You can do this. You might even like putting yourself out there."

Reluctantly, I take a seat and face her. She gives a finger slash and, "You're on."

I clear my throat. "Hi. I'm Evan Bailey. I'm about to get my first pedicure." My mind turns fuzzy. I can't do this. "Um. I'm spending my day at a spa. That's all."

Her face is encouraging, but I know I bombed. "That was good. Slightly on the stage fright side, but a start. Do you want me to post?"

"I don't care what you do. Don't you want to do more with your time?"

"Don't you want to do more with *yours*?" She hands me my phone. I sit back and cautiously submerge my toes in bubbly warm water.

No one else seems concerned about strangers paid to touch their feet. I didn't like making a video. It felt too personal.

I cock my head, getting a better look. "What are the beads in the water?" The nail tech turns on the massage. I jolt at the assault of machinery and a shaking chair jiggling all my parts. "How the hell is this relaxing?"

"Don't ruin this for your feet," Lexi says, slanting her head to face me.

The chair beats me into submission along with subtle floral vapors released from the water, which isn't *so* bad if the massage could stop rolling over my lower back like a lead pipe. Lexi's shorts give my gaze plenty of skin to follow.

I want *her* to tell me she was asked not to come to Bailey's.

She opens her eyes with a thoughtful expression. "I have to ask you something."

"If it's about why I hate intelligent appliances, then no. Otherwise, ask me anything."

"Don't act like you don't love a house with perks. My house isn't even the most luxurious of all my father's properties. You should see his vacation house in Vail. The guest bathroom has an open-walled shower to the outdoors. There's nothing like it."

I see Lexi in her bathing suit in that scenario. Lexi in her bathing suit, my hands braced on either side of her, then shoving aside those tiny triangles up top. Steam infiltrating to moderate the snow, all of it in front of snow-capped mountains. That erotic scene aside, I'm not on board with the other thing she told me.

"Your dad owns your house? You're okay with that?"

Lexi tosses an irritated look at me. "I guess no one passes the Evan Bailey work-hard-or-die test. I bet your father is proud of you."

"My father died when I was in high school. Heart attack."

"Oh. I'm sorry."

"Why are you really here today? This isn't in your budget and I'm not paying for you."

"I told you. I thought you could use support. I know this terrifies a guy like you."

"A guy like me? What does that mean? You think I can't handle my toes getting massaged?"

"I think you despise anything indulgent."

"Big surprise."

My nail person looks back and forth between us.

"Never mind, you're right, I shouldn't have come."

"You should have told me why you're really here. Not because I need a friend. Alec didn't give you the day off. *Ow.*" My foot retracts at the sharp pain of her digging around my nail beds using a tiny weapon of torture. She ignores my pleas and repeats the brutality on all ten of my toes. I check my pinkie toe to make sure it's still there, poor guy.

She looks caught in a trap. Her cheeks flush pink and her breath stills. She looks away and her hand clenches the armrest. "He asked me not to come in." Her voice chafes with humility.

"Why didn't you tell me yesterday?"

"You're the last person I want to tell that to." I'm surprised by the modesty in her voice.

I reach across and touch her hand, struggling not to touch more of her. "Then show up tomorrow and try again."

"What color do you want?" the nail tech asks Lexi.

Lexi takes one of her feet out of the water, resting it on the cushioned stool, and holds up two colors to me. "Hot Pink

Crush or Killer Kiss?"

"I don't care," I grumble, sneaking a glance at her choices, choosing an instant favorite.

She sets the polish on the small tray. "I'll go with pink."

"Go with the purple," I say offhandedly.

"Pink." She reinforces a smile at the nail lady. "I thought you didn't care."

"Purple," I say beneath my breath, earning a frustrated Lexi sigh.

She flashes me a dirty look. "You'll pick the opposite of whatever I choose."

Resting my head back, I whisper with enough volume for only her to hear. "The dark color will look hot against your white sheets."

She maintains focus ahead, her expression never wavering, faint streaks of blush creeping up her cheeks. She's a blusher. She has no idea how sexy she is.

The rigorous foot scrubbing causes me to lurch forward. "Hey. *Stop that*. It tickles."

The nail tech grabs my foot harder and my toes retract at the sensation.

Anything else I want to say to Lexi is shut down by the procession of searing hot towels and a leg massage I don't want to end.

Lexi goes with the purple polish. She catches me staring. "I liked the color for me, not because you suggested it."

"If that's what you believe, then we'll go with it." I wiggle my toes and whistle, garnering a few looks. "My feet look good."

The receptionist enters and walks over to me, speaking quietly in my ear. "Mr. Bailey, when you're finished, Rupert will handle your eyebrow wax."

I look to Lexi. She offers no support.

"My body, my brows," I declare firmly.

Her mood is tense when we leave, entering the muggy air. I say nothing of her use of my funds to pay for this.

"Before you go," I say. My breath is a hot ball in my throat.

I'm worried that I have pulled at the first thread of a complicated, tangled knot. My fingers claim her hip gently, adding subtle pressure. I'm taken aback by my body's reaction to her.

Our physical contact is an issue. Even the slightest touch and I feel her. *Everywhere.* I have to be thinking with my brain. Not acting with my other parts. "Thank you for being here today."

She doesn't back away. I don't move my hand. I could stay here all day like this.

Her phone rings, pulling her away, and she slides it away from her mouth. "I'll see you later, Evan." She walks away, down the sidewalk when I catch her words, "Hudson, hey. No, I'm not busy."

I don't want to think badly of her, but she let me put my hands on her five minutes ago and now she's moved back over to Hudson.

Her games are hers to play. I read the physical connection. The way her shoulders sharpened when he called and the excitement in her voice. Lexi is undoubtedly hooked on Hudson and that's going to be a problem for us.

A shiny Bentley slides into the parking spot ahead of me. A car like that could never go unnoticed but I keep walking.

"Evan Bailey."

I turn at the sound of my name. "Yes?"

A man looks at me from the back passenger window, his face familiar in a way I can't place. He has dark gray hair and an air of commanding authority I can see from where I stand. "Get in the car. It's time we meet in person."

My hand motions in front of this guy with oddly familiar eyes. "I don't do the whole 'get in a stranger's car' thing."

His unrelenting stare is patient. "If you want to waste my time, fine, but this affects your niece."

Now he has my undivided attention. No one dangles my niece in front of me like a bargaining chip. I get in the car and close the door. "You have thirty seconds before I get out. Who are you? And to clarify, this doesn't involve you blindfolding me, does it?"

"Edward North," he says, extending his hand. A faint similarity to Lexi's exists in his gaze. A deep vibrant brown. "I'm Lexington's father. Call me Edward." He runs his hand over his bold blue tie. "How do you like Lexington's life?"

Lexington doesn't fit her at all. It's like she was named after a battle in the 1800s. "I'm adjusting. What were you saying about my niece?"

"Parent to parent, you understand how important Lexi is to me. This bet she made is for her best interest, but she's my only child. If any harm comes to her, there will be consequences. Your brother is struggling to make rent at Bailey's."

His implications about Bailey's are from a man who has done his homework and his claim of his daughter's importance doesn't hold water. He says her name like a robot and shows about as much emotion as one. He's a little late to roll up now.

"Was that a question?" I ask through clenched teeth.

"If something happens to her, I'm going to make you responsible. Understood?"

"Lexi's safe. The guys at the shop are respectful."

"Since we're discussing family, there's also the issue of the Hoffmans," he adds. My blood goes from warm to cold. "Specifically, Hudson's older brother, Craig. He's your niece's father, right?"

I hold my breath.

"I would hate for a scandal to unfold in the middle of this and young, innocent Cecelia be affected."

He knows. And if Lexi finds out, other people will. CeCe

will know. She can't know her father is a man capable of providing everything for her and who chose to give her nothing. It wouldn't crush her; it would destroy her.

CHAPTER FOURTEEN

Lexi

Low Point is a bar. Not a mctaphor, mind you. The Bailey's crew meets here on Fridays. The location is a seedy establishment in a strip mall.

I inhale like my life depends on it. Guys wearing sleeveless jean jackets. Women with eyeliner for days. The customers at the bar sit with hunched shoulders, shady over-the-shoulder glances, and abundance of butt crack.

Just this once, I'm allowed a grace period for coexisting with paneled walls and dusty decor. Oh yes, and the live band. My spine wants to slink into a cold, dark corner.

I wish Talia were here or Elena, or anyone who knows not to pair leather with leather.

Tia's five-foot-nine-inch height makes her easy to spot. "Look who's here," she says and nods at the spot next to her. "We have pitchers of beer."

I reach for an empty glass and Josh beats me to it. "These are for Bailey's employees."

Half the employees are here, milling around the pool table, with their gazes communicating: *Go home.*

"I'll get a drink from the bar." No. I'll make it look like

I'm ordering a drink and leave immediately.

Josh hands me a beer foaming to the tippy top. "Just take the glass." His mouth parts in a wry grin, showing off dimples that contradict his *If you steal my girl, I'll chase you down with a bat* appearance. "You can explain why Evan texted me about a blanket warmer. What's that about?"

"Exactly what it sounds like." An amenity I had to have and didn't use. Turns out, blankets are good on their own.

"My last girlfriend dumped me after I bought her a neck massager for her birthday," Brandon says.

"She dumped you because you forgot her birthday," Tia says.

"Don't bring that up." Brandon's face is cute in a bad-boy way, but I have good-boy tendencies. "I'll tell you a secret about Evan."

I lean in, ears wide and my glass poised at my mouth. "Go on."

"His ex-girlfriend is on Alec's Do Not Serve list. She was a while ago. I'm sure he's mentioned her."

"I haven't." Evan's distinct, rough voice has me turning on my heel.

Our gazes unmistakably collide. My heart flies and crashes. This is not a twin-switch situation. "Evan," I say out of frustration that I cared if he's here. "I leave you with VIP party access and you're out for an evening of wings and watered-down beer?"

An elbow to my side jolts me forward, spilling beer down my shirt like Karma's sticking her two cents in.

"You look like you're enjoying the cheap, watered-down beer just fine," Evan says, torn over what part of my beer-spilling mishap to comment about.

"Don't you dare say anything." I wipe my shirt furiously, only making this worse and leaving me with a huge wet spot mid-chest. The music dies down.

"About which part? The beer or you asking Brandon about my ex?"

"Gooooooood evening folks," the lead singer says into the microphone. "I'm the lead singer of Rat Tail." Cheers and hollers erupt like we're at a concert. "Right on. Right on. I hear you." He puts his hand to his forehead like he's searching the crowd. "Some beautiful people are out tonight. Who's in the mood to get laid?"

"That's what I'm talking about!" someone yells.

Evan's gone, already hand-clasping and man-hugging Josh and Brandon.

"They aren't used to being apart," Tia says, toying with a ring on her thumb. "None of them are."

"How long have you known Evan?"

"Since he first took CeCe in. He went from freedom to overnight parent. Evan used to be this fun-loving, outgoing guy. He traded it for sidewalk chalk art and buying bike helmets."

I shy away from looking at Evan. The heart-wrenching intel says so much. He must have given up everything. *Would I have given up the allure of my early twenties?* All signs point to no.

"Who wants to lose this next game?" Alec pokes his head between us. "Bets begin at twenty."

Evan throws down the gauntlet. "Not Lexi."

I ignore Evan's smug expression. "Anyone comfortable in Prada can work a stick and a ball." I slap a twenty on the edge of the pool table. "I'm in."

Plus, they don't know I'm a closeted Billiard player. This will be fun, watching Evan eat his words.

I beat Alec twice and a few other guys, too, before my reputation draws spectators and new competition: a guy named Sticky.

Evan is deep in conversation with a woman hanging on

his arm. Sticky takes the first move, silent and serious; he smells like pot masked with cologne. He has the names of four different ladies tattooed on his arms. Three of them have lines through them. His face turns angrier and angrier as I happily take my winnings and shoot down his angered gaze.

When no one else steps up, I grab another beer. "Who's next?"

Evan stares at me with a peeved expression. Guess the woman on his arm had to leave. "Are you drunk, North?"

"No." I hiccup. "Are you going to throw your pool skills into the ring or do you need to go after your girlfriend?"

His mouth remains firm.

"Hold my beer." I plop it in his hand, overcome by the need to pee, and follow signs to the bathroom. I sway slightly from the major buzz I'm enjoying.

The signs to the bathroom lead me outside to a building near dumpsters. The door to the bar closes behind me, muting the music. What kind of place makes you leave the bar to use the restroom?

A familiar face steps in front of me. Fear strangles my lighthearted mood at the knowledge that we're outside and alone.

"Sticky," I say distastefully, pushing him aside. "Move."

He doesn't.

His hand clamps an ungodly powerful grip on my arm, pulling me toward him. "Give me my money back."

Panic rocks my center. Shaking my knees. A fight-or-flight level of adrenaline pumping through me. "No. Learn to play pool better."

He hoists me closer, terrorizing me with the look in his eye and his strength. "I said,"—his voice is slimy, his eyes, void of feeling—"give me my money." His hand gropes my pocket.

"Stop," I shout, the music too loud to hear a scream. *"Stop."*

A powerful hand grabs Sticky's shoulder, tossing him

against the brick wall. He crashes against it, getting up, ready for round two.

"Don't embarrass yourself," Evan's guard-dog voice is nothing compared to the firm grip he has on my hand. His fingers squeeze mine back. "Get out of here."

"Pussy." Sticky spits on the ground and saunters away, pulling up his saggy jeans.

Evan turns to me with eyes full of bold protectiveness. His hand changes spots, settling at my waist. "Did he touch you?"

"He grabbed my arm," I say in a daze, my heart thumping against my ribs.

"Are you okay?" Evan's fingers slide down mine until he drops his hand.

The aftershocks aren't pretty. "I will be. I want to go home."

"There's *no* way you're driving."

I'm too shaken up to care.

Evan has to grab clothes from his house, which I don't mind him doing, since he can go ahead and check to make sure no one has broken in.

We enter the house and he flips on the light and goes ahead of me until we're both in the kitchen. I open one of his cupboards and grimace. "Do you have anything besides canned ravioli?"

"Can I interest you in borrowing some compassion?" Despite his chastising, his lips hold the slightest grin. He pulls out two glasses for water while I rummage through the pantry. I open the bottom drawer and his hand grabs mine. "That's my private drawer."

"There's no lock on it," I state the facts. "No do not enter sign. What's in here? Pot? Porn?"

"You do remember CeCe lives with me, right? Besides, this

is the digital age, North. Guys don't buy nudie magazines." He holds a finger up. "Know your audience."

I snicker at the use of the word nudie. "Where is CeCe, anyway?"

"With my mother. I wasn't going to miss a night out so I could stay home and obsess over your bath products."

Evan moves my hand away, but I open the drawer hard and stumble back into his arms.

My gaze settles on the supply of Oatmeal Crème Pies and Cosmic Brownies. "What is this? An underground Little Debbie trading ring?"

He closes the drawer and gives me an irritated double take. "You're so nosy."

"I've never had any of those."

"I'm not even going to touch on that wrong." He leaves me standing in front of the open pantry, my stomach no longer growling. "Stay out of my treat stash."

I find Evan in his bedroom, the dim bedside lamp on. The sheets on his bed are rumpled. He opens and closes drawers swiftly as I saunter in and kick off my shoes. "Who's your ex?"

Evan sighs, opening and closing one of his drawers and slapping a couple of shirts on the top. "No one you need to concern yourself with. Are you going to leave your shoes in the middle of the floor?"

I crowd him and start rifling through his drawers, taking the shirt he's about to grab. "You have soooo many T-shirts."

"What am I supposed to wear? Tuxedos every day?" Evan lets out a bark of laughter. "Go away."

I move around him but he turns at the same second and we bump into each other, blocking the other's move forward. Evan shuts the drawer with one hand, never taking his eyes off me, undressing me with an unapologetic gaze. His impossibly firm gaze makes it hard to look anywhere else.

"You look like you want to ask me something."

Evan stares at me. "Do you get tired of being alone in that big bed of yours?"

I scoff harshly. "My bed gets plenty of action."

His gaze flickers. He grabs his large T-shirt pile and starts to walk away. "Solo action, maybe."

I reach around my back and tug at the dress. The zipper isn't budging. I try again impatiently. *Oh come on.* Evan's out of the bedroom. "Wait. Evan. Come back."

He appears and leans casually against the doorframe. "What?"

This is going to sound like a ploy, but it isn't. The darn thing is stuck. "Help me with my zipper."

"*No.*"

I grab at his shirt. "Please. I'm trying to get into your pants."

He cracks a harsh laugh. "You mean *you're* not trying to get into *my* pants."

"That's what I said." Wasn't it? I love the deep vibration of his laugh. "I'll pay you."

He stands in front of me. He's all muscles and defiance, making me aware of how much I want him to stay. He points at my chest. "You can't afford me." His low, husky voice is entirely too smug.

"You're wrong." To prove my trustworthiness, I reach down to my dress pocket and grab my pool winnings, fanning it out in front of him. "I'll give you one hundred dollars for five minutes."

His fingers crumple around the cash and promptly sets it on the dresser. "For what, North? Be specific."

I'm tongue-tied and motionless. The maddening pulse beneath my skin doesn't help. "I want to know what your stubble feels like."

The mood changes into crackling, bold need splitting wide open between us. "Go on," he says roughly, molding his fingers to my hip. "Feel it."

My hands rest on his chest. We both hold our breaths. "What about my zipper?"

"I'll handle that in a sec." His suggestive, heavy tone is unmistakable as his hand slides around my waist. His gaze focuses on me. "Where'd you learn to play pool like that?"

I swallow hard, needing him to kiss me. "No one asks me that." My throat is suddenly dry. Strange—my feet won't move. Evan tilts my chin up.

His searing gaze pierces me with sharp need. "I'm asking."

"When I was at boarding school, I couldn't sleep. I started playing to bridge the gap of time before sunrise."

"That wasn't so hard, was it?" Warmth flushes my cheeks at his fingertips brushing against my collarbone. His hand falls to my waist, spreading wide, straddling lower to my hip.

"You paid for me to take off your dress. I'm going to collect." His gaze is as dark as his voice.

"Yeah," I breathe the word out as a light rain taps against the windows and the crack of lightning flares in his bedroom.

Heat rolls off my breath, my chest, the spaces between us.

He slides his hands up slowly, brushing past my breasts and around back, sliding the zipper down without issue. Looking at my mouth. He pushes the straps down, then the dress. His fingers trace the lacy bra. My breasts strain against the fabric, ready to pop out. He drags his fingers between them, turning my legs to mush.

Whatever they put in the beer at Low Point is working. If his hands go any further, he will feel the dampness between my legs.

"Kiss me," I whisper in a needy plea.

Evan doesn't kiss me. His eyes do that, trailing me like hot silk, down to my matching lace panties. He cups his hand beneath my jaw, evoking a shallow gasp, confusing my needs and wants. The strong, deep ache between my legs thickens.

Hatred burns through me at how much I want Evan's mouth on mine. How much he *knows* it.

"Not tonight."

My heart cries in stunned protest. "You bring other women back here, but you won't kiss me."

"Does that frustrate you?" His voice is soft as the rain against the window.

None of it is cutting the tension between my legs.

"Not at all." I thought Evan's kiss was a sure thing. I crawl into bed and pull the sheets up to my chin. "It wasn't worth the money?"

He looks down at me and tugs the sheet from my hand. "You're wrong. You think I bring any willing woman home from the bar with me and roll around in these sheets. *You're* the first woman to sleep in my bed."

A dry rasp leaves my mouth. "But I thought—I *thought*..."

"What did you think? I would fall all over you because you asked me to undo a zipper?"

Evan's rejection washes over me.

"So what if I did? Is it so bad to have me throw myself at you?" I turn the light off and move away from him, cocooning myself, inhaling traces of his scent in the sheets that only contribute to my frustration and disappointment. "Your sheets smell like you," I say softly, feeling Bowser jump onto the bed near my feet.

"And how do I smell?" Evan's voice has a sharp edge.

Warmth cradles me and calms down my spinning head.

"Like cool summer nights. Like smells you can never get enough of," I admit to my pillow, thinking he's gone. "I want to kiss you. It's all I think about when you're talking and I look at your mouth. I'm always so distracted by your mouth and your hands—"

"North." His voice is a warning.

The blanket is situated over me and I pass out.

. . .

I wake up to the sound of someone puking in front of my house. Sunlight outlines the window, framing the closed blinds. Bowser purrs next to me.

The fuzzy details of the night are clearing up with a thumping headache at my temple.

The guy accosting me at the bar. Evan taking me home. Evan not kissing me. Evan's rough voice and fingers teasing the ridges of my bra.

You're the first woman to sleep in my bed.

Evan's words spear pleasure right to the heart of me, and the empty bed is all I notice.

I do something I haven't done in a while.

I let myself think of my family. My father hasn't called to check on me. *A drop of hurt in the bucket.* My mother and I don't speak. *Another ball of pain falls.*

The three of us are like arrows shot in different directions.

I wipe away a tear when my attention refocuses and a tearful smile manages to break through.

Evan did not stay, but there's a box of Little Debbie Honey Buns on the nightstand.

CHAPTER FIFTEEN

Evan

I am in a foul mood. For good reason. Seated among twelve women each holding a glass of bubbly in hand (their word, not mine). This is a pearl-wearing, cardigan sweater convention.

Saturday morning brunch with members of the Alexandria Board has me turning my thoughts inward and zoning out at the white linen tablecloth.

It took a force of nature to not kiss Lexi.

The timing was all wrong. I wish I were at the shop with a wrench in my hand instead of a mimosa.

My actions were far from the smooth Evan Bailey variety. Smooth Evan would have been breaking in his bed. Uptight, concerned Evan does not.

My decision does not stop me from imagining the noises she would make as she grips me. Lexi was dangerously soft, like a slide of silk sheets slipping off the bed. I would claim her hips and kiss her where my fingers roam, showing off my skill set when it comes to paying attention to detail. But not when she's that drunk.

Lexi is not an easy woman to navigate. There are missing pieces around her of who she is. The heart of her, what makes her, *her,* isn't something I have figured out. The million-dollar question is, do I want to?

I used to have free evenings and weekends. Those things I gave up when Craig's lawyer watched me scrawl my name across the nondisclosure agreement to keep quiet about Craig's paternity.

Of all the choices I have made in my life, that one still rears its ugly head.

Did I do the right thing? For CeCe's sake, I did. No question there. It doesn't mean I'm not human. I wish I could stay out late or go to bed without wondering if CeCe's sore throat is allergies or a cold.

Craig has been out of our life for so long, I have no reason to be worried he would ever want in. My lawyer made it clear my mother, Alec, and Craig are the only ones who know he's the father. What's stopping Craig from stepping in and reasserting his rights?

Did he ever tell his family?

Thanks to Edward North, an ominous feeling pools in my stomach, spreading like spilled ink.

I run my hand down my Better Than Ezra shirt and focus when Elena's hand flutters over my arm.

"Thank you all for attending this morning," Elena says, smiling her pearly white smile. "I'm not alone when I say this is the first time we're starting on time." Polite laughter follows but I privately recoil at feeling the jab was made at Lexi's expense. "You know him from social media, but for those of you who haven't met our Lexi substitute, this is Evan Bailey. He's going to do a fabulous job working on the Alcott Gala."

The group of women offer their welcomes. I don't remember any of their names.

"We're going to start with where we are on catering." Elena glugs down a large sip of her champagne. "The lobster will be flown in from Maine. Same goes for the scallops."

I look at my phone and immediately open the text from Lexi. *Thanks for getting me home safely.*

My heart beats a little faster. **Me:** *Are you aware you just thanked me?*

Lexi: *Yes, I am*

I stuff my phone in my cargo shorts pocket in time for Elena to announce, "My apologies. Before we go any further, let's go around the table and introduce ourselves. I'm Elena Wilshire, I do nonprofit financial work for large corporations, and this is my sixth year cochairing the foundation."

The women go around the table and the more they speak, the less I know what to do with my hands or how often I should nod. My heart rate picks up. I gave Lexi a hard time for not having substance to her life but by the time the circle of trust comes around to me, I can't think of one thing I do outside of work that doesn't involve hanging out with Alec or making sure CeCe eats three meals a day.

"Go on, Evan, tell us about yourself." Elena signals the waiter to bring another round of mimosas.

"You all know I'm a mechanic."

"Could we tour the shop sometime?" a blonde at the end of the table says, and the other women snicker.

"We should get a photo with him," another says. "For the gala publicity."

They start talking all over each other like squawking geese, and I put my mimosa down, deciding I hate the flavor.

"Ladies," Elena says, ripping them one with a chastising glare. "Evan's our go-to man for the swag bags. This year we have three hundred confirmed yeses for the event and we're working with a tight budget of $500,000."

Rumblings break out among the ladies.

"What the fuck?" I say, causing Elena's smile to falter. "Half a million?"

The ladies pause their drinks midway to their mouths.

"Our budget is carefully maintained." She passes me a list. "These are Lexi's contributions for the swag bags. You're in charge of making sure the orders arrive."

I read the list.

Platinum smartwatch wrist bands

Two passes to Tannigan Island

A brainwave-sensing headband

Bitcoin surprise token

A robotic dog

"What is Tannigan Island?" My interest piques about the robotic dog. Do they make robotic cats?

"A billionaire's playground off the coast of southern Florida. The owners open up their island for three nights only to those with an invite. Anything you want is available. Parasailing, scuba diving, spa treatments. The nightlife is nothing but the stuff of fantasies."

Sitting at my neighbor's front yard bar and watching the sun go down has always been my version of paradise.

I know my place at Bailey's, but I sure as hell don't know who I am seated at this table.

I have seen enough. No one at this table sees what I see. *The excess.* "Excuse me, but I have to pick up my niece," I lie and stand up so fast I almost knock the chair over.

The one place I want to go—to the shop, is not an option. Not while I'm fresh off the heels of spending time with Lexi's "friends."

By the time evening rolls around I get out of the pool and towel-dry just as a text from Lexi appears. *Your washing machine is leaking water.*

This is the third time in the past six months the washing machine is acting up.

Me: *Don't touch the washing machine.*

Me: *I'm heading over.*

Lexi answers the door wearing a tank top with a loose

swoop, revealing cleavage my hands want in on. The wide, silky bow on her shorts is begging to be tugged loose. Her eyes are splashed with golden brown and I can't find any reason to look away, especially with her hair piled off her face.

"I'll be quick," I snap, walking around her.

She closes the door. "I hope that's not your opening line."

Lexi's lazy ways clash with the effort I put in to keeping a clean house.

"Did a bomb go off?" I ask, stepping over clothes strewn around the room. The table is full of forgotten bowls of half-eaten popcorn and snacks. Mutual disrespect irrevocably takes hold and pulls us close with a gravitational force.

"You're trashing me for the way the house looks? I've been at work since the butt crack of dawn and do you know how I spent my time? Cleaning tools. Hundreds of tools, and my hands ache."

"The only difference between me and you is I don't complain about it."

She squares her shoulders, evoking a ruffle of fabric at her chest I'm having trouble not looking at. "No one asked you to stop by. You don't get to show up and fault me because you nickel-and-dime every repair. You should buy a new washing machine. They aren't *that* much." She points a hard arm to the laundry room.

"You want to go there? Fine. I'm going to win this one, sweetheart. Do you know how much a new washer costs?"

"Yes. I've been doing my research. I was going to handle it. If I take money out of next month's stash, I can get a dryer to go with it."

"It doesn't work the way you think. You won't have money next month. You buy what you can afford. *That* was our deal. Didn't anyone ever teach you how to budget?"

"I didn't think you'd be such a schoolmarm about logistics, and no," she says with a touch of prideful scorn, "I don't know how to budget."

"Maybe you should." I switch modes of blaming her to making a list of life skills this girl needs if she wants to make it to thirty and play adult. "Your father did you a major disservice. He runs a multi-million-dollar company and he didn't bother to teach you about finances?" I feel outright frustration toward learning the members of the Alexandria will spend more on one gala than I will make in years. The entire morning puts my mood over the edge. "I bet you don't even check receipts."

The specs of gold in her eyes darken. Her mouth clenches like she's about to explode. "I don't need to check receipts!"

"When you can't afford apples next week, you'll want my help. Move out of my way." I stalk past her with my teeth grinding over one another.

I go straight to the laundry room and shut the door.

This was a mistake. All of it.

The bet. Both coming here and seeing what's in front of me.

Hanging from the metal shelving is an entire row devoted to bras. Lacy, padded bras. Some of them see-through.

I think of Lexi's beautiful tits filling up the lace. Her hard nipples, rough from my touch, straining against the fabric. A private groan escapes the back of my throat.

I take them down, pile them in the laundry basket, and cover them with a shirt.

She opens the door and squeezes into the small space. There's enough room for the washer, the dryer, and Lexi's ego.

My gaze scans the bottom of the washer with the ring of water escaping with dollar signs. "Grab towels from the bathroom."

"You're using the bathroom towels to clean up the mess? I use those." She makes her case known. "Looks like I'll have to order new ones."

My head cocks. My gaze is curious. "From what I've seen,

the only thing you've changed about your life is your address. By the way, *your* towels are overpriced."

She leaves the room with a blazing hot gaze, returning with an armful of towels she ceremoniously drops at my feet. "You think everything over five dollars is overpriced."

She is different than she was the other night. Less, *Evan you smell like summer nights* and more like the day I met her.

I pull the washer away from the wall and scope out the hose, giving her a side-eyed glance. "What's with you today?"

"Me? It's your life, Evan. Your couch has stains. Police patrol your grocery store and I hate how fast food affects me. I'm counting the days until I get my house back."

"Then quit," I seethe, hating the way my life sounds. "Let's be done. Give me the $100,000 and walk out the door. You don't think I see every eye roll? Hear every huff? Aren't you exhausted from treating everyone like they're beneath you? *I see it all*. Do you have any idea how stuck-up you come across? Do you even care?"

She drums her nails on the dryer. "I don't have to care."

"You do," I roar, the two of us moving closer together.

"I see all *your* eye rolls. Hear *your* huffs. You do the same to me. You're the most arrogant man I have ever met. Have *you* spent any of the money I left you? Have you made an appointment for a tux fitting for the gala?" Lexi does a 180, her eyes turning patient and her voice tender. Her anger is gone, leaving only warmth. "This goes both ways," she says with unearned softness. She runs her hand over my jaw, resting her hand against my stubble. "Stop acting like you don't have to try either."

My hands slide over her hips, pulling her close, lifting her onto the dryer.

The energy between us shifts, it deepens, surrounds us, trapped in this tiny room with no airflow. I run my hands over the tops of her thighs, fingertips pushing up the fabric of her short shorts. "You said I'm arrogant."

"You are. That wasn't a question."

"I am when it comes to things I want."

"And what is it you want, Evan?"

My hands fall to either side of her, my head bows, and I suck in a sigh.

I want her.

I want her mouth on mine, her hands on me, and mine sliding down her hips.

Our gazes meet with held breaths. The air in my chest is tight. One tug of her closer to me and I could capture her mouth in a kiss.

Lexi makes the choice for me.

Her mouth slams into mine in a burst of fiery movement. I seize her lips in a rough kiss, exposing my need for her, wrecking her mouth until she gives in with heart-shattering fullness. Her tongue moves with mine, her hands slide up my jaw and into my hair. Her mouth is soft, yielding entirely to my claim on her lips. My tongue works over hers, around hers, demands her willingness against my harsh strokes, determined to taste her, feel her hips rise to my fingers.

I crush my mouth to hers alternating between firm and soft. Our lips explore, our breath turning choppy, the scent of laundry detergent hovering in the air. I am hard for her, an urgency rising within me.

I slow down the kiss, finding our rhythm, my hands sweeping over her rear, hauling her closer, hearing the first beautiful moan break from her mouth.

"You like that?" I whisper.

She pushes her hips into my hands. My fingers swipe over the bow. I have it untied, my fingers at the ridge of her waistband, and I break away, stepping back.

We stare at each other in silence, breathless and wired, her eyes full of lust and cheeks flushed pink from a kiss outranking any others.

I retie her bow and I angle her face up to mine, planting a kiss on her mouth, ignoring my own desires. "I'm going to show you how to fix the washer."

"Fix the washer?" she repeats.

I leave the room to grab my tool bag, giving myself space, and come back. "The leak isn't new," I explain to her.

She gets off the dryer and stands next to me, our shoulders bumping. The pipes are old. The repairs are expensive. I check the water hose valve and feel at once that it's loose.

"I can fix this," I say and dig around in my tool bag. "I'll show you what to do if this happens again."

Her brow furrows and she slides her mouth into a frown. "I thought I broke the machine because I did something wrong. I was trying to figure out how to wash my clothes."

I tighten the hose and push the washing machine in, her words belatedly registering. Tilting my face to hers, I give her a thousand-yard stare. *"Wait.* Are you saying you've never done your own laundry?"

She crosses her index and pointer finger, holding them up like an honor code. "I have never done my own laundry. Judge me all you want."

I'm calling her bluff. I set down the wrench, giving her the full brunt of my attention. "How's that possible?"

"My parents employed a housekeeping team. All my laundry was done by someone else. I never needed to learn."

Kissing her again is in the forefront of my brain, working in tune with my other parts, but I'm invested in how she squeaked through life without doing a single load of laundry. "What about during college?"

"I paid my roommate. She was on scholarship. We had a good system. And I dropped out after a couple years."

"She did your dirty work." I grab the detergent and unscrew the cap. "We're going to take care of this right now." Moving to stand beside her, I catch her hard swallow in my side-eyed glance. "This is concentrated. Use the cap to measure," I overexplain how to do it. An ember burns through me at her gaze, slipping to my mouth and back to the washing machine controls. "Go on. Your turn."

She fills the liquid in the cap and chooses the correct load size, her polished finger pressing the start button. "Thank you for not laughing at me."

"I will never laugh at you for learning. You have to start somewhere, North. In the meantime, how would you feel about attending an art fundraiser? There's to be a wine tasting at the event and I'm clueless about the proper way to drink wine except when chugging. Do you think you could come with me and translate?"

"You are clueless," she says, "and, since you helped me with laundry, I owe you one."

CHAPTER SIXTEEN

Lexi

Holy shit. Evan knows what he's doing. On the dryer no less, my mouth exploring his, my hands running over his hardness, all those angles.

The tightly wound, luscious knots haven't left.

Tonight's an early light's-out kind of night. My lower back hurts from a day spent cleaning shop mats, mopping floors, and restocking supplies.

My hand goes to flip off the lights and I spot Bowser's face. Something's not right. "Hey," I say, going over to her and freaking out. "Oh no."

Her left eye is enlarged and glassy. I try to get a closer look and she scratches my arm. What am I supposed to do? I grab my phone and call Evan.

"Bowser's eye doesn't look right. I think she's in pain," my words roar into the phone. "What should I do?"

"There's a twenty-four-hour vet number on the fridge," he says, laughter and music loud in the background.

I suck it up and ask him. "Could you come over?"

"Can't, North. I'm at a pool party with the foundation members."

Oh.

I wasn't invited. Even with this switch, I thought I would still be included. Not that I would rush to join even if they did ask. I have an injured cat and a body of sore muscles. "I'll figure it out."

I end the call before he can say he knows I'll be fine.

My plans to park my rear on Evan's couch becomes a night leaving me at a loss for what's next.

Here's what happened. The vet clinic didn't have an appointment until ten. Evan didn't have a crate to transport Bowser. An emergency trip to Walmart was needed (first dip into next month's cash). After I returned, Bowser threw up all over the carpet. Evan doesn't have pet insurance so I paid out of pocket for her scratched eye (second dip into wallet).

We return home after midnight with Bowser subdued on drugs and wearing a cone collar and antibiotic cream (third dip into wallet). I situate her on a bed of blankets. "There's really no good way to wear that look, is there?" I speak gently to her, getting into bed.

Evan's kiss is wiped from my mind. Legs parted, one arm over my face, my thoughts are wound-up with my fast-beating heart. How will I afford groceries?

I wish I hadn't done the pedicure with Evan or all the overspending on groceries for ingredients I let go to waste. I ran through Evan's money faster than I thought.

Now, I'm in trouble.

In the morning, Bowser receives her eye drops.

A text from Evan at one o-clock a.m. *How's Bowser?*

Was he awake at home when he sent this? Or was he still at the party riding a blow-up flamingo, half-drunk riding double with Elena?

Me: *She's on meds*

Me: *Do you have any idea how expensive her care was?*
I don't send this text. Instead, I delete the words. I don't have

time to complain.

I get ready for work, using the last of the toilet paper. No seriously—not a single roll exists in the house. I go through every cabinet and I already used the last of it in the second bathroom.

Wanting to come home after my shift and crash on the couch won't happen if I don't go to the store. My cash flow is a problem. I work it out the way I always do. "I just won't go to the store," I tell myself as I scrub whatever funk is taking up residence at the base of the toilet in Bailey's customer bathroom. "I'll live on Evan's treat stash."

This is the moment I reach a new low.

While refilling the toilet paper, I take an extra one and stuff it in my jumpsuit and put it in my handbag when the break room is empty.

Soon as I get home, guilt is dripping thickly down my spine. I stare at the roll of toilet paper. "I'll return it," I say to Bowser.

This means I need to go to the store now, instead of putting it off until I'm back at home with my personal shopper.

Halfheartedly pushing my shopping cart around, I'm weak in the knees. Time to see the damage.

The self-checkout aisle seemed like a good idea until I swipe the last item, a fresh block of Asiago from the deli, and the AI harasses me to put the item in a bag.

I have $163.00 on me to buy groceries for the next two weeks, a whopping total of $320.87, and death stares from the customers waiting in line.

Anxiety blooms in my chest.

The items are bagged and I don't know what to do. I can't pay for the groceries.

"I'll be there when I can," the woman behind me says,

snapping her gum. "Some girl's holding up the line."

A child is crying.

I'm frozen with what to do, numbly raising my hand. An employee trots over, ponytail swinging, and whips out an ID card.

"I have to put stuff back."

An uproar of gripes and sighs detonate like a bomb. Someone throws their hands up.

The employee is nice, she doesn't say a word as I hand her the salon-grade shampoo and conditioner, the pet toys for Bowser, and start downsizing my purchases without making eye contact.

The grocery store incident is how I ended up at my actual house parked curbside and deliberating about knocking on my door.

If I go in there, I admit I need help with finances. Sitting in Evan's car, I am afraid if I look at my spending, I won't like what I see.

Secondary thoughts creep in. What if he tells me *I told you so*?

I run my hand over the steering wheel and give him a head's up I'm stopping by. Evan, for all his faults, would never be in my position. "Get your butt to the front door and ask him for help."

I get out of the car. Time's up.

CeCe answers the door in her bathing suit and with a towel flung over her shoulder. "Hey, Lexi," she says. "We're about to go for a swim. You should join us."

"Oh," I say, clearing my throat, feeling like an intruder on their tight-knit world, "that's okay." I chicken out, not wanting to crash their plans. "I'll be in and out. I needed to grab some clothes."

"Can I come see Bowser tonight?"

"Tomorrow," Evan says, appearing at the top of the stairs,

shirt off, muscles out, bathing suit blocking my view of better things. My heart does a tiny flutter. *I kissed this man.*

CeCe stays put with her hand on the door.

He moves quickly down the stairs, giving me nowhere else to look. "I'm classing it up, North. I have a six-pack of Stella's. Stick around."

"You splurged, impressive. Watch out, CeCe, he might buy a Rolls-Royce."

The house is immaculate but still full of their presence. CeCe's sketchbook with fine-tip markers is on the table and Evan's Caps hat hangs off a chair. The place feels big as an open sky and being back in my space is like having a pair of tight arms around me.

"How's your summer going?" I ask CeCe. Evan grabs the glasses for the beer.

"Boring," she says, picking up her tablet. "At least this year I didn't have to go to summer school. My friends are all at camp together this week."

My summers were rarely at home. "I went to overnight camps."

"See?" she says to Evan.

"I'm not leaving you with strangers for a full week," Evan remarks, pouring our drinks. He's tipping the glasses to avoid foam.

There is no way to take the *pretentious* out of my next sentence. "Mine was for a full summer...in Europe."

Evan looks up at me sharply.

CeCe's clearly enamored with the idea, resting her chin in her hands, her pretty brown eyes with thick lashes. "Really? What did you do there?"

"Hmm, I haven't thought about it in some time. We took day trips, traveled, and played sports." All of it meant to keep me out of my father's hair.

"I'm going to go in the pool," she grumbles, "maybe I

should get my floaties."

"Not funny," Evan calls after her, handing me my beer, his fingers gently grazing mine. "She's like this all the time now."

I take a sip of the refreshing beer, saying what's in my heart, what I see in her. "She's dying to try new things. Can't you see?"

"She's not—"

I put my finger to his mouth. "Don't you dare say I have no idea how to be a parent. I won't fight you on that point, but I was her age once and I wanted to do everything."

"Yeah?" he says briskly. "What happened to that girl?"

My hand molds to the glass, and I look at the thin layer of froth. "She changed." I don't meet Evan's gaze. "She realized her last name would open any door." Her credit cards became her safety net.

Lonely? Swipe the card. Bored? Call up friends and pay for them to join you. Feeling good? Celebrate with a trip to anywhere.

"Didn't your parents worry about shipping you across the ocean?" he says coolly. "Didn't you care?"

"I cared." Emotion winds up my voice. He's picking at scar tissue. The thing about scar tissue is, it hurts when irritated. "Where were your parents? Didn't they want more for you than spending your days in a garage?"

His mouth parts as if I've nettled him. "They wanted me to be happy about my choices."

Which is more than I can say for you is embedded in his eyes. His reaction weighs on me.

"You said your father died of a heart attack. Were you close?"

He clears his throat, and his eyes turn glassy. "Very much."

I move my hand to reach toward him but stop myself.

No longer in the mood to deal with budget woes, I retreat into introvert land laden with unrest. Bitterness about my own family crusts over my mood.

My father hasn't bothered to check in on me and my mother probably doesn't even know about the bet.

Setting the beer glass down, I get to my feet. "I have to go."

His hand curves around mine. "You didn't say why you stopped by."

To ask for your help. Instead, I take the easy way out. "I was going to grab clothes, but I don't need them."

Evan's kiss was a straight shot to my heart. There's more there, between us, but it feels messy, dangerous even, like he could get me to spill my pain.

One kiss wasn't supposed to change anything. It brought us closer, and I don't do *close*.

Not with a guy I won't talk to once this is over. I am kidding myself if I think there is a place for me in Evan and CeCe's life. This will be over in a matter of weeks and I will be left in my same situation. *Alone.*

Maintaining a bored face, I fight the urge to put my fingers on his jaw, feel the satisfying scratch of his unshaved face. "I was thinking about our kiss."

"I was too," he says in a way that will make it difficult to stick to my plan.

"Let's not do that again."

There's a flicker of surprise in his eyes, but also understanding. Evan stands at his full height, respecting my choice and taking a step back. "Understood."

I get in the car and exhale a long breath. It's everything. Bowser. Money. Evan's house. *I stole a roll of toilet paper.*

I can't do this.

I hold my breath and type *I quit.*

My finger hovers over send.

CHAPTER SEVENTEEN

Lexi

I did not quit. I wanted to, I really did. The toilet paper was returned and I feel bad about how I left things with Evan last night.

Karma didn't let me off so easily. I'm stuck behind the rear end of an Accord working on buffing an exhaust pipe like I'm prepping a cow for labor.

I am literally nose-close to the car's smelly fume hole using tar removal. My arms *ache* from the repetitive motion. I take what I can get. "Umbrella" blasts over the speakers. Just one of many pop songs on my playlist.

Garcia's tapping his foot.

Josh is hunched over the open tool drawers digging around for the good mood he must have lost. "The asshole tried to get out of here without paying," Josh says to no one in particular. They all just talk, put their voices out there, and hope someone hears. "He thought two drink coupons to Minx was a fair trade for replacing his brake pads."

Brandon stretches his arm with the tattoo over his chest. "That's where I took my date."

"That girl who never texted you again?" Josh comments

offhandedly.

I poke my head around the taillight.

"We were having a great night." Brandon's hands spread wide. "She asked about a second date and then nothing."

"Maybe her ex came back into the picture?" one of the techs asks, reaching for a pry bar hanging on the wall.

Their conversation is far more interesting than listening to my inner thoughts about why this place hasn't sent an SOS to a makeover show. "What's Minx?" I ask.

They stop talking.

"Are you about done?" Josh says.

"If you're asking if I'm done losing my sense of smell, then yes."

Garcia does a slow shoulder roll and peeks out from under the hood of the Camry.

Brandon turns his back to me and continues talking to Josh. "I thought the date was going well. She even said she wanted to join me next time I go hunting, then she never texted me again."

Brandon needs a female perspective—the second-date hunting suggestion aside. This is my chance to get more from them than a cold shoulder. I take off my gloves and text Evan.

Me: *What is Minx?*

Evan: *Applying for a second job?*

Me: *Just tell me*

Evan: *A strip club*

"Oh my God," I say loud enough for Josh and Brandon to turn abruptly toward me. "You took your date to a strip club?"

"When we were talking online, she said she liked their cheese fries," Brandon says with a combative raise of his voice. "Where was the last date *you* went on?"

He flew me to Chicago for a night at the Four Seasons. I come out from behind the car, dirty rag in my hand. "You sound like you liked her."

"Not anymore," Brandon says. "I'm over it. I'm over dating. All you want is for us to make fools of ourselves just so you can turn us down."

"That's not true."

Josh scoffs. "Yeah, coming from someone who thinks caviar is food."

"That's not fair," I say, not hiding my irritation. "All anyone wants is to feel special. If you think ordering her cheese fries while women wrap their legs around a pole and slide upside down is the way to do that, then that's on you. You didn't like this girl. You wanted her to reject you just so you could stand here and complain. I listen to you guys all the time. You're lazy when it comes to dating. You pick up a date by swiping and you expect the evening to go just as easily. When was the last time you got off your butt and really tried?"

Brandon's entire body stiffens.

"You don't know what you're talking about," Josh says.

I keep my gaze on Brandon. "Brandon does."

Alec's voice booms over the speaker like a god. "All of you. *Get back to work*. Lexi. I need the new shipment of parts sorted. You're done with exhaust cleaning."

There is no downtime at the shop. I'm relegated to the shop room to organize a new shipment of parts.

I put my earbuds in and listen to a financial management podcast. When I was on the cusp of quitting last night, I did something that surprised me. I downloaded a step-by-step guide about achieving financial freedom. The first episode was about spending within my means. I even filled out the online worksheet about wants and needs.

Needs: Food, shelter, clothing (within my budget limit).

Wants: Hermes cashmere scarves, micro pore cleaner, thermal-regulating bedding.

Today's episode is *Your Paycheck is Not Your Therapist*. "Money will never fill emotional voids," says the calming host.

Volume up. Ears open. I want to be ready for the quiz at the end.

My biceps ache and my lower back could use Evan's firm mattress. I don't like the way I left things last night. Instead of opening up to him about how I was overwhelmed to start a budget, I found a quick exit.

Taking a break, I sit on the storeroom floor.

I hold my phone tighter and my pulse picks up. *Just tell him why you came over last night.*

Me: *So about this budgeting stuff.*

Me: *How do you factor in grocery shopping?*

Me: *I don't know what I want to eat until I get to the store.*

I wait for his response, clutching the phone in my hand.

Evan: *Think ahead before you go to the store.*

Evan: *Make a weekly meal plan.*

Evan: *Stick to your list. No unplanned flowers or six dollars for one avocado.*

Evan: *Have you taken a look at what you spend each month?*

Me: *I think you know the answer.*

Evan: *Start there.*

Me: *I'm afraid what I might see.*

Evan: *You should be more afraid of being ignorant.*

Evan: *Have you checked out my latest video?*

Me: *You're not supposed to ask people if they saw your video. That's like a laugh track.*

I pull up the video anyway. Sure enough, Evan and his shaky grip, talking his followers through his experiences at the country club. I can't watch. It's not *him*, but his followers love him. #HangInThereEvan #CountryClubVibes.

My gaze moves over the hundreds of auto parts wrapped in plastic bags. I press play on my podcast and think about Evan's advice.

The no-kissing rule I put on Evan and me is flapping

around my head like a noisy bird. It won't go away. I send Evan one more text. *About last night.*

Evan: *There's nothing to say*

I step into the customer lounge with a growling stomach, prepared to get my low-budget packed lunch of store brand PB and J. My nose crinkles at a smell wafting around me.

When no one is watching, I give a discreet armpit sniff test. *Oh no.* It's me.

I grab a cup of coffee and add two powdered creamer packets. Stirring my hot drink, I notice a flyer posted on the community bulletin board.

LADIES, HAVE YOU ALWAYS WANTED
TO LEARN HOW TO CHANGE A TIRE?

"Nope," I say, removing my gloves and giving the flyer a second look. Bailey's is offering a workshop on how to change tires?

"What do you think?" Alec says, tacking up another flyer.

His earnestness is commendable. "Do people want to know how to change tires?"

"What if you're stuck on a highway with a flat?" He taps his finger on the flyer. "You have no cell service."

"I would say why are you limiting your customer base to women? Almost every person in this city has a car. Tire changing seems like a useful skill for anyone with lungs and a heartbeat."

The likeness of Alec and Evan stops at their identical faces. Alec is extremely private and Evan is always up for chucking his opinion. Alec lives and breathes Bailey's. I swore he slept here last night. The telltale sign was the coffee was made when Josh and I opened.

He runs his hand through the fringes of his side-parted hair. Nothing compares to the depth of green in Evan's eyes. The way they burst with color after he kissed me.

"It would be the start of other workshops, changing your own oil, basic car maintenance."

My father would never give property buyers trade secrets. "Doesn't this hurt your bottom line? Customers doing maintenance on their own?"

"Not really. It takes people time to trust their skills when it comes to their vehicles. What's your female perspective? Would your friends sign up for this?"

I choke on the thought.

Talia with her four-inch heels. Elena in her dresses that could double as lingerie. I stop thinking of my life from Lexington North's POV and from the auto shop janitor's view. The cost gets my notice. "Fifty bucks is going to be a deterrent unless you're offering perks."

"What kind of perks?"

"At all the events I help coordinate," I plug in my experience, "we offer swag bags. Your demographic doesn't need silk scarves and electronic feather dusters. You could offer lattes or chilled drinks." Help me, I'm on a roll. "Or a Bailey's koozie and a T-shirt."

Tia's lightning-quick reaction has us turning toward her. "Told you, Alec," she croons. "I said throw in a free bottle of wine. The $3.99 red zin from Liquor Up is a gift to wine drinkers."

The door opens and a guy holding a vase of flowers struts over to the counter. "Delivery for Tia Carter."

"Those are pretty," I say, having an infinite love of florals and not a dime to buy any for the house. "Who are they from?"

She rips open the card and reads. Her eyes scan the handwritten text. "I don't know." She hands me note.

"Tia, just because you're you." I flip the card over. It's blank. "Are you seeing someone?"

"No," she says, bewildered by the gift. She runs her stiletto nails over the rose petals and my manicure-loving heart

squeezes with jealousy for wanting to pamper my dry, rubber-scented hands. "The last guy I dated stole fifty dollars from me. He wouldn't spend it on flowers."

I slide the card in the plastic note spike. "Well, someone is trying to get your attention."

"Lexi, the guy who pulled up is asking to see you," Josh says, late in noticing the flowers. "What are those?"

"Roses," Tia deadpans and grabs the vase, moving them next to her computer.

"She has an admirer," I explain to Josh. Tia's flower delivery is the most interesting event to happen at the garage.

Josh does a finger whistle and Brandon looks up from the hood of a Civic. "When Lexi's done in the stockroom, show her how to make the oil spill mixture."

"You just complimented me," I say, jabbing Josh with my elbow.

"I did not," he gripes, but he so did. "Just focus on your next job. You'll need sawdust and paint thinner, in case you've been waiting all day to mix toxic chemicals and breathe them in." The hard line of his mouth relaxes into a grin, showing off his dimples. He gestures to the SUV in the car queue. "The customer specifically requested you."

The car door opens and a shiny, masculine shoe appears, then another, until my gaze settles on the slim-fitting suit and Versace sunglasses. Leaving the car door open, he stares at me and rips off the sunglasses he wears as religiously as his aloe oatmeal face mask. Hudson strides with long steps over to me, sticking out like the golden egg he is. "I had to see for myself."

I don't like him here. At once, I'm uneasy. Embarrassed, too. "What did you need to see?"

"Is there someplace we can talk?" he demands, his gaze taking time poring over my face, my shoulders, down to my boots. "Tell someone you're taking a break."

"No breaks!" Brandon calls out and I whip my gaze around,

finding the staff conveniently keeping busy.

This is Hudson, going out of his way to see me.

I fall back quicker than I thought. Did I really get upset about groceries? Or think I should take a tire-changing class? This deal with Evan is getting taken too seriously.

"Ten minutes is all I have. He's getting an oil change," I say loudly at Brandon sauntering over, giving Hudson an eye full of mistrust. "The platinum package."

We go out front and stand beneath one of the few trees and avoid the scraps of trash tumbling around us. The garage doors are all open; the guys can see us.

"How are you?"

His gaze turns squinty. "Things are hectic. My cases take up all my time."

"You've wanted to be a lawyer since I've known you. It can't be all bad." And Isabella? Is she still part of his dream? The heart can set a horrible example of self-control.

His gaze locks on mine with a ripple of unease. An air of effortlessness settles between us. "The truth is, I've been worried about you. I wanted to call."

"Your girlfriend doesn't care?" I'm allowed to be snarky for this occasion. "How's Isabella adjusting?"

He sighs like the world is on his shoulders. "It's not going well. I didn't want to admit it to myself. We were perfect in California. Now I'm not sure."

"I'm sorry." A fizzle of excitement follows. This is easier than Evan. Evan and I are confusing. "Is there anything I can do?"

"No. I've got to work it out. I want to be able to call you and talk."

I put my hand on his arm. "It's always okay. I'll be back in my life in no time." And then what? What is he asking? Stillness registers in my peripheral vision and I look at the garage. Garcia and Josh are suddenly busy.

"My mother doesn't like her. Isabella is so outspoken. It's why I needed to see you. To get perspective." He laces his fingers through mine. Our palms press together and raise to his chest. He untangles them at once. "What's on your hand?"

"Unnatural compounds."

"Craig's been asking how you're doing. He wanted to talk to you."

How odd. Craig and I are close as a cat and a mouse. We talk to each other but don't hang out outside of the Alexandria social scene. "About what?"

"He didn't say."

"Lexi," Josh booms, holding a blowtorch and looking at Hudson like he may not want to stick around to see how it's used. "Break's over."

"I have to go." I don't want to. Hudson is back to the man he was when we were together. "At least you can't say I don't like to get my hands dirty."

He winces. "I feel awful about what I said. Let me make it up to you. Do you need anything? Money? My credit cards? A dinner out at your favorite restaurant?" He doesn't give me a chance to answer. He pulls out an envelope from his back pocket. "This is on me. *Enjoy.*"

I am all too aware of Alec in the garage, taking in the entire scene. I open the envelope to see crisp one hundred dollar bills.

Hudson's thumb chucks beneath my chin. "Anything you want. I've got you covered."

CHAPTER EIGHTEEN

Evan

Swimming in the idiot lane is not my comfort zone. Yet I feel like one. "I look like a salesman," I gripe, pulling at the powder blue button-down and navy slacks. "I did have my Pearl Jam shirt paired with jeans." My hand slides over the back of my head. "I went formal with the man bun instead of a ponytail."

Her mouth turns up ever so subtly. Lexi leans close, her hand touching the side of my slacks and she rips off the vertical XL sticker. "Might want to take this off next time."

I grab it from her fingers, twisting it because she won't let go. My cock is impossibly aware of her. I was willing to let her straddle me and pin my wrists down, be however high-handed she wanted. Her mouth was perfect and nothing was sweeter, but she prefers chasing after Hudson.

I am not making this up.

She told me she didn't want to kiss again and the next day Hudson is at Bailey's. The information came courtesy of Brandon, Alec, *and* Josh.

I let out a long, quiet scoff. "Do you know why these men suffer through wearing pastels and pocket squares?"

Her gaze holds mine. "Interesting, Mr. Bailey. I didn't think pocket square was in your vocabulary. Be careful where you fling that term, I might think you're hanging out at tailor shops and cigar bars."

"Look around. This doesn't get worse." I am back with the cardigan lineup of the Alexandria Board. We are hosting an artist's fundraising showcase at the Hillwood Estate with a wine tasting. Sweat pricks the back of my neck as I watch the guests strolling in the flower garden.

Lexi steps away from me, wearing a short dress that's hard to ignore. She's missing only my hands on her. The fabric opens and flutters around her mid-thigh, drawing the eye to her smooth legs and heels. I've barely scraped the surface of her curves, of her needs. "Do you think you can survive tonight?"

"Depends, if you feel ready to handle my art issues."

"Art issues?" her voice croaks.

"Possible aversion to discussing lines and texture. My fear that the Mona Lisa is actually a time traveler and how I will say the wrong thing when surrounded by beautiful, wealthy women forcing me to make conversation about things I know nothing about."

Her crinkly brow smooths. "What things are twisting your panties, Evan?"

I run my hands over the front of my shirt. "The usual topics I might find myself engaged in. The pitfalls of purchasing a castle in Scotland. Dividends. Neurosurgery."

"You're scratching the underside of your chin like you do when you're uncomfortable."

I drop my hand. "Am not."

I can't look away from the deep burnished brown of her eyes highlighted by the golden evening sunlight. "You know what your problem is?"

"No. Could you tell me?" I deadpan.

"Why don't you give tonight a chance? I think you're afraid to put yourself out there. You've grown too comfortable at Bailey's. Did it ever occur to you, you have things in common?"

I drum up my best southern gentlemanly accent, hiding the growing fear that her observation of me isn't entirely wrong. "No, it did not occur to me, Ms. North."

She straightens my collar with disdainful scorn. "Talk about cars or having a seventh grader."

The estate is an ode to gardens and prestige, and involves a string quartet, tables set up with food and drinks and an art display. "Can I also talk about that art? Bowser could have accomplished the same picture with her paws."

"Kindness is your best asset."

I lean in close to her ear, my fingers aching to wrap around her hip. "I beg to differ, North."

People are moving around us, commenting on the beauty of the estate, but all I see is Lexi's face, all I want to sample is her mouth, her curves, and watch as she whimpers my name. "Go easy on me," I speak for only our ears. "I'm an art virgin."

"I highly doubt anyone looks at you and thinks you're a virgin—about anything." Lexi's focus makes a drastic shift and she holds her breath.

Talia is standing close by. Her black hair falls to her shoulders and her ever-intriguing eyes are looking at us.

"I haven't seen Talia since the night I met you." Lexi's worried voice gets my notice.

"Did something happen that night?"

"I charged her for taking a selfie with me."

I do a double take.

"I know, not my finest moment. I don't think that's the whole story, but she won't return my texts."

I put my hand on the small of her back. "Both of you are here now. You should talk to her."

"I can't."

I lean in close to her ear, my hand unmoving. "You can."

Lexi steps toward Talia and raises her hand, mouthing the word, "Hi."

Talia steps closer and I hang back. "How are you?" Talia asks.

"I'm good. I'm working at an auto shop."

"I know," Talia says, pausing with her drink in hand.

"I would love to talk. If you want that." Lexi puts her heart right out there. Right on display.

My breath catches at her vulnerability. I don't think this is a friendship strained by one night of Lexi behaving badly but a string of mistakes over time. From where I stand, they look like two friends who have more to say to each other.

"Sure. Not tonight though." Talia's gaze moves to mine and back to Lexi.

Lexi introduces me to people whose names I forget. They ask questions I don't know how to answer. A few new things I learn about Lexi. She has two different laughs. An etiquette laugh and a genuine one. She lets people finish their sentences and she doesn't leave my side.

"I need a drink," I finally admit the moment Elena enters the party. Her bouncy, honey-colored hair is distracting.

Lexi's a show of sighing and pressing her lips together as Elena moves around the party full of easy smiles and sneaky glances at me. "Watch out for her. My friends will use you for one thing."

"Only if it involves props."

Her mouth crumples adorably. Lexi pauses and turns to me, my hand still on her, sliding and cupping her hip, my thumb gently moving back and forth. "The night you took me home from Low Point," she states seriously.

One of my favorite nights with her. "The night you threw yourself at me."

She balks in complete denial, tucking strands of hair

behind her ear. "I wouldn't put it like that. You told me no one's ever been in your bed."

No one but Lexi is taking up mattress space. A fact I'm acutely aware of.

I dig my fingers a little deeper against her skin. "How long have you been thinking about that?"

"Why don't you bring women back to your house?"

"To protect CeCe." It was necessary when she was much younger, and even more important with her astounding ability to hear everything. But my rule morphed into the control I needed to not get attached. A self-employed strategy to make sure no one gets hurt. "And because my walls are thin."

Lexi's mouth parts, her throat making a sexy noise. "Your headboard is—"

"Loud, North. It's loud slamming against the wall." It will be once I have a chance to test that theory.

A grin breaks out on her beautiful mouth, and her voice is like a whisper from a pillow. "Don't worry, I already thought it would be."

"North—" I manage a strangled sound at the thought of Lexi pleasuring herself while caught between my sheets.

Elena gives a speech and introduces the artist to a round of applause. "Please, everyone take their seats for dinner." The table setting uses more plates than CeCe and I use in a single day. I am about to take my seat and bullshit my way through a place setting requiring three forks, but then I pull out my chair in time to see Hudson striding through the crowd like he's walking on water.

Hair slicked back, tan suit and brown shoes, an ensemble I would never wear. I have no idea what Lexi sees in his aerodynamic nose and lack of facial hair, but he's headed toward her like a plane about to land.

This is no longer about Lexi and Hudson. This is about being around anyone with the last name Hoffman. If Hudson is here, is Craig? Fear strikes a tender nerve. I search the room with a heart ready for a fight, but Craig isn't here.

Hudson says hi to no one, looks at no one, and sweeps down, pressing a kiss to Lexi's cheek and stretching his hand to mine. "We haven't officially met, I'm Hudson Hoffman."

Upon first meet and greet, Hudson doesn't appear to register who I am. He could be hiding this for the sake of appearances or...he doesn't know he has a niece. "Evan Bailey," I answer, keeping it brief.

Hudson steals the chair I was about to take and snags the spot next to Lexi.

What's the deal with this dude? I thought he had a girlfriend. Now he's hanging his arm over the back of her chair and annoying me with his white-as-bleach teeth. I walk around to the other side of Lexi and take a seat as Hudson pours himself a glass of wine and makes a private toast to Lexi, shutting out the rest of us with his voice meant for her.

Elena takes the seat next to me, plopping down and tilting her face at me thoughtfully. "Looks like I got the best chair."

Lexi's face turns to mine.

Hudson, who hasn't heard a word I've spoken, breaks off from hogging Lexi's attention, and I'm tempted to throw her a life raft. But that's before Hudson speaks. "You don't know the Hartwell family by chance, do you, *Ev*?"

Everyone in the auto industry knows the dreaded Hartwell name. Bailey's was hit hard by their presence thanks to the national chain eating us up like Elena's hitting the appetizers. "Never heard of them."

"No? Too bad. The owner's son and I spent a week in Hawaii at a private golf course last year. It worked out, considering both our families put in a bid to have our name on UVA's football stadium."

"No one's interested in size wars," Elena says.

I look to Lexi, but she's staring ahead, her face pale, and

drinking champagne and shooting me a coldhearted glance.

I pick up a piece of cheese from the tray in front of us and break off a section, accidentally dropping a chunk into my wine.

Am I supposed to fish it out?

Hudson picks up his glass and sticks his nose in with a hefty sniff. "The bouquet is incredible," he says, pausing like he's reading scripture, "fruity and oaky. Wouldn't you agree, Ev?"

I look at my own glass with Hudson's patronizing tone ringing in my ear.

I shouldn't care, but he started this. Baileys do not have it in our blood to shut up.

I take a sip and swallow the cheese, my tongue recoiling. "It tastes like bark."

"Do you not know how to properly taste wine?" Hudson says smoothly, a glimmer of *we're doing this* situated in his expression.

My jaw coils as tight as my accelerating pulse. Lexi does nothing to come to my defense. So that's how it is.

Hudson's eyebrows lift in a challenge. "Server," he says, snapping his fingers, "pour the next wine."

"Sir," the server answers calmly, "we aren't onto the next selection."

"I don't care. Go get the wine. I'm going to make our resident mechanic a deal."

"Hudson, don't," Lexi finally says.

"Evan's not offended. Are you?"

"Not at all," I say swiftly, completely offended Lexi chooses to hang out with this guy. Hudson and Craig are definitely related. No denying their relation, but half their blood flows through CeCe, an unsettling thought I've never had to face before.

The server returns, hovering and waiting.

"Pour him the wine," Hudson orders. "If Mr. Bailey can guess all the ingredients, I'll pay him five hundred dollars and he can run off and spend it any way he wants."

My teeth clench and my hand pinches the wineglass stem hard enough to break it. My calculated gaze collides with hers. *Say something. I'm your guest. Stick up for me.*

Lexi shrinks in her chair, shoulders pushing forward, and I am on my feet, napkin falling to the floor. The server puts the wine bottle in my hand.

A hush falls over the conversation. White lights strung between the trees sway in the breeze.

Staring at Lexi and *only* Lexi, I chug the wine from the bottle and set it down in front of her. "That's what I think of wine tasting."

CHAPTER NINETEEN

Lexi

Something has got to give. In more ways than one.

First screw-up was at the wine tasting. No amount of work will wash away the stomach-curdling way Hudson treated Evan. I need to make this right. But how? I let him down.

I let myself down.

Despite the lack of posting I've been doing, my follower numbers have never been higher and Evan's developed a cult following.

Second screw-up. The stack o' cash Hudson gave me is a wad of five thousand dollars, with a note for accessing his credit card. All of it stored in my bedside drawer. Right next to Evan's big box of condoms. His still sealed, unopened box.

I'm a financial mess with half a pack of lunch meat and a loaf of bread to my name and Bowser's graduated to no cone but still needs the eye drops.

To top off this royally inconvenient summer, tonight's the Fourth of July.

Not a single invite to an event. Where are my friends? Where are the designers fighting to dress me? They can't all be lost in Elena's infamous champagne and bubbles party.

Not making the cut to this event is like a snubbed Oscar nomination.

I showed up anyway.

The Wilshire property is ten acres outside the city limits. Expansive green lawns stretch on and on. Stepping into the grand, storybook entrance, the place is loud, the deafening, pulse-thumping music vibrates from the walls. Not five steps into the obnoxious shoulder-bumping crowd and bubbles float down from machines above. I look for Evan in between shirtless male models wearing wrist cuffs and tuxedo bowties, but he's not here.

Dressed in heels and a maxi dress with an open back, I feel like my old self, but also not. Guests hit the champagne fountain. Not me. I want to be clearheaded, drive home safely, and sleep in without a headache in the morning.

Three conversations in, I find myself looking at the entrance more than I should, the apology I practiced on the drive over sitting like a lump in my throat.

Lost in my thoughts, I don't immediately notice the person taking a place beside me.

"Hey stranger," Craig Hoffman says, his expression tranquil.

"Hi," I say back. It's been a minute since we've spoken. He has the same eyes and cheeks as Hudson, but Craig's taller and he threw himself into a lucrative position in the finance world. He was engaged at one point. His social résumé took a hit after his fiancée up and left him. "How are you?"

He rocks back on his loafers. "Keeping busy." Hudson chose law and Craig accounting. "I bought a condo in Manhattan. I'm splitting time between D.C. and there. I've been following posts about your bet."

"Who hasn't?" Never before have I wished people would find something else to post videos about.

His serious expression parallels Hudson's when he's got something on his mind. "I'm curious how things are going."

It's not weird he is asking, unless he's warming up to what he wants to talk about. Small talk isn't a crime.

"I'm here, so it's not all bad." I have nothing against Craig, he's always been Hudson's older brother. He's more private, more competitive, and he gets whatever he wants.

"What about this Evan guy? What's his story?" He puts his glass of liquor to his mouth, watching me with similar brown eyes as Hudson's.

"There's not much to tell. His house is small. He's raising his niece."

"A niece?"

CeCe's face comes to mind. The way she and Evan go together. They're quite a pair.

"Yeah, a niece. He's overprotective of her. Their neighborhood is sketchy. They don't have what we had growing up." It doesn't hit me until I talk about her, how much I see how good she has it. He takes care of her, even if he's the least likely candidate to be a single dad.

"What's she like?" he asks casually.

"She's exceptional." She duped Evan and me into this. "She's smart. She seems well-adjusted. Her parents aren't in the picture." CeCe doesn't need someone gossiping about the specifics of her mother's location. My gaze settles on the entrance with a wide arch of red, white, and blue blooms. I press my hand to my mouth.

Evan's here.

He sets foot on the carpet of digital stars. He appears as himself. Shorts and an AC/DC shirt among a fashion show of linen suits, a mustang who broke free from his natural environment.

You know the moment you really *see* someone?

My heart stands at attention in a way it doesn't do for anyone. From here on out, I will remember this as the moment I fell for him, accompanied by muted breath, a violent heartbeat, and hands I suddenly don't know what to do with.

"And the father?" Craig continues a conversation I was done with five questions ago.

I'm too focused on Evan. "I don't know anything about the father," I say offhandedly. I do want all the facts, but Evan's a role model in privacy. He doesn't talk about his past much, about any of his exes. There had to have been women before CeCe.

Evan makes eye contact with me. Annoyance is clear in his gaze.

I turn to Craig, but he's gone. Where'd he go?

This is my chance to get to him early. What was my apology? *I'm sorry I didn't stick up for you?*

He turns his back to me and goes in another direction.

Evan doesn't give me a chance to approach him. Elena doesn't help, snatching him up, keeping him close. Evan doesn't let anyone lead him around like a dog on a leash, which is why he isn't fooling me. He's doing this on purpose.

Initially, I wasn't worried about Elena...*but then you rejected his kiss, took Hudson's money behind his back, and watched while Hudson made fun of him.*

I wince at my own string of bad choices.

Here's the lowdown on the party. An R&B star and backup singers have been flown in from L.A. and are serenading a group of guests in their underwear making out on the steps into the pool. Laughter explodes like sparklers. People bump into me, grab my hand obnoxiously, pull me into conversations. Half the gossip I'm ignorant of, having been out of the loop.

My feet are tired and the one person I wanted to see is making a point. *You win, Evan. Enough is enough.*

A couple hours before the big show goes off, Elena, Evan, and Talia are standing near the pool. They turn to me with buzzed smiles and pretty faces. Evan's the odd man out with his glower.

"I'm leaving," I tell Elena.

"No, you can't leave," she says in a breezy voice. "You're going to miss the surprise guest!"

Chin held high, my heart is dropping low and reinforced with a grateful smile.

I'm too chicken to look down at Evan's hand to see if his fingertips are brushing hers. Guests around us get louder, laughing and fake pushing one another into the pool.

"I was hoping I could borrow Evan for a second." I raise my voice over the distant baby-making crescendo of the singer.

"No business tonight, North," he says, bringing his drink to his mouth.

My mouth twists like my father's. "Okay. Another time, then."

It happens before I can flail for help. Someone rams into my side, my feet lose their grip, and I turn around, screaming and silenced by the whoosh of water as I crash-land in the pool.

I come up with a shot of shocked breath and water in my mouth. No part of me isn't wet.

"Someone's starting the pool party," the singer sings a high-pitched tone into the mic, his gold chains thick around his neck.

Evan is crouched on the side of the pool. His hand is stretched out, fingers wide.

"Elena's getting towels," Talia says.

I put my hand out to Evan, stunned by his smug expression. His hands close around mine and I reach up, catch him at the wrist, and yank forward hard. He comes barreling at me, crashing into the water, briefly pulling me under. The two of us bob up like buoys.

His thunderous, dark eyes widen and narrow. He pushes his hair back. "You're unbelievable," he says shortly.

"Me? *You've* ignored me all night."

"I'm sorry that my night doesn't revolve around *you.*"

"Lovers in the pool…" the singer's voice, smooth as melted

chocolate, sings into the mic.

"I could have been camping with my friends," Evan says, treading water, drops of pool water sliding down his face. "I could have been ten different places I would rather be than in this pool with you."

"I came to apologize to you." He's not going to let me. This was a waste.

"You should have saved the gas money." The singer changes his tune, the backup singers leaning into their mics singing "Sexual Healing."

"Thanks for the tip. I'm sure Elena will be happy to get you out of your wet clothes."

"At least she knows what she wants."

My palms smack the water. "I'm going."

Soaked to the bone, messy wet hair, and pissed-off, I leave the party.

I go straight to Evan's house when I want to be in my own bed, waking up to a gourmet breakfast and a day wrapped in designer fabrics.

Before I can dive into full-time lazy mode, Bowser's litter box is in grave need of changing. I do the work first, then prop my feet on the couch with cheap canned beer.

Elena's fancy party has been upstaged by solitude and a temperamental cat.

A party in the street is going strong. Fireworks snap and screech. The lights turn the walls green and pink and then fade.

I felt like an outsider at Elena's. The beat of the night was off. "And just how much did she even spend on the VR booth?" I tell a bemused Bowser. My mouth is crammed full of words. "I wanted Evan to know how sorry I was. That I wasn't interested in hookup rumors and cheating scandals. He didn't want to hear what I had to say."

Someone knocks on the door and I wait, watching the loose brass doorknob move. I put my beer on the table.

Evan walks in; his gaze goes to mine. His lean, broad frame gets my notice. Everything about him since kissing him seems sharper, more muscular. His unimpressed gaze moves over the house.

I'm on my feet. In front of him, I'm noticing his wet clothes stick to him, showing off every groove in his abs.

"What are you doing here?" I ask.

"Getting camping equipment." He stalks over to his bedroom. "Joining Brandon and Josh on their camping trip like I do every year. Like I should have done this year."

Ooh, he's testy.

I follow Evan to his bedroom, feet moving quickly to keep up. Hurt and determined to get him to listen. A puff of air leaves my mouth. Glancing at him, I can't punish him for something he didn't do. "I've been wanting to apologize to you."

Evan's lamp flickers and dies as he's opening his dresser. A stray firework explodes overhead, bathing his face in light. "I don't want your apology."

I've never forced an apology on anyone. "There's really no other way to do this?" I ask, respecting his wish.

"There're lots of ways we can do this," he says, shutting the drawer, facing me. I am in his way. He will have to go through me.

Evan places his fingers on my hips, squeezing gently.

"It's not easy to admit people aren't always who you want them to be. I've been looking at Hudson from the wrong angle."

"He's all yours, you don't need to sell me on him."

"Evan," I say hoarsely, splaying my hands on his chest, "please, stop. I let him be rude to you and I said nothing. I'm sorry. I'm rusty on the basics of friendships. I'm relearning how to be one. I should have been your friend and I wasn't."

"Friends, North?" His hands tighten on my hips. "We are not friends."

Another firework goes off and I take a chance. An unsatisfied ache fills the space between my legs. I squeeze the hem of his shirt.

"Then what are we? Two people destined to hate each other?" I ask.

His gaze trails down the length of my front, stopping at my chest. "We're not that either."

I'm not up for a round of Evan and me fighting about *fighting*.

"Tonight should have been a post-worthy spectacular filled with irreplaceable memories on a hot summer night. And yet, the only place I want to be now is here, with you, like this."

"Like this?" His fingers inch toward my inner thighs. My breath is frozen, but Evan's is, too.

"Do it!" a man yells from the street, followed by an idiot setting off a firework and a horde of footsteps thundering away. It feels like someone is going to wind up in the ER soon.

Light erupts in the room. Fireworks shriek outside his house.

It takes me a second to decide what I want. *What I really want.*

I start to peel his shirt up, the chlorine scent overpowering. He lifts his arms to help. I put my hand on his almost-dry chest.

The feel of his defined muscles, interrupted by a smattering of chest hair, is like heaven on my hand. His hand overtakes mine, his gaze hot as he kicks off his shorts.

I gently push him onto the bed and bend my knees around his thighs, straddling him.

His calloused palms wrap around my inner thighs, spreading them wider. The bluntness of his arousal is thick against my sleep shorts.

His hand pushes my hair back and glides down my shoulder. "What was all your talk about not wanting to kiss me?" he says, bringing his mouth dangerously close to mine. "Because I can't stop thinking about you."

I gasp silently, riding him tenderly, overcome by longing, by desire, by him. "A defense mechanism," I say, running my hand down his chest.

"I need more than that, North."

I am going to admit something I never saw myself confessing. Words sometimes take time to get right. Humility is so inconvenient.

I like Evan. A lot.

"I thought not kissing you would be easier. Turns out, it's harder." It happens like a shot to the heart. I want this to continue when the bet is over. I'm going to show Evan I can fit into his life. I can be grounded. Lazy, complaining ways will be behind me.

Showing Evan he's wrong about me is my new goal. Evan's hands move down my sides, slipping lower, cupping my rear, dragging me taut against him. He is giving me a second chance.

From this point on, time to pull a reverse and do *me* differently. Evan wants someone who sticks up for people (done), who doesn't fall into the lure of parties with singers flown in from another coast (check).

He cares about what's on the inside, and I haven't shown him my heart. Not really. I've given previews and snippets, but no more holding back. I bring my mouth close to his, our lips lightly touching. I move with him gently. He gasps against my mouth.

My plan of attack is simple. No more will I be a woman overly concerned with how I dress or where I shop. Evan needs to see I am real and *grounded*.

From this moment on, I'm rethinking everything. This might be the end of five-star restaurants and standing monthly spa appointments. No more splurging. I am trading in my super-secret party apps for coupon apps.

I grind against him harder, sucking in a breath at the sound of his groan. The summer is going to end and I want more of Evan when we're done.

I only need to change everything about who I am.

CHAPTER TWENTY

Evan

I swipe my hands over Lexi's rear, squeezing her against me. "Ride me," I command her. Lexi's fingers press lightly into my jaw, moving closer to my mouth, her warm breath mixing with mine. Her thighs flex on either side of me.

I stare in awe at her. Her rich, velvety eyes flare with specks of gold. Even in the shadows, I'm versed in the details of her eyes, her mouth, her face. Heat laces between us, scorches us, connects us. A cord of tension runs from my mouth to my cock, imagining how wet she is.

"Let me feel you, Lexi." I grip her shirt but don't take it off. I move my hand to her collarbone and drag a steady line between her ample breasts to the spot where she straddles me. Briskly, yet firmly, caressing the place between her legs, impatient to hear more of her gasps.

She stretches over me, shifting, runs her lips over mine, and I lose control. I seize her lips in a crushing kiss, pushing my tongue inside her mouth. She gives back, her tongue wrapping around mine, gently sucking me.

We open our eyes, our mouths still connected. There is nothing sexier than her heightened, vivid gaze. Her hard nipples scrape against my chest through her thin shirt.

My hand glides down her sides and around, gently slipping beneath her shorts, swiping wide over her core to the burst of her moan. Gently, I stroke her, touch her, watch storms fill her eyes and her mouth slacken. I bring my hand back up and slide my finger into her mouth.

She swallows hard, my own needs building in response. Her kiss is different this time, firm, soft, but with a rough edge. Her intoxicating scent is sickly sweet air. "Lexi," I whisper as fireworks go off, the multicolored sparks throwing her golden skin into sharp relief.

I place kisses up the crook of her neck; my lips skate lower. "I'll show you why we're not friends."

I roll her onto her back, our feet clumsily tangled together.

"Show me," she demands, sprawling both hands down my lower back, kneading the slope of skin at the top of my butt.

"I'm obsessed with your mouth," I say with a husky tone, sliding my hands beneath her shorts, flexing my fingers toward her center. "And other parts, too. God you're wet." I dip two fingers beneath her panties, groaning at the slick feel of her. Her panties trap my hand right where I need it to be.

She grips my shoulder and presses into me; my size and weight dwarf her. She pulls me even closer and this time, as my finger slips inside her, I thumb her clit relentlessly. Her every movement is clinging to me and evoking the smell of her sex, as I circle with my fingertips, her hips bucking helplessly in response.

"Evan." She says my name with a voice dripping with desire.

All our bickering becomes something else, turning over a bright new leaf underscoring the undeniable attraction we share. Our issues are worked out in this space, under our rules.

"Is this what you want?" I take care of every inch of her, rubbing my finger over her hard nub in the opposite direction, colliding with her slick, smooth warmth.

Her head falls back, one hand reaching up, fisting the pillow. My hand strokes her, torments her. I watch her hips arch and push forward with a needy edge, my other hand steadying her hip.

"You're gorgeous when you're like this," I say, surprised by the vulnerability in my voice, applying more pressure, more speed, to her quaking lower half.

Her thighs tense around my wrist, her skin slick between her legs, my fingers thrusting inside her, pulling out, pushing back in. "Do you want me to take you right here?"

"I want us to go slow." Her voice cracks. She does something I'm not expecting. She reaches for my ponytail and takes out the rubber band, letting my hair loose, another first she's snagged. First to be in my bed. The only one who's seen me with my hair like this.

My mouth closes on hers again, capturing her in a controlled kiss. Slow can mean many things. It's my job to make sure I understand.

"How slow?" I whisper between breaths.

"With limits," she says, pulling my mouth back to hers, "nothing involving a condom."

Message received loud and clear. "I can work with that."

She returns her mouth to mine, her kiss dissolving into me. I'm right there with her, forgetting how to breathe.

My fingers move faster, gliding over her damp heat, strumming her with chaotic movement, then precise, her breath hitching and thighs clamping. I fight to control my own reaction, but I can't help the smile that spreads across my face at the sight of her.

Lexi jerks her hips, raising them, molding her body to my fingers. "I want you in so many ways." She groans, thrusting her hips forward. "Places I want to put my mouth on."

She runs her hand over my hardness.

"Positions I want you in."

I want this for her. I want it more than with anyone else. Harder, my fingers work over her clit, all my attention on giving her what she wants.

Lexi erupts in a series of moans and movements, her body bucking beneath me and fitting to me, riding my hand wave after wave, breath after sinful breath, release after release, my name like a claim on her mouth. She crumples forward, breathless, and releases her hand from the pillow.

She turns toward me, her face lit by a series of fireworks, the orgasm afterglow in her creamy complexion and crystal brown eyes.

"Did I prove my point?" I push my thumb against her heart. My own needs are going unmet, but her hand flattens over my chest, and I keep it there.

"More than once," she says, fitting against me.

I press a kiss to her forehead. Now, more than ever, I could never just be her friend. I want more.

And that's a game-changer.

She's here. With me.

Thick, warm air is trapped between the sheets.

Lexi moves against me, her breath warm on my chest. One of her hands is plastered halfway down my abs like she hasn't moved all night, and her knee is hiked between my legs.

I'm rock hard, stir-crazy horny, and she stirs against me.

I owe her an apology also. She came to the party. I pulled a move from high school and I treated her like an outcast.

Why hasn't she quit this thing? Why haven't I? *Because I don't want to.*

My fingers drift over her shoulder. *Because there is so much more to her I haven't uncovered.*

This isn't post-sex weakness for the woman in my arms

igniting protectiveness unlike anything I have ever felt. Hell, we haven't even had full-blown sex.

She's been hurt. A lot. Starting with the parents she never talks about.

Lexi glides her hand with a sleepy motion over my abs, evoking an internal struggle to stay put. The pillows push against the headboard.

Her hand skims down my abs and lower, causing me to tense. She looks asleep. Displays all the classic signs of sleeping. Eyes shut. Mouth a little open. A natural peacefulness. Her shirt is back on. I could have been talked into sleeping naked. No bra though, so I won't complain.

Her hand rests above my wide-awake appendage and stretches over it. Her warm breath is on my abs. She makes a quiet moan and yawns. I look at her hand, at her face, and clear my throat.

Her eyelids fly open. The position of her hand is well in view, resting below my belly button.

"Good morning," I say pointedly and stiffen.

"It's a holiday. Sleep in."

"With your hand like that? Yeah, not happening."

She doesn't move her hand away. "You didn't have to stay the night."

"I did. I missed my bed." I do my best to imitate Lexi. "A true hostess would have offered to take the couch."

"A gentleman wouldn't let me take the couch," she says, perfectly at ease, a tinge of pink on her cheeks.

"I never promised to be gentle."

At that, Lexi moves her hand over me again. Just when I don't ask for more, she locks her mouth against mine, pulling her body flush to me. Her hand flies to my hip and starts to push my boxers down. I finish the job with racing adrenaline.

She moves over me and kisses me like the devil I want to know. The heavy-lidded look in her eyes is my undoing with her fingers closing around me. "Lexi," I say her name deliberately, loving how it sounds coming off my lips.

She looks at me as if she, too, is caught off guard. Her mouth bends into a soft grin and she strokes me with her hand, down the length of me, back to the tip, her lips leaving mine. "Is this what you want?" she says, brushing a slow kiss against my lips.

"Fuck yes." A flutter of her eyes at me and she works her way down my chest. I close my eyes the moment she takes me again in her hand.

A reflexive groan, my head dropping back, and my hips thrust forward, moving with her, her other hand monopolizing my thigh. I'm hard as a brick, rigid and helpless except to let her have me. Heat spreads through my pelvis, my muscles, my tense torso.

"Lexi." A guttural moan causes her to take me harder and faster, her fingers working. "I can't hold back."

And I don't.

I let go. She clings to me until I'm done and out of breath, drawing her close, my heart raw with things I didn't know I'd been missing.

We stare at each other, making no assumptions.

"Normally, I would leave," I manage to say dryly. "But this is my house."

"Is it? I pay the bills," she says, pushing the covers back. With a self-important slant to her mouth, she gets out of bed. "Does this mean you'll bend your rules, Evan?"

The door closes and the shower begins.

Coffee seems like a safe bet.

I withhold opinion on the pigsty condition of my abode and the two feet of grass growing in my front yard.

The list I left her is stuck to the fridge. Wiggling my feet reminds me I miss the heated tiles at Lexi's. Along with the lattes. Especially when Chef Sofia creates crossbow latte art.

Purple and navy plates and cups are on the counter, CeCe's favorite colors. I overlook the metal marks on the pans and the dishes stacked in the sink.

Boxed pasta, jars of sauces in the fridge, printouts of recipes. A notebook on the table has my attention and I slide the document toward me—a handwritten budget with updated balances.

I make the coffee, gagging at the flavor of my generic ground coffee. Does it always taste this bad? Never mind about the coffee. I crouch and stare down at Bowser. "She didn't."

Lexi finishes crumpling her towel-dried hair and reaches at Bowser's faux gem collar. "What's with your grumpy cat face toward her?"

"Her neck is sparkling. Do you have any idea how gross cats are? They piss and crap in a litter box and then walk all over your kitchen counter." Bowser swipes her paw at me. "My shirts turn into sweaters after she lies on them."

Lexi grabs a mug and eyes my ponytail. "You're sure it's her hair?"

I stick my nose up. "You weren't complaining about it last night."

She walks over to the table with her phone and starts browsing.

Lexi surprises me by purchasing tickets to the firemen's carnival. Technically, this is our first date. At a place where no one looks attractive and lemonade costs fifteen dollars.

"I could take you out to dinner," I tell her once we reconvene at the fairgrounds in the evening.

Alec rides over with me and CeCe. She ditches us immediately for friends and she doesn't look back to acknowledge me telling her to make good choices. Alec's buying an unnaturally large refillable drink cup.

"Where've you been?" Alec says, folding cash into his back pocket. "You've been MIA."

"I've been busy," I say, admitting I haven't had time for Bailey's. Texts from Josh and Brandon go unreturned. I keep an eye out for CeCe. She's congregated by a Tilt-O-Whirl, the vomit maker.

Lexi appears. Her midriff-baring shirt and frayed shorts aren't like anything I've ever seen her wear. She...fits in.

Alec eyes me like a blade to a target. "Busy my ass. Tell me you're not losing focus."

"Focus?" My attention is entirely on Lexi. So are a bunch of other dudes, giving her looks, staring at her backside as she walks past.

Alec's brotherly punch to my arm causes me to face him. "The money, Evan. If you don't get her to quit, the shop will close before Thanksgiving."

"I haven't forgotten," I retort, having lost track and knowing it, unwilling to restore his confidence.

The money is important, the heart and soul of why I'm doing this, but something else is also happening. It's out of my control, unnamed, and all I want is to get through this night without Lexi being too traumatized by the smell of cotton candy and hordes of screaming children and hawkers yelling in her face.

Alec is correct. I am getting used to the clean lines and freshly folded and put-away laundry done by housekeepers.

"There are so many people here," Lexi says, standing in front of me and whisking me back to early high school when I didn't know how to tell a girl I liked her.

"You kids have fun," Alec says, "I have a date."

"He does?" Lexi says, watching him disappear into the crowd.

"He doesn't want to be the third wheel. Not to worry, he's

meeting friends and simultaneously making sure CeCe hasn't discovered cigarettes, or vaping, or anything else that needs to be inhaled."

"What do we do first?" she asks, eyeing the water gun squirt game.

"We battle it out, North. You asked me on this date. Do your best to win me a prize."

We hit up three challenges and she's the one applying the brakes to our good time because the games cost extra. She eats the funnel cake like she's orgasming, stealing all of it and leaving me with a few sad bites, and holds my hand with powdery, sticky fingers.

"What was it like when CeCe first came to live with you?" Lexi asks, strategically walking around a toddler in the middle of a meltdown.

It doesn't take much arm twisting. I want to tell her. "I was dating someone at the time. My ex had gotten to know CeCe, but when CeCe moved in and all my focus was on her, my girlfriend left me—she was a gem." She would have fit into Lexi's social vortex. "I was clueless and I overheard her on the phone telling a friend she could never bring home a mechanic with a kid."

"Ouch."

"The thing about rich girls is, they want rich husbands."

Lexi doesn't deny this.

"CeCe was a grieving five-year-old. Natalie was alive, and CeCe didn't understand why she was *gone*. Everything was minute to minute."

"I assume you and Natalie were close, since she left CeCe with you?"

"We all were, but Alec wasn't an option. He was just getting the business off the ground and all his money was tied up in it."

"You're not jealous he gets all the freedom?"

I shake my head in denial, but her question hits home. "I

was resentful, especially in the beginning, but I couldn't let my family see. What's done was done."

Lexi stops walking in front of the pirate ship, the ride with no other purpose than making people nauseated and guaranteeing screams.

The sunset casts her eyes an intense brown. Not for the first time, I keep thinking she's too good for a place rife with corn dogs and sweaty backs.

"Where's CeCe's dad?" she asks, holding her breath. "Why isn't he involved?"

Tension works an impressive knot in my right shoulder. The irony of all this is my turning the other cheek at Lexi's social proximity to Craig.

If you knew, whose side would you be on?

Lexi could stand with me, or she could easily walk over the line and support the Hoffmans. I don't want to find out. And, let's be honest, we won't be together long enough to get there.

"I don't know who CeCe's dad is," I lie and cringe at my dishonesty. The NDA is in place, but I don't trust anyone enough to break it and face unwanted consequences. All it would take is for Lexi to tell one person. Gossip would spread like a virus in an incubator. "Do you want to go on the big slide?" I gesture to the burlap sacks people carry to the top and ride down.

"*No.* You're finally talking about her. How can you not know the dad? Didn't Natalie tell you?"

"My sister had a one-night stand. Some guy she met in a bar," I say, digging a bigger hole. "Do you want to go on the Ferris wheel?" I ask like a consolation prize.

"I'm still working out your relationship issues. It might take a while. We rich girls have no heart."

It happens without warning. A teen straight out of the Typhoon staggers forward, arm wrapped around his waist, his face white as an eggshell...and pitches forward, vomiting all over Lexi's sandals.

No. God no. As if Lexi needed to experience any more of the quickly spiraling trashiness around us.

"Dude," I say, pushing his shoulder like he needs propping up. His glassy eyes look at mine, and he hurls again. Lexi moves back, but he hits her once more, splashing her legs this time.

An unnamed pressure overcomes me, one I cannot ignore. The one building slow and steady, like the clicking sound on the incline of a roller coaster.

I act quickly to find napkins, and one of the vendors is near a hose. Lexi is grimacing and simultaneously trying to smile. She's forcing an uncaring reaction when I am as grossed out as she is.

Bringing her to a place to get barfed on is not going to make a case for me when this bet is over, which it will be.

Once we break out of our deal, she's going to think of this moment and recoil. This, along with my dumpy house and low-rated life, is what she is going to remember.

We are tipping over the halfway mark of the bet.

I swore I wouldn't change a thing about how I was, but the reality is here, staring me in the face. I need to try harder than I ever have.

No more carnivals. No more Evan the Cheap.

My reasoning is crystal clear. I am falling in love with her. A rush of emotion shocks me to admit this. My mind says *not true* and my heart says *stop fighting me*.

What Lexi and I have is new and fragile. How can I get her to see I am worth more? I need her to see beyond my house and my job. And the clock is ticking.

A plan takes form. One that guarantees I get a fair shot. Lexi wants someone she's not embarrassed about.

I need to be a replica of Hudson and all the men she's used

to. Suits, fine dining, and someone capable of fitting into her world, because she does not fit into this one.

Everything about me needs to change.

CHAPTER TWENTY-ONE

Lexi

I want my holiday weekend back. The mini vacation was too short and Monday morning has me counting the days until the weekend.

I inhale traces of campfire in Bailey's break room, full of Gatorade bottles and chip bags leftover from camping. I scroll through the IG account @TradingPlaces.

The puke episode is going viral in edited, slow-motion movement choreographed to Star Wars main theme. #AreTheyDating #WatchYourShoes #TheScramblerGotThem.

A recent poll shows only 71 percent of @TradingPlaces followers think I will quit.

I take a screenshot and send it to Evan. *The tides are turning.* Despite Evan's profuse apologies and buying water bottles to wash the vomit off my feet, I insisted we get the money out of the rides. He was quieter than usual on the Ferris wheel, and afterward, we checked on CeCe.

Evan: *Funny, North.*

Evan: *I was sleeping.*

I take one from his playbook, grinning at my phone.

Me: *Life doesn't sleep in.*

Evan: *Get your own motivational sayings. That's mine.*
Evan: *I've been looking into this gala thing you do.*
Me: *What about it?*
Evan: *It's a formal dinner.*
Me: *What's the problem?*

I don't need to see his face or hear his voice to understand why. Evan doesn't know his way around a table setting. He needs my help.

Evan: *I'm having a cutlery problem.*
Me: *Happy to enlighten you.*
Evan: *Let's do this miserable thing at your home.*
Me: *Yeah, in about eight hours. Some of us have work, you know.*

The customer lounge is pathetic as far as welcoming spaces go. I straighten up the room and clean the coffee area. Tia is occupied fanning herself over her latest delivery. All the "oohs and aahs," coming out of her mouth cause Alec to step out of his office.

His gaze moves to the counter.

"Bailey's is not a dating service," Alec says to Tia. His increasingly testy mood is making Evan look like a sunbeam.

"It could be." I showcase the magazine I was putting back. "If you didn't have articles about where to get the best lube job."

One of the customers snickers.

Alec runs his hand over Tia's latest gift. "What guy sends a coffeemaker just because? *In teal?*"

"Why is it you and Evan have an aversion to colors outside of black and brown with faded logos?"

Alec shakes his head. "Don't you dare tamper with that handsome SOB's style." He tidies his polo. "If he's making any fashion changes, he'll take notes from me."

Tia's strangled laughter causes Alec to take the coffeemaker out of her hands and examine it.

"Are you saying I'm not good enough to receive this

beauty?" Tia puts Alec in his place, giving her coffeemaker a game show host style sweep of the arm. "And where are my repair forms? You said you'd have those an hour ago."

Alec beats a hasty retreat to his office.

As part of my new mission to win Evan over (makeup is down to the bare minimum and my shirt was purchased at Dollar-Be-Good), I accept he will be who he is.

This will not be a makeover story. The guy doesn't get put through the wringer at a salon. There will be no big shopping spree on Rodeo Drive and then hand him over to a team of people, experts in body types and cheekbone structure. If I want him to love me without the frills, I must—sigh—do the same in return.

The single pot coffeemaker arrived for Tia with a note from her admirer with no real intel, but her guy or girl—guy, I think—is the talk of the garage.

Garcia sticks his head into the customer care center more than ever, on the lookout for customers doubling as her admirer. The technicians have a betting pool going and I throw my five dollars in and put Felipe's name as my guess. He's the newest hire, keeps to himself, and is the underdog with this sketchy shoulder-hunch thing he does.

Tia smiles at her computer screen with her mouth closed. One can only wonder if those are hearts or stars in her eyes. She's falling for someone she's never met. It's more exciting than swiping to find a date. This person is good, clever, and putting himself out there.

This isn't what has Alec in a mood-killing bind.

Tia is *not* the only one receiving flowers. I've come out of my gasoline hideaway to be presented by a delivery guy wearing a thick silver cross around his neck.

"Lexi North?" he says, handing me the vase. A heavy waft of cigarette smoke emanates from him.

"For me?" From Evan? The hammer in my heart beats

wildly. Nothing about Evan screams he is a flower-giving guy. The bouquet is a blushing beauty of pink and red roses chopped and tight in a short vase. A thrill runs through me and I open the card with a mix of disappointed breaths. "There's no name."

Tia scoots back fast in her chair. She snatches the card from me. "I knew this guy was too good to be true."

"Your secret admirer is already cheating on you?" Josh says, poking his face between our shoulders. "Told you no one is that good."

I grab my ringing phone and almost don't answer Hudson.

We haven't spoken since we saw each other at Hillwood when he acted like a five-year-old in front of Evan. I'm also not above taking any reason to get a break.

A push of the door and I press the phone to my ear.

"Lexi, I didn't mean to interrupt your work. I know you're busy," he says.

Ah. We're dealing with tail-between-the-legs Hudson. "I have a minute. What's up?"

"Did you get my flowers?"

"Those were from you?" My heart crashes and burns. They weren't from Evan. My gaze coasts to Bailey's garage. The employees are keeping an open ear. I can tell by the way Josh is lingering around the tool shelves. "Thank you." I can't help using please and thank you.

"Flowers don't fix how I acted. I was a huge jerk at the wine tasting. Ever since coming back to town, and with Isabella, I've been stressed. My cases at work are overlapping, we're off when I'm used to you being my rock, and I made a huge mistake asking Isabella to move here with me. We...broke up. For good."

It's over?

How I feel about this is irrelevant. Hudson is back to being single. It's what I have been holding out hope for. I pick at the inner corner of my eye, something's in it.

"Lexi? Are you there? I think this can be good for us. If you want a fresh start, meaning we get back to us. Friends for now so you don't question my actions."

The thing about Hudson's voice is, I'm sucked in like an insect to a web, my feelers looking for a catch.

"I understand how this sounds," he adds quickly. "I need time to process the breakup. I won't put you through thinking I'm jumping from one bed to the next. I want you there when I'm through all that."

More waiting.

"We start small. An occasional dinner. After this case I'm on goes to the jury."

More and more waiting.

"Give us a chance to be there for each other." Hudson is speaking clearer than ever, working his fine-tuned speech over me like this is a graduation address, and I keep thinking about how doing the same thing always lands me in one place. Nowhere.

"Lexi?" Hudson says. "I won't push. The flowers are to let you know I've been an ass and I want things to be okay between us."

Evan's name flashes on the screen. He *never* calls. Is he okay? Oh gosh, is it CeCe? My apologizing ex-boyfriend is going to have to wait.

"Hudson, let me call you back." I swipe the screen. "Evan?"

"I need your help with something," he grumbles.

My rapid heartrate subsides. "You're okay?"

"I'm fine," he says like I offended him by asking. "I was thinking about the gala and how maybe I should do more than show up in jeans and my favorite flannel."

"You have only one flannel. It's not even cute in the farm-boy-lifts-hay-bales kind of way. It looks like squares of fabric were bred with the wrong color thread and some buttons were glued on."

"Er—yeah. Whatever. How do you know about my flannel?"

It's important to know what's in your man's closet. "You're telling me you haven't spent time in my closet or going through my drawers?"

"No." He pauses. "Except for the drawer with the lingerie."

Evan's rough hands letting the silky, lacy numbers slide through his fingers. "What do you need?" I say impatiently.

Josh signals me over. "Today, Lexi."

"Evan."

"All right," he blurts, "fine. I need a tuxedo for the gala. Some new pants. Shoes too, because no one at these events wears sneakers." His voice gets quieter and quieter. He's waiting for my reaction.

I want to squeal in excitement, I do. But I'm not so sure. Evan *is* who he is. His hair on his pillow was sexy. The scruff around his jaw makes my hands desperate to feel the prickliness. If he starts changing, then my goal of winning him over is less likely. He doesn't give me the opportunity to answer.

"How do I get an appointment with one of your designer people?"

He sounds crabbier than ever *and* certain. "Are you sure this is what you want to do?"

"Yes."

I suppose an external makeover won't change who he is on the inside. "You leave the logistics to me. Oh, and Evan?"

"Yes?" he says with a voice full of dread.

I don't let his woe-is-me tone ruin this. "The best stylists are in New York."

I'm not sure, but I think he hangs up on me.

"He's getting a makeover!" I shout as I reenter Bailey's, scaring the cell phone right out of one of the customer's hands.

Tia stands straight up with military precision. "Who?"

"Evan."

Tia makes the sign of the cross and forms prayer hands.

Alec happens to walk out of the office and crooks his finger at me, oblivious to my double-barrel smile. He takes another look at me. "What's wrong? Oh no. Why are you smiling?"

I don't have the heart to tell him. "Nothing."

"I need a word with you."

"What's going on?" I ask, peering over the stack of paperwork on his desk. Office management is not his strength. "You should hire someone to take care of this paperwork."

"No room in the budget," he mutters and hands me paper with a perforated edge. "This is for you. It's your paycheck."

My eyes roam over the numbers. The amount won't afford me a replenish of my favorite skin care products, but wow. Awe catches in my throat. I throw my arms around Alec, shaking him and stepping back. "This is my first paycheck." Bewildered and a teensy bit crushed, I stare at the small amount. "Evan left me cash, though."

He looks over at me from his computer. "We couldn't work around the regulations once you signed your employee forms. This is the money you earned based on the hours you put in. Evan's money is separate."

Roll out the banners. I'm officially a working girl. Who knew one paycheck could cause my heart to tip and overflow? This feels like nothing else. I have money of my own, that I earned.

I have unfinished business.

Something I should have taken care of before today.

After my shift, I go home to get the money Hudson gave me. I drive over to Hudson's office, making a dramatic entrance. The girl from the auto shop with her swaying ponytail making her way through the pristine hallways of the law firm. The envelope is in my handbag, shaking around due to my pounding steps.

"You can't go in there," his assistant says, swiveling out of her chair and balking as I enter his floor-to-ceiling glass office.

Hudson is on a call. He looks up, his face never more handsome, and holds up a finger.

A spasm squeezes my heart. How many times had I thought I'd be stopping by this office with our kids in tow?

His assistant goes in before me and she returns, mollified by his instructions. "He said to go in."

"Let me call you back," he says to the person on the phone and is out of his seat, closing the door behind me. "Lexi, hi." His voice is calm sincerity. His cologne is alluring, scents of success and crisp nights. "Is everything okay? I worried the flowers were too much, too soon. Sending them was inappropriate."

The flowers don't bother me. He has sent me flowers for no reason before. This time, he had one. "What happened with you and Isabella?"

He takes my left hand, rubbing over my ring finger, studying my skin. "The truth is, I knew things with Isabella would never work. My parents didn't like her; she said we were elitist," he says, sighing and running a hand over his tie. "She wanted me to be the person I was in California, and I wasn't prepared for how fast I would be reminded of who I am." Hudson's eyes are full of clarity, looking right at me. "Coming home does that to a person. We're never more genuine than when we walk through the door of our childhood home and grab drinks with friends we've known since we got our driver's license."

This is the part I struggle with. The all-or-nothing with Hudson feels more like a real goodbye than a welcome home. We can't be halfway anymore. "I came to tell you not to send me flowers or ask me out on a date."

Hudson is never at a loss for words. Right now, he looks like he isn't sure how to pull off a sentence.

For Evan, I set the envelope on his desk. "I can't take this."

Hudson doesn't hesitate. He doesn't blink. "The money was a gift for you. I can't stand the thought of you needing a dime."

Maybe struggling is not all bad. If I made one paycheck this month, surely I can make more. "I don't need your money."

He draws in a stiff breath. His neck pulls back. "You're falling for Evan."

My heart raises a hand. "No."

"You are, Lexi. How can you go there? Tell me you haven't slept with him." He moves closer to me, calm anger in his expression. "He's using you. He's a joke at the parties. And he's going to leave you, mark my words, he will, and he'll ask you for money before he does."

Turning on my heel, I leave, refusing to give him any information.

A text chimes as I make my way to the elevator.

Hudson: *I'll be here when you get bored with him.*

CHAPTER TWENTY-TWO

Evan

'm coming in hot, riding in the Norths' private jet flying high above the network of farmland. The sun pushes a slow path around the overcast sky.

"Once we touch down, we won't have a minute of free time," Lexi says from across the narrow aisle. Her head tilts back, resting into the cushy leather seat. Her frown deepens. "I still can't believe you asked for this. If this is a reverse psychology to get me to quit, I will only reverse the game."

"You can't reverse a reverse. Everyone knows that."

CeCe tips her head forward. "Why are you talking about UNO?"

"We're talking about other games," I answer, stretching my legs, my inward grin expanding.

She is going to love the new me. This is part of my master plan to show her I am more than a mechanic. I lift the new tablet I bought for myself and continue reading the autobiography I downloaded by a New York socialite. The insights are valuable. For example, receiving secret party links at two a.m. and the dangers of declining.

"What are you reading?" Lexi leans toward me, her skin

glowing and her eyes like she's doing a victory lap at getting me on this plane.

"You haven't told me your code name to get into private parties." I tap the top of my screen. "I want in."

As soon as I say it, her mouth tilts upward. "Keep on wanting, Mr. Bailey."

"This is so cool." CeCe guzzles her cranberry ginger ale like the soda police are going to take it away. We pass over a quilt of mild turbulence. Her sun-kissed straight hair falls over her shoulders like Natalie's. The resemblance to Natalie pains me, and grief hits when I least expect it. We're living our lives. What about her?

I have been out of touch since this bet. Visiting Natalie isn't easy. I leave the prison with a persistent loss and sense of failure for my family. My mind races with how we could have prevented her from doing what she did, and there is never a good answer.

I am not sure how to feel about it. With CeCe backing away from visiting Natalie, maybe space from going myself wouldn't be a bad thing.

"No more soda," I say, watching her gobble another maraschino cherry. I'm not one to talk. The flight attendant set a bowl in front of us and I am on my fifth, having a distinct love for preservatives and sugar.

Lexi clears her throat and points to my lips, then traces over hers. "Do you need a wipe?"

"Your lips are so red." CeCe's like a squirrel with her attention diverted to the window. *"Oh my God*. Do you guys see this? Is that New York?"

She has me out of my seat, sticking my face in her window in awe, looking at the scene like a grand entrance to Earth. A thin layer of clouds sweeps up to the skyscrapers like a silver meadow and I dig in my pocket for my phone. "I think so."

CeCe's hands are *gimme gimme gimme*. "We need pictures."

I photo bomb her picture with a thumbs-up and she pushes my face away, only to get me to take one with her, the two of us squeezing in for a selfie with my forehead cut off.

"Lexi, get in our picture," CeCe says.

"I'm good," Lexi says as my hand reaches out for her.

She crashes butt-first into my lap, hitting my sensitive guys with a jolt. Her arm slides around my neck and CeCe gets in front of us, holding the phone out with both hands, angling the camera down.

My hand curves around Lexi's hip, giving a gentle squeeze to let her know I'm here by choice.

I reclaim my phone as the stewardess informs us we're about to descend.

Descend, we do.

CeCe and I arrive in the city like Jay-Z's "Empire State of Mind." Big and flashy.

The vertical city flaunts her features. Buildings reach up into the sky. The private driver maneuvers the SUV through the streets. The only finger I've had to lift is to buckle my seat belt.

"I want to see everything." CeCe's face is glued to the window, her mouth hanging open. "Look at the buildings. All the people. *Oooh* did you see the woman holding a cute dog? What are we doing first?"

"Going to the house." Lexi doesn't look up from her phone.

The city is used goods. Her been-there, done-that attitude is a sharp contrast to our touristy lack of shame. My gaze sweeps up her bare legs. Her denim shorts are more like we're going to the carnival. Her nail polish is picked off.

The only thing true to Lexi are her oversized sunglasses. "It's on the Upper East Side."

"What's that?" CeCe asks.

I make a money motion with my fingers, to Lexi's disdain, and grab my ringing phone.

A silent groan clogs my throat. *Of all the times for this number to appear.* The number belongs to Aiden Cho, the family lawyer and the reason for my chest fogging up.

He calls for only one reason. To relay new information about CeCe.

Worry falters my mood like a crack in the Earth's crust.

Not now. Not this time. Lexi gives me a probing glance and I flip my phone over.

"Everything okay?" Lexi's voice is coy.

CeCe twists her head in our direction. "Who called?"

"No one. A spam call." From a spammed life. With unwanted problems showing up on my turf instead of knocking on someone else's door.

Not today, I decide. Not. Today. Let the voicemail absorb it.

When Lexi mentioned her home located steps from Fifth Avenue, I had no idea what to expect. But I didn't expect this.

I am not an expert on what makes a house a brownstone, but there are five levels wrapped in brick and trim work. She unlocks a door painted the color of garnet.

I am out of my league stepping into the mammoth entry with gleaming wood floors and a grandiose staircase pushed back to the left. The entry table is circular with a tall bouquet of white roses.

The North family has money.

I am not talking about millionaire wannabes with a riding mower and a backyard fire pit. They live on a different planet.

And, hold the applause, not once have I asked who picked up the tab. I want to, I do; this goes against my nature and a small mutiny in my brain breaks out. The men in Lexi's world don't ask how much this trip costs. Therefore, I do the same.

"I've been living in the servants' quarters," I say, as we check out the residence with CeCe. "You have only seven bedrooms to choose from," I tell her.

"This one," CeCe says, entering a room with wainscotting

up to the ceiling and a window seat with pale blue cushions. "OMG I have to show my friends." She takes out her tablet and promptly acts like I'm not in the room.

I could see her here. A book in hand. Bowser next to her.

If my plan goes well, do I think I can ever fit into this world? To be with Lexi, can I truly give up who I am?

There isn't a choice in the matter. I am already here, switching positions once more, wanting to show her I belong. I just need to buy a robe and slippers.

"Your father owns this place?" I join Lexi in the kitchen, walking across the black-and-white diamond floor pattern. CeCe's already taking over her bedroom.

Lexi concentrates on pouring the water. "It's part of my trust."

I whistle. "No feet on the furniture then? How come you didn't mention this place?"

"I left it in my notes. Way *way* down in my notes. You could have been living it up here all summer."

"Maybe CeCe and I will stay here." I blow a quick breath across the back of my knuckles. "But only if I can attend gallery openings and grab brandy with the Wall Street dudes."

She snorts and laughs, opening the fridge with shaking shoulders. "I'd stick around for that."

No, seriously. This place. Pristine as new-fallen snow. And just *lying* here, empty.

I smooth my hand over the quartz countertops that reflect the enormous wrought iron double chandeliers on the ceiling. "Do you ever stay here?"

"Occasionally. I have friends in the city. My mother is here."

She mentions her mother with a ghostlike voice, clearly hoping I don't hear. On the topic of her mother, I don't push. "You can live here and you stay in Virginia? *Why?*"

Her look tells me she's sensitive about the topic. "I always thought this would be a great place to live with my husband.

Start out our lives here. Immerse ourselves in the city." She pours glasses of water for CeCe and me and adds fresh-cut lemon slices. "I've been saving the dream for when I get married. I thought Hudson was that person."

She doesn't talk about him anymore. Come to think of it, not at all. Still, she has thought about the possibility of living here with him.

I don't want to ask, but I must. "Why him?"

"I'm sure you already have the answer figured out."

"Be kind, I'm sensitive."

"If you're sensitive, then I'm down to earth."

She is, more than she thinks. "What about Hudson made you see him as husband material?"

"It was a feeling. No matter what we went through, our script was already written. He was always the one person I looked for in a room. The unexplainable feeling like we got each other."

This isn't what I want to hear. Mild fear permeates my voice. "And now?"

"I feel like maybe we don't know each other like we used to." She hands me a glass of water.

Gingerly, I take it from her hand and set it away from us, molding my hands to her hips. Her eyelids flutter. She bites down on her bottom lip.

"*Christ*, North. I barely put my hands on you and you look like that."

"What do I look like?" She balls my shirt with both hands.

Lexi slides her hands up my jaw, resting on the parts in need of a shave. She rubs methodically, igniting a string of fire down my spine. I want to lift her onto the counter and push her thighs apart, fitting myself between her legs.

Neither of us makes a move. Not with CeCe in the next room.

"Keep this," she says, running her hand over my stubble.

"Don't let them take this."

If I didn't have my thoughts wedged between her legs, I would give her comment some serious attention.

A chime on Lexi's phone has her grabbing it, taking her hand off my jaw. My instincts want to pull her back, but CeCe's loud footsteps make me stop.

"The driver's here," she says, meeting CeCe in the hallway.

"Already?" I take a step back.

"No turning back," Lexi says.

"What's the designer's name again?" CeCe asks.

"Fiona Arnaud. She dresses Hollywood A-listers."

My heart thumps on the drive over to Fiona's shop. I can't get over the buildings and the sheer number of people moving to the city's beat.

Would CeCe fit into this place? Would I want her to? Talk about breaking out the jump-to-conclusions mat. I blow out a long exhale, unable to ignore the underscore of stress suddenly gnawing at me. This isn't like me, to tack expectations into a future with someone whose heart I haven't yet won.

"Relax," Lexi says, mistaking what must be the stress in my jaw.

The driver brings us around to an alley with dumpsters and delivery trucks. What a sketchy place to park. "Is your family connected to the mob?"

"I can't spoil all the surprises." Lexi gives a satisfied smile.

Any doubt is erased by a man waiting for us at a rusted door. He stares down his nose at me through large square glasses. He barely comes up to my chest in height, but his sharp voice is a man who isn't to be messed with. "I'm Christoph," he says, full of gallantry I haven't seen since Josh and I binge-watched Downton Abbey. A curt nod and he turns around. "My team is waiting."

"Just remember," Lexi says, as we step into a warehouse-style room with randomly stacked boxes and dusty windows.

She's clearly enjoying my misery more than she should. "This was your idea."

Look at me, destroyed by my own tactics. My spine straightens at the impending sound of doom disguised in high heels. "Were we supposed to bring shovels?" I ask, following Christoph around a corner and to another door leading to the inside of a clothing store.

Lexi's hand slaps against my stomach with a gasp. "Fiona's here."

From around the corner, a woman appears. Hair pulled back in a bun so tight, it may twist off. Friendliness is for no one, a limited commodity as her gaze briefly meets Lexi's, then rises from my sneakers to my athletic shorts. With each article of clothing she scrutinizes, she becomes scarier. Her eyes settle on my Nine Inch Nails shirt like I'm carrying the plague. I try not to retreat in terror.

"Oh," is all she says and then snaps. Six people appear from the next room.

"Evan Bailey." I hold out my hand.

Fiona turns her cheek. She turns her attention to CeCe and I step alongside my niece, ready for a throwdown, if necessary. "And you," she says with an uptick to her voice. "You are stunning." She and Christoph exchange a hundred words between them without saying a word.

Christoph's fingers are furiously typing on his phone, probably some secret designer code.

I get the awful feeling that things are getting snipped today. I move my hand discreetly over my junk. I just hope I'm still in one piece when this is done.

He takes a photo of me.

"What was that for?"

"You don't know? We need a *before* to go with the *after*. There. Posted."

Fiona does an about-face, embracing Lexi with hands

grasping her elbows, and goes in for a kiss on each cheek. "Times must be tough." Her appalled voice is long as a runway and turns quieter. "I'm sure you've tried."

I lift a finger to protest.

"Evan. Describe your reaction to the word fashion."

Lexi's finger prods my lower back. I pinch my shirt and waft it. "It's pointless. Clothes cover the body."

Her mouth twitches. "You're a purist. Clothes have a basic function." She turns to her crew, rattling off instructions. An occasional pitying glance is tossed at me like a bread crumb.

"CeCe's with me and Fiona." Lexi stands closer to CeCe. In a show of what should be family loyalty, my niece is quick to jump ship and sail with the enemy.

"I'm not leaving her with strangers." She could get lost or go hungry or need me.

Lexi's hand cups my shoulder. "I'm not a stranger. I won't let her out of my sight."

CeCe was done with my rules an hour ago, and I remind her Lexi's in charge.

Fiona sends me off with Christoph, who increasingly feels like a chaperone. I am whisked away through shiny floors, glitzy lights, and tables of pleated pants in every shade of blue. No one seems to care about personal space.

Christoph and his team put me in front of a large, three-way mirror. Arms spread out straight, a man near my ankle takes measurements. The room is outfitted with dark navy walls and gold accents, far from the dressing rooms at the bargain stores making up my retail experience.

I'm allowed a lettuce wrap, and in his no-nonsense voice Christoph warns me, "I was told to shut down any bitching and moaning."

In no time, I'm in a salon chair with a black cape secured around my neck and a staff deliberating over highlights and lowlights—whatever those are. Christoph takes out my rubber band and fans my hair. Low volume club music plays from hidden speakers.

"Are you attached to this?" he asks, like I have a say in the matter.

The ponytail. The last of my rebellious stand against fatherhood. I grew my hair out after CeCe came to live with me.

A defiant move that said *I'm still young, I'm not entirely responsible*.

I wiggle in the chair at Christoph's impatient eyes in the mirror. *Hudson would never grow a ponytail*. "Not at all. Ditch it."

The haircut is only the beginning.

Once finished, I'm shown to a room with a cloth-covered slim bed and the smell of hot honey. I'm working out the direction of this next stop on the makeover train with rising apprehension.

This is more of a personal nature. The kind involving a woman and body hair and neither is appealing. None of this is part of my standard grooming practice.

I scratch my jaw. "Is this some kind of ultimate shave experience?"

The staff member is conspicuously absent. Then I see the brochure. Blood drains from my heart. STYLING YOUR SHAFT: EVERYTHING YOU NEED TO KNOW ABOUT THE MALE BRAZILIAN.

The brochure drops out of my hands along with a half-baked cry. The words stick out as I swoop down to pick it up: CHOOSE YOUR LOOK…FULL OR PARTIAL…

CHAPTER TWENTY-THREE

Lexi

I wonder how Evan is doing.

CeCe's knee-deep changing into more outfits in the dressing room. The runway-style space in Fiona's wing of the department store with lighting could make a warthog look pretty.

"I'm keeping this one," CeCe says from behind the pink and gold curtain.

I chuckle despite my nerves. CeCe makes it easy to focus on her and not her uncle.

We've been at it for an hour, first each of us walking around one another on eggshells and then, joking freely and making comments. After a tray of chocolate-covered strawberries and an assortment of tiny pastries, CeCe eases into it all. Shy at first, then beautiful, with awkward limbs yet to settle into a deeper graciousness. The depth of her struggles is reflected in her eyes, but she is a good kid, has a good sense of herself all because of Evan.

Does he know how good he is with her? He must have sacrificed everything to get her to this point. My gut wrenches as I compare our lives. My cheeks turn cool. Evan will never get his twenties back.

I can't shake the thought and shrink like a flower after the sun goes down.

Could I ever be there for someone like Evan is for her?

CeCe steps out from behind the elaborate dressing curtain, a look on her face I can't decipher.

Fiona is not short on maternal prowess. She sticks to CeCe's side, her rapid-fire voice overbearing. "The shirt is too cropped. The skirt too short. The legs must remain mysterious." Her golf-club double clap signals her assistant, and more clothes are brought.

CeCe stands in the middle of the floor with that same odd look on her face. I bolt from my seat and go to her. Something is wrong.

"Is everything okay? Do you need a break? Or food? We're about to go to the salon. We're almost finished with this part. Unless you want to be done."

She straightens her hands behind her back. Her eyes sparkle like two brown crystals from her framed, thick lashes. "My stomach started hurting this morning and, I mean, it's not my stomach." She points her hand beneath her belly button. "There's blood. It's never happened."

She got her period. I grip her shoulders, breaking all sorts of personal space decorum. "Do you want me to get Evan?"

"*No*," she says it so fast, with so much force, I take a step back. "What am I supposed to do?" The borders of our situation crumble. No time for awkwardness.

CeCe is asking for *my* help when she could run over to her uncle.

Here I am, fully circled back to when puberty tossed out her ace card and my mother was not around. One more event I had to go through alone.

I don't know what Evan would do, what he wants me to do, but I won't let CeCe go through this with a frivolous reaction.

I can be here for her, if only this one time. Her mother isn't here, but I am.

"Of course I'll help you." Hugging isn't in my nature, but I put my arm around her. "I'll get you everything you need."

The great advantage of a day spent with Fiona is she has assistants. I give one of them a list and instructions to be discreet. I give CeCe what I have on hand and wait outside the restroom door.

CeCe and I take a break for snacks, until the assistant returns and leaves us alone in the dressing room. "I think I'm done trying on clothes," she says, glancing at her keep pile.

"Ms. North," the assistant says, knocking on the doorframe. "I have your items."

The gift bag is over-the-top, with sparkly fuchsia tissue paper like she's at a bachelorette party instead of getting a period pack.

CeCe takes out the items. Hygiene products, a sleeping mask, fruity lip balms, warming gel for cramps, a stress ball, and cozy socks.

I put my arm around her, taken aback when she folds against me. How good it feels to be needed. "Are you in pain? I have ibuprofen."

She shakes her head vigorously. "Not really, a little." She moves her hand over her stomach.

"Those would be cramps and they are completely annoying." I offer a reassuring smile and leave out the part where she will have to deal with this for eternity. "Ask me anything, I've been through it."

"I didn't want to say anything because I didn't want to miss getting my hair done."

"There's more fun to be had." I had no idea she would be afraid to miss out. "If you're still up for the salon, then so am I." I pause, waiting to figure out what to say next. "What do you want to do about telling Evan? Yes? No? Do you want me to call your grandmother?"

Her cheeks turn pink as watermelon. "Could you...talk to him?"

I will. I will because it is going to be harder for him than her.

I keep a solid eye on CeCe at the salon.

Her long locks are chopped off to her shoulders. We skip the highlights. She honestly doesn't need any color, and sparse strings of tinsel are added to her roots.

It feels like days later instead of hours. I'm running low on energy and a stomach telling me it needs to be fed, and I am seconds away from seeing post-makeover Evan.

CeCe is with one of Fiona's assistants, showing her how to play a game on her phone, when Christoph opens the door looking like he's been worn down to his soul. "I've done my good deed for the year."

The nerves I had been fighting earlier swell in my chest.

The private dressing room area is empty. The dark walls and dimly lit room could be turned into a swanky bar.

"You owe me."

Spinning around, my jaw drops. The breath is knocked hard out of my chest. His rich, surly voice matches the man in front of me.

Oh. My. God.

My hand smacks my chest.

A moment is required to let this version of Evan settle in.

A dark navy suit covers his body, highlighting the breadth of his shoulders and the powerful, muscular set of his thighs. The crisp white shirt open at the collar is meant for a hand to slide into, feeling the smoothness of his chest.

Lowlights bring out the color in his styled, gelled hair. The ponytail is gone, yet a tiny ache persists in my heart. Maybe I liked it more than I let on.

The new haircut opens up everything about his face.

The controlled stubble, shallow as a veil, begs my hands to touch it. His eyes are piercing and trained on me, exuding another realm of confidence with the corner of his mouth upturned. My heart is spilling over.

My hand is frozen at my mouth. I go to him and rest it on his chest. "I'm afraid to touch you. You might wrinkle."

"You can always touch me, North." His mouth twists and his voice tolerates no argument. "Preferably not when I'm wearing something called a modern fit and am fresh off a lecture about hair texture."

We're back to Evan being Evan. "You look very handsome, Evan Bailey. Do you want to talk about what they did to you?"

He snorts. "Obsessed over my height. Took measurements. Made me try on a full color scheme." Evan's rant is only starting. He stabs his finger into his chest. "I've been to a salon. I've been shaved, plucked, and thanks to a woman with hot liquid and an intimidating face, *waxed*. And tortured. Do you know anything about what estheticians actually do? Do you know what goes on in these places?"

He is making it hard not to grin. "I have a good idea."

"I have twenty bags I'm supposed to take home. None of them have jeans."

I splay my fingers over his lapel, desperate to touch him. "Progress, Evan. *Progress.*"

His mouth does a twitchy thing. "Where's CeCe? How's she doing?"

"She got a makeover as well. Not as dire as yours. She had quite a day."

"What does that mean?" He jerks his neck like a chicken, the scrape of a stiff collar against the back of his neck.

"She got her period," I drop the news on him. "She told me to tell you." Ten different emotions cross his face. Disbelief, horror, and acceptance.

"Is she okay?" He takes my hand without delay, like he

doesn't want me to let go. "What should I do?"

"Do nothing. Let her come to you. I can help her while we're here and have your mom take over once you get back. Just be there for her. She'll tell you what she needs. Don't make it awkward."

He makes a face. "I wouldn't do that."

I'm not convinced of this, but he probably needs some major chill-out time after his transformation. "Why don't we get dinner?"

"Wow," CeCe says, startling us both, causing us to turn.

"What do you think?" Evan says, making a fuss about bending his elbows. "Are the Baileys ready for a night in New York?"

The Baileys, yes. I feel on the outside of a club I want to be invited to join.

"What's in your hair?" Evan's parental admonishment breaks the spell.

"Tinsel," I speak up for her as my phone rings. It's the last person I want to talk to. My mother's name is on the screen. *Ignore*.

She texts: *I heard you were in the city. I want to see you.*
Me: *No*

"What now?" Evan asks. "I need food to be involved."

"Fiona's assistants will deliver our purchases in the morning and we have dinner reservations at The Plaza."

We dive into the rest of the evening, not leaving a trace of food on our plates before we see the city at night.

I don't have to ask what they think of the place. They are two buddies, walking either ahead of me or behind me. I've stood in Rockefeller Center in all seasons but never with two people who make me want to see the lights and skyscrapers through their eyes.

Like all spell-binding nights in NYC, the party comes to an end.

CeCe is dead on her feet at the apartment. "I want to do it *all* again tomorrow," she says.

I check on her, making sure she is okay. She closes her door, and I turn out the light in the hall, stopping in front of Evan's room.

"It's me," I say, knocking softly.

Feet shuffle. "Door's unlocked."

I open it, finding him removing the button-down shirt, his muscles taut, a smattering of chest hair. The light from the street is coming in through the window. He lowers his hand to his belt, never taking his eyes off me. "If you're wondering, I skipped the Brazilian."

My eyebrow arches. "Afraid?"

Stop ogling him. I look at the bed, annoyed I'm staring at the pillows and the duvet. All I see is Evan in it.

"Hardly." He removes the belt and his pants, kicking them off. Evan fills out every inch of his boxer briefs. His boxers are more him. He's not a boxer brief guy, they're too everyman. He stretches out on the very bed in which I was just imagining him. He dwarfs the space. Takes it over. Owns it.

"I came by to say good night."

He lifts his head from the pillow. "Stay, North. I'm mourning the loss of my boxers."

It's what I have wanted all day.

I get beneath the covers, turning and facing him, my heart on fire.

He glides his hand over my cheek, moving closer to me. His mouth seizes mine in a slow, but greedy kiss.

Moonlight and streetlamps bathe the room.

His mouth works over mine, his tongue invading me, taunting me, taking me. His chest and thighs push against me, and I lean into his hardness, all of him. Heat spills between us and around us.

A noise from the back of my throat is his undoing. He

kisses me with fresh urgency, but then stops. He rolls onto his back, swearing softly.

What happened? "Evan? What's wrong?"

"I want to know about you. About the *you* before you were with Hudson. The Lexi who never talks about her family."

"We could always sleep together and skip the backstories."

His breath evens out, his choice made. "Not this time, North." The familiar hesitation sweeps over me. Evan's hand touches mine. "Sometimes having courage isn't doing something life-altering and remarkable. Sometimes courage is saying a word or two."

Maybe it is the long day, or maybe, for once, I'm too tired to pretend my life hasn't been without disappointment and rejection. In his arms, this is real. I don't want to put on a show anymore.

With Evan, I feel heard.

Something about Evan makes me want to be braver.

I don't think about the emotion. Listlessly, I recite it to get through it.

"My mother's name is Dara Arnold," I say, not expecting Evan to know or care that she's worth over thirty-five million. "She's a cliché. Had an affair when I was thirteen. Next thing I know, my parents are divorced, and my mother remarried and she moved to Manhattan to be with him. She didn't even try for full custody."

Evan's breath shudders. "Did you ever spend time with your mother?"

"Occasionally, I did, during their divorce. I would go to Manhattan and we would go shopping and hang out. I was angry at her for having the affair, but she was different when she moved in with Michael and his son, George." I pause and breathe. "I have a stepbrother."

This is the hard part. Fearing what I'm about to say is frivolous. That there are worse things in the world, and I have somehow been hanging out on the bank of this excuse for too long.

"I never understood why my mother didn't want full custody until I found a letter from her lawyer on my father's computer. Not only did she not fight for me, she didn't want me. She stated in her letter she wanted to put her entire focus on her new family. She knew my father traveled for weeks on end, and she saw no problem leaving me with a string of nannies, whom I spent holidays with half the time because my father was gone."

Evan goes still. His arm hardens against my side. "Go on."

"It was a long time ago."

"Doesn't make it any less relevant. Did you have other family?"

"My grandmother died at the start of their divorce. We were close. I would have begged my parents to live with her. She wore that bracelet all the time. I still miss her. Without her, I tried for so long to figure out why I hadn't been good enough. So I stopped trying. If my own mother didn't care about me, then who would? The worst part is I didn't want people to see that I cared. I bet I sound like a brat."

Tears slide down my neck and onto where my head is wedged against his jaw.

"How can you think I would see this as shallow?"

More tears leak from my eyes.

"Pain is pain, Lexi, and loss is still loss. Both hurt in any form. You weren't abandoned once, but twice. By both parents." Anger takes shape in his voice. "I would never be okay with letting CeCe be alone for holidays. I would never leave my child because a better family came along. There's nothing *okay* about that."

Evan stays eerily silent for a long time and I move my hand over his chest. He covers mine with his. He places a tender kiss on top of my forehead, whispering, "I'm sorry. You deserved better. Thirteen-year-old Lexi deserved better."

Someone shouts on the street below; my breath sticks in my throat at how much I miss my own mother. Despite what she did, I am always her daughter, and what I wouldn't give to be mothered, for real, for five minutes instead of longing for a ruined relationship.

Evan says nothing, does nothing when more tears slide from my eyes onto his chest.

I close my eyes, my leg fits between his, and I stay in his bed. My heart is a little cooked around the edges from talking.

Evan holds me close the rest of the night.

CHAPTER TWENTY-FOUR

Evan

I smell good, if I do say so, like sandalwood and fresh air. I'm a man dressed in slacks and a Ralph Lauren polo in the throes of indecision, torn between which luxury box Caps seats I want for the upcoming season. Food service or no food service?

This is only the beginning. I put away cash for CeCe's savings account, but there's plenty left over to immerse myself in Lexi's world while we have the chance.

I take a video of the swag we're putting together for the gala and hashtag the hell out of it. The video thing is growing on me. "Did you see how many likes I got after Christoph's *before* and *after* post? I even got a marriage proposal."

"Your uncle is in high demand," Lexi says to CeCe like I'm not in the room.

"I said no."

"Make sure each box is filled exactly like my sample," Lexi says, adding a thank-you card into embossed Alcott Gala packing with real platinum-infused bows.

CeCe leans forward from sitting on her knees. "What about the rings?"

A fashion magnate donated a round of diamond bands with diamonds the size of dust specks.

Lexi tries different placements of the rings inside the gift bags. "It just doesn't look right, but they may not see the ring and accidentally toss them out."

"What if we tied a ribbon on each ring?" CeCe suggests.

"Yes," Lexi's eyes light up. "That's it."

What the hell. I go for the seats with the food service. "What if the ring size is wrong?" I ask, stretching my fingers wide. "What if...you have man hands?"

"There's a contact email to replace products, which there shouldn't be because we're the quality control team. We should get to work."

Lexi's sample box is easy enough to follow. A mini robotic dog is a token for a real one. "Are you aware these dogs retail at $7,000?"

"I am," Lexi says plainly.

CeCe tries on the brainwave sensing headband and the smartwatch. "It feels like something's missing."

"We also need to add the lip gloss and the mascara."

The makeup was overnighted to us by a celebrity looking to promote her new makeup brand.

"No, I mean something unexpected. Don't they always get the same kind of stuff?" CeCe says.

"They do, but that's why they love these bags."

"I was thinking when we're done here," I stop to look at CeCe, ready for her reaction to what I'm about to say, "we could check out the stables."

CeCe's gaze flies to mine. "Seriously?"

I'm touched by how quickly Lexi's expression softens. "How about we finish these tonight and tomorrow we meet at the stable after I get off work."

"You heard her," I tell CeCe, tearing my gaze away from Lexi. "Swag bags first. Horse riding tomorrow."

We work through glittery white tissue paper and products like an assembly line. All the boxes are placed in black-handled gift bags and moved to large cardboard boxes.

"I'm going swimming," CeCe says, leaving us to get changed and eventually shutting the back door when she heads out to the pool.

I pull Lexi on top of me on the couch, my hand moves down her side, coiling the hem of her shirt. Her mouth moves over mine and I crush my lips against hers. Our tongues move together, twisting and sliding. I lose track of time.

"I could take you right here," I whisper against our kiss. Her body rubs against mine, her throat breaking with her moans.

I curl my body against hers, feeling her breasts and hips, and relaxing, knowing that's not possible.

"I should get going," she says, moving off me and glancing at my cock. I sit up. "What made you change your mind about the stables? The last time I brought it up you said, and I quote, 'I like her spine functioning normally.'"

Doesn't she know?

You changed my mind. All this. This house. Your life. "I figured I might as well use what we have at the moment." Before it's gone. "I'll walk you out."

I lock up after Lexi leaves and join CeCe in the pool for a battle royale on the newly purchased blow-up swans.

We stay out past midnight, until CeCe is dead on her feet and goes to bed.

I am too restless to sleep. Staying outside on the lounge chair, I look up at the night sky. My thoughts are not wrapping nicely around Lexi's family. Dara Arnold and Edward North— don't get me started. They are no better than Natalie. My blood pressure rises, fluctuating between cold hatred and disbelief. No wonder she doesn't answer to anyone. There's no one there.

CeCe getting her period put things into perspective. Another invisible shift out of my wheelhouse. This day was always a *one day in the future when she's older*. She *is* older. We're here.

I'd never been more thankful for Lexi's presence. To have someone there for those moments. I have been keeping women at bay for years in CeCe's best interest, but what if I have been holding her back from having support?

Allowing myself to think about a future with someone hasn't been in the cards. I've made sure of that. Maybe I've been avoiding relationships for CeCe's sake, using that as an excuse.

What happens if I do date someone more seriously?

What happens if Lexi is it for me?

I don't know what one wears to the stables. Asking Lexi means I'm not man enough to figure this out on my own. She wants a guy who doesn't send messages like *Is the preferred collar position on a polo up or down?*

Tailored pants and a button-down are my final answer. Life without my ponytail is settling in and with hardly any facial hair, there's a high likelihood I look fifteen.

I pull the car into the dirt lot at the North Star Stables.

"I think you're overdressed," CeCe comments, tucking her hair behind her ear, and a strand of tinsel sparkles. "Where do I pick up my outfit?"

"Lexi said the stable manager would have everything waiting for you. And I'm not overdressed; we have dinner reservations after at a Michelin-rated restaurant."

My mother is stopping by to surprise CeCe and watch her first riding lesson.

I tweak my hair in the rearview mirror. No matter what

CeCe thinks, I like the air my new look communicates. I am someone. An injection of this is long overdue.

I'm still young.

I have never been resentful of raising CeCe, but I'm not even thirty.

CeCe and I get out of the car.

The dirt parking lot is at the edge of a path leading to two pristine red barns connected with a muddy walkway in the middle. A horse is led away by a woman in riding gear, and CeCe and I get out of their way.

"Grady Strauss," says the tall, big-muscled guy who comes out from a doorway in the barn to shake my hand. His collar is turned down on his North Star polo. "Welcome to the stables. I'm the manager. Are you Evan and CeCe?"

"We are," I answer, shaking his hand.

Grady steps away from the barn and signals us to follow. "I hear this is your first time riding."

"First time on a horse," she answers without hesitating.

"Come with me. I'll introduce you to your instructor and get you set up."

The country road is flanked by horses and hay bales. Expansive land is touched by nature's golden, deep green mid-summer brushstrokes. This is good. This is nice.

I want more of this.

The dark green compact car pulling up is my mother's. Barbara Bailey is easy to spot with her height, two inches shorter than me. She has bangs always too close to her eyes and a hurried rush to her movements.

She has not seen me since the makeover. Her jaw drops. "Look at you," she says, reaching out to touch me as if I'm a newborn cub lost on the way to his den. "I didn't recognize my own son. You're even better looking than your brother." Her attention swivels to the stables. "Where's CeCe?"

Judging by the practical look in her eye, she can't wait to

comment. "How much did your makeover weekend cost you? How much is all this?"

The bad Bailey habit strikes again. Price is put before the value of human life. The bottom line is our beginning and end. "The trip was taken care of."

"You don't have money like that." She makes sure CeCe isn't around and cranes her neck. "I don't care about this bet. This isn't good for CeCe."

We are not having this conversation. For CeCe's sake. "Mom. Stop."

"Well, I'm sorry. You shouldn't have taken her to New York. When I mentioned we should meet at the community pool, she said she hopes Lexi lets her swim at *her* pool next summer."

My teeth grind lightly. I don't blame CeCe. Not one bit. "Buying CeCe three pairs of shoes instead of two isn't a bad thing. This will be the first year she doesn't need to wear the same coat two years in a row. God forbid she finally gets braces."

My hand scrubs my forehead. Maybe inviting my mother was a bad idea.

"Do you know what people say about Lexi?" My mother's voice comes back into focus. "I'm on the Instagram now."

My mother also screenshots her phone's app screen. Most likely, one of her friends has followed the bet and showed her.

I have made a mistake. One I'm only realizing now.

This is Lexi's first time meeting my mom. Another first for Lexi.

"When you meet Lexi, don't mention money."

The insulting ream of a glare I get from her is too much. If my mother is displeased, everyone will know it. "What's gotten into you?"

Lexi's here. That's what.

With none of her generally superior attitude, Lexi comes to us. Her face strikes a chord. A connection I feel every time

I look at her. Lexi's plain shirt and frayed jean shorts are her new norm. Minimal makeup graces her face, none of it *her*.

My jaw unclenches. "Lexi, this is my mother, Barbara."

Mom is in her personal space like Bowser gets in my business. "I can't believe you set this up for CeCe. Thank you. Isn't my son wonderful?"

I squirm. My mother never misses an opportunity to put in a plug for her sons. My eyebrow lifts. *Really, Mom?* I do not, under any circumstances, make eye contact with Lexi.

"He has his positive points," Lexi says politely.

The assessment wins Barbara Bailey's approval. She squeezes her shoulder. "I want to go find CeCe. I promised my friends I'd post a photo."

I cast my mother a furtive glance.

Lexi's fingers snatch me by the hem of my shirt and pull me aside. "You invited your mother without telling me? And why are you dressed like you're going to prom?"

"We have dinner reservations. Did you forget?"

She wiggles her shoulders, stepping closer. "No, but I'm exhausted."

Her eyes are not loving me right now. I rest my hands on her shoulders, defusing her with a persuasive grin. "My mother's not going with us, if that's what you're worried about."

"I'm not up for a fancy dinner. I would need to leave now and shower. We could order in at my place. CeCe could see Bowser."

Right. Just like every night of my life. A sullen note swings my mood. The city is full of restaurants I have walked past but never been inside. "We'll just do our own thing tonight."

CeCe comes out from one of the stables and I need a moment. She's in her riding hat and boots. Tan pants and a white shirt. She looks so happy.

She's keeping up with Grady and he walks her toward the training ring. "How often can she come for lessons?" I ask, knowing I can't take this away from her.

"As long as you want," Lexi says, bumping her arm against mine.

I give her a side-eyed glance. "I could talk to Alec, see if you can have reduced hours."

"Reduced hours? I can't believe you're even suggesting that. I would rather earn overtime."

"Order anything you want."

Our meal is small portions on big plates. Without acknowledging it, CeCe and I practice our newfound cutlery skills. She giggles when I pick up the wrong fork and I correct the error.

"There's so much to learn about riding horses," she says, sliding her fork through the buttery mashed potatoes with chives. "Grady said next week he'll try me out on different horses to see if I bond with any. You're cool with that, right?"

"I told Grady I'd email tomorrow, and we'd figure out lessons."

"You could take lessons too."

I'm more Viking than cowboy. "I think I'll stick to tennis and golf. Do you have any interest in attending a golf camp later this week?" Her smile disappears.

"What's wrong?" I ask, finishing the last of a juicy steak with sauteed mushrooms.

"A man keeps looking at our table."

Casually, I look over my shoulder.

My fork drops with a loud clatter. Dread folds in my stomach, settles in, and seeps into my quickening pulse.

Craig Hoffman is three tables away. A woman is across from him, her attention on him. He always looks the same. Plain brown hair slicked in a side part and a distinguished look in his eyes. Time has not changed him. Or me.

He watches me watch him and purposefully makes a point to move his gaze to CeCe.

To my knowledge, he has never laid eyes on CeCe. His flesh and blood, eating buttery mashed potatoes. It comes back to bite me, taking her here, putting her in harm's way.

The two of them seeing each other for the first time, and me, powerless to do anything to stop this. One of us knows the importance of this and thankfully, the other does not. His face gives away no response except unremitting silence.

Their appearances are uncannily similar. Their eyes are same in shape. His are darker, and hers, light as her heart.

If anything, my hatred of him has simmered and grown stronger—the harder things got, the more I cursed his name. Now he is in front of me, the same cookie-cutter, boring, infuriatingly same. We stare at each other. Neither of us move.

Do not worry. Nothing will come of this. He is not interested in fatherhood. He gave her up. If only I could keep telling myself this.

I am the one unable to look away. The one who can't move.

Their identical noses and chins. His expression is riddled with strong observation. Craig's eyes slide back to mine. A silent struggle unfolds.

My heart is thundering rapidly and nearing a breaking point. Craig with his superior expression. Me with enough fight to stay put until he understands CeCe is not his concern.

"Don't be creepy, Uncle Evan, you're staring," CeCe says innocently. "Do you know him?"

"Never seen him before in my life." I signal the server for the check. CeCe makes a move to get out of her chair. "Where are you going?" I say with undue worry.

She pushes in her chair. "Jeez, easy. The bathroom."

"Can't you hold it? We're about to leave." Any more time spent here increases the chance of Craig not staying in his seat.

Nervous, heart-pounding breaths fill my chest. I don't like the guy. Or his family. Especially Uncle Hudson. I have nothing to say to him. I never will.

"Do what you need to do," I mutter, not wanting to draw more attention.

As soon as she's out of sight, the unthinkable happens.

Craig comes over and takes CeCe's chair. "I want only thirty seconds," he says, his hand open in front of his chest.

"Talk to your lawyer." I glance in the direction of the bathroom.

"She's beautiful."

"*She's* none of your business." *Take your time, CeCe. Don't come back.*

"I think about her," he says like he has *any* right. "About how she's doing. What her life is like."

My life-force drains like a slow leak with time crushing us. Seconds until CeCe returns. "If you don't get out of that chair and leave, I'll be sure to tell her next time she asks how her father signed away his rights and left her before she was born. Leave us alone, Craig. You've seen her, your curiosity is satisfied. There's nothing left for you to know." I glance in the direction CeCe will be coming from. Any second she will return. Any second...

I think it's time I call my lawyer.

CHAPTER TWENTY-FIVE

Lexi

What was *up* with Evan at the stables?

Maybe an Evan doppelganger was roaming around North Star property.

I thought he would be eager to ride instead of arriving in ironed pants only to whine like Hudson when the temperature rose a degree above seventy.

He suggested I cut my hours at the shop *and* he sprung his mother on me.

Why does meeting Barbara Bailey matter? This was my first official mother meet-and-greet of someone outside my social circles. It was a big deal to me.

Evan brushed off the introduction and rounded out his actions by leaving me with the oddest feeling that he was repulsed by the idea of going to his home. That can't be right, *right*?

Moving on. I measure out spices for a casserole. A neighbor was taking meal donation requests for a family with two children receiving chemo and I need to put this together before work tomorrow morning. Am I supposed to bake ahead of time? Or deliver the meal uncooked?

Mixing the ingredients, I spot Tia's latest text, which is all digital warm fuzzies and hearts galore. She snapped a shot of someone's IG account @LovingThisSocialite, who posted a photo of me washing windows at Bailey's.

No matter how much I'm changing on the inside, I'm never going to love the smell of dirty soap water.

HOWEVER. Public opinion is changing, with 58 percent on one poll predicting I will quit.

Bowser saunters in, and executes a high-arched stretch with paws forward, looking at her food bowl expectantly.

Another message pops up. **Hudson:** *Any chance you're free for dinner tonight?*

The last thing I want to do after breaking an all-day sweat in the scorching heat is to be wined and dined by *him*.

No thanks, Hudson.

I have better plans.

Someone must be handing out lucky stars because one of the neighbors put out two camping chairs with a FREE sign and I seized those bad boys.

With sweetened iced tea and a gloriously braless minute to myself, I rest my head back, my hair dripping wet from a cold shower. I finally get around to texting Hudson.

Me: *Sorry, busy day. Dinner another night*

Hudson: *My plan was to ask you to the Alcott Gala*

Hudson: *As friends*

The "as friends" piece doesn't run smoothly from his lips.

Hard to believe in no time I will be back in my groove. This also isn't bad, watching couples walk dogs and watching what I think is an affair across the street. Every evening at the same time, my neighbor's husband leaves and twenty minutes later, another man shows up.

I am about to text Evan again and stop myself.

After a few breaths of emotional grunt work, I rest my head back. Waiting is what I did with Hudson.

In the beginning, I checked my phone for texts. After he was home for a visit and the usual *I miss you* sex and *where is this going* routine, I turned down dates and checked his feeds, wasting so much time. Time I can't get back.

Turning my phone off, I close my eyes, sucked in by the oppressive heat, but too limp to move. Evan has my number. He knows how to text.

A car engine pulling into my driveway causes my eyes to open.

"Oh. No."

Evan's here.

In a silver Porsche.

Turning off the car, he checks me out and exits the car.

I get to my feet. "What did you do?"

"It's nothing," he says, leaning against the hood casually before making his way over. "I've always wanted to test drive one of these babies. I leased her for forty-eight hours."

"What do you think?" I say, watching his gaze travel over me, stopping at my chest. If only my nipples could behave themselves when he's doing the direct stare thing. *He* is dressed to impress. Ironed pants. A polo the color of violet. Hair styled. Who is this guy? "Are you sure you didn't get lost on the way to a croquet match?"

"Why is there a chair and a table on the porch?"

"You had no porch furniture." I make a ta-da gesture.

"I get that, but why?" His gaze zeroes in on my shirt.

"I like to sit out here in the evenings. I chat with the neighbors. You never did that?"

"I do. All the time. Is that my shirt?" He points at the Iron Maiden tee. He looks different, good, but a swinging pendulum in my soul misses the excess scruff and the ponytail.

He's too...pretty.

"You should get a porch swing. Use some of your fun money to refurbish this space." I don't have the heart to tell him there's a solid chance his water heater is wonky.

"Not with this roof." He pushes up from the car and stops, both of us flinching at the ominous *creak*.

"Don't leave me hanging. To what do I owe the pleasure of Evan Bailey standing on his doorstep?"

"I've had a complaint. About that." He points a hard finger to the rolling green pasture that has become my front lawn. "One of my neighbors texted. I'll have someone come out to take care of it. Consider this my gift to you."

"Don't do that. I want to do it."

"Why?" he asks cynically, his voice like last night when he declared we would do our own thing for dinner. "We could use the time to spend the evening at the country club pool. Tonight's wine night. All bottles are from local vineyards."

"I'm not in the mood for going out," I insist, getting up from the chair. "Now that I know someone's complained, I want to get the lawn done."

Evan sighs heavily. "Why don't you let me call someone?"

"Doesn't that go against your moral code? Paying someone to do something they can do themselves?" I can be touchy, too.

"I'm trying to do you a favor."

"I don't want favors. I want to mow the lawn."

"Then why wasn't it done weeks ago?" he blurts.

"I've never mowed a lawn." My tone rises, but then the embarrassment subsides. This is Evan. Champion of do-it-yourself. He doesn't seem impressed. Just irritable. "I know it's not brain surgery. I watched a tutorial. Everyone has an opinion on how to do it correctly, and I'm sorry, but who cares about lawn striping? AND when I tried to start the mower, nothing happened. It's broken." I grab my iced tea and punch the straw in the cup. "Like everything else in your house."

Evan's disarming gaze makes my heart race. "Aside from the washing machine, what else is broken?" He waits, folding his arms. "That's what I thought."

We glare at each other until the tension is palpable. God, I want to jump this man. I can't believe we've actually not had sex yet. It's killing me.

The corner of his mouth quirks. Evan's adept. He knows. *Knows* my reaction to him. He's at my side in less than a breath and slides his hand around my waist, hauling me against his hard chest. "Do you want me to do it for you? Just ask."

"Aren't you afraid your shoes will get dirty?"

"I'm okay with dirty." His gaze is full of fiercely wicked promises. He brushes his mouth against mine with a delicate stroke.

"Lawn first," I mouth the words, kissing him lightly.

"Can't. I have dinner plans."

I pull away, searching his eyes. Longing overcomes me. For what, I am not sure. Evan hasn't invited me to "help" him with much of anything since we got back from New York. I didn't realize how much space he took up until he stopped asking me for advice.

"With Elena?" I ask like a jealous girlfriend.

"Yeah," he says nonchalantly but doesn't meet my gaze.

An aggravated sigh leaves my mouth. "You don't want to be late. I'll figure it out."

He glances at the watch. His *Cartier* watch. A timepiece I was born able to spot.

"I'll show you everything you need to know."

"If it won't throw off the rest of your schedule." I give him a haughty look over my shoulder.

A lightning round of teeth brushing and slapping on deodorant is not optional. Completing those must-do's and changing into dollar-bin athletic shorts and a tank, I meet Evan in the garage.

Hyperaware of his nearness, we stand in the garage with the door trudging up on a belt making a low-key screeching sound. Evan goes right for the mower and crouches down, unscrewing a black cap. "Grab the red container. It's gas."

Noxious liquid fills the tank as I get my footing and pour.

"Show me what you were doing so that it wouldn't start." His tempered attitude is an improvement, but he's not himself, either. I step back, my throat dry, wanting to touch him. To satisfy the heat between us. I pull weakly and look over my shoulder.

"I pulled the cord like this." A huge, bicep-bending maneuver is added for effect. Nothing. "See?"

Evan stares at me, arms adoringly crossed. He puts one of my hands on the thin handle I thought was for appearance. Like handbags with keychains. "You have to push this toward you for the initial start."

"I must have overlooked that step." It wasn't my fault I got caught up in the sexy lawn mower guy in the online tutorial.

"Try again. Harder."

The second time gives off a sputter. Nothing, again. I take another look over my shoulder at Evan's face.

"Pretend it's the day we met."

I pull the rip cord like it's nobody's business.

A shriek and a flood of excitement startles me into a giddy expression. From there, I go. Lexi on the loose. Walking forward. Gripping the handle. Pushing it across the lawn, loving the rewarding ache in my limbs, my muscles doing their job. The energy inside me is unstoppable. I might mow every available yard.

Evan stays off to the side, occasionally pointing his finger and shouting, "You missed a section."

My neighbors come out to watch.

Eventually the heavy humidity sucks the life out of me. Stone-faced and in desperate need of cooling down, I march behind Evan's house, turn over the gross baby pool, stick the hose in, and sit my butt down while the water fills up.

"Ahhh," I say, uncaring that I look like a sunbathing seal.

No sense in opening my eyes. The cold hose water feels like heaven and turns me boneless. I lift my hand slowly like raising a flag. "You're welcome to join."

He extends his hand and I take it, tempted to pull him in. His eyes flash in distrust as if he's thinking the same. He locks his grip harder, his strength overpowering my urge to make sure he's still faded-Caps-tee Evan. "I need to get going," he says with brutal honesty.

I step out of the pool and drop my hand from his, stamping my feet into the house, leaving him to do whatever he wants. "I wouldn't want you to be late. Enjoy the Porsche."

Evan's bedroom turns dim as stormy gray clouds gather outside.

I get together a change of clothes as he enters the room. Right in time for rain to hit the windows. He walks over to me, takes the clothes out of my hand, and sets them on the dresser.

"I didn't think anything could drive me crazy as much as you in a sundress." His hand drops to my waist. "Then I had to watch you mow the lawn in these." His hands skim down the sides, clutching the edges of my shorts, his knuckles grazing my thighs with a flicker in his eyes.

I move my hands up his chest and over to his shoulders, taking my time, holding on to the devoted way he looks at me right before he kisses me. I touch his jaw, guiding his mouth to mine. Slowly at first, my mouth slants over his. Keeping his hands beneath mine, we both drag my shorts down until they're off. "Touch me, Evan."

A noise breaks from his throat.

I love feeling his tenseness reduced to agonizing need. The slightest touch of my tongue to his lips and he snaps, crushing his mouth to mine.

His bruising, sensual lips fill me with pleasure coiling tightly in my body. "You won't need this." He takes off my shirt, discarding it impatiently, and slides his hands up my back. The bra straps hang loose at my shoulders.

He traces the outline of my bra with his finger, dipping into the cups, pushing the fabric down, exposing my hard nipples as I arch forward, pulling his face against my chest, running my fingers through his hair. His breath is hot on my skin. His tongue follows the curves of my breasts.

He reaches around and unhooks my bra like he can't get it off fast enough. I dip my mouth against his, kissing him thoroughly, taking control, exploring his tongue, his mouth, trailing kisses down his neck. He swipes his hand down my side, between my legs, pulling my underwear off. His fingers take me one, two strokes at a time, inside me, circling my clit, anticipation tearing through me. I'm damp where he touches. Needy when he takes his time. I gasp on weak legs.

"Do you want this slow?" he says, his voice dark as midnight, driving his finger against me, "Or fast?"

"Both," I say softly, cut off by his mouth.

It's my turn to take off his clothes.

Shedding all of them, I see him naked for the first time. Taking my time, moving my gaze over his torso and lower. The size of him, swollen and hard. I let him see me look. And damn, I am looking. Evan's big.

His hand grips my waist, guiding me to the bed. I'm on my back, stretched out, as his eyes drink me in. *Christ,* the look on his face as he watches me, spread out on his bed. I can almost see the moment the need to touch me overwhelms him, and then he's on top of me.

He drags his hand over my nipples, swiping each one with the pad of his thumb. His fingers spread hard over my breasts, circling them, feeling them, sucking each one with his mouth, his stubble scraping my skin. His hand slides between my legs.

"I just want to touch you. All the time," he whispers huskily. His mouth is working down my neck, his other hand plunging between my legs, again and again, his fingers stroking me, owning me, taking me in the perfect rhythm.

His hand swipes over my breasts, his movements firm, tugging and pulling, smothering both of them, rubbing his palm back and forth over my nipples.

Gasps escape my mouth. Evan pulls me on top of him, his erection grinding against my lower half.

"I thought you wanted to sue me for hitting your car," I whisper mindlessly.

His mouth withholds a kiss, keeping his face close. Our lips are frozen less than an inch apart. "Are you finally willing to admit you were at fault?" He moves his fingers slowly and purposefully between my legs.

My breath holds. "Maybe."

Evan's fingers retreat. They are tantalizingly close. Enough to drive me wild. "Maybe?"

He withholds his fingers, resting them on my thigh, then returns his finger to me, but only touching me lightly, delaying my pleasure.

I have no willpower when he has me like this.

My words blow out in a huff. "I was distracted. That's all I will say." About Hudson dumping me. About trivial problems I haven't thought about much lately. Those thoughts are fleeting while Evan's putting that behind us with his sinful fingers, giving me what I want at the cost of admitting I might be wrong.

"I'll interpret that my own way." His tone is all irony. All of it a tease. He kisses me again, soft and hard. Urgent, then slow. He backs up on the bed, resting his hands on top of my knees and beneath. His gaze takes in my nakedness.

A steady, piercing lust builds in his eyes.

I love that I do this to him. My head drops back, hair sweeping over my back, knees pushing against his hands.

"Any rules?"

I say what I feel. Plain and simple. "There are no rules

when it comes to us." Us means something different now and has something more profound than just butterflies in my stomach. He is right. He's the one I want.

Evan presses kisses up my leg, moving his hand behind my knees, scooting me toward him in one move. He looks at me, running his hand between my legs and lowering his head, moving his mouth over my inner thighs, his hot breath caressing my flushed skin, dangerously close to my center.

His hands grip the backs of my thighs. "Let me fuck you with my mouth."

I blow out a thin breath, pressing my hand on top of his head. Evan kisses his way down my legs and back up, his eyes on me the whole time.

And then he's at my center and his possessive mouth takes over, covering me, gliding his tongue along my seam, sucking gently. He shifts, follows my thrusts, curses against me, devotes his lips to me. "Christ, Lexi, you're so hot when you come. Do you want that now?" He says, increasing the pressure. His voice is rough against my dampness.

The smell of my sex clouds the air. I grind against his mouth, softly, carefully, losing my breath, my sanity, to the feel of his stubble scraping my thighs. A low growl breaks from his mouth.

I moan, wriggling against his rigorous mouth and tongue. He takes my clit hard now with deliberate, hasty rhythm. My resistance vanishes and I come fast. I explode against him, riding his lips until my orgasm is an ember of radiant heat.

Evan reaches for the nightstand drawer, but my hand is faster, closing around him, stroking him as he backs away from me, stopping briefly at the low growl from his throat. I slide my hand over him, firm strokes, then softer ones, my hand slick with his need. "Is that what you want?"

"I want all of it." This time, he opens the drawer and wrestles open the box of condoms. He rolls it on and pushes my thigh to the side. Our gazes click. He enters me in a heart-pounding, delicious shudder.

His groan is stifled by my kiss.

Evan moves inside me, hard and fast and urgent, his mattress shaking. The comforter drops off the side of the bed. I move my mouth over his, my orgasm in reach again.

I have never been so badly in need of a shower and he's taking me, adoring me like none of that matters.

I move to kiss him, stopping short of his lips, our gazes locked with each other. My mouth touches lightly at first, then without restraint. Greedy, hungry kisses take over, my hands clench his strong biceps, pulling him closer, his beautiful body connected to mine.

His every breath hinges on this orgasm. It's just him and me and this moment. It's instinctual like it's never been before. I barely hear my name right before Evan shatters inside me. His shoulders shake. His arms quiver. The aftershocks of his release ripple through the moment, claiming us.

CHAPTER TWENTY-SIX

Evan

My bed is a hot mess. Our clothes are on the floor. The bedding is half hanging off.

Lexi's face is smashed into my side, her hair crumpled, mouth hanging open. Sheets are twisted around our legs.

We woke up around midnight. Lexi's mouth had found mine. That's all it had taken. I fell back asleep to the sound of hard rain and noises outside I didn't have the energy to investigate.

Waking up in my house, in my bed, should be a welcome feeling. But now, not so much. The air is damp, the hour is early.

The bedroom has a grimy feel. The furniture is inexpensive and old. From now on, we will do this at Lexi's house. In a bed that doesn't squeak.

Without waking her, I grab my phone off the nightstand. My lawyer, Aiden, called and left a message.

I don't want to call Aiden back.

I don't want to deal with anything about Natalie or running into Craig. How can I, when Lexi's fingers open over my chest?

Elena sent me a meeting invite for a pre-gala meeting. I accept without hesitation. My body shifts to accommodate Lex.

The endless repairs this place needs. The way certain spots in the hallway sound like the foundation is snapping.

The gloomy tile and faucet of my own shower need to be dealt with. Lexi is too good for these patched walls where the previous owner put his fist to them.

CeCe is, too.

"I have to get to work," she says with a hefty sigh and manages to open her eyes. "You look wide awake. What's on your mind?"

"Shower sex."

She yawns. "Give me five more minutes."

"Not in my shower. In yours. I'll make a playlist and coordinate the water color."

She lifts her head. "But we're here now."

I slide away from her and start grabbing my clothes off the floor. "I can't be late for my golf lesson."

She sits up on her elbows, watching me. "Because you're going pro later this month?"

I make a face. "Golf takes dedication. You could always come with me." My arms do a mock swing.

"Sorry. I'm fresh out of nine irons."

"These are your golf lessons."

"Yes, and I have a job. You had one, too, once upon a time. I don't feel right calling in sick. And where's CeCe today?" Lexi's sloth-like movements get her out of bed, offering me full view of her, slowing down my hurry to leave. Unfortunately, she then wraps herself in her robe.

"She's at my mother's and then has her riding lessons." I walk over to her, pull her close, and kiss her goodbye. "I'll see you tonight."

Turning the doorknob, I pause before stepping outside. The Porsche key fob is in my other hand. Should I go back to the bedroom and explain to Lexi about the shower? Should I tell her I see this place with clear eyes? The way she did when she first arrived.

I open the door and push the fob. "Son of a bitch!"

The Porsche is on cinder blocks. The wheels are gone.

I break out in a frustrated body shake and call Alec. "I need a tow."

"Why would someone steal a catalytic converter?" Lexi asks, hours later, fresh off her shift at Bailey's. She and CeCe sit at the kitchen counter. Chef Sofia's spread of cheeses from France and homemade butter crackers with seared scallops are in front of us.

CeCe's newest purchase, a friendship-bracelet-making kit has their full attention, a pile of threading successes and failures between them.

"They're made with precious metals," I explain, removing a defective grape from the fruit bowl. "They go for a couple grand." The one from the Porsche was stolen.

I filled out twenty different forms and spent my morning at the private office of the car rental filing a report.

"Did you have to pay?" CeCe asks.

"Yes."

Admittedly, I'm blowing through Lexi's money faster than I anticipated.

CeCe pulls up a video tutorial and watches a girl her age demonstrate how to make the bracelet. "We didn't make the string long enough."

"I still like this one." Lexi starts to loosen the bracelet to put on her wrist.

I run my fingers over my shaved jaw. I miss my stubble. "Bringing the Porsche to the house was a mistake."

"Or renting it in general," Lexi adds with a less-than-tactful stare.

Never mind that. I take out the infamous teal bag and set one in front of Lexi and another in front of CeCe.

"What's this?" Lexi slides the friendship bracelet onto her wrist.

She opens the box with wide eyes and her mouth hanging open. "It's beautiful." She holds out the strands of the diamond bracelet.

"Since your grandmother's is at the shop a little longer, I thought you could use a replacement."

CeCe is quick to open hers. A white gold chain with a connected arrow. "Oh my gosh, I love this."

I'm quick to put it on her, admiring how the diamonds look on her tan skin. CeCe is making a fuss over her necklace as Lexi swivels her wrist to show hers off. "You can't afford this," she mouths.

I dismiss her concerns with a wave of my hand. "I bought it while we were in New York."

"You bought me jewelry with my own money?"

CeCe stops running her thumb over the arrow. "Do I get to keep this?"

"Yes," I tell CeCe and to Lexi, "I thought you'd like the gesture."

"I do, but— Thank you." She closes the box and reaches for her handbag. "I wish I could stay longer. Your brother's offering 15 percent off oil changes before noon tomorrow."

I resist the urge to ask if we're cool. The bracelet seemed like the right purchase at the time, but she is heading toward the front door and I ignore the awkwardness of whatever just transpired.

"I'll take the bracelet back," I say, standing with her on the walkway to her car. Children's laughter carries over from her neighbor's lawn.

"Evan. What's going on with you? The Porsche, the bracelet, they don't feel like you."

"It is me, North. Aren't I allowed, for once, to buy a woman a piece of jewelry or joyride in a car I've only ever worked on? This is the first time I get to be *me*. The guy *I* want to be. The man who doesn't look at the bill before signing."

"I thought you were a guy raising his niece without comparing his life to the rest of the world."

"I didn't ask to raise her. I didn't ask to give up my Friday nights or weekends or dating life."

I didn't ask to be the one to save my brother's auto shop, either.

"I'm trying to understand, but I don't." Lexi's gaze moves over my shoulder. "You better hope she didn't hear any of that."

The door opens and CeCe's holding my phone. I panic for a second, wondering if she overheard. "Someone named Aiden Cho is calling you," she says, handing it to me. "Who's Aiden?"

Lexi turns and leaves without a goodbye.

"No one," I say, doing a poor job of disguising the frustration in my voice. I take the call with rattled nerves, closing the door and hiking upstairs. "Hey Aiden," I say, closing the bedroom door.

"Craig's lawyer contacted me," Aiden gets right to the point. "He wants to meet with you about CeCe."

The declaration shakes me. This wasn't how things were supposed to work out. Craig was supposed to stay in his narrow minded lane.

Fury churns in my body like smoke, and rises.

My stomach is choppy and my tunnel vision tight.

I should have known he wouldn't leave well enough alone at the restaurant. "What does he want?"

"I'm working on finding out," Aiden's voice is always a baseline of calm. "Craig hasn't demanded anything. He wants to meet with you. He could have any number of reasons. Until we know his purpose, you don't have to agree to anything."

The only question for which I need an answer is the one

hardest to ask. "He can't reach out to her, can he?"

"No, he can't. You know this. But guardianships are tricky, as you know." Adoption wasn't an option, but that would have sealed off Craig's rights. Natalie wanted an easy fix and she got one.

"Give me time to find out what he wants. Do not, under any circumstances, contact him or approach him."

"I have no problem doing that."

"Your situation isn't helping." I had explained to him about Craig running into us and how we've been loosely connected, socially. "Maybe it's time to go home and reestablish clarity, for everyone's sake. Out of sight, out of mind is the best-case scenario."

That's the thing. I can't go home. Not yet. I am so close to getting everything I want. Here is a small piece of the truth I also don't want to admit.

I don't want to go home.

CHAPTER TWENTY-SEVEN

Lexi

The latest in my ever-evolving social media presence is that Evan is now the subject of negative attention.

The latest photo from @mechanicVSsocialiate boasts 700,000 likes. "Impressive, Bailey." I zoom in on the shot. Evan was spotted like a lone wolf leaving Tiffany's. He's clenching his jaw and wearing Dita's Mach Five sunglasses. He could be a jet pilot or a porn star. The jury's still out.

I do something I haven't done in a while. I look at my own IG page. My follower numbers exceed millions, but I look through the posts from before the accident. In one pic I'm on a random guy's lap wearing thigh highs and a rhinestone-studded bra.

In another I've got my arm draped around Elena and pointing at her bikini-covered boob. I log out of my account, unable to see myself as nothing but a lost girl with no ambition, living one party to the next.

I asked myself at the beginning of all this if I was that bad.

Yeah, I was. What's weird is this photo of Evan reminds me of *me*.

I stuff my phone in my back pocket and put my gloves

on. Whatever is happening with bizarro Evan isn't going to detract from the job in front of me, paying attention to Garcia showing me how to read the engine scanner.

"This number is for the electrical—" He looks over his shoulder.

An irate woman with too-dark lipstick against her pale skin is shaking her head at Josh and tightening her hold on her purse that says GOACH instead of COACH.

The lounge door opens and Alec walks out with a pissed-off expression and goes over to the customer and Josh.

We know it's bad when Alec makes an appearance.

Brandon's head is jammed up the underbelly of the same car I'm working on. He lowers his hand with the wrench and stuffs a dirty rag in his back pocket, eyeing the evolving situation.

"What's going on?" I ask Garcia.

Brandon makes his way over to the scrap metal counter and pretends to be looking for something when I know he's getting the down-low.

He comes back over. "Get this. She brought her car in last week because the back passenger seat belt was stuck. We fixed it. She's back, demanding a refund because it happened again." He gives a stealthy glance over at the woman and Alec. "Her kid's been using super glue, but she doesn't believe us."

I take the opportunity for a break, wiping my forehead with the back of my hand. "I'll check on Tia."

"I'll go with you."

Brandon opens the door for me, and I go through in time to see Tia's hand over her heart. Her face in full awe.

"What is it?" Brandon asks as Tia holds up a simple gold necklace with a small circle and the letter *T* inscribed in it. "It's from my admirer." She hands over the card.

I take it, eager to read. "Tia, you're beautiful."

"First flowers, then a coffeemaker, now a necklace." She

wastes no time clasping her gift around her neck. "It better not be you," she says to Mr. Colfax, an elderly customer.

He waves her off with a head shake and a raspy voice. "I would have taken you to dinner by now."

"Why doesn't this person ask you out?" Brandon goes over to her to get a closer look.

"He's scared," Garcia says, running a hand over his crew cut. "Tia, do you want me to track this person down? My cousin's girlfriend is a stripper with connections to an ex-detective on parole."

It takes me a minute to work out what he's said. "Er—"

"I'm not going to do a thing," she says. "I like not knowing."

We watch as Alec breezes through the door and takes one look at the necklace. "Get back to work." He looks at me last. "You. You're learning how to change oil."

My heart does a tiny somersault. "Are you sure?"

"I think you're ready for something other than cleaning the breakroom fridge. Well done."

Tia gives me two thumbs up.

Gathered around the popped hood of an SUV, Josh gives me a mini tutorial on engine terms. Brandon's elbow brushes mine as he stands close, adding his expertise. "First, locate the drain plug," Brandon says.

"No, you check the oil level," Josh says.

Brandon's pulled away by a text on his phone and grimaces.

"Is something wrong?"

"Nope. Just Evan. We were supposed to hang out and he bailed, again. He invited us to your country club's pool, but then he sent this. He holds his phone in front of my face.

Evan: *Sorry, I can't bring guests*

That's a load of crap. Guests are welcome. Like a strong magnet, my mind goes straight back to thinking about Evan.

Sex is off the charts, with gasping and moaning and his voice whispering dirty things against my mouth. I would not change a darn thing about that. I love waking up half on top of him, aware of all things Evan. So what's bugging me?

Ever since the makeover he's been different.

"What happens when this is over?" Brandon's voice is like a siren in the distance.

My fingers clench around the wrench Josh hands me. Isn't that the million-dollar question. "Nothing. We go back to our lives."

"Are you going to be friends?" Brandon asks, reaching for his Big Gulp.

Evan and I could not switch off and become friends. At least, I couldn't. Do we have what it takes to make our time stretch further? Do we actually have a bond strong enough to go back and forth between our residences and frequent the other's events?

"Of course." I brush off the disdain in his voice.

Josh pushes the button for the lift and signals me to grab one of the floor rollers. "Evan's having the time of his life. He's probably been getting plenty of puss—action."

All that action is taking place with me. We never said we were exclusive. Why does that communication oversight bother me?

"He posts every day. Yesterday, he posted a photo from a polo match," Brandon says nonchalantly, and hands me a dirty towel. "Not sure what's up with that. Our man's just pretending not to stress about his job."

It doesn't take a financial wizard to figure out Bailey's isn't rolling in the dough. But Evan still hasn't mentioned anything. In fact, he doesn't talk about the shop anymore.

"Why is he worried about his job?" I take a seat on the roller next to Brandon's and stretch out, prepared to move beneath the car.

"Well, the auto shop needs a serious infusion, you know."

"How much money do they need?"

Brandon shrugs. "You didn't hear this from me. About $100,000."

Ah. I see. Clearly. How did I not put two and two together?

This is why Evan agreed to the bet. The money wasn't for himself or CeCe.

"Lexi," Alec chirps, suddenly in the doorway like I'm called to the headmaster's office. "When you're done, I need to talk to you."

I take my time, following Brandon's instructions. Opening the oil tank, letting it drain, and taking off the old filter.

Brandon punches my arm when I'm done. "Good job. We'll work you into more."

I have a hard time looking Alec in the eye. I wish I had money to help him.

"I was thinking," he says, the chair creaking as he leans back. "You're good with social media. Do you have any experience with public relations and ad sales?"

Yes. My heart responds first.

It's a question I didn't know I wanted him to ask until he presented it to me like an appetizer I'm hungry to try. "I know more than a few tricks. I sit on the board of the Alexandria Foundation. We put on charity events and community activities. I have been in boardrooms and behind the desk."

He looks almost shy when he asks, "Do you have any ideas about how to expand our customer base?"

I brace my hands on the table, eager for him to listen. "I have several ideas. You have to ask yourself what you're doing to incentivize people to walk through the door."

"We offer discounted services."

"Your advertising doesn't reach anyone past the end of the block. When was the last time you looked at Bailey's social media accounts? They're free advertising you're missing out on."

"What?" he says, a touch hurt. "Tia updates the accounts regularly."

"Tia is doing the job of three people." I take out my phone and pull up the screen. "You have less than five hundred followers. Your last post was two months ago. Those weekly specials you offer should be blasted the week before. Make people feel like they're missing out if they don't get their car an appointment. You could hold a community event with food trucks and rope those classes you offer into something bigger."

Incredulity forms around his mouth as he nods. "I didn't ask because I didn't think you cared—initially. Would you be interested in helping until you leave? I couldn't pay you." His voice drops at the last part. A truly regretful look plays out across his face.

"I can do it for free."

He pulls his chair forward, inviting me to do the same. "Here's what I'm thinking..."

CHAPTER TWENTY-EIGHT

Lexi

My mind is on brainstorming overload for how to help Bailey's. I plop my keys down and open the fridge, ready to drink my first-ever homemade margarita. Dinner plans include a salad from scratch. That way I can use the ingredients for other meals.

Un-showered, my hair pulled back, I pour my drink. Evan won't be home until later.

A knock on the door interrupts me and I go to answer. "Talia," I say, aghast.

"I got your address from Evan," she says, her smooth black hair matching the silky tones of her black silk romper. "Is this a good time?"

I momentarily freeze. No one from my old life has been inside this house. A little scared, I open the door. "I haven't had a chance to take a shower or clean."

She steps her calfskin ankle Valentino sandals onto the matted patch of the carpet darker than the rest. "We've known each other long enough to not worry about any of that."

"Do you want something to drink? I just made my own margaritas."

"I'll take one," she says, taking in the beat-up couch and Evan's television with cables connecting to a box. "This is where you've been living?"

Apologizing for Evan's house doesn't feel right. To him, there's no apology required. This is the place he lays his head at night. Who am I to judge where he does that? "The kitchen has good bones and I like the coziness."

"It's great," she says, and we leave it at that. "Okay if I sit?"

"The couch is yours. Any good plans tonight?" I ask, returning to her with plastic margarita cups in both hands. "I got the whole set of these for eight bucks. Not bad? I think the blue rim is cute." She takes a sip and I do the same. "Oof," I say, my tongue recoiling.

"They're not bad," she says, taking another sip.

"But not good either," I say, letting go a sigh of relief, my stomach unclenching. We both have a surreal moment. The two of us. *Here.*

"How's life at the auto shop?"

"You're looking at the newly appointed PR staff member." I felt like Alec gave me two big wings. "I'm busy in a way I didn't know I could love. I feel out of the loop, but I'm not sure I want to go back to being in the loop." That is the truth. Even if I didn't know this until Talia was in front of me.

She stomachs another sip and finally sets it down. "Pre-bet Lexi wouldn't say such things."

"No, she wouldn't."

"We haven't been friends for a while. You know that, right?" Her voice is delicate enough for me to be afraid she's come to tell me we'll never be friends again.

"Not on the surface, no. After the auction, when you didn't return my calls or texts, I realized why. I couldn't put blame on anyone but me. That was rough. I've been a crappy friend and I understand if you're here to say your piece and go."

"I'm not here to end our friendship." She grabs my hand

with an earnest gaze. "I'm here to support you. This Lexi, the one in front of me, is *real*."

A tear plops from my eye onto my leg. "I've had no one to talk to about this except a group of guys in an auto shop who can't seem to find love…and Evan. He encouraged me to talk to you at the wine tasting."

"I'm glad he did." She sheds a few tears and we hug. "You smell like oil."

"All part of the job."

"Come to my birthday party. It's on my parents' yacht. I won't let this year be the first time you're not there. Evan's invited, too. Now, tell me everything."

We spend some time catching up and making fun of my terrible bartending skills. Talia takes a turn mixing a batch and hers are even worse. After she leaves, I take the place in. Evan is coming over later; he's stuck at a gala meeting. This place needs major TLC.

The house is warm. I turn on the AC units and grab the bucket of cleaning supplies.

My intention is to scour the place to make it presentable, but my motives change.

I blast wall-thumping volume levels with nineties rap and get to work.

Rain hits the window, sweat forms on my brow.

The yellow plastic up-to-the-elbow gloves are on. This is the mother of all cleanings. The kitchen is tackled first. As I clean away the dirt, toss the wrappers, and wipe down the countertops, my thoughts turn to the things I need to put in order in my mind. Bursts of childhood memories are like logs on a fast-burning fire. Scrubbing the sink edges with a toothbrush, I work hard, my thoughts bring me to a turning point.

I think of all the names I have been called in the past.
Spoiled

Fake

Selfish

Snob

Maybe I've been okay with them, but no more.

Before this summer, I was never alone long enough to do this kind of soul-searching. I have put off taking a closer look at my life.

I think of my mother. I think I need help—the professional kind—facing her and working up the nerve to ask her why she chose a new family over me. But this time, do the work. Stop skipping the pain.

Shadows darken the sky as I finally give these thoughts the spotlight. It's getting harder to push the feelings down.

Bowser looks like Alec keeping an eye on the shop. She retreats when I get out the lint roller and the vacuum.

The couch is next. Cushions are washed, clothes are put away, tables get a thorough wipe-down and I break out the duster like a swag bag must-have. On my knees, sticky gloves rest on my thighs. I wonder: who do I want to be when this is over?

I can't go back to the person I was. I can't go back to the person waiting for everyone to kiss her hand and make things easy.

I'm having a mic-check moment. I don't *want* easy.

The notion presses urgently on my heart. What I have been hiding is who I am. The last name North is deceiving. Sure, I was raised in a different tax bracket, but this new version of me eats cereal with marshmallows, and my budget is in order. The fridge has food, and my clothes are folded and put away.

This doesn't mean I can't love the finer things.

The flame inside me burns strongly.

Long-term generosity is on my mind as I take a photo of my sundresses and two thousand dollar shoes. I text Talia. *Is there an app to sell these for charity?*

Talia: *I'll send you the link*

Talia: *We can do it together*

CeCe's on my mind with this. Not just CeCe, but all humans her age, when appearance is important. When things are changing inside and out, having a good haircut and well-fitting clothes matter.

Thunder crashes by the time I toss the used sponges in the trash and shower the funk off me. Exhaustion settles in as Evan arrives, not missing a thing.

"What happened here, North?" he asks, almost tripping over a skittish Bowser.

"I cleaned." More like my heart just cleaned house.

Out with the old Lexi, in with the new and improved. This is no longer about being Evan's perfect woman. This is about my own personal fresh start.

"I had reservations downtown." His gaze looks over every surface, the scent of disinfectant with a lovely lemony chemical smell filling the room. "Do you want to change?"

My hand touches his biceps and I pull him close, hanging my arms loosely around his neck. I can't wait to tell him about who I want to be and the starting line of a new direction for my life. I stare into his eyes, wiped out and ready for bed.

"I want to stay in. Could we skip a night out?"

He has been spending money like water flowing from a tap. His finances are none of my business but I am afraid he will run out of cash.

He puts his hands on my arms, gliding his fingers down to my waist. "We could go to your house and open a bottle of wine," Evan says.

"You're already here. There's no point in driving to my place."

His eyes seem to prickle with frustration.

Releasing my hands, I go toward the bedroom. Over my shoulder, I call out, "Stay or go. It's your choice."

Evan instantly notices the Tiffany's bag on his dresser. The bracelet is still packed away inside. He doesn't say anything, but he has a perturbed look in his eyes. "Your closet is empty. What happened to all your clothes?"

"I took them out. I'm selling them for charity. I can't wait to get my hands on the outfits at my house. They'll go for thousands."

"You love your clothes."

His room is bathed in early night shades. It's too pretty to turn on a light.

It reminds me of never-ending summer nights, bittersweet memories, and strangely, innocence. "They don't exactly fit into this scene." I try to make light of it, but he's standoffish.

I look at him, unblinking. Maybe he is waiting for me to say what I'm feeling.

We watch each other. My heart is swimming with emotions, pulling me further into him. Time stops. My breath halts.

No matter what happens next for us, I need him to know one thing.

I take his hand tentatively, innocent middle school style, and whisper, "I love you."

He does nothing.

I threw the words up in the air and they are hanging, waiting for him to catch them. Because what I needed was another person to disregard my feelings.

Evan does not say it back. He offers a hand squeeze. "Thank you."

Thank you?

"Tonight's not going as planned," he says, looking around his room. "Feel free to donate any of my old clothes to charity. They're just taking up drawer space."

Soon after, he leaves.

He does not kiss me before he goes.

I close the door behind him, sliding down the wall, knees up and head resting forward. It all comes out in one unstoppable breath. For the mother who raised me but abandoned me, for the father who doesn't see me, and for Evan and all my bone-drained fatigue, one tear falls, wetting my eyelashes. Then another.

Some of the tears are for me, for not having anything about my life figured out and wanting to, but not knowing how to take the first step.

The tears do not stop. Not with my heaving chest, my rocky breaths, and the gut-spilling, soul-cleansing tears falling freely.

I cry until I am drained. Until there is nothing left.

CHAPTER TWENTY-NINE

Evan

C urse at me all you want. I froze.
I came to tell Lexi about Craig and when I opened my mouth to bring up the subject, she said *I love you*. A few heartbeats passed and I said nothing. If I had told her, it would have sounded like an afterthought.

I blew my big moment. I wish I could take that moment back.

The notification on my phone sets the romance in motion with a delivered gift basket including tickets for a weekend trip to Vegas in the Penthouse Suite at the Venetian with the remote-controlled Roman shades.

She left the money for me to do what I want. I'm spending it on her and CeCe.

My hand slides lower on the Callaway 7 iron. Knees bent, feet wide, I use what I've learned from my private golf lessons.

The tenth hole is in the distance, marked by a white flag and Alec's nearby voice. "You're going to choke."

I set up the shot. One, two, three, *whack*.

The ball launches like a cannonball, disappearing into the sky and landing nowhere near the hole.

"Worth a shot," Alec says, taking his turn on the green turf of the tee box. He blends in like a golf native with his visor and frustrated frown. "I never thought I'd live to see the day you picked up a golf club."

"See it. Believe it," I boast, stepping out of his way.

Alec is light-years away from making his PGA debut, but he took up golf with his ex-girlfriend, right up until she cheated on him. "Not sure I want to."

His ball flies high and long, driving with better accuracy.

"I booked us both private masseuses by the pool. You can meet Elena and the other board members."

A line creases between his brows as he rests his club on his shoulder. "You're joking, right?"

"I don't joke about working out my strained calves." I flex my foot for effect at the same time as my phone chimes. The text from Lexi is what I've been waiting for. This should set right the botched "I love you."

Lexi: *I received your gifts*

That's right. Love it all, sweetheart.

Lexi: *You booked a trip before I could ask for time off?*

Me: *I'll take care of it*

"Can Lexi take a couple days off?" I ask, hopping into the golf cart with Alec's trigger-happy foot on the pedal. The golf cart lurches forward down the paved path with a clunky start.

"I don't think so. She's eager to work on a customer event over Labor Day and help with our social media reach. I'd like to utilize her as much as possible. She brings a fresh perspective on advertising."

I stare at expansive views of the country club's sloped hills and a manicured fairway bordered by rough tall grass.

Lexi's planning an event? She didn't say anything.

My hand steels on the roof's edge and my weight shifts from Alec's increase in speed. "Slow down, this isn't like renting the golf cart at Hidey Ho's Campground."

Alec lifts his foot, mocking me and driving at a slow, painful speed through a winding path of weeping willows. My ball is nowhere in sight. Another golf ball casualty. "This slow enough?"

"Just try to act normal, can you?"

He pushes the brake hard and the cart lurches forward and settles into place. "What the fuck, Ev?"

"Look around. We're not at Bailey's."

"Bailey's is our life."

"Maybe I'm tired of everything revolving around Bailey's." There. It needed to be said.

"You can go to any other shop whenever you want. Don't put this on me," he says, clenching one hand on the wheel.

We're doing this now, in a place far removed from the grit of our lives. "I stayed for CeCe."

"Do *not* use her for the reason you're suddenly ignoring my texts and only hanging out in a place you can't stand." Alec's open palm hits the wheel lightly. A bitter laugh leaves his mouth. "Look at you. You're so desperate to be one of them, you're going to screw me over. The whole goal was to get Lexi to quit. But that's not happening, is it? When you go back to your life I'm still in the hole. At least have some decency and tell me to my face."

Hearing it from Alec sends me into resistance.

"She's going to drop you faster than this," he says with a poof, his fist closed and open, fingers spreading. "You'll be back in your work shirt and boots like the rest of us. Tell me if I missed anything." He named my biggest fear. She will step back into her life with fresh eyes directed at me.

I sigh, resting my head back, frustrated. "I ran into Craig."

Alec's pissed-off glare reduces to rapt attention. "When?"

"At a restaurant. I didn't want to say anything." Stress flows out with my words and my throat feels as hollow as my stomach. I swallow nothing but air.

"You spoke to Aiden, right?"

"Of course I did. He said Craig wants to meet. Aiden's figuring out why. That's all I know."

The rumble of another golf cart behind us has Alec moving and abandoning our last hole.

"And you didn't tell me or Mom?" Alec's eyes close and his chest heaves in a grand sigh.

"I'm taking care of it."

Alec has been with me every step of the way, commenting on Natalie's choice with resentment only a few times. "You're not. You're acting careless and irresponsible. Uprooting your life for the summer was your choice," he says, picking up speed, the clubhouse breaking into view beneath a blue sky with fluffy clouds. "Dragging CeCe along was a mistake I shouldn't have let happen. Has she seen him?" His neck whips a sharp right, and the force of his green eyes is on me. "Has he seen her?"

I pinch the bridge of my nose and close my eyes.

Excuses come to mind. Throwing myself into gala planning, pursuing something real with Lexi, avoiding Craig and Hudson. Each one is barren, unable to hold a drop of reason, and CeCe's been relegated to my mother's more than ever.

These so-called excuses tag along with my choices. They don't hold water, and Alec will see through my explanations. "He saw her."

"Son of a bitch." Alec's regard for my answer is sewn in revulsion. "So you screwed more than me this summer. You did the same thing to CeCe."

"Alec—"

"Save it, Evan." He silences me with his hand, crossed over his chest like a blade, and pushes his foot on the pedal. "Get your priorities straight."

The golf attendant jogs over to help with our bags.

I slide him a tip and pull the golf bag over my shoulder.

Alec walks ahead of me, making it to his car without a goodbye. He doesn't glance in my direction on his way out, and I pop the trunk on Lexi's Audi and put my clubs in the back.

The electric hum of a golf cart passes behind me with a *creak*.

"Look who it is. *Ev*."

I whirl around at the most nauseating voice in the world.

Hudson is in the driver's seat, leaning to the side to be seen. His buddy, a near duplicate version of Hudson, except with his hair pushed off his forehead and a power gaze, is watching me, both of them looking like they have nothing better to do than pick a fight.

I stand taller, make my chest broader. *"Hud,"* I fire right back.

His gaze moves to Lexi's car, as if her vehicle triggered his sudden dislike of me. "Is Lexi golfing?"

"No, she's not here."

He smacks his friend's shoulder. "Yet here *you* are. Do you see this guy?" His friend looks at me with a superior demeanor. Hudson's hand casually grasps the wheel and his legs stretch farther. "I give you credit, Ev. I didn't think Lexi would stick out role-playing this long. Then again, a little help along the way was in her favor."

The hairs on my neck stand up. His ego doubles in front of me. The voice. The look. The same sucker punch hits me the way it did when I learned Lexi and Hudson had history. Same feeling. Same animal instincts.

Hudson's eyes are a caseload of bragging. "Do you still think she's going to stay at your pathetic auto shop?"

His friend sneers.

Hudson leans toward me, the atmosphere flipping like a switch, churning around us, inside me, my sixth sense hanging off a cliff I've only just realized is coming. "Do you know where she'll go first?"

"Somewhere smarter than you."

Hudson's snarky grin mellows, but his gaze is sharp as the tip of a nail. "You still think Lexi actually took this thing seriously." His voice is winding up. "Good thing she took the money I gave her. Oh, and the credit card. I almost forgot about loaning her that. It was no problem to put her name on the card. It was one of those without a limit."

The betrayal hits hard and fast, knocking my breath to the curb.

Hudson's jeering gaze eggs me on, the truth too real to even think about saying *you're wrong*. He's right. He knows it. I know it with a vibrating breath.

"You didn't know?" he tacks on like a postscript. "Wish I could stay and explain, but we're all out of spare time. Unless you want to carry our bags?" Laughing, he speeds off, high fiving his friend.

Motionless, I stand at the back of Lexi's car, keys dangling in my hand.

The day I got the call Natalie had been arrested, I was in the middle of replacing brake pads. Customers don't realize that the daily stress put on brakes wears them down until they aren't safe to drive anymore. I felt worn down before my mother finished explaining to me that my sister was in custody. I knew it would change everything.

Lexi's been going behind my back, preaching about honesty without being *honest*.

The cooking, the lawn mowing, even the budget she created were all part of an act. The more she spent Hudson's money, the greater the lie she presented to me.

I slam the trunk shut, my jaw compressed and my mind seeing this bet as clearly as Hudson's words. She was cheating the whole time. Scamming a behind-the-scenes level of comfort.

The changes I have made to my life, they were for her,

and she's been lying to me, using me, and I was caught up in convincing myself we were really that good together.

Did she and Hudson laugh about me? A rush of anger strikes my pulse, raising it, sharpening it. *How often have they been seeing each other?*

I toss my phone onto the passenger seat and reverse out of the spot.

My heart isn't going to be the victim of someone jerking it around. Throwing in the towel is tempting. I come within an inch of backing out of Talia's birthday party, but doing so would let Hudson and Lexi win at their game and I would be the fool everyone will talk about.

CHAPTER THIRTY

Evan

Three days later, Lexi and I are traveling by helicopter to the superyacht parked off the Virginia coast to attend Talia's birthday party. I wait for her to arrive at the airport, rethinking how I did not see what she was doing. The more I go over our time together, the less sure I am about the small moments and the bigger ones. *I love you, Evan.* She really pulled out all the stops with that one.

The door to the aviation building pushes open and Lexi appears. We haven't spoken since I found out about the money, making a point to ignore her until this moment couldn't be avoided.

She walks toward me with the hem of her sundress swishing at her knees and her hair gently hitting her chest. All I see is Lexi from before. The woman who rear-ended me and looked at me like I was beneath her.

Maybe I am. Lexi had the chance to try on someone else's world and she was too scared to give this a real chance. Disappointment crushes me with a low blow. I would rather feel anything other than being let down.

Looking at her, I can't help but scrutinize her steps. Neither anger nor wounded pride feed my growing bitterness at her lighthearted disposition.

"Ready for the party?" Lexi says, stopping in front of me with faint traces of my body wash on her. "Talia's excited you're joining. She wants to get to know you." She lays her hand against mine and I pull away. "If you need any help, I have been attending parties on yachts since—"

"I don't need your help."

Her eyebrows scrunch. "I thought you might be nervous."

"Nervous? No," I bark. I don't need her next to me, whispering in my ear how to make conversation while mocking me behind my back. "I'm not your puppet, North."

Her shoulders draw back. "Excuse me?"

I make it a point to walk ahead of her toward the pilot motioning us over.

Buckling in, Lexi's arm touches mine and I move away. We wear headsets with attached microphones. The whir of the helicopter blades obliterates the steady silence.

The pilot takes us off the ground like we're beamed up in a vertical column, the bird angling and gliding into the clear blue skies.

"Your first time in a helicopter. What do you think?" Lexi asks, touching my arm and pointing out my window.

I shrug. How much of Hudson's money did she spend? Thousands?

"Come on, this is exciting, I know you think this is cool." Her smile makes me only angrier. Hudson's voice cracks in my ears. *One of those cards without a limit.*

"Is that what you think? This ride must be the best thing to ever happen to me?" I say curtly, holding her gaze, seeing only lies reflected in her eyes.

"No," she says, taken aback. "I didn't mean—"

"It's a helicopter, not a flight to the moon."

Her shoulders round forward with her mouth closing and

forming a straight line. "I'm sorry. Did I miss something? Was flying on a private jet your new standard?"

"Newsflash, North. People have actual problems other than starting arguments about helicopters versus private jets."

She stares open-mouthed. "A birthday party *you* could have stayed home for. If this was such an inconvenience to you, I would have been happy to relay it to Talia."

"Whatever." I lean my head against the seat and look at the patchwork of hazel fields below. "I'm here to see my new friends."

"You mean Elena," she says briskly. "Or did you think I didn't notice you're with her all the time?"

I look at her, our gazes erupting like a bonfire. "And you aren't with other people?"

"What's that supposed to mean?"

"It means I want to enjoy the rest of this ride."

It's a chilly descent to the airfield. The pilot lands in an abandoned parking lot with a small building on one side and the ocean on the other. The entire facility is wrapped in a chain link fence.

Lexi and I continue giving each other the silent treatment, which extends through the hired car ride to the yacht. She looks out her window and I keep a vigilant focus on the stretch of highway and houses until we arrive at the marina.

Talia holds out both her hands for me and squeezes and pulls me close, my gaze lingering on the swatch of freckles down her nose and those dark inviting eyes of hers. "So lovely you could make it." She does a cheek to cheek kiss.

"Happy birthday," I say, handing her a gift.

Lexi looks around my shoulder as Talia opens the professionally wrapped bag. "Evan." She gawks with a thrilled voice. "*Evan*. It's beautiful."

It's a change tray etched in glass and goatskin, with a hand-painted tiger striking a stately sitting position on soap bubbles. The saleslady knew Talia and said she would love this.

"Since when do you shop at Hermès?" Lexi's cold voice is like an ice cube swallowed whole.

"Since now," I say flatly, keeping my focus on Talia's overjoyed reaction. But now spending Lexi's money feels like a giant waste.

"It's perfect. Thank you." Talia's grabby hands pull me into a hug. "Make yourself at home. Drink, eat. Have sex. No rules. Swimming is bathing-suit optional."

"A month ago you would have made fun of such a gift." Lexi grabs two glasses of a drink with edible violets and a fizzy base with raspberries. "Clearly you're comfortable in your new skin."

I take one of the glasses. "Comfortable? Yeah."

She purses her mouth so tightly, I'm not sure how her drink slips through.

Hudson comes into view, and my lips buckle and roll inward. Insecurities fire off inside me. He has had Lexi's heart from the get-go. This is the guy she wants. Hudson, with his suave steps and inner circle acceptance. The man who manages to ignite a look of admiration in her eyes I can't compete with.

She leaves me playing a never-ending guessing game as to why she bothered to say *I love you*.

I refuse to be the odd man out and waste more time with her. They deserve each other, which I want to believe wholeheartedly. Lexi and I step back, our cold shoulders parting at the accidental touch.

"I would say enjoy yourself, but I can't even do that," she says, taking the drink out of my hand. "Unless you want to apologize for how you acted on the flight over."

"Apologize for what?"

She whirls around. Her dress hem slaps her thigh. "By the way, I hate Vegas," she blurts, grabbing another drink.

"I'm sorry it wasn't Cannes or the French Riviera." I put so much thought into the gift basket. The money I spent on the trip and the gifts far exceeded my comfort, but I did this for her and she shoves the gesture back in my face. Nothing is ever good enough for her. *Including me.*

"Cannes *is* on the French Riviera."

"Fine. Don't go. I'll take Alec." I make it a point to look away from her and assess my options, because hanging around her is not one of them. My eyes catch the notice of a blonde I have seen at the country club. "Don't hang around on my account. I intend to have fun."

Why shouldn't I have fun? This was how it was supposed to be all along. Falling for Lexi was never part of our terms. In fact, I'm sure a solid make-out session with one of these women—or Elena, will make the night far more interesting.

"Be my guest. You're winning at the whole pinky's up thing." She turns and walks away while another woman descends the stairs. A splash of fabric glittering in the late sunlight begs my eye to look at Elena taking one step at a time. Her short dress hugs her curves.

My focus breaks at Lexi, far enough away to look from Elena to me. Her mouth opens a little bit more and any other expression is blocked by Elena standing in front of me.

"You made it," Elena says, showing off slender legs and feet tucked into heels that are giving her an extra few inches. "Why don't I show you around?"

I offer her my arm. "Please do."

My loafers make a quiet *click* with each step. I duck beneath flowery paper banners, making my way across the multi-deck craft.

Elena doesn't leave my side. She introduces me to her friends among a subdued crowd sipping champagne. A dude wearing a jacket with his naked chest beneath sits with legs wide and a drink in one hand while the bikini-wearing woman tucked next to him laughs when he takes off her captain's hat. Music pulses from the speakers, and the sun slips lower into the horizon.

"Evan's been such a help with the gala," Elena says, her hand touching mine.

I have already forgotten the name of the guy we are talking to. My cocktail glass pauses at my mouth. Across the deck my attention rivets to Hudson, studying Lexi from a barstool like he's on a mission to establish himself as hers.

But it isn't their interactions causing my teeth to clench. My nerves tense for another reason.

Craig is here.

Only this time, there is nowhere to run.

CHAPTER THIRTY-ONE

Lexi

Evan is a snob. I should have seen what was happening. The clues were right in front of me.

Evan's foul mood, his ridiculous gift basket. The present for Talia is like something any of these men I'm staring at would put together.

Completely unoriginal.

Evan's talking with power hands, his gestures contained between chest and waist, to a group of guests with tanned faces and open shirt collars.

Like he's one of them.

White roses adorn the deck, flown in just for the party. Servers walk around with trays of champagne and I grab a glass, sipping quietly with my newfound thoughts.

Evan's silence about the *I love you* was worse than the second-rate *Thank you* that followed. Words squandered on a phony giving his attention to Elena. She's next to him and won't leave his side.

"Your date seems to be finding a new date," Talia says, taking a spot next to me with her unfiltered observation. "I overheard Elena inviting Evan to the Hamptons for Labor Day."

Instant, full-blown irritation swings my patience meter into the red zone. My face turns sharply. Playing clueless has never worked with her. "I'm not surprised." No wonder he's been short on love.

The wind rakes a steady breeze through my loose curls. My fingers stiffen around the champagne glass.

Sex, clubbing, partying, sum up Elena's Hampton bashes. Two things are always guaranteed immediately following the weekend: Someone winds up pregnant and someone files for divorce.

Evan tips his head back in laughter at whatever magical thing she said. The champagne goes down smooth with a blasé, "I'm sure they'll have fun."

Talia's line of vision follows mine. It's quite possible my friend has a scannable microchip in her brain that reads my thoughts. Her skeptical eyes are like a ticking time bomb. "Fun? You're okay with Evan, Elena, and bunk beds?"

A half shoulder shrug and toffee-nosed laugh plead my case. "Why wouldn't I be?"

She looks at Evan, taking off his aviator sunglasses, and de-smudging them with his shirt. "What am I not seeing?" she says severely.

"Your birthday, my dear, is about you. What's on the agenda for tonight?" I haven't had a chance to scan the QR code for the list of activities and food.

A server catches Talia's notice. "Excuse me one sec. We're not finished talking about this."

I am done discussing Evan. Trouble is, everyone else has nothing better to talk about. *Evan's expertise about cars? So interesting. Does Evan restore vintage cars? I have this lovely Jaguar. Do you think Evan would be interested in consulting? Give him my number.*

The yacht glides over waters calm as the sky and I retreat to introvert status, confined to the upper deck. My gaze lowers to the deck below, finding Evan and Elena standing close and talking. Without trying, friction tightens my every breath. This is not how I saw our evening going.

His impressive mood swing could be tied to the financial stress at Bailey's. He must be embarrassed or worried about what I might think if I found out.

No, it's none of the above.

He laughs with Elena at the same time I decide to end our standoff. Turning on my heel, I run smack dab into Hudson with a muffled cry. "How long have you been standing there?"

"Not long," he says. "I didn't know if you would show."

Hudson is by my side at the exact moment I need him to be, handing me a drink like nothing ever went wrong between us. My face angles to his. He can tell at once something is wrong.

"I wouldn't miss Talia's birthday."

He squints at the cluster of women across the deck paying attention to Evan and Elena. "When you first made this bet, I thought it was a joke."

I hiccup and hit my fist to my chest. "So did I." Elena pulls down on Evan's shirt and whispers in his ear. Evan's sly grin is a look I thought was reserved for me. I was so wrong about him.

"Are you ready to come home?" Hudson's voice is neither arrogant nor assuming. He asks with a warmth I haven't heard from him in a long time.

"I don't know," I say honestly. My shoulders draw back. "There're so many things I want to do at Bailey's and with my life. I want to figure it out."

"You can do anything, Lexi." Hudson's hand rests on mine.

Strange how I thought Evan would be the one saying those words. They sound misplaced coming from Hudson, but he's the one saying them. "Thank you."

Evan and Elena are leaving the deck. Worry swishes through me like a bag of bricks falling. She leads him with her hand. Past the table of card players...behind the bar to the hallway. They are headed to... My jaw falls open.

I stay put, immobile with a heart of glass struck by a hammer and I'm left standing among the shards with tiny cuts. They are headed for the cabins.

Evan, whom I trusted.

Evan got what he wanted and is moving on to blonder pastures.

Hudson touches my arm idly. His observant eyes take in the same scene. "You're almost to the finish line. Don't quit now."

"Why not?" I say vacantly, hurt beyond belief. My inheritance is back in sight. A couple short weeks to go.

"You proved me wrong about you. I want to get to know this Lexi. Of course, I thought because of Evan's connection to our family, he would take advantage."

Take advantage. Hmmm. What did Hudson just say?

Craig appears from the lower deck. A beer in hand and heading across the deck with the same Hoffman swagger, like the world bends to their needs.

"Why would Evan take advantage of your family?"

"You don't know?"

Cool silence settles between us. "I haven't kept up on your family."

"Craig is CeCe's father."

The impact is an instant one-two punch right to the gut.

My fingers fasten around Hudson's bicep, our gazes meeting. The drink glass in my other hand slides between my fingertips, dropping and intercepted by Hudson, who puts it safely out of the way. "What did you say?"

"I thought Evan would have told you. My family found out only recently." He turns his hand over, crooking his index finger for me to come closer. "Lex, believe me when I say this. We're still in shock. *I have a niece.* My parents have a granddaughter. He has no idea what this has done to my mother."

It's true, Cecilia Hoffman would love nothing more than to dote on her grandkids, a gift I had thought Hudson and I would someday give her, but those were juvenile thoughts from a version of myself I don't recognize anymore.

This isn't about me.

Evan explicitly told me he didn't know CeCe's father. How would Natalie and Craig have known each other? *My sister had a one-night stand* were his words. Is that even true?

I need to be careful about what I am willing to believe and what's a rumor. No one is allowed to spread gossip about CeCe if I can help it. "Evan doesn't know who CeCe's father is."

"And you believe him?" he says like the joke is on me.

Evan lied to me. I want to see the good in him and think there is a reason, but he is not standing with me to contradict Hudson. He's *not* here. He's with Elena. Tears form, not out of sadness, but out of anger. I can't see straight.

Hudson jumps on my reaction. "Why would I make this up?" His volume drops even lower. "We're not sure about all the details. Craig's been reluctant to share, but we think Natalie's been blackmailing him. Who really knows the extent? Evan's made sure my family doesn't see her."

Bursts of laughter around us sound far away.

Talia catches my eyes and motions me over. My breath chokes on the possibility. Evan wouldn't purposefully keep family away...would he? Has he? He already lied once about this.

Reeling from the news and failing, my feet get involved. I move past couples and friends reaching for my arm, oblivious to my determined steps down the stairs and giving the hallway with bedroom cabins a ferocious glance.

I march over to Craig, who is standing twenty feet away.

Evan appears on one of the couches. Is his shirt button undone? His sunglasses are off. Our gazes collide like our hearts were always meant to.

Ten feet away...

Evan sees the direction I'm headed. Right toward him. He's on his feet and heading this way.

In a blink, I fear Hudson's telling the truth. The few odd questions Evan has asked about Craig. The reason he is never in the same room as him.

His gaze checks mine. Both of us pick up speed in the same direction. Evan's longer strides get to me first.

"Craig's her dad?" I cry loudly. "Craig is CeCe's father? You told me you didn't know, and this whole time, you've been lying to me."

Pale-faced, Evan stands tall like he can't move.

A stray long laugh dies down in the distance, and a hush ripples over the guests. Hudson is standing behind me. He puts his hand on my shoulder. A look of disgust is in Evan's eyes. "Let's not do this here," he says, his mouth constrained and tight.

"Where are we going to do it? We're on a boat."

"You're drunk," he says distastefully.

"Do you blame me? How could you lie to me? Look at you." My fingers shake in front of him.

Evan is infuriatingly uncaring. "I bet Hudson was the one who told you."

I get in Evan's face. "Who cares if he did?"

"The thing about casting stones doesn't work if you're the one in the wrong."

What? He's not even a smidgen sorry. "You're saying I'm the liar?"

The music has stopped, furious glances and whispering rotate around us.

"You've been taking money from Hudson."

The money was weeks ago and not a dime was spent. "No."

"You didn't think I would find out you've been seeing him

for financial support? Lying about everything? You didn't need to buy the instant rice for effect."

"*You're* well versed in sneaking around. I said I loved you and how do you react? By having sex with Elena."

Evan's face turns red. "I didn't have—" The captain blasts the foghorn.

"You did." My words proclaim as the horn ends. "You're a—"

The foghorn again.

I give the upper deck a mean glare. "We were supposed to be honest with each other. Look at you. You're the one who's unrecognizable, dressed up like the very people you've mocked. He's a mechanic," I say with a raised, buzzed voice, "he wants to be one of us so bad, he's hoping you can see past that." I ignore Evan's rapidly increasing hostile expression and my pounding pulse. "He never will be one of us. No one's inviting you to golf or to a birthday party when this is over."

I look around until I find Craig. He's twice my size with an unforgiving gleam in his eye, but I march over to him and grab his sleeve.

A few cell phones are raised.

Talia touches my arm. "Lexi, stop."

I can't see past my own anger. Craig's sleeve is clutched in my fist. "Are you CeCe's dad?"

Evan's mouth twitches.

I turn to Craig. "Well?"

"It's true," Craig says, his guard up like the rest of us.

Anger pounds through my veins. Tears swell behind my eyes. My heart breaks for CeCe. For all the intricacies of how this came to be. The details I am not privy to. I think of her, worry for her, want to jump ship and be there for her.

"I was wrong about you," I say to Evan, scrambling to pick up the pieces of my pride. They're tiny as shattered glass. If only my heart wasn't so soft, I might be able to keep the fight going, but I find my voice is tired.

"I don't recall asking you to be right about me." Evan comes closer. The two of us are an arm's reach of each other. "You used me, too. You think I don't know the second we're done you'll run back to this guy?"

Craig and Hudson simultaneously stand on either side of me.

"Don't talk to her like that," Hudson says.

Fists clench at my side. The urge to slap him comes on strong.

Evan rises to the challenge. "You're the one who publicly dumped her."

"I've got this," Hudson says, holding Craig back. It happens before I finish my breath. Hudson clocks Evan in the face.

Evan stumbles back into the guests, knocking champagne glasses over, spilling alcohol down dresses and shirts. Evan regains his composure, pressing his hand to his jaw, working his tongue along the inside of his cheek. He's going to hit Hudson back.

I step in front of him. No more. I can't do this one second longer.

"I quit." I say it louder. "I. QUIT. You win. We're done."

"Good," Evan says. "I always knew you would."

My hard stare is reserved for him. "Be out of my house by six a.m. If you're there, I'll have you arrested."

Mini earthquakes hit my nerves. My trembling hands won't stop.

All of it was caught in cell phone recordings, the entire scene likely already going viral. #YachtProblems #LexiQuitFirst #NotTheChampagne.

I need air, but we're already outside. I need to be alone and there is no place to go. We are stuck on the yacht for the next several hours.

Hudson puts his arm around me. "You did the right thing.

Doesn't he know who you are? Doesn't he know how much you're worth?"

Worthless is more appropriate.

Two things are clear: I never had Evan *and* I just kissed my inheritance goodbye.

CHAPTER THIRTY-TWO

Evan

If there was a sublayer beneath worse-case scenario, last weekend qualifies. Stuck on a yacht for hours, I kept to myself in one of the guest cabins. Lexi was right. Her friends took immediate sides. I don't need to spell out which side they took.

So did the rest of the world. I declined an interview invite for three talk shows. The video of our fight is reaching viral heights thanks to @HesNotAllThat and @LexiLost, two teens not much older than CeCe posting nonstop videos. My outfit was picked apart, to which one of the designers posted the comment *Our brand is not affiliated with Mr. Bailey.*

I can tune out social media.

I cannot erase her words and snobby tone. *He's a mechanic.* Called me a loser without saying it to my face and embarrassed me.

Lexi accused me of having sex with Elena, which wasn't true, but I go on letting her think what she wants. It makes it easier.

We circled back to our first impressions and now we're back where we started. Hating each other. Lexi left nothing to interpretation.

The bruise on my jaw changes from black to a sickly yellow. Each time my mouth opens, the tender skin pulls.

It isn't like I haven't been in a fist fight before, but I wasn't going to hit Hudson, even though I wanted to. CeCe was the reason I held back.

Nothing spells stellar parenting like throwing punches in front of the man eager to find a reason to take her away. I came close. Too close. My blood pressure soars and peaks, my hands doing a jerky motion with the wrench.

"What the hell are we listening to?" I shout and roll out from beneath the car, shoving the dirty rag in my back pocket.

Brandon and Garcia don't look up from the hood.

"Material Girl" disrupts my mood. Impatience stalks me. I walk over to the computer and switch the music with my grease-stained fingers to Guns N' Roses. "There. Much better."

Tia sticks her head in the garage. "Alec needs you."

I toss the wrench on the counter. "Now what?"

The waiting area is uplifted by another bouquet of flowers for Tia. Roses again. Same blooms, different colors. She runs her finger over a white petal.

"You realize this person is stalling. They're too chicken to tell you who they are."

"They can stall all they want," she responds, eyeballing me from behind her computer screen.

The flowers are not the only change.

The display cases underwent organization. The new "smart" coffeepot talks to customers. I prefer a dumb coffeemaker. Is there no end to Lexi's influence? Magazines are strewn about with flirty covers and advice about quilting.

Everyone is acting like this is normal.

I rip off one of the Labor Day posters she had printed and toss it in the trash.

"You're going to pay for that." Tia's voice carries into

Alec's office. My brother is in the middle of pushing up his glasses and rubbing his eye.

"What's up?" I remain standing, our power play taking shape, only this time I am in the penalty box.

"I need to know what your plans are for the $100,000. If you don't want to put the cash into Bailey's, tell me. I would rather tell them business is about to take a turn for the worse and give our staff chances to find other work. You did the work. I shouldn't have allowed you to do this for the shop."

"I'll get you the money," I say through bitter lips. I don't want a single dollar. CeCe and I were fine before the bet. "Every last cent is yours. I'll send Josh to collect." I have no interest in ever seeing Lexi again.

"That's horseshit, Evan. You need to finish this. Get the money yourself. Don't send Josh." Alec's hand rustles around his desk drawer like a disappearing act and places the sleek black box on the desk. "Give this back to her."

"She quit," I say testily. "We keep the loot. Pawn the darn thing for all I care."

Alec pauses thoughtfully. "Do you know if this is special to her?"

"It was her grandmother's." The one person she had in her corner, who died. I think of Lexi in my arms after the makeover and trusting me with her pain.

"You two are even. Don't keep this from her."

I shove the box back. "You're more than welcome to drop it off."

Losing myself in calipers and brake pads is my world, topped off with replacing antifreeze. All of it is welcome.

"And about CeCe? Has Craig contacted you?"

"No." Thankfully. I'm still not breathing a sigh of relief, but out of sight, out of mind may work in my favor. "I'm heading home. I'll see you tomorrow."

A few other notable changes happened.

Elena was quick to remove me from the planning committee. Elena's name causes upheaval in my breathing.

The notice from Marmont was as follows: *Dear Mr. Bailey, you are no longer on the guest list. If you are interested in a membership, contact guest services.*

Chef Sofia removed me from the cooking app.

Pulling into my driveway, a stomachache forms. The lawn needs to be mowed and dinner made. The dishes need to be done. I need to investigate why our water is staying lukewarm. I'm right back on the hamster wheel.

I hate coming home to this dump.

Lexi's fresh, floral scent will take time to go away, even with the air freshener I spray, coughing at the overuse.

"CeCe, I'm home," I announce, going to her room and knocking on the door.

"Come in," she says, seated on the floor, legs stretched out and crossed at the ankles. A book is nestled against her chest protectively.

"I'm making your favorite. Baked tortellini."

Her smile is forced. "Sure."

"Sure is the most unexcited answer." Sadness fills my breath. Neither of us want to talk about how much we liked Lexi's house. Baileys have the genetic code to retreat internally.

"You don't have to cook," she says. "I'm not really hungry."

Neither am I.

I take a seat next to her, knees up, grease-smelling hands resting on top. "How are you doing?"

She shrugs. "I miss her house."

What's the point in missing something that was never ours?

CeCe can't hear that. A lump forms in my throat. "We can go to the pool tomorrow. We'll order pizza. Do it right." I nudge her shoulder. "What do you say?"

"Nah. I want to hang out with my friends. Do you think Lexi misses us?"

"CeCe," I say firmly, "it was always going to end. Lexi has her own life." She has everything a woman could want, and she hates me. *Good,* I hate her.

Soon as I think it, I know it's not true.

Tears rush down CeCe's face. My arm is around her, pulling her close. "I hate this house. I want to go back."

"We can't. It's not our life. We got to live in someone else's world. That's all."

She rips herself out of my arms and scoots away. "We have nothing. We're poor." Emotion throttles her voice. Her face is puffy from crying. "When I was staying at Lexi's, everything was better."

"I can do better," I plead; her heart-wrenching voice holds me captive, wishing she would look at me with the same awe as when she rode her bike for the first time. "I'll get another job. I didn't before, because you were too young. I want you to have nice things, CeCe. I don't like saying no to everything."

A puff of air breaks through her lips. "You don't understand anything. Grandma's old and you're a guy—I *liked* Lexi hanging out with us. I thought you guys liked each other and I thought…"

My heart breaks. "You thought we would date? Get married?"

"You never date."

"That's because I don't want to bring someone home only to have you get hurt."

She stares at me with all she has. "Maybe *you* don't want to get hurt."

"I hate that you're getting smarter than me."

Her mouth bends into a smile.

"We were always going to come back here. We can't go back to Lexi's, but I'm here for you and I love you, sweetheart." My voice breaks. "You *are* my world. Do you understand that?" I fight back my own tears. Every sacrifice is worth the privilege to be here, sitting on the carpet next to her. A thousand memories of CeCe overcome me. "The first moment I held you, you were this small." I show her with my hands. "Your eyes were open, like you didn't want to miss a thing, right from the beginning."

She sniffles and wipes her nose with the back of her hand.

"I just held you and I promised myself I would always look out for you. I promised myself you would have a place in this world. I couldn't wait to see what you would do." I nudge her shoulder with mine. "When you don't fight me about putting away your clothes."

She smears another tear away with a soft laugh. Bowser's paw sticks out from beneath the bed. Her claws snag the carpet as if she's been waiting for a break in the conversation to let us know she's here.

"Then why won't you tell me about my dad? I want to know about him. Even if it's not good. I want to know. I saw him on the videos from the yacht. But I wanted you to tell me."

Shit. Of course. She's always a step ahead of me.

CeCe moves back closer to me, resting her head on my shoulder. She rests her hand on my arm.

I look around her room and I think about all we have been through.

How things change when we least want them to. That's the thing about raising CeCe, she is always changing me, shaping me, making waves in my heart when I am the one who is supposed to be in control.

It is the wrong time to think about Lexi, but I wish she were here, so I wouldn't have to do this part alone. Because I got used to her, being here, with me.

I am angry at myself for thinking that. I take a deep breath, then another. Taking a minute to sort my thoughts and put my words in the right order. Lexi and I are over, but CeCe's story is beginning. Am I scared?

Yeah, I am.

"Your father's name is Craig Hoffman and he lives here in Alexandria..."

Bowser pounces forward, finding her spot in CeCe's lap, managing to stretch her claws and stab my skin. The dark horse in emotional support has emerged. Both of them snuggle closer to me.

CHAPTER THIRTY-THREE

Evan

Tia throws me a welcome back party at Low Point.

It's really another Friday night in my life. The discussion with CeCe about Craig is still on my mind now, days later. She asked a lot of questions, all of which I answered truthfully. I'm still not comfortable talking about Craig, and I look over my shoulder everywhere I go, afraid he is going to be there with a lawyer and a court order.

A brunette with a gap-toothed smile and a pretty face is buying me a drink. "We can go to my place," she says, touching my arm.

"I have to steal him," Alec says, his hand on my collar, saving me.

"Thanks," I say.

"You looked miserable from the moment she talked to you."

Low Point never changes. The place is a reminder of where I came from and who I am. A guy who, in time, will get over Lexi and put this summer behind me. I look around the room, half expecting to see her, to feel my stomach lurch at the sight of her face and the irrefutable need taking over every time she's in a room.

She's not here. But the brunette is, and maybe the best way to forget Lexi is to occupy my night with someone else.

His hand clamps on my shoulder. "This isn't easy to tell you, but I saw Lexi having lunch with Hudson this afternoon."

I sip my beer with a stubborn mouth. "That happened fast."

"Have you talked to her about the money?" he shouts over a whiney rendition of "Here I Go Again." Spittle sprays from the lead singer's mouth.

"I will," I say, prolonging making contact. "This week," I fib, "I'll get in touch."

"Bullshit. You're chicken. Why don't you just talk to her?"

"I told you," I retort, running my hand over my neck, "I will."

"No, not about the money. About your fight. Did you tell her you didn't sleep with Elena?"

The lead singer pulls back from the mic, eyes closed, and claps his hands over his head waiting for the crowd to do the same, but this isn't center stage at the Capital Arena.

"It doesn't matter. She's going to think what she wants. This whole thing was a joke to both of us. We wouldn't have lasted."

"If you say so."

"I do. It's done. I'll get your money."

"Prove it."

"No."

Alec snaps his fingers. "Get out your phone and text her."

Lexi and I are business-only from here on out. I did not go through the past weeks and give up my summer out of the kindness of my heart. "No problem."

Me: *I need to collect the money*

My heart beats fast and my razor-sharp focus is on the screen. *Tell her you want to talk. To set things right. About Elena.* My fingers hover over the keys.

Lexi: *You'll get it by the end of next week*

Lexi: *You and Elena can spend it in the Hamptons*

She had to go and say that. **Me:** *My plan exactly*

Where was that brunette? Ah. Over by the entrance. Giving me come-hither eyes. With CeCe away for the night, I don't need to keep my rule.

But all I think about is my time with Lexi in my bed doing just that. An ache filles my chest and my cock is partial, too, showing favoritism to that scenario. It's just going to take time, I tell myself.

She told you she loves you.

I take another step toward the brunette.

She told you she loves you and you said nothing. Then you acted like a world-class jerk.

She does not love me. She was talking to Hudson the whole time.

Five feet from the brunette...

The entrance to the bar opens. I blink hard at the suit brigade and styled hair. The brunette swings her gaze in the same direction. My jaw ticks.

The thing I was most afraid of when this began was Craig. Yet here he is, forcing me to confront his presence. I am too scared to take a step toward him.

"Folks, someone's dad is here to get them," the lead singer says, starting up another song.

I don't move. I don't have to.

Craig sees me and I nod, still unwilling to move. The women do plenty of looking on his way over.

"I was told you come here on Fridays," he says. "I didn't want to show up at Bailey's. Can we talk?"

"Not without a lawyer. Go home."

"Evan, give me five minutes. That's all I'm asking."

"No."

His hands flinch. "It was worth a shot."

Craig is out of here, the door closing behind him. The crowd fills the space where he stood. What I should feel is relief, but I don't.

Alec comes over. "What was that about?"

"He wants to talk."

"Then go talk to him."

"Why should I? You know what he's capable of doing."

"I do, but I think you should hear what he has to say before he drags his entire legal team into it. Ignoring him won't stop that."

Alec holds out his hand and waits for me to decide. I put my beer in his palm.

I hustle after Craig, finding him almost to the street corner. "Craig. Wait."

He turns around. The two of us are nearly the same height. His face is shaped like CeCe's. "What do you want, Hoffman?" It's all I have the nerve to ask.

"Thanks to you and Lexi at the party, everyone knows I'm her father." His gaze moves over my shoulder. Alec, Brandon, and Josh are standing near the bar entrance.

"It wasn't my intention to have anyone find out. You admitted it. I never broke the NDA."

A car with a thumping subwoofer drives past us, distracting us until the noise fades. "Does CeCe know?"

"Why the hell do you care? Did you suddenly get a heart? Why are you here when you're the one violating the parameters *you* put in place to distance yourself from CeCe?"

"They weren't all my terms," he snaps. "You and your family walk around like I paid off Natalie."

"You did. I have fifty pages in your rambling legal document to prove it."

"You think I did it to absolve myself of raising an unwanted child."

"That's exactly what I think."

"I liked your sister. She was beautiful as hell and exciting." Craig crinkles his hands in frustration. "I didn't even know

CeCe existed. Not until Natalie was in handcuffs. I learned about CeCe through her lawyer."

My breath catches like I've swallowed too much air. This is not the version of the story Natalie told me. He must be lying. "You abandoned Natalie when you found out she was pregnant."

"I didn't *know* she was pregnant. I was in the middle of planning a wedding to my fiancée. CeCe was about six when I found out. It was around the time of Natalie's trial."

This doesn't add up. "You knew about the trial?"

"Of course I did. Natalie was selfish. She wanted me to testify that she didn't mean to rob the store and that I left her to raise a daughter on her own. When I wouldn't, she withheld CeCe from me. She took the plea deal before I ever had the opportunity to be involved."

The blame my family put on him squeezes around me. I want to hold on to Natalie's version as tight as I can. Her explanation of Craig's disappearing act has been my justification for hating him. "No."

"*Yes.*"

A string of expletives leave my mouth. I'm not ready to believe him.

"My fiancée at the time wouldn't have accepted CeCe. Both our families would have been hurt. Natalie knew this and she used it against me. I tried to do the right thing and explore legal options. *Your sister* blackmailed *me*. She told me I was never to see CeCe again and in exchange, she would keep my identity as CeCe's father a secret. If I didn't, she would go to the press." He rubs his hand methodically over his baby-smooth jaw. "Natalie's terms were the solution I needed to keep my fiancée. We called off the wedding for other reasons and I was busy dealing with the fallout. I honored the NDA I signed. I never sought you out. I didn't look for CeCe until I ran into you and then I saw her."

It takes me a moment to realize Alec is behind me. Hearing everything.

"You have no reason to believe me. I'm asking you only to consider the possibility. Natalie gave me an out and I paid for it. I've *been* paying for it. Not a day goes by that I don't think about CeCe. First, I find out I have a daughter, and then, I made the choice to leave it that way. It still fell apart. All of it."

Alec's hand lands on my shoulder.

"My family now knows, as does everyone else."

"What do you want?" I ask the question despite my fear of the answer. Knots roll over in my stomach.

It's here. The moment I never wanted.

"I want to get to know her," Craig says flatly.

"That's a hard no."

His fingers expand in front of his chest. "Hear me out. I understand this isn't easy for you." He looks at me and Alec. "For either of you or your family. CeCe has another half to her family, grandparents desperate to meet her and to know her. They are grieving at only recently learning about her. They are furious with me and with Natalie." His hands push out in front of him. "She also has my brother."

"That's a definite no." I don't want Hudson anywhere near her.

"If you are willing to meet with my lawyer and me, you'll find I want to work with you. I want to introduce myself and my family to her."

Before I say no again, Alec presses his hand onto my shoulder.

"She stays with you. I won't break her stability. You're still her legal guardian."

Eye to eye, we both know he could flip that over in a snap. He is her biological father. That will hold more weight than all the work I've put in. It terrifies me. Leaves my thoughts scrambling.

"We would start slow. See each other with you or any of your family present. If she's comfortable, one Saturday a month without you. If she doesn't want to continue, I back away. If she wants to see us more, we make room for what she wants. Either way, I want her cared for financially. In any capacity. Private school, clothes, doctor visits."

"I was the one in the trenches driving her to school, taking her to Urgent Care and back-to-school shopping. Where were you this whole time?"

"I thought about her"—he raises his voice—"more than you could ever understand. If I could go back, I would have scooped her up the second Natalie was put away. That's a regret I must live with. Please don't stand in my way now. I want to do the right thing."

"CeCe has to agree to it," Alec says abruptly.

I shake my head at him. Every muscle in my heart shreds. I could see CeCe wanting that.

Craig eyes me carefully. "I know what I'm asking. All I want is a chance."

"You should go." I don't trust myself to be rational.

We wait for him to get into his car and drive away before Alec turns to me. "We need to talk to Natalie. Verify what he's saying," Alec says, putting his hand on my shoulder. "I'll go with you to talk to her."

Tears fill my eyes.

This is no longer about CeCe. It's about the fact that deep down, I feel I've already lost her.

CHAPTER THIRTY-FOUR

Lexi

Two universal truths exist in my world. I owe Evan money and I'm flat broke.

Evan and his cold-hearted text when I immaturely suggested he spend the money in the Hamptons with Elena. That was an impulsive reaction to things I haven't gotten over since Talia's party.

The single source of money in my life is my father. So, this is how it has to be.

I show up at my childhood home, a sprawling château mansion nestled behind acres of lush green lawn. My phone is lost in the bowels of my Walmart purse and dinging.

Messages from my so-called friends sending me screenshots from IG and TikTok. Friends, who didn't reach out once while I was in the thick of the bet, but who are now flooding my phone with invites and messages of support.

I just want visual silence. No more screenshots sent with #ILoveLexi and #MechanicChicks.

I unbuckle my seat belt and round my shoulders into the driver's seat. Starting with the way I mishandled my grandmother's bracelet.

Then I look through all my social media accounts. I'm not that Lexi anymore. Not entirely. Holding my breath, I delete each account. Thousands of followers and likes disappear from my line of vision.

Panic beats in my heart. *Was that necessary?*

One look at my father's gabled roof and I know I can't turn back.

I didn't fulfill my end of the bargain, and Evan and I are meeting later. He wants his money and I have forty dollars in my wallet.

"Come in, Ms. North," my father's house manager says. Yes, he hires someone to run the estate. "I'll tell him you're here. Would you care for something to drink?"

The last thing I need is for her to announce me like I'm a pauper asking for money because my crops died. "I'll go see him."

I step into the library complete with a portrait of him above the desk Evan would comment on, and I wait to be noticed.

My father looks up from his desk, his eyes pensive. He rolls back in his chair and gestures to the leather couch. "You're on time," he says.

"That would appear to be the case."

"I was just thinking of you."

"Were you?" I counter, giving the couch a once-over and remaining upright. Years of pain creep to the surface. Words I can't hold back. "Are you ever thinking of me?"

He squeezes his hand and drops it to his side. "Lexington—"

"Did you ever ask yourself if you did the right thing? Letting my mother discard me for another family. Did you, even once, feel guilty about spending two months in Europe closing business deals instead of opening Christmas presents with me?"

His mouth parts in surprise. "What?"

My hands grip the top of the wing-backed chair and I push into it, leaning forward. "You were gone. All the time."

"I had a business to run."

"You had an obligation to make sure I was doing okay. You had the audacity to make me go through with this bet when you're partly to blame. Maybe you should have been there all the times I needed you. I've been irresponsible, I admit that. But I can't look you in the eye and not say how disappointed I am in you."

"I tried."

My tearful, head-shaking eye roll keeps my voice in check. "No, you didn't. I saw that letter from Mom's lawyer to you. She wanted to be with her new family, and you acted as if life could go on like normal."

He takes a long breath. "I didn't know you saw the letter."

"How could you? You were never home and when you were, you were holed up in here. You abandoned me and we have never gotten over it. *I* have never gotten over it. And yet, I still look at you wishing you would be my father. For once."

The humility in his eyes and creases around his mouth pull at my heartstrings.

He closes the distance between us. He pulls me into his arms and folds them around me. He gives a shuddering sigh and I cry. I cry like a baby, letting the tears soak his suit. "I'm sorry, Lexi." His own tears cloud his throat. "I made so many mistakes. I didn't know how to talk to you. I didn't know what to do. The longer time went on, the more I stayed away."

"Stop staying away," I burst out. Swiping the rest of my tears away, I see he can't hide his watering eyes, either. Both our noses are puffy and red. "I need you to be my dad. I need you to ask how I'm doing and call me. Help me find a plumber if I need one or check if I lock my house at night." Mascara stains my fingertips from rubbing it away. "Get to know me."

"I want that," he says, pulling me into another hug and

wrapping his arms around me. "I should have done this years ago."

He pours me a glass of water. Both of us look at each other with regret.

I still have another hurdle to leap over. "I also came about my inheritance."

A distrustful glimmer is in his eyes, but he would be used to that from the old Lexi.

"I'm not asking you to go back on your word," I say up-front. "I lost."

"I saw the video and the fight with Evan."

A bad memory I want to go away. "If you plan to give away my inheritance, I want to put the money into a charitable trust to help our city's youth. I would like to oversee the program in a paid position as part of the North Foundation."

He stares at me, the request registering with pride in his eyes. "I would love nothing more than to see you make this happen."

"Don't make this too weird and try to make up for lost time. We don't need belated father-daughter trips to a baseball game or anything. Okay?"

"What do you suggest?"

"Starting small. Dinner once a month, for now?"

"Twice a month."

My head is spinning from my father's loving hand on my shoulder catapulting me back to a time when anything was possible. Maybe two of the three North arrows have a better chance at traveling toward the same target.

"I also need something else from you, for Evan. I don't have the money to pay him for the bet. Or the three thousand dollars I promised him to tow my car." I shudder at the thought of my inflated arrogance that day I showed up at Bailey's to get my car.

"I'll pay the debt," he says, wrapping me in his arms once

more. "You won't owe me. And Evan? The two of you had quite a fight."

Nope. Too soon for this conversation with my dad. "The stress of the switch got to us."

My head rests against his chest and for a few minutes, everything feels okay. "We should have done this a long time ago."

"Would you like to have lunch here, while you wait for the check?"

I nod. "Yes, I would."

Why is it whenever I need to see Evan, Hudson appears? Stalker seems like a natural conclusion, but he's seated at an outdoor café I had to walk past on my way to my meeting with Evan. He's with another man in a suit.

No sign of Evan yet. The check is in my purse. I have no reason to be nervous, but my stomach drops like a fast-moving elevator.

"Lexi," Hudson says, signing his name on a credit card receipt, "hang on. I'm paying the bill."

He shakes hands with the guy at his table and strides over, hand in one pocket, suit jacket disturbed by the pose.

"Hello beautiful," he says, stopping in front of me with glittering, late-afternoon sun in his eyes. "What are you up to?"

"Personal business." *Go, please, just go.*

"How long will you be? We can grab a cup of coffee."

I spot Evan's car pulling up to a metered spot and the brakes flicker. The car gives a lurch forward. "I can't meet you."

"Dinner, then?"

"I can't," I say, exasperated. Evan's door opens.

"Could you at least look at me?"

My gaze swings to his. "This isn't a good time."

"I got a job offer back in California and I didn't take it because of you."

I stare at him. "You shouldn't have done that. *You* came back with Isabella. I'm sorry things didn't work out, but you treated me like a second choice. What we had was over a long time ago." His gaze catches Evan making his way over.

Evan's hard eyes are directed at Hudson, then me. He stops and folds his arms. His shirt and cargo shorts shouldn't melt my heart, but they do.

"That's it? You're going to throw away the second chance I'm offering?"

"I thought I made myself clear when I returned your money." I lift my hand to touch his chest, but I stop myself and keep it at my side. "Good luck with whatever you do. You'll find someone."

Evan doesn't move a muscle and I stay put, waiting until Hudson leaves.

We stare at each other, feet apart, like a duel. Neither of us are moving.

"Right back to where you left off," Evan says.

"Why don't you say it louder? Then everyone can hear our business."

We both move closer. If our postures were any straighter, we would break in half. Those piercing green eyes go right for me. His jaw is tight and wound. "Did you bring the money?"

"Yes. Did you bring my bracelet?"

"Nope. Wasn't part of the deal."

His voice doesn't have a trace of humility. He's as full of himself as ever. "I thought you would be reasonable."

"We're all entitled to our own opinions."

Reaching in my handbag, I grab the check and hand it to him.

He takes the check without touching me. He looks at the amount and flicks his gaze to me.

He turns around and walks away.

"Un-be-lievable. You're going to walk away? I fell in love with you," I say, uncaring who hears.

Evan stops.

"You were the most ridiculous man I had ever met. You had no manners, no sense of flexibility, and yes, you were beneath me. I wasn't going to kiss you. I swore I would never like you." The woman next to me gets off her phone. An elderly couple leans into their walkers, their interest rapt through large bifocals. "How could an heiress love someone who spends their days working on car engines?"

"Oh honey," someone close to me says.

Evan turns around, scolding me with his scowl. My frown is equally impressive.

"Then I got to know you. I slept in your crappy, cheap bed. I learned how to make a casserole. From canned soup. I pulled a hair clog the size of a rat from your shower drain and I slept in your shirt and boxers. I changed your cat's litter box and scrubbed your gross baseboards." I take the slightest step forward.

He does the same.

The onlookers blur like wallpaper. "I learned to love the position of the sun in your kitchen in the morning. I loved the way I smelled after using your stupid multi-everything body wash and how satisfied my muscles felt from being on my feet all day. I even stole toilet paper from the shop."

His mouth parts.

"You rooted for me. Even to do the ordinary everyday things. The chores no one gets credit for. You didn't make fun of me or dismiss me. You showed me how to function."

"Bob, put your phone down," a woman hisses to her husband.

Evan doesn't flinch. His eyes flicker.

"Then you became the same boring version of every guy

I've ever dated. You did it so quickly, I almost didn't catch on to what you were doing. You thought I needed a guy who uses hair gel and wears loafers without socks." I take another step closer. "You sold me a lie when all I wanted was the guy who helped me learn how to do laundry. I said I loved you. I've never said that to anyone before. And what did you do? You went to a bedroom. On a yacht. With another woman."

"I know who I'm rooting for," a voice chimes.

"Bastard," a man says scandalously.

"For the record." I cast him a mixed bag of resolve and a giant chunk of my heart, getting a good look at the man I will forever miss. "Hudson did give me money. He showed up at Bailey's and gave me an envelope I didn't have time to check because I had to clean up an oil spill. I didn't know he'd given me cash until later that night, and I gave it all back. Before the art fundraiser, I showed up at your house."

He nods, remembering.

"I was embarrassed I went through most of your money. I was going to ask you to help me budget. So, congrats. You won. You got the money. You got everything you wanted. We're done, Evan. Don't ever call me again."

This time, I walk away.

CHAPTER THIRTY-FIVE

Evan

There are three hours until closing. Tonight is the gala and the bulk of summer is gone.

The SUV is jacked several feet high on the lift. Underneath the belly with a cordless drill, safety goggles slide down my nose.

A triple helping of regret weighs down my mood, splitting my thoughts like frayed threads. My back and arm muscles are locked in an uptight mode, my breath is strained from lack of sleep. There is too much churning in my stomach. Craig's offer. Lexi's speech.

Since I excel at holding on with a death grip, loosening my thoughts is proving tough. What if I let go even a little?

These days, walking past CeCe's bedroom causes my heart to divide. If he turns out to be good, she will have more with him than I can give her. One weekend a month might turn into every Saturday, then weeknights, and finally, full parental custody.

I hold back sudden emotion.

Wanting what's best for her has never been more difficult.

I remove the cylinder head, unable to think about Craig.

As soon as I move on from that beast, thoughts of Lexi drown me, submerging me beneath heavy waves. I look at myself the past few weeks and I can't breathe. The damage is done, and shutting out the look in her eye and the passion in her voice is pointless. Replaying that scene is automatic.

I miss her.

CeCe misses her. A light is out in each of us.

Only Lexi did not screw things up. This one is on me.

Out from under the car, I glance at Josh, who's busy with a muffler. I check my phone, thinking a text will be there from Lexi. Of course not. She put herself out there. She did everything right.

Maybe tonight I'll see if Alec and my mother want to come over for dinner. I have to do something to keep busy.

I wipe the back of my neck, the heat ever-present and grueling.

Josh whistles. "Ev. Someone's here to see you."

Caution laces my steps when I see Talia at the garage door. What's she doing here?

Talia waits expectantly, scoping out the garage with an observant gaze.

I go to see what she wants, stopped by a delivery guy with a hearty basket of chocolate-covered fruit, waiting for me to indicate which entrance he should use. Another mystery gift for Tia. The secret admirer is constantly on my nerves.

"Are you short on clients these days?" I ask Talia, stuffing a rag in my back pocket.

She points to one of the cars lifted on the jack. "I'm not a personal injury lawyer. I'm here to see you."

"Did I forget something at Lexi's house?"

She pokes my arm with her white-tipped nails. Her friends are all so touchy-grabby. "Elena said you bailed on the gala. I came to change your mind."

I snort and cross my arms. The tuxedo is still hanging in

my closet. "I didn't bail. She told me not to attend. I didn't want to attend eight weeks ago."

"Funny you say that. Your eyes lit up when I said gala. I saw it. I represent liars, Evan. Don't be on my naughty list."

"What do you want, Talia? I have work to do."

"Okay. Lexi does not have a date. You don't have one, either." She starts her hands wide and pushes them toward each other. "Let's fix this."

Let's not. Showing up to an event for a woman who told me to f—off is not my style. "I have no interest in acting the part of a third wheel between her and Hudson."

Talia is having none of my excuses. "Stop with the weak arguments, sir. She said goodbye to him. Those two have been wrong for each other since the start. He liked showing her off. She liked someone who didn't expect much. Lexi needed someone to help her find her way. Hudson was never that person. They would wind up divorced, hurt, and lost. You helped her find her way. Are you going to make her walk the rest of the way alone?"

I am too afraid to consider what she is saying. To disagree would be a lie. Lexi knows herself now, she won't settle. She'd be settling with me. "She can do better than how I treated her."

Talia taps her foot and rests her hand on her hip. Her back is straightening like she's nowhere through with me. "Did you ever ask Lexi why she didn't quit sooner?"

Doing this bet for the bracelet did not make sense. "I didn't figure that part out."

"Lexi's father gave her an ultimatum."

I still.

Momentum fills her voice like she's rounding the corner to an indisputable argument. "Edward was tired of her antics. He told her to finish the bet or he would cut off her inheritance. She quit because of you when she was near the end. She lost… everything."

My own recklessness crashes around me, sweeps over me, leaves me stunned. Pieces click into place. Gears shift and show me answers to questions I had asked myself. I suck in a heartfelt breath tied up with blame.

"That's right. You know I'm not pulling one over on you." Her voice tinges with pride.

"I didn't know." I lose my voice, catching the guys looking over. She walked away from the money...she gave up her lifeblood, her cushy life. My modest gaze meets Talia's certain eyes. "She picked a life without money for—"

"For you?" Talia touches my shoulder. "I've known Lexi a long time. I've never seen her look at someone the way she looks at you. You two say so much without a single word. The rest of us are a bunch of spare tires around you and Lexi. We're way past bullshitting, Evan. Don't do it now. Go to the gala or don't. Stay here and prove me wrong. Pack up the story of you and Lexi for a rainy day when you can't stop thinking about this moment and how you could have gone after her."

Someone—Josh, I think, cues the music. The evocative notes of "Come As You Are" fill the garage.

I look inside myself. I look at Talia's expectant expression. It is hard to get the words out. If I put myself out there one more time, will I have a chance? Resisting the urge to turn my back for the sake of my inflexible ego, I have one more thing to say. "I don't have a ticket to the gala."

"You leave that to me."

This is not a done deal. Second chances are not guaranteed.

I'm not sure how this will go. The tailored tuxedo covers me like a shield. My fingers don't toy with the bowtie and I ignore the tight fit of my shined shoes.

The gala is at a historic mansion downtown.

The property is surrounded by gardens and high wrought iron gates. A valet takes my car and I use the digital invite Talia sent me.

Lexi walked away with her head high and determination in her eyes.

If only I had told her how I felt—if I had been brave enough to be myself, I wouldn't step into the night unsure about how this will go.

Lexi could decide she wants to dive into her next chapter alone. She may look at me like a has-been fling. All I have to go on is knowing if I don't step up, if I don't set this right, it will take me forever to get over her. Showing up is a make-or-break chance.

Soon as she looks at me, I will know if I'm too late.

Volunteers man the tables at the entrance. They're faces I recognize from our meetings. The line for the media wall is long. People put on big smiles and pose in front of the foundation's logo.

Attention turns to me with cell phones and whispers catch on like wildfire. "Evan's here?" "Oh my gosh." "Where's Lexi?"

"Evan," one of the board members comments, coming around from the swag bag table and extending both hands to me. "Look at you. Perfection." She holds up a bag, one of the bags that Lexi, CeCe, and I put together. All of us in the kitchen. A moment I didn't appreciate. "Grab one of these on your way out."

"No thanks," I say and continue ahead with chaos in my stomach.

A scent similar to Lexi's floral body wash tricks me into thinking she's close. I whirl around, not ready to see her and crestfallen to find an older woman.

She's close though, I can feel it. Nail-biting close. The guests angle their heads toward the door.

The place is dripping with elegant flowers and white

lights. Jewels sparkle from around necks and wrists. Shoes are shining. Every man is in a tuxedo.

Talia, in the middle of talking with friends, sees me. She gives a slow, approving nod and points her finger in the direction of the large white tent set up outside with the band playing music inside. The singer's voice carries like a soft breeze on an evening with fireflies and early stars in the sky.

My heart is in my throat crossing the manicured lawn and elegant torches making a path to the dance floor.

Ten seconds in, I stop walking. She has no reason to listen to me.

I wouldn't listen to me. The best outcome is she gives me a chance to explain, but I don't know if I have earned even that.

The committee transformed this place into a white light, flower-filled event. The music entices a crowd of dancers. Almost not a square of spare dance floor exists.

My heart beats faster and louder. My eyes searching...

Then I see her.

Actually, I noticed her dress first. The color of midnight, the fabric hugs her body like she's stepped into satin. Her shoulders are bare and the halter around her neck continues in two long trains of silk down to her exposed back. Her hair is down, caressing her shoulders.

She is dancing with another guy. *Someone my age.* Decent-looking and probably knows the difference between Louis Vuitton and Dior. But what this guy has on me is she is offering him a smile and the respect I managed to lose.

This is going to be harder than I thought.

The lead singer's voice fades and the song dies down. Lexi and her dance partner stand face-to-face talking. Her hand touches his shoulder in the same split second her gaze strikes mine.

Her eyes are cold.

My plan was to ask her to dance, but nothing about her

reaction invites me closer. Another song begins and her partner begins to put his hand around her waist. I step away and turn around, stopping at the edge of the dance floor and giving myself a swift mental kick.

Go back and try again.

"May I have this dance?" My tone is riddled with uncertainty.

Lexi's partner gives her a solid eyebrow raise.

"Not interested," she says, securing her hand in his.

Couples dance around me, and Lexi moves away. Dancers glance at me and my awkward presence. I have my answer.

I leave the tent, sticking to the less crowded pathway, and allow myself to be impressed at the aesthetics of the evening coming together. Maybe I even had fun putting this night in place.

There is no reason for me to stay.

"Evan."

I spin around at the sound of Lexi's voice.

She keeps her distance. "Why are you here?"

Her chilly voice is not a welcome mat, but she is giving me the smallest of openings. "To ask you for one dance. May I?"

She nods. "Half a dance."

My hand slides around her, resting all five of my fingers on her skin. A blaze of heat teases my fingertips. Holding her is like finding home. "I bet you're wondering what made me put on this tuxedo."

She lifts her chin. "Not really."

I take a breath and close my hand around hers, careful to keep space between us as we dance. "I didn't come to apologize."

She stops moving.

I spread my hand wider, my fingers grazing her lower back.

"You deserve more than an apology. You deserve the truth."

"Evan, let's not do this."

A crowd is forming at the edge of the tent. "I came to tell you I failed you." I find my strength. She pauses with a look of indecision but doesn't release her hand from mine. Tears overcome my eyes. They hold on as tight as my breath. "I fell in love with you." The words come out fast, fearing this isn't going in the right direction. "The night of the carnival."

She looks like she doesn't believe me. "Was it the vomit on my feet?"

Tension spans the length of my spine and holds onto my breath. When I can't find the words, something clicks inside, and I regain my composure. "It was, actually. I saw how you must see me. A guy attending events where people throw up in public."

She cocks an eyebrow. "You think that won't happen tonight? Do you know how many guests I've witnessed puking in the bushes?"

"I get that now." My fingers coil around hers, bringing our hands to my chest. "The carnival was the last straw. I saw the end of the bet approaching and I kept thinking how you would feel incorporating me into your life. I needed to be someone who has more than a thousand dollars in the bank and a house without central AC. The thought of you embarrassed by me was too risky. I wanted to show you I could make the most of our time in your world."

The last sentence drops like a bomb, scattering pieces of my vulnerability.

Her fingers flinch against mine.

"I *failed* you, and I *know* it." My fingertips cling to her hips.

Her pain-filled gaze doesn't leave my face. Her eyes are flickering like her earrings.

Keep talking. Keep trying. You're nowhere close.

Lexi's hand opens over my shoulder. Her voice is unforgiving. "That's why you were willing to get the makeover."

"It was part of my plan to impress you." Somehow, we're

dancing again. Our feet are shuffling. "I never meant to hurt you, Lexi."

"I didn't think anything could break who you were. I didn't want you to change. Couldn't you see that?" She breaks her hand from mine and pokes me in the chest. "You didn't seem to have an identity crisis with Elena. Or lying to me about Craig."

Pressure beats a steady pulse. "I didn't sleep with her or kiss her or hold her hand." I move my fingers over hers. "What you saw wasn't what you thought. She was upset about a guy who told her he was in love with someone else and she was emotional."

"She was so emotional you disappeared into a bedroom with her?"

"One second she was flirting, I admit. Next thing I know she's crying. I accompanied her to one of the cabins and got her water." I feel Lexi's hand clench mine. "As she was crying and trying to hold onto me, I came to terms with how much of a jerk I had been to you and how tired I was of not being myself. I went to go find you to set things right."

This snags a hint of softness at her mouth. "Talia went out of her way tonight to tell me the same story. Elena moved on to be comforted by one of the waiters."

I don't quite breathe a sigh of relief, and it's a good thing, because she continues. "What about Craig?"

I unlace my fingers from hers and look at her like the first day I saw her. "The short version is, there was an NDA. Lexi, I'm so sorry. I...I got off track from what I wanted."

"We both wanted the same things."

"To be loved for who I am."

"To be seen for who I am." Lexi and I speak at the same time.

"Give me a second. There's something I need to do."

CHAPTER THIRTY-SIX

Lexi

Where is Evan going?

He leaves me on the pathway. My gaze tracks him through the crowded tent and to the side stage. He pulls the music coordinator to the side. She listens with rapt attention to Evan while my gaze strays to the bar and the guests standing close and laughing.

I see my "friends" hanging around the sidelines of the tent. They were absent all summer, but as soon as the yacht scene went viral, I've received nothing but invites and apologies. *I was so busy I forgot to check on you… You are one of my closest friends… Can we get together for brunch?*

They have been nothing but attentive since I broke up with Evan, but they weren't there when I was getting yelled at by Alec or watching videos on how to mow a lawn. For that reason, I almost stayed home tonight.

Look at them, cameras up, welcoming gazes. Their shoulders no longer cold. They are the same. I am not.

I wake up in my big empty bed and start my day making my own breakfast, but my house is so terribly quiet, and CeCe left a few clothes and a sketchbook I've flipped through more than once.

My eyes shift to Evan returning to me.

He is not out of the woods, but I haven't exactly walked away. I watch him approach with my heart beating a little faster. All his height and broadness get special notice, but the humble expression keeps me from bolting.

My gosh, the guy takes my breath away.

The timeline of his actions makes complete sense. The makeover was the starting point. Every time we were together afterward was like he was holding himself to a standard I couldn't see.

He was changing in front of me, for me, when I was doing the same. Maybe not to his extreme, but I sacrificed parts of me, too.

He stands in front of me, leaving hardly any room between us. "Did you know, in hockey, there are three periods."

This sounds like the Evan I fell for. I clear my throat and stand taller. "I've never been to a hockey game."

"That is the saddest thing I've heard all day," he says with a guarded voice. He holds out his hand.

"Where is this analogy going?" I say skeptically.

"I've used up two of my periods and I would love nothing more than to have the other half of this dance. I am dying for a reason to hold you close, and we're almost at game over." He extends his hand. "What do you say, North? Do I get the second half of this dance?"

I take his hand to a tune I almost don't recognize. The song is slowed down. The melody is breathtaking, or maybe it's the warmth Evan's hands bring out in me.

A tear traces one of my cheeks at the vocals of "How Will I Know" with one difference. The pronouns of the song have been changed from "he" to "she." "That's what you were doing over by the stage? Requesting a song?"

He angles his face to mine, and the rough pad of his thumb

wipes my tear away. "You know I love three things in this world. Music, hockey, and sex."

Before I get distracted by the music and his confidence, I run my hands up his arms, resting them behind his neck as he pulls me closer. "And Craig? How could you not trust me?"

He manages a hefty wince. "All of that got out of control. I didn't trust myself to tell you and then have you side with the Hoffmans," he says, pausing like it pains him to finish his thought, "Fine. I was also jealous of Hudson."

"I thought *nothing* could make you jealous."

"I have my moments."

I had heard through the great rumor mill about Craig and Evan talking, but I need to hear this for myself. "Where do you and Craig stand now?"

"We're talking." Evan's reluctant to say more. His finger draws small circles on my hip as the music spins around us. "Craig wants to get to know CeCe and I'm having trouble accepting it."

My fingers tap lightly against his neck. "She was going to find out someday. Isn't it better she knows?"

"I don't know, but we can't go back. I'll do what CeCe wants."

According to one source, Cecilia Hoffman is overjoyed at the prospect of meeting her granddaughter, and I try to imagine Evan showing up on her doorstep.

I press my body against his and get lost in the feel of his big, strong hand spreading over my back. Heat infiltrates my skin. When I picture such a scene, I am there with him.

He holds me close and I inhale his body wash, a total weakness of mine, and I think about how I can either walk away or I can stay like this.

The song ends.

My feet don't move. I stay, ignorant of the party and laughter around us. I reach up and straighten his bowtie.

"Now I have a few things to say."

"Go on," Evan's husky voice brings my gaze back to him.

"I adore cheap makeup. I have a love-hate attitude about grocery shopping. And there is nothing more satisfying than getting my own paycheck." My glossy frown falters. "I like you better with your ponytail."

Evan's fingers dig into my hip.

"I love the way you kiss."

His posture straightens a notch. A gleam shines in his eyes.

Moment by moment, I surrender to accepting where I want this to go. I could never give up on Evan.

He reaches into his pocket, making me wait to open his palm and reveal a homemade bracelet. "This one, I made for you."

He holds up his wrist, showing off a matching one. "It doesn't go with your dress. According to style blogs, neon is never acceptable."

I take the bracelet. Evan's fingers brush over mine.

"This one's a limited edition."

My heart falls into a head-over-heels crush. "So, what happens if I put this on? I won't see *Ev* again?" I mimic Hudson's tone.

"That version of me fell off the yacht."

I hold my wrist out for Evan to slide the bracelet on. His hand lingers at the base of my palm. "When it's you, CeCe, and me, you guys are the only invite I want to accept." The words roll off my mouth and my heart seizes. Maybe it stops, the beats waiting for me.

Evan pushes my hair off my shoulders. His hands slide up my jaw with heat exploding in my belly. "You love the way I kiss."

"I'm not sure. It's been a while."

Evan tilts my face to his. His thumb swipes slowly and purposefully over my chin. The vivid hunger in his gaze is directed at my mouth, but I can tell he's keeping it muted. "Let me refresh your memory."

The first brush of his mouth is slow and gentle, his lips brushing over mine, soft as can be. His palms flatten over my jaw, giving him all the leverage. I am easily influenced by Evan's mouth.

I don't give him an inch to think he's won. "That was a nice kiss."

His eyes read mine. "I don't do nice kisses, North."

"Maybe all my late-night thoughts of you were better in my mind—"

Evan's mouth seizes mine in a heart-pounding embrace. His mouth crushes against mine with an explosion of heat driving straight to my thighs. His lips take on an urgency full of wicked, delicious need.

Our tongues collide in fast, needy thrusts and coils. Evan's unyielding mouth softens me into a heart-stopping, slow-burning kiss that has the makings of our story going well past tonight.

"That nice enough for you?" he whispers with a smitten but cranky edge.

"I haven't decided." I mouth the words against his lips, going in for another kiss. My body rises to him, seeks out his touch. Rough-padded fingertips swipe low on my back where skin meets silky fabric. I imagine Evan balling this dress into a fist and taking it off me the second we're alone.

"I love you," he says with aching tenderness. "I'm going to do everything to be the grumpy..."—Evan pauses to spoil my mouth—"stubborn..."

I move my mouth against his.

"T-shirt-wearing man you love. I'm going to complain about the price. Of everything. I won't shave for days. I may or may not position my cutlery between ten and four o'clock to keep you in suspense and I won't balk when you force me to ride in a private jet."

"Is that all?"

"No. Not even close." His voice is as somber as the dark night. "I will be there if you ever call your mother and I will hold your hand if you decide you can't. I'll come home filthy, in need of you yelling at me to take a shower before my skin touches the sheets. Then I'll take you in my bed and again in the middle of the night."

I shudder pleasure-filled shivers at the thought of Evan stretched out as he is when he comes home from work on just-washed sheets.

My heart is kind of stuck on something more from such a fantasy. Evan coming home to me.

CHAPTER THIRTY-SEVEN

Lexi

Here's where things ended.

Summer remains my favorite season. This might be the best one yet and I'm holding onto the very last day of it. I was forever changed by a grumpy guy in a faded Capitals shirt and a whole world I knew nothing about. *Myself.*

I've found a lovely former heiress-turned therapist who understands the dynamic that pushed me over the shallow edge. I talk about points in time I stopped caring about who I was and what I want for my life. Good stuff. Hard stuff.

My dad and I have a standing date twice a month and he's been texting me. I love to read his messages, even if they're in paragraph form.

He did reinstate my trust, but I asked him to not make it available to me until I'm thirty-five.

Next week I start my new role at the North Foundation.

Budgeting is major trial-and-error and will be tested when I move into my first apartment next week. No personal staff. No big house. All of it goes away.

I drive my Audi down the familiar street and spot the familiar brick building. The month has kept me busy planning the Bailey's Labor Day Community Fair.

The stay-up-late hours I put in with record time paid off, looking at the balloon arches, food trucks, and discounted oil changes with cars lined up around the block—all at no cost to Alec.

I have a real job. One important enough for me to go to bed at a decent hour and attend only the occasional event.

Once I park, I walk over to Bailey's carrying boxes. Evan's most likely in the garage getting his hands nice and dirty.

Tia works behind a table, talking to customers.

Sometimes, it's good to be a North.

We skipped ten different hoops at the city permit office to use the sidewalks and block off the street to give it a festival feel. Families are out, there are kids with ice cream cones, and the sign-up for the tire changing classes has a waitlist.

Tia looks up, lifting her hand. "Look at all these people," she says, wrapping me in a hug. Her hoop earring hits my jaw.

"Any big reveals?" I ask, setting down the box of Bailey's merch full of car service coupons, pens, travel mugs, and fidgets and tattoos for kids (CeCe's suggestion).

"Nothing yet," Tia says.

Tia received a mysterious note yesterday that her secret admirer would be here. Fresh off the heels of my own love story, I am waiting with nail-biting, Lexi-level meddling to see hers.

"I still think Alec should have taken my suggestion to auction him off for a date night."

"You'd have a better chance at Brandon reading poetry."

I spot CeCe at the table with Alec, talking to customers. She's grown another half inch, joining the tall-girl club in a matter of weeks, and stops short of Evan's biceps.

I feel a little off about how things are changing for her and

Evan. After the gala, and after Evan showed me how much he missed me, we stayed up talking through the night and he told me everything about Craig and Natalie.

"Do you want to put these bags out?" I ask CeCe.

She takes the box and looks in. "Awesome," CeCe says, straightening the tissue paper of the swag bags.

Good girl, not letting delicate paper crumple. "Where's Evan?"

Evan appears at the door of the garage. Scruffy face, signature confidence, and Bailey's polo with rugged jeans.

Oh. My heart.

He looks at me like he is trying not to notice me and casually slides his hands in his pockets.

"What's going on?" Tia's worried voice calls out.

I spin around as Evan makes his way over to me. "Huh?"

Brandon is dressed in a suit, holding a bouquet of flowers.

From the corner of my eye, I see Josh coming from a different direction, wearing a vintage suit with a bowtie and a bouquet.

Evan stands next to me, his leg touching mine.

"Why are they dressed like they're going to a wedding?"

Evan's eyebrows lift. "You'll see."

Brandon hands Tia the vase of mixed blooms. "I'm your secret admirer."

Her hand slaps over her heart. Her smile forms. "You've been leaving me the gifts?"

Josh butts in, also handing her a bouquet with the same flowers. "I sent you the fruit and the necklace."

She looks from Josh to Brandon. "You both were sending me gifts."

"He stole my idea," Brandon says.

"I've liked you since before he did," Josh says. "Why do you think I'm always hanging around your desk? I knew what Brandon was up to. I wanted my shot."

Tia takes both bouquets. Bless them, they must have shopped at the same store. "You're telling me you both have feelings for me?"

"I'm crazy about you, Tia," Brandon says, taking her hand. "Go out to dinner with me."

Josh rolls his eyes. "I'll take you to breakfast."

Tia smiles at them equally. "I loved all my gifts, but you are like brothers to me."

"Ouch," Evan says, wincing, rocking back on his shoes.

She squeezes each of their hands. "You can still send me gifts."

The poor guys, they tried.

"Speaking of mysteries," I say, watching a line form at the snow cone truck. "You didn't tell me who Bowser is."

"If only there were a way to look up information," he says wryly, slicing his gaze to mine.

"I want to hear it from the horse's mouth. You would be the horse."

"Bowser's the boss at the end of every level of Super Mario Brothers. Have you ever played? Even the French version?" Evan says with snooty undertones.

I snort. "I know what Super Mario Brothers is. I don't live under a rock entirely. And no. I haven't played it. Ever."

My heart jumps at the sight of Alec standing next to Tia. Oh wait. His hand is on the small of her back. She's looking at him the way I look at Evan. I slap Evan's chest with the back of my hand. "Are you seeing this?"

"Why do you think he's been in a bad mood since she started receiving flowers?"

"I thought that was because of me."

"Yeah, well, Bailey men are easy to read. The grumpier we are, the more we like a girl."

I am about to ask if she likes him, but I watch with a dumb smile on my face as her hand brushes his shoulder.

Evan wraps his arm around me. "When does this thing end?" he says impatiently. "I want to get home."

Later that evening, CeCe is quick to ditch us for her bike, friends, and holding onto summer same as me. With her in school we will be here more.

"I'm anxious to see how Bailey's did today," I say, squishing against him where his couch sags in the middle. Bowser hops up, filling my entire lap.

"Alec promised he'd text once he and Tia figure out the totals," he says, tapping several buttons on his remote, and opens a box leaning against his thigh. He seems worried. "Craig called earlier." Craig and his parents are having CeCe over for lunch on Saturday at their house.

This will be the first time they meet her. "What did Craig say? Is everything okay?"

"He called to make sure my mother and Alec were invited. They all want to be there. Do you think that's too many people?"

"I think CeCe will see how many people she has ready to take this next step with her. I'll be with you in case you forget how to answer when Cecilia asks you about your pedigree."

"I haven't asked you to be my date yet." He flashes me a shit-eating grin.

While Evan and Hudson will never get along, Hudson isn't a factor, since he moved out to the West Coast. His parents *are* good, generous people, and they are eager to get to know their granddaughter. "We'll see about that."

The video game appears on the screen, theme music and all. He hands me a black plastic remote with a toggle switch. "Here's your controller."

"What's this? I thought we were going to do some major

porch sitting." I take the controller out of his hands. There are a lot of buttons.

"We're going to rectify one more wrong in your life. We're going to play Super Mario." Evan walks me through how to use the controller, explaining in detail which button does what. "Let me play a round. To show you an example," he adds with a boyish look that warms my heart. "Your turn, North."

I take the remote and move my fingers over the raised buttons. "People play this without cocktails?"

Ten seconds into the game, I die.

"Why is there a moving mushroom?"

My gaming skills suck. It's obvious from the start.

Slowly, very slowly, Mario moves across the screen. The strange mushroom creature moves toward Mario. I'm killed on the spot. "That wasn't fair."

"Jump on him next time," he says too late.

Now we have a turtle. Or goose. Mario might be slightly cuter than this Luigi guy. I can't tell. "Who designed overalls for their outfits? What do I get with the coins?"

Evan fights a smile. "Eventually, an extra life. You're not there yet."

"I like the mystery question marks. No! I died again." I still haven't seen this alleged Bowser. Nor do I make it to the end of the level.

It's a little addictive.

An hour disappears and I'm snug against Evan's side. I hand the controller to Evan, his hand covering mine.

Bowser takes offense to all of it, jumping off the couch and hiding. "You ready to move this operation to the front porch?" I ask.

"Definitely," he says, reaching for me, pulling me onto his lap.

He brushes his hands over my jaw, stealing my mouth in a long, drawn-out kiss, undressing me with his lips. We are on borrowed time if CeCe comes home. His heady, warm breath mixes with mine. I plant my fingers on his jaw, kissing him back, reciprocating everything I'm getting.

"You are the best thing to happen to me, North," he says, slanting his mouth over mine, "even if you steal my bodywash." Evan's grown partial to wearing a robe after showers and tried to downplay purchasing house slippers. "I'm going to miss your shower."

I kiss him fully, from the deepest parts of me. "Can I get that on record?"

"If you promise to take advantage of me," he says, expelling a knowing breath.

Evan grabs us a beer and we move out front to our camping chairs and front porch for people watching. CeCe and her friends race by on bikes.

Evan and I are sitting here, nothing is rushed.

Muggy air ruins my hair and glistens my skin.

The comments posted about us are changing. Evan shows me on his phone, since I created a new private IG account for just my close friends.

75 percent of his followers are in favor of us getting engaged.

There is plenty of time for that.

#MaybeOneDay

My favorite stories are the ones nobody sees.

CeCe asked me to teach her how to shave her legs without it looking like a war zone and confided in me the last month of school she was having problems with friends. They didn't leave space for her at the lunch table and she wound up eating alone.

Turns out, when I left the filter off my life, it was pretty good to begin with. I just needed to adjust my point of view and see the vibrant colors staring back at me—and of course, have one person believe in me. That's it. One person.

Thank you, Evan Bailey.

Without my family's money and last name, I will be *fine*.

I will also master cracking an egg without shells falling into the bowl. One thing at a time, right?

And the future?

I don't want to presume to know how anything works out.

Evan takes my hand, thumbing mine softly. I clench his shirt, pulling him into a kiss, letting our mouths speak louder than words.

It's a foretelling of our future for a socialite with a beating heart like the rest of them. Only this time, the beats are louder, more genuine.

Our lips meet, soft and sure, his hand keeping me close on this one night in a summer I will never forget.

This, my friends, is only the beginning.

ACKNOWLEDGMENTS

Here I am, writing my favorite part of the story process, the one which extends beyond the pages and into the real world. Behind the scenes is where the real work happens, and *Trading Places* was a team effort by all the incredible team at Entangled. A big, heartfelt thank you to Liz Pelletier; Editors Jessica Turner and Molly Majumder for giving this story developmental edits to get Lexi and Evan *there*. For copyeditor Nancy Cantor for her attention to detail. But none, *none* of this would have happened without Jen Bouvier, for "seeing" this story and giving me a shot.

Thank you to Elizabeth Stokes and her gasp-worthy cover and to Curtis Svehlak for production work.

This story did not happen overnight, and I owe shout outs to those who saw early drafts, Andrea Mallozzi, Adrienne Oudenampsen, Mona Shroff, and Steve Bradham. To Christi Barth for your support (and story problem solving) for those of us who signed up on purpose for this writing thing.

Love and gratitude to my supporters both near and far. My family and friends who are on this ride with me and still think talking about story ideas is normal dinner conversation. To Brian for, well, everything and Nolan and Abby who make an *ew,* so-not-cool face when I say I write romance, I love you guys. To Jen Beck—oh my gosh—can you believe it? Thank you for cheering me on. Finally, to Sonal Patel, dear friend and motivator who tells me to keep going, keep trying, and don't forget to use the right hashtags.

To all the readers—*Oh my heart.* This is for you.

Fans of Christina Lauren and Tessa Bailey will adore this witty and unforgettable rom-com about skyways, highways, and all the perfectly wrong ways to fall in love.

Turn the page to start reading for FREE...

CASSIDY

I jolt upright and whip my head left and right. Recognition of my surroundings dawns as my sleepy brain flickers to life. *Airport.* The lights are dim but not out, like a theater just before a show.

And here I was hoping the diversion was a dream.

My attention falls to a foreign bundle of gray fabric in my lap. A tired squeak leaves my mouth as I shove it off my legs.

The heck?

With a pincer grip, I pluck it off the ground. It has a hood, but no drawstring. The cotton is threadbare and faded. A quick peek inside reveals the tag is missing.

This is the baby blanket of sweatshirts, worn to death.

I lift my chin and search the area.

Of the hundred or so people camping in this gate, there's only one I could pick out of a lineup. And the last thing Mr. *Is This Your First Time Being Right?* would do is offer me a sweatshirt. His dislike of me is so intense he chose to argue with me instead of conceding that I was right about the hotel situation, even after we'd achieved a mutual understanding and respect as our plane landed.

Or so I thought.

That's what I get for attempting to turn over a friendlier leaf: Luke sass. A glimpse at his ego. I bet if I told him the airport was on fire he'd have to google it to be abundantly sure rather than trust my assessment.

So what if he doesn't like me? I didn't like *him* first. I've got squatter's rights on this grudge.

And yet, I have a sweatshirt in my clammy hands.

I spot Luke and his tousled shock of hair across the walkway. It appears he's ransacked it with his hand a time too many. Even the WASPyish among us are susceptible to the harrowing realities of an all-nighter, I guess. He's putting the *lap* in *laptop* as he pecks away at the machine perched on his thighs. His glasses reflect the glow of the screen.

I could ask him. But if it isn't his and belongs to a random good Samaritan who saw I was uncovered—or a random person who intended to smother me in my sleep and failed—I'd be mortified.

Playing *The Sims* until the airline provides an update is safer.

My phone lights up at my touch. *Five twenty a.m.* The drained battery icon winks at me.

I scan for an open outlet. Too many people have fallen asleep body-blocking their charging phones. All plugs are taken except for the top half of one.

The bottom half has been claimed by Luke.

This ought to be fun.

I gather my stuff, cross the crowded space, and approach with my chin lifted and the sweatshirt tucked under my arm. "Can I use the top half of that outlet?"

He looks at me for approximately half a second before returning his gaze to the keyboard. "Sure."

I'm reveling in the ease of this interaction when he adds, "I mean, I don't own it."

"Could've just left it at yes," I mumble as I dig my charger out of the front pocket of my suitcase and plug myself in.

Muscles tight from the plane and sleeping upright, I extend my legs. I've got enough room for a full straddle, but I don't push it far. Just a half. My hamstrings hum in objection, which means it's all the more important I do this to avoid injuries. Even a small one could put me out of work.

"What are you doing?"

I glance to the right as I stretch further. Luke's face is aghast.

I keep my voice low to match his. "I'm stretching my legs."

"*Here*?"

With the scandalized tone of his voice, you'd think I stripped naked and bent over. "Sure. Why not?"

He slides his glasses off his face and buffs them on his shirt. "I've never seen anyone do a *split* in the middle of an airport."

"This isn't a full split, nor am I in the middle of anything. We're on the side of a room where barely anyone is awake. It's not like I dropped down while in line for security." I lean against my elbows, and my muscles sing. "Does this bother you?"

"No."

"Then why do you sound bent out of shape?"

"I'm not." He returns to his computer, peck-peck-pecking.

"Great." I shift even further until my legs are almost a perfect 180, which I had no intention of doing until he questioned me. There's something about his tone—that there are right and wrong ways to do things, and his ways are right—that makes me want to poke him until he snaps. "It's part of my job to be flexible. I'm working, too. Just like you are with your type-type-typing."

The typing ceases. "Your job?"

"Choreographer. Dancer. Professional stretcher, as it were."

He swivels his head roughly ten degrees, runs his gaze up my body, and returns to working. He could weaponize that sharp jawline. "Fascinating."

Heat creeps up my neck. "Astounded by my talent?"

"Moved to tears."

"I'll get out of your way soon enough."

He lets out a strained sigh and scrubs his hand over his mouth. His hoarse voice suggests a lack of sleep. "I didn't say you had to move. Forgive me for asking a simple question."

"Speaking of simple questions." I cross my legs and hold up his sweatshirt. "Any idea where this came from?"

He freezes for a good four seconds. The volume at which his silence yells rails against my eardrums.

I purse my lips and lift it to my nose. The scent is vibrant and refreshing, evocative of California with a hint of citrus, like cold lemonade sipped on a beach. I'd know it anywhere thanks to a summer in high school working at JC Penney and huffing enough cologne to jump-start puberty: Ralph Lauren. "Smells good."

While he continues to ignore me, I lean sideways into his bubble and sniff the air around him.

His gaze remains firmly on his computer. "Did you just smell me, Cassidy?"

"Absolutely not." The delicious scent lingers in my nose as I breathe deeply. "Gosh, it's just the strangest thing. I woke up and it was *on* me. I guess I'll have to go ask every single person in this terminal individually so I can thank—"

"You were freezing." His brow furrows. "Your arms were going to fall off."

I grin, pleased that he admitted it. "So it *is* yours."

He shrugs a shoulder. "It's not a big deal."

I scoot a little closer. At this angle, I get a peek of a color-coded spreadsheet filled with numbers on his monitor. Gag me with a calculator. "That was very nice of you."

The words leave my mouth and heat trickles across my cheeks.

It *was* nice—unexpectedly so.

"Can I do something in return?" I scan the darkened room. "I don't know, buy you a snack from the vending machine or something? You a Doritos guy? Wait—blue bag or red? This is a crucial distinction."

"Not necessary."

"Okay, no Doritos. Soda? Chocolate?"

He pushes his glasses a fraction of an inch up his nose. "You were in danger of frostbite, and I'm not even sure this town has a hospital. Consider it a public service."

"That's actually a perfect comparison. I put out a huge basket of Snickers and Cheez-Its for overworked delivery drivers every December. To thank them for their service. I wish you'd tell me what zero-nutrient crap you like so I could thank *you*."

He eyes me warily. "Not a big fan of snacks. Can we drop this, please?"

"Who isn't a fan of *snacks*?"

His laugh is incredulous. "Have you ever had a conversation that doesn't end in frustration?"

"Actually, my conversations usually reach a satisfying conclusion." My lips arrange themselves in a smile. "Except with you, apparently."

He presses his eyes shut. "And to think, I could've been sleeping this whole time and missed out on all this fun."

I swivel toward him and push up on my knees. He tenses and rears back, hitting his head on the wall.

"I'm not going to smother you with it, Luke." I reach for the suitcase standing upright near his feet, loop the sleeves through his handle, and tie it in a knot. "There. Tiny soldier has returned home."

I catch his eye, and my stomach twists. My neck heats as he studies me.

"You're something else," he says quietly.

I've been on the receiving end of that tilted-head, appraising look before. Like I've rattled off a complex riddle and forced him to solve it against his will.

It's fine being something else—until someone goes out of their way to point it out. It then becomes a judgment. A branding.

I drop back into my seat and angle my body away.

We co-exist in silence long enough that an inkling of color threatens the cloudy horizon. It is the La Croix flavor of sunrise, an almost imperceptible taste. In the interest of letting my battery fully charge, I forgo *The Sims* and dig a notebook out of my purse. I'm halfway done filling the page with pointless doodles when my and Luke's phones light up in unison on the ground between us.

Atlas Airlines JLN to LAX. Canceled. Stand by for updates.

"No." I topple back into my stretch of carpet and snatch the phone off the ground. "No, no, *no*. This can't be happening. How can they just *cancel*? Oh my god, how long are they going to leave us here?"

"That's the airlines for you." His voice has precisely one degree of heat. No urgency.

"This is a nightmare! I can't just wait around here forever."

"Exactly why I'm not counting on a plane." He nods toward a hallway. "The car rental place opens at nine if you're looking for an alternate way out. The desk is near baggage claim."

A few people have stirred in the area, all glaring daggers at their phones.

Our eyes lock.

In unison, we scramble to gather our stuff.

If this entire terminal is trying to escape, I need to be *first* in line.

We blaze into the quiet baggage claim area, collecting a few looks as we skid to a stop at the back of the rental line.

Luke beats me by a hair.

"I would've been here even faster if you didn't kick my suitcase over," he grumbles.

"You must have me confused me with someone else. I'd never disrespect Samsonite luggage that way."

"Must've been another pint-size redhead with an agenda."

There are eight people ahead of him, and we've still got an unholy amount of time before it opens. My breathing calms as we file in, with two people already queuing up behind me.

Luke's neck hovers just above my eye-line, his perfectly precise hairline hitting like visual ASMR. Smooth and weirdly satisfying. This one doesn't skip his monthly stint in the barber's chair. The strip of tan skin above his travel-rumpled collar brings dull friction to the tip of my finger, like I accidentally traced it.

His physical presence is overwhelming up close. Long legs that perfectly fill a pair of dress pants. A lean but strong back that tests the seams of his shirt. Broad shoulders, perfect for throwing a girl over. For swing dancing purposes, of course—

My phone stirs to life, sending a pulse through my hip. A peek at the caller sounds my internal alarm.

Isabelle, calling at six a.m. her time.

Admittedly my nervous system is hair-trigger sensitive this morning, but this doesn't bode well. "Hey. You okay?"

"Cursdy," she slurs. "You were supposed to call me back!"

I inhale a sharp breath. "Are you drunk?" At six in the freaking *morning*?

"Nope! I slept for two hours. That cancels the drunk."

"Yeah, not how it works. What's going on?"

"This wedding is a *disaster*. I should cancel the whole stupid thing."

My stomach plummets. "Slow down, Bells. Did something happen? Did you and Mikael have a fight?"

"The caterer can't get salmon because of some kind of boat problem, the florist's cooler broke and all my flowers died—*died*!—and I have to go find more and make my own bouquets I guess? Wait, what about the table flowers?" She groans straight into my eardrum. "Mikael's been mostly MIA working on a big, dumb lawsuit. It's like he doesn't even care we're getting married."

"You know that's not true. He's obsessed with you."

"We haven't had sex in three days. *Three*. And two of those were weekend days!" She sucks in a fast gulp of air, a pseudo-hiccup. "Guess he's not attracted to me anymore. I stayed up all night waiting for him to get home from work, and he just passed right out! I had wine and everything. *Gah*, fucking florist, stupid caterer—"

"—Isabelle—"

"—I'm in way over my head with this stuff. And my PTO is *not* time off because my boss is a fuckwad. Mom is useless because she's being so *Mom*, worrying about random stuff I don't care about."

She sighs, regaining composure before adding, "I need you."

I saw my lips together. I *knew* I should've come home a week sooner. I could've been attacking the smaller to-do list items, leaving this week free for the more important stuff. But Isabelle is always so meticulous and competent I hardly thought we'd find ourselves in meltdown territory. I never expected we'd be on doubting-our-fiancé's-attraction terrain.

She's losing it. My mother, as a result, is going to lose it. It'll be fire and fury when I get home. The makings of a panic attack simmer at the base of my brain, threatening to alert the rest of my body.

This is my fault. Not much I can do about her tragic three-day sex drought, but the rest of those problems I *must* fix. Somehow.

"Bells, you still got your drink? I want you to put it down."

"But—"

"Down, girl."

I wait until I hear the faint *thud* of a glass. I don't often get to be the boss—little sister problems—but Isabelle needs a firm hand.

"You're going to be okay. We're going to get through this. The wedding is not a disaster. I'll call the caterer and florist today. You need to go back to sleep."

A beat of silence passes. "One more thing. Dad's not coming. Called him last night, which—you know I don't *ever* call him. And… no-sir-ee. No answer. Just a text back. 'Can't make it, Isabelle. It'll be all the better for it.' What does that even mean?"

My heart pangs. "You called him, though. That's the important thing. I'm happy you tried."

"What's it matter if he's not even bothering to come?"

"If you want a relationship with him moving forward, it matters. He's just being stubborn because he's terrified of Mom's wrath, and he doesn't want to upstage you on your big day."

"He's punishing me for Mom being Mom."

I let my head fall back. It's not the time to have this discussion yet again about our biological father. That's a conversation best left for when she's stone-cold sober and we can give it the unpacking it deserves. "I'll call Dad."

"I mean, I don't want you to *drag* him to the wedding."

"It's clearly important to you. You only get one wedding, and he should be there. Let me handle this, okay? Sleep. We'll talk soon."

"What time is your new plane coming?"

Like the time I borrowed and promptly lost the Ariat boots she bought for Coachella, I have to pick the perfect words to soften the blow. "About that. I'm going to be a bit longer getting there. Having a slight transportation issue. It's looking like tomorrow at the latest. I'm going to get a car and drive straight through."

"*What?*"

"I know it's not ideal—"

"*Not ideal?* Sixty percent humidity is not ideal. You not being here right now is a crisis! I swear, if *one more thing* goes wrong, I'm calling off—"

"Whoa." I jolt at the mere mention of calling anything off, even if it is just tipsy threats. "Don't even say those words, Bells. Everything is always more okay after a good sleep, I promise. I'll make calls to vendors as I drive. I'll even call your boss if he doesn't back off the bride."

"Jack Astaire would drop all the way died"—hiccup—"*dead* if someone talked to him about anything other than profits and numbers."

"Then I'll speak to Jack *Ass*-taire in binary code. Jack Ass Tear. Wow, what an unfortunate name."

"Promise me you'll be here soon, please? I can't do this without you, Cass."

Determination snakes its way through me until I'm nodding. It's more important than ever that I show up for her. Even if it's just for this week, to check off all one hundred to-dos. To talk her off ledges. To keep my stepfather's side of the family distracted so they don't accidentally perceive Mom's blood relatives and how poor they are, the shame of Mom's existence.

Isabelle, pillar of human perfection, needs *me*. Trusts me to be there for her.

"I'll be there," I say firmly. "I promise."

And when I get there, I'll be the best fucking maid of honor that has ever maided or honored. I may have chosen the wrong flight, but I will do what it takes to get this job done. I want to show Isabelle, Mom, *everyone* that I can be good at this.

Because if I'm not good at the role I've trained for my whole life—standing by while Isabelle shines, helping her look good, and building her up—then maybe I deserve Mom's constant criticism.

We say our goodbyes, and I perch on my suitcase, studying Google Maps for what feels like an eternity, until the desk opens.

When the clerk materializes, she scans the now *long* line of waiting patrons and anxiously fluffs her short salt-and-pepper hair. She receives a lot of intense stare-downs from people awaiting their turn as she works with the first two customers, the kind of impatient scrutiny that would turn me into a blubbering mess. After observing her pace as she hands out the seven rentals in front of Luke, I almost want to climb over the counter and help the poor thing.

She raises her voice to a solid 30 percent intensity when it's Luke's turn. "Next."

Luke lopes to the counter and draws his wallet like a sword. I'm close enough to hear his measured tone. "I'd like a vehicle, please. Something bigger, if you've got it."

She clacks chipped mauve nails against a keyboard.

"Oof." *Clack clack clack.* "This is, um…"

Luke, already gripping the speckled countertop, slides his hands farther apart, bracing himself. "Really, anything will work. Size isn't important."

Her thin, pursed lips and wide eyes suggest she's on the verge of a meltdown. She glances past Luke at the line, catches my eye, and quickly drops her gaze to the computer. "We've only got one vehicle left."

To read more, visit EntangledPublishing.com

Trading Places is a hilarious, heartfelt, fish-out-of-water rom-com which features a rich heiress trying to make it on minimum wage and a salt of the earth mechanic trying to figure out the intricacies of hob-nobbing with the elites. However, the story includes elements that might not be suitable for all readers. Poverty, minor road accidents, sex, foul language and parental abandonment are shown and discussed in the novel. Readers who may be sensitive to these elements, please take note.

AMARA

an imprint of Entangled Publishing LLC